MORE THAN MEMORIES

N. E. HENDERSON

PROLOGUE

WHITNEY

I suck at writing.

This was crap. All. Crap.

I pushed my notebook away in frustration, and a twinge of disgust ebbed inside me. When that didn't help, I threw my pencil at the white wall in front of my boyfriend's bed.

I had been lying on Shane's bed for twenty minutes or so, working on lyrics to a soon-to-be song that wouldn't leave me alone. Phrases kept popping into my head, distracting me from school, my friends, and everything else—pestering me. If I didn't get this song out, I felt like I was going to go crazy.

Music was my second love. My boyfriend was my first.

Shane Braden was one of a kind and, simply put, a great guy. I wasn't sure how I'd lucked out with him being mine, but I thanked the Heavens I did. He had been the best thing to come into my life, yet we were polar opposites. You know the saying opposites attract? Well, it was true for us. He was good, and I was the bad girl. The one that got into trouble almost daily. Shane was the sweet one, and I was the bitch—or so Kylie told me on a regular basis.

Kylie Morgan was my best friend. She was also dating my boyfriend's best friend, which made the four of us pretty damn close. Our group was made up of six at one point. But a year ago, two of our close friends—Chance and Eve—dropped out of high school and then moved out West, making us a foursome. It's funny how I only clicked with those with different personalities than my own. Kylie was the sociable one. Friendly to everybody and loved by all. She'd go out of her way to make others happy, even if that meant doing something she didn't particularly want to do. She was a true sweetheart.

I wasn't like that. I wasn't a follower. I did what I wanted when I wanted to do it.

"What's that look about?" I glanced in the direction of his smooth voice. Shane was walking into his bedroom. As he closed the door, my eyes roamed his lean body of their own accord. He was wearing a long sleeve black Henley with denim pants. His deep, dark brown hair looked almost black, and his blue-green eyes stood out as though they had a glow to them. His eyes were his best feature—they were beautiful. My good boy certainly looked the part of a badass, dark, and dangerous guy, but he wasn't. And that was the way I loved him. His heart was pure.

Mine, maybe not so much.

My own parents seemed to think I was the spawn of Satan. I could never do anything right in their eyes. So I stopped trying long ago.

Rolling onto my back, I took my eyes away from the guy who'd captured my heart back in eighth grade. He didn't know that then. At least, I didn't think he did.

I had fought him tooth and nail, not agreeing to go out with him for nearly a year until I finally caved. And not because I didn't like him back. I did, maybe a little too much, and that scared me. I didn't think he could possibly like me *that* way once he got to know me more.

I was stupid. But I know myself well. I'm difficult.

We ended up having an on-again-off-again relationship for years because of me and my dumb insecurities. I don't like feeling vulnerable. I don't like being on display for everyone to see. I'm not shy, just reserved.

Unlike Kylie and her boyfriend Trent, who were all about showing as much public display of affection as they could, I only got touchy-feely in private with my boyfriend.

When I'd break up with Shane, it would never last longer than a week. I couldn't go more than a few days without him being near me. Without his touch. He was my anchor. And I was lucky he put up with all my crazy.

"This song," I finally sighed. I was over it already. I wanted this shit out of my head, done with, but my brain wouldn't cooperate. Maybe it was broken. I didn't know.

"What's the problem, Love?"

See what I mean? Sweet. Love is my middle name, but Shane called me that instead of Whitney most of the time. He said he wanted to remind me as often as possible that I was *his* love. But he also used to tease me by calling me that when we were in Elementary school, so...

His face came into view as he stepped next to the bed. Shane moved his Fender acoustic guitar from where it was lying at the head of the bed, placing it in a standing position against his nightstand. Once he finished, he climbed onto the mattress, straddling me. I won't lie; I enjoyed the feel of his heavy weight on top of my small frame.

Another way we were opposites. He was tall, and I wasn't. At five feet, three inches tall, I looked tiny next to my boyfriend's six-foot height. He was not only tall but lean too, from running. So was I. It was one of the few things I liked about myself. That and my long, straight black hair and unnatural-looking eyes. But everything else... eh. I had no curves and small breasts. I wasn't supple and soft like Eve.

Besides music, running was another thing Shane and I loved doing together. I found it was how I could best free my mind. Maybe that was what I needed, but at the moment, I didn't want to move.

"This song won't leave me alone." I glanced over to where my notebook was lying. "I have most of it written, but it doesn't sound right when I read it back to myself."

"This again?" He looked down at me with those beautiful, patient eyes of his. "You're a brilliant songwriter. You need the melody to go along with it before you'll like it, Love." He paused for a short second as he peered down at me. "I want to read it." He didn't wait for me to agree. He never did, but that didn't bother me either. This was how we worked. I wrote the words. He created the music.

Leaning forward, he grabbed my notebook, then rose back up. He wasn't looking at me; Shane was looking at the page with my scribble written on it.

I can feel you from the outside in.
From my beating heart, down to my toes.
You're an ache I can't shake.

And I don't think I want to.
Just the touch of your lips can bring the girl inside me alive.

I can feel you from the outside in.
From my beating heart, down to my toes.
You're an ache I can't shake.

You love me like no one else ever has.
You're the only one that can reach inside and break down my walls.

I can feel you from the outside in.
From my beating heart, down to my toes.
You're an ache I can't shake.

Believe me when I tell you
You are my forever
Because baby, no one can break through the way you do.
You're an ache I can't shake.

"Is this about me?" His smile was infectious. And cocky too.

"Aren't they all about you?" I smiled up without shame. He was the only one that got to see my affectionate side. With him, I wasn't guarded. I was free. I didn't trust many people. At seventeen, I'd been burned too many times by my parents—mainly my wretched mother.

"And people say you aren't sweet." I rolled my eyes at his dig.

"I'm not trying to be sweet." I rose onto my elbows. "I'm trying to stop this useless chatter in my head."

His smile left his face rapidly, and then I watched as his eyes turned darker. The green faded to allow the blue to burn into my violet irises. This stare made me want to cower and look away, but I didn't. I wasn't weak, and I'd never show weakness to anyone, not even to the boy above me.

Shane tossed the notebook where I heard it land on the floor, then he lowered his head, bringing it down only inches from my own.

"Nothing inside your head is useless. Your mind is as beautiful as your angelic voice. It ticks me off when you say shit like that."

"Ohh. He cusses," I mocked. It was rare to hear a bad word come out of Shane's mouth. That wasn't a bad thing because I said enough of them to cover us both.

I had a potty mouth.

My parents didn't like Shane, or any of my friends, for that matter. They didn't know him either. If they did, they would've loved him like I did. He was impossible not to love.

A few years ago, my parents met Eve, back when she and Chance still lived here in Mississippi. They took one look at her and immediately judged her as 'bad news.' She didn't even have tattoos back then. After she had moved away, I heard she finally let Chance convince her to let him ink her skin. From what she has told me when we talk on the phone, she's addicted. I missed my friend so much. But we were graduating high school in a few weeks, and both of them were going to come home for a few days.

"Just because I don't see the need for excessive cussing doesn't mean I don't, Whitney." He lowered his head further, making me slide my arms down the bed so my head could fall to the mattress.

"Your little brother cusses more than you do, and he's a kid." I grinned, trying to get a rise out of him. One thing I knew how to do well was to get under this boy's skin.

"Shawn's an immature little prick." His palms slide slowly up the mattress about a foot away from my head on both sides.

"He's cute. Get off his ass. Besides, he's only that way when Trent's little sister is around." Which was a lot. Trent took overly protective brother duties to a whole new level when it came to that girl.

"Why are we talking about Shawn and Taralynn?" His lips were inches away from mine, and all I wanted him to do was press them against me. Okay, I wanted him to do a lot more, but we had to start somewhere.

"No idea. Kiss me." His eyes glanced down to my mouth, a smirk forming on his lips seconds before he planted a swift kiss on my nose.

He was rewarded with a glare.

So not what I wanted, and he knew that.

"Kiss me properly, dammit." I lifted my head an inch or two off the bed, trying to line my lips up with his. All he had to do was meet me halfway.

He didn't. Instead, he moved to my left, where he pressed his lips to my cheek, then slowly made his way to the shell of my ear.

"What do you really want, Love?" he whispered, tickling my ear. "My lips or something more?" He pressed his hardening cock against my center, making my head spin and my body shiver with anticipation.

"I want everything." And that's exactly what he gave me.

Whoever thought premarital sex was a sin hadn't been with Shane Braden. There was nothing about him that was sinful. He was everything right in my life. Those blue-green, ocean-like eyes were where I saw purpose, love, and happiness. I didn't get lost when I looked into them. No, I saw everything clear as a cloudless day. Shane was my now and my future. He was *my* calm to the raging storm swirling around in my head. That is unless he was making my heart race like it was doing right then.

The second his tongue met mine was the moment the ending of the song played out in my mind.

You're the one I can't shake.
You are the one.
My foreverly after.

CHAPTER 1

SHANE

Pain.

For me, that word is a double-edged sword. I seek it. I chase it just to make it stop. And that method was working just fine until one year ago today. *Or so I thought.* That's when I saw *her*. That was when I saw the source of my agony staring back at me from the screen of my cell phone. Her beautiful face shattered every brick I thought I had carefully crafted around myself all these years.

All humans know pain, some more than others. I'm sure some people know greater pain and loss than I do. Kylie, one of my best friends, is one of them. Where my other half was stolen from me and living a completely different life from what I saw in pictures—one without me in it—Kylie wakes up every day without the hope of ever seeing hers again.

Her agony is much bigger than mine.

She doesn't have hope left. Even the little sliver of it I do possess is enough to get me through the hardest of days. She doesn't have that.

Ten months ago, a guy I grew up with, my best friend practically my whole life, was killed. Kylie and I witnessed the senseless accident unfold right in front of us. We were in her car, and she was driving behind Trent. He was on his motorcycle. The three of us were headed home on New Year's Eve night when a man, driving drunk, swerved into our lane—into

Trent. He was thrown from the bike and died on impact.

That scene isn't something I like to think about. It hits too close to home from another wreck that occurred a decade before the one that ended Trent's life.

For most people, high school graduation night is a celebration and looked back on with fond memories. For me, it was the worst night of my life. Maybe even the end of my life if I'm honest with myself. The way I'm living now isn't exactly living. I'm merely going through the motions, looking for distractions from the pain that has been clawing at my chest for so long—too long.

Pain.

That's why I'm sitting where I am now. Because of pain. Because I need a different kind of pain to mask the other one. Only it isn't working like it used to.

"Are you purposely jabbing me with the needle, Shawn?"

I'm sitting in my brother's tattoo parlor, Wicked Ink, in Oxford, Mississippi. He's hovering over my leg, inking the vacant real estate.

My younger brother isn't usually this rough when he's working on me or anyone else. He's a very skilled tattoo artist, but something is bothering him. I see it plain as day. I saw it when I walked in. But Shawn's not exactly the most open person, so I kept my mouth shut. And it's not like I want to talk about the things rolling around in my head either. I need the hurt. I crave the sting of the tattoo machine heating my flesh as my brother creates another piece of art that bares a soul—a dark reminder of what I've lost.

I'd imagine this would hurt an ordinary person. Fuck, I hope I'm not becoming numb to the physical pain of getting a tattoo. If I have, then what the hell am I going to do now to ease the burning sensation in my chest?

No, I'm just thinking too hard. I'm not giving myself over to the needle.

"What?" He stops, retracts the tattoo machine away from my body, then glances up, looking me in the eye. There is a moment of confusion on his face before his brown eyes slide down, viewing the red, inflamed area on my thigh that now displays a black pocket watch with the time of

1:53 stopped on it.

That was the exact time—one fifty-three in the morning—when my heart stopped beating, and the world crashed down on top of me. I remember because it was the exact time I was staring at, from across the living room at my parents' house, when my mother wrapped her warm arms around me and told me my girlfriend was dead. I wanted to die too. It felt like I was dying. Too bad I didn't, because then I wouldn't need this pain. I wouldn't have to live with so much despair and anger burning inside me if I'd died that night.

That happened a little over ten years ago, and it turned out to be a lie. Not on my mother's part; she unknowingly told me something that wasn't true. Whitney wasn't dead. She was very much alive.

"Stop being a pussy." Shawn gestures with his hand that's holding the tattoo machine. "Isn't me torturing you the reason you come here?" His question comes out more as a sarcastic sulk than an actual question. "I don't know why I even agreed to do another one." He places his equipment down on the tray next to where I'm reclined on his table.

"Because I asked you to." This is on me. I should've never divulged the reason behind inking every surface of my body, but a couple of months back, Shawn and I got drunk, which is a rarity, even on my days off, and we got to talking. He confessed everything that had gone down at the beginning of summer with Taralynn, his girlfriend, and the stupid reason he almost lost the best thing that's ever happened to him. I, in turn, told him too much about my past. "And if you refuse, I'll go to Vegas and get Chance to do them."

It's an empty threat, but the "eat shit and die" look he gives me tells me he doesn't know that, and it works. It's not that I'm against getting tattooed by my buddy, Chance. He's an equally talented tattoo artist as my kid brother. I can't explain why I only want Shawn to do mine. Maybe the answer is as simple as he's my brother. He's someone who won't question the whys or the meanings of each tattoo; he just does as I ask. Any conversation during the ink session is monotonous, although I would miss this time together if he were to refuse me. It's the only way we really know how to connect.

When Shawn was in high school, he started apprenticing at a local tattoo parlor in our hometown of Tupelo, Mississippi. During my first year in medical school, I was home visiting, and that's when he finally talked me into letting him ink my skin. That night, tattooing became an outlet, my release when the pain and pressure inside became too heavy.

Shawn has only been tattooing for a few years, although sometimes it feels much longer. He dropped out of college his first semester to become a full-time tattoo artist here at Wicked Ink. Now he's the owner.

"Why don't you tell me what's bothering you? Because it's not me or my morbid need for your torture." He gives me a look that tells me he doesn't find my humor very funny.

"I'm fine." His words come out as a bite. His voice intimidates most people—even grown men. To me, he's still and will always be my kid brother, who, if he needs it, I will drop on his ass when he gets out of hand. He's lucky I didn't find out about the mess he put Taralynn through until long after it had been said and done. He was the one that told me everything. Had I not been so drunk, I probably would have whooped his ass. The punk would have deserved it too—still deserves it, if you ask me.

"You're not fine, Shawn. You're stressed, and you look as old as I feel." At twenty-eight years old, I feel as if I should be in my late thirties. My little brother is six years younger than me at twenty-two. He has dark circles under his eyes as if he isn't getting enough sleep, or maybe he's back to drinking more—possibly both. I don't know. "Are you planning on speaking today?"

The tattoo is complete. He just has to clean it, then wrap it, and I'll be on my way.

As if thinking the same thing, Shawn glances down at my leg before he pulls in a deep breath of air through his nose.

"I haven't gotten laid in five months, asshole."

He and Taralynn still aren't in the clear, although they aren't broken up either. I don't know what they are really; I'm not sure anyone, including both of them, knows. Neither one talked about what happened, nor did they speak of the future. It's like they're in limbo, neither wanting to make any move for fear of making the wrong one. "I'm wound a little tight, okay?"

"Try being dry for over a year, and then come talk to me, dickhead."

His facial expression changes to one of shock. He clearly wasn't expecting that to fall from my mouth.

"I know why I'm not getting any pussy. What's your excuse?"

"Do you think you could not use the word 'pussy' when referring to someone I think of as a sister?" Jesus Christ. I look up to the ceiling, then back to him. I should have never opened my mouth. He's waiting for an explanation. One I don't plan on sharing. I'm going to have to steer this conversation back to him, or he won't stop pushing until he gets something out of me. "So, what? She still isn't allowing you into her bed yet?"

"I'm in her bed almost every night. And if I'm not, she's in mine. We just haven't moved past cuddling." He says the last word like it's the most disgusting word in the English language.

"Has she cut you off completely? What's the deal? I thought you both were making progress, wanting your relationship to work." When I first found out about my little brother and Trent's little sister hooking up, I was pissed. Granted, Trent had always been adamant about there being something—or could be something—between them if Shawn would just wake up and pay attention long enough to see it.

I have to admit, though, I didn't see it. My brother has never been the love 'em and leave 'em guy, just the screw 'em and be done with 'em kind. Love had never been in the equation for him, and I didn't want Taralynn to be one of *those* chicks. I see now, that she isn't and would never be. He is in love with her—something I never expected to see. He surprised the hell out of me.

"No." He shakes his head. "She didn't cut me off."

"Then what?" This may be a worse topic to roll with. It's not like I want to know he and Taralynn have sex. "Are you even trying to have sex with her?"

"Not exactly." He twists his upper body, grabbing a spray bottle from the tray, then turns back, spraying water over the ink on my leg.

"Spit it out, Shawn. What do you mean? Do you not want to have sex with your girlfriend anymore?" I breathe hard. "Is that the problem? Because if you're planning on breaking up with her *again*, I will beat your ass this time." He tears a clean paper towel off the roll to wipe the soap, water, and excess ink off my skin.

"I'd like to see you try." He laughs while tossing the dirty paper towel into the trash bin.

"I don't think you do." Shawn and I are matched in height. We're both six feet, two inches tall, but where he is bulkier from weight lifting, I'm leaner from running and the Jiu-Jitsu training I used to do. I have no idea if I can take my brother down or not. Outside of a wrestling match—which I haven't done in years—I have never been in a street fight, whereas Shawn has. But I'd bet money on myself that I can hold my own. "Do not break her heart... again. Do you understand me?"

"I'm not planning on it." Anger flares briefly in his dark eyes. He's always been quick-tempered. "Look, have you seen Tara? Because if you have, then you know how smoking hot she is. Of course, I want to fuck her. She's a goddamn animal in the bed and out of it."

"Dude!" I say louder than I should. "There are some things I do not want to know. That is one of them." Christ.

"Well, don't bring my sex life up then." He turns again. This time he grabs a half-drunk bottle of water, twists the cap off, then takes a long swig. "You're not getting out of this conversation. Spill your shit. I know you aren't getting laid for the lack of bitches trying. Who was that one last month? The blonde. She was definitely trying hard to get into your pants."

"She isn't a bitch." I grab the nearly empty bottle of water from his hand, downing the rest.

"I didn't say she *is* a bitch. I was just referring to her as a woman." He looks at me like I'm the stupid one. He's unbelievable at times.

"Then say, woman or chick or whatever. You don't have to call every woman a bitch, man. Jesus." I don't know how Taralynn deals with his mouth. "Her name is Roxanne. She's one of the interns I'm supervising through the end of December, and she is just a friend and neighbor. I have no interest in a relationship with her."

"She does. Or at least has an interest in your dick." He laughs, but I don't find this subject funny at all. Before I can tell him to leave it alone, Taralynn's voice catches both of our attention, causing us to turn our heads in her direction.

"Goddammit, Kenny, this is a workplace, not a fucking playground." From the look of it, Kenny and another guy I don't know were just tossing a foam football back and forth inside the open space here in the shop. Kenny must have bumped into Taralynn when she was walking through. She shoves at his back, forcing him to stumble forward. He and the other guy look at her with stunned expressions on their faces. "Take that shit outside. No, better yet, take that shit home if you want to play like five-year-olds instead of working."

I glance at my brother with an eyebrow raised. He looks equally shocked and perhaps even a little scared of his girlfriend's actions.

"Great, now your colorful mouth has rubbed off on an angel." I shake my head. Taralynn is not one to cuss. She's also never one to fly off the handle and go off on anyone. "Precious," I call out the pet name I started calling her when she was five.

She looks over at us. First at Shawn, then when her eyes land on mine, she forces a smile. This isn't good. Taralynn isn't happy. Not even a little bit.

After a beat, she heads over, stopping next to me.

She's dressed in light-colored blue jeans and a black sleeveless tank top that is cut low in the front. Taralynn is well-endowed, so it's impossible— even for me—not to notice all the cleavage she has on show today. Her blonde waves are longer than usual, so the length helps to cover them up somewhat. She is a beautiful woman, and I love her deeply, but in a far opposite way than my brother does. She and Trent came into my life a long time ago. He used to drag her everywhere we went, so somewhere along the way, I started feeling like a protective brother toward her.

She'll always be a precious, sweet girl to me, and it bugs me that Trent isn't here to watch her blossom into the strong woman I see her becoming.

"Hey," she whispers as her features soften.

"You okay?"

"Just fine." Another forced smile emerges from her lips. She looks over at Shawn. "Can we talk in the office?"

"Uh... yeah," he says, sounding a bit unsure of himself, which is unlike him. Without looking at me, he tells me, "Be back in a minute." Then he stands, following behind his girlfriend.

"What's up with those two?" I ask Kenny, one of the other tattooists, when they're out of earshot. He bends down, picking up the soft football from the floor.

"Man, who fucking knows?" He shakes his head as I sit up, reaching for the wrapping material on Shawn's tray. I've watched him do it plenty of times, so it's no problem to wrap myself. "They tiptoe around everything with each other. With everyone else, they act like they're pissed off at the world."

He walks to his station, tossing the ball on the counter as I wrap my leg. When I'm finished, I stand and pull up my jeans.

A loud bang comes from the back of the shop where the office is located. Seconds later, music flows into the studio from the speakers on the walls. I chuckle, shaking my head. Something tells me their dry spell is officially over. But I don't stick around to find out. Time for me to head home—back to an empty apartment.

The pressure in the center of my chest didn't so much as lift a little while I was sitting in Shawn's chair. I don't know how much more of this I can take. I like to think I'm a strong person, both physically and mentally, but these feelings inside me will start to seep out and affect my job if I don't find another method soon to take the edge off.

CHAPTER 2

WHITNEY

"**M**om!"

"MOM," my oldest daughter shouts.

I close my eyes for a needed reprieve. It's going to be one of those days. I can feel it. I can feel it all the way down to my bones.

I breathe in deep, then exhale in a rush, blowing the air out of my mouth as I wish it would take away the hardship of being a parent with it. If only for just a little while. It shouldn't be this hard...

"Hello," she continues, her voice returning to a normal volume. But I can hear the irritation even without looking at her. Always so irritated.

What do I do? How do I fix this?

Turning away from the counter, I take in my daughter's appearance. She's standing at the entrance to our designer kitchen—that I hate—with her arms crossed over her chest. Her long, dark, almost black hair camouflages her anger. Almost. The eyes show all, though. Her blue-green eyes are both stunningly beautiful and haunting at the same time. They always have been from the moment the dark pigment shed and her real color sparkled to life. I remember that moment like it happened yesterday. A strange feeling had pierced my chest, and for a split second, I felt pain, longing even. I had thought I was about to have a heart attack. I think it must have been new mom emotions. I had them often when she was a baby.

Today she's dressed in a red and white checkered flannel shirt with the sleeves rolled up to her elbows. It's unbuttoned over a white tank top with dark blue jeans tucked into her favorite pair of cowboy boots. Why on earth she's wearing warm clothes this time of year is beyond me. It may be early fall, but it still feels a lot like summer in Tennessee.

"If you have something to say to me, then you need to do so without an attitude, young lady."

On the one hand, I feel as though I shouldn't say things like that to her. It only fuels the fire between us. On the other, I can't sit here and let her speak to me the way she sometimes does.

She pops off at the slightest thing she doesn't like or at something that doesn't go her way. It's her outlet, I guess. And maybe I envy that occasionally. I wish I had an outlet for everything bubbling inside my belly.

Her stare darkens. She hates it when I use pet names. Anything other than her name, or Ev for short, seems to tick her off these days. And people say the terrible twos are bad. I disagree. She was sweet as pie at two.

Slowly the anger fades, replaced with a sadness that catches me off guard.

"What's wrong?" My voice turns to motherly concern for my little girl. It doesn't seem that long ago that she was in diapers crawling around and climbing into my lap just to be close to me or wrapping her fist around my hair as if it were her safety blanket. I miss those days.

"You promised." Her tone is an accusation.

Confused, my eyebrows turn inward as I ask, "I promised what?"

"If I got all A's on my report card, I'd be able to take guitar lessons after school. Why can't I?" she whines.

I sigh, shaking my head, remembering the exact conversation at the start of her third-grade school year this past August.

"What I said was, 'I would convince your dad to allow it.'" I knew it wouldn't be an easy feat. Blake, for whatever reason, hates music and is adamant he doesn't want anything to distract our children from their education. He and I disagree wholeheartedly on this. *We disagree a lot.*

Music is often a lifesaver for my sanity, so I understand our child's need for it. It is often times an outlet—an outlet I feel she needs. I know I do. "Did you say something about it to your father already?" I cringe at the tone of my voice. I didn't mean for it to come out the way it sounded. Harsh. Accusing.

"Well, yeah. I wanted to start lessons this week." Her arms fall away from her chest, only to be placed on her narrow hips. She's like me in this way. When she wants something, she wants it now, five minutes ago. "Why?" she demands.

Lord help me.

Had I not been able to convince Blake, I had still planned on letting her do the lessons. I just wasn't going to tell my husband. But I can't tell her any of this. She doesn't understand the trials and tribulations of marriage—and she shouldn't at her age. I pray when she grows up and decides to marry, things will be different for her than they have been for me.

I shake my head of these thoughts. I have no business thinking like that and every reason to be grateful for my two girls. And I am grateful—very grateful, but sometimes...

I sigh, letting my thoughts die with the air coming out of my mouth. "I'll talk to him," I finally tell her as I stride over to stand in front of her. I place my palms on each side of her cheeks, then tilt her head slightly up. After I plant a chaste kiss on her forward, I say, "I'll find a way for you to take the lessons."

Her frown turns into a small smile. "Thanks, Momma." I drop my hands, taking a step back.

"Grab something to eat before it's time for you to leave for school," I tell her. "Your dad will be down any minute to take you."

I get an eye roll but choose to ignore it. My relationship with her is strained, but I don't have a name for what Blake's relationship with her is. They seem to always be at war with each other these days.

Honestly, I can't blame her. It seems nothing either of us does is ever good enough for Blake Lane, except maybe Emersyn, our three-year-old. She is his pride and joy. To him, she is perfection.

While my daughter grabs a granola bar from the pantry, I go back to fixing Emersyn's oatmeal that she eats most mornings. A minute later, the temperature in the kitchen turns cooler. It always does when he enters a room.

I turn my head just as my husband comes up behind me. He places one hand on the curve of my hip, squeezing gently. I've mastered not cringing when he does this. "Morning," he offers before placing a kiss on my temple. "I forgot to give these to you when I got home last night." I take the prescription bag that's stapled closed with my birth control pills inside.

"Thank you," I reply, sitting the white bag on the countertop. I am one day from needing to start a new pack. I never take the sugar pills during the last week. What's the point? "Are you busy this afternoon? I thought Em and I might grab you from the office so we could have lunch together."

He blows out a puff of air that ruffles the back of my hair before moving away from me to make himself a cup of coffee.

"I can't today," is all he offers.

"Oh, you have a meeting?"

"Yes, Whitney." His voice is firm. It was a simple question, not one I meant to irritate him. "I work. I don't have time for play dates."

I catch the angered glare my daughter throws his way out of the corner of my eye before she abruptly turns, leaving the room. I have to bite my tongue not to return a remark that will only piss him off more. My fingers curl around the edge of the countertop, and I have to close my eyes for a few seconds. It burns in my stomach to hold my tongue. It feels wrong. Always has. Instinct tells me to kick him in the dick for the way he just spoke to me, but I can't do that. I know I can't do that.

Once the need to lash back is gone, I release the pressure and tell him, "Maybe dinner, then? Do you think you'll be home in time to have dinner with us tonight?" Last night he was late and didn't bother to let me know until he was en route home—after eight. After the kids were already in bed and dinner was long gone.

"Yes, I'll be home by six thirty. A nice cooked meal would be great." I watch him take a sip from the travel coffee mug the girls got him for Father's Day this past year. I'm surprised he still uses it. He wasn't that thrilled about the gift when he received it. "I'm off. Have a good day doing whatever it is you do." He grins, but it doesn't reach his eyes. Not even close. *It looks fake.* But finally, he turns away from me, heading out.

Relief expels from my body, exiting my mouth. It always does when he leaves for work.

My head turns toward the door leading to our garage as my daughter yells, "Bye, Mom." My lips tilt up automatically at the sound of her voice, but the smile wanes almost immediately when I hear Blake reprimand her for raising her voice in the house. At that, I grit my teeth.

He needs more than just a good kick to the crotch. So much more.

I am a stay-at-home mom. Always have been since my oldest daughter was born. It isn't something I love or hate. I enjoy my time with my girls, but I know something is missing. I just don't know what.

There's a void. A part of me feels hollow. And no matter what I have, I know deep down it isn't enough to satisfy. It's been that way for years—since I woke up in a hospital without a memory.

I've yearned for my past for over ten years now. Maybe mourned for it even. I don't know. But something isn't whole inside me. Then again, maybe it never was, and I just didn't remember always feeling this way. Still...

My thoughts are cut off when I hear Emersyn running down the stairs, yelling my name. Time to start *whatever it is I do all day.*

CHAPTER 3

SHANE

Treating kids—of any age—isn't easy. I don't know why I thought it would be when I decided to be a pediatric physician at the beginning of my senior year of high school. My mom's a general practitioner in pediatrics, and my dad is an adult cardiologist. I've always wanted to be a doctor. There wasn't a moment in my life when I wanted to do anything else.

Every summer back in high school, I worked in my mom's clinic doing various non-clinical things and fell in love with all the kids that came through. Following in my mother's footsteps, going into pediatrics was a no-brainer. But every time I treat a child with a confirmed or life-threatening disease, I question if I can do this for the rest of my career.

"Judy," I call the charge nurse's name as I exit room three. "Order a full set of labs and a CT of the chest with contrast on my patient." I stop in front of the nurse's station.

A palm lands down, gripping my shoulder. When I turn my head to the side, I find the residency director, my boss, Dr. Forsythe, standing next to me.

"Gavin," I greet him by his first name as I hand the patient's chart over to the nurse. She nods, acknowledging my requests.

"So," he starts out. "I'm having a holiday get-together Saturday night.

I can expect you to come, right?" He squeezes my shoulder, letting me know he isn't asking if I can make it or not. My presence is expected. He may have quickly become my friend a few months ago when I transferred to Memphis to finish out my residency, but he is, first and foremost, my boss.

"My brother and his girlfriend are coming up from Oxford tomorrow and staying the weekend..." I let my reply hang in the air, hoping he folds, letting me out, but I know there's a slim chance of that. I have two days scheduled off this week. Friday and Saturday.

"Bring 'em," he tells me. "The more, the merrier and all that."

"Yeah, I guess I could."

Halloween is this coming Saturday, and Taralynn told me last week she wants to go out clubbing when they come up. I know the real reason they're driving up for a visit, just as I know the reason they insisted I come to Georgia with them on Labor Day weekend last month to ride ATVs. Trent's death is still fresh for everyone—me especially. He and I had been best friends since we were ten years old and roommates since the summer we graduated high school and enrolled in college. Kylie was practically living with us even though she technically had a dorm room. We had one too, freshman year. We just didn't use it since my grandparents let us live in their old home now that they were retired, living in Florida.

After grad school, the three of us lived together again while in medical school. Every holiday not spent back home in Tupelo, Mississippi, was an excuse for Kylie to throw a party. Halloween has always been her favorite.

If I had to guess, Shawn's best friend and Kylie's youngest sibling, Mason Morgan, will head to Orlando, Florida—if he isn't already there—to spend time with his sister for the same reason Taralynn has insisted they're coming to see me.

It's not that I hate them coming. I enjoy seeing Taralynn and my ass of a little brother. But going out to a club is a hassle I'm dreading. It just isn't my thing anymore. Really, it never was. Hanging with friends, I enjoy. Hanging out in a loud and crowded place... not so much.

"Why aren't you taking the kids trick-or-treating?" I ask. Gavin has toddler-aged twins, so it surprises me he and his wife won't be doing the family thing instead.

"Maria's parents are handling that this year. The kids are going to their house tomorrow night and staying through Sunday."

I nod my head, letting out a soft laugh.

"So, this get-together," I pause, turning to face him, "are the interns coming too?" A coy smile graces his face, and I know before he speaks, they will be.

"It's going to be epic." His eyes dance with delight, making me chuckle. I've heard of *his* idea of amusement. And I want no part of it.

"And costumes...?" I leave the question hanging. Kylie's thrown a Halloween party every year since our first year of college, and I've never worn a costume. I haven't worn one since I was a kid, I don't think. If I wouldn't do it for my best friend's girl, I'm certainly not doing it for him. Boss or no boss, it's not happening.

"Only if you want to be my source of entertainment for the night."

"And I'm guessing you aren't planning on informing the interns of this?" Of course he's not. I'm just surprised none of them have heard of his yearly "initiation," as the other residents call it. But maybe since he's only been the residency director for the last four years, the stories haven't circulated enough.

"Mum's the word." He places his index finger over his lips to stress his point. "See you Saturday, Braden."

I shake my head as he walks off.

"Shane?" I hear Roxanne call my name. Looking over my shoulder, I see her walking out of room one toward me. "You got a sec?"

"Sure." I turn, facing her. "What do you need?"

"My patient complains of stomach pains, but the x-ray was clear. I ordered a lab panel, and those came back normal." She looks back toward the patient's room. "I'm not sure what else to try. They don't have insurance, so I don't want to order a procedure if he doesn't need it."

"Want me to take a look at him?"

"Please," she sighs in relief.

"Come on, let's go figure out what's wrong with your patient."

CHAPTER 4

WHITNEY

A *happy husband is a man with a wife that does her wifely duties, Whitney.* My mother's obnoxious voice plays in the back of my mind, making me want to vomit all over the porcelain sink in my primary bathroom.

Looking in the mirror, I remove the teardrop diamond earrings from my lobes. *I can do this.* I place them off to the side, making a mental note to put them back into the jewelry cabinet in my closet when I'm done washing my face. I stare at the eyes looking back at me. They often appear violet even though they're technically a shade of blue. Tonight, they definitely look deep and much darker than usual. *I can do this.*

It's just sex.

And guitar lessons would mean the world to my daughter. *I can—*

"Dinner was... edible." I turn the faucet on to allow the hot water to heat as I cut my eyes over to him through the mirror as Blake saunters in. "Why didn't you place a delivery order from Macaro's? You know I love them, and I told you this morning I'd be home for dinner." He removes his watch, placing it neatly on his side of the vanity. Everything in his small bubble has to be orderly. *Everything.* My fingers itch to move it—move anything—just to watch his face twitch like it does when I leave my shoes scattered about or when I have the laundry dumped on the couch.

Oh, he hates that. I laugh internally.

"Because I wanted to cook." He may not like my cooking, but I like it. I happen to think I'm pretty good. Sure, I'm not great. I'm not a chef, but I don't suck at it.

Leaning over the sink, I gather warm water into my palms. After splashing it onto my face, I pump facial soap out and lather, creating suds to rid the makeup I put on before my husband arrived home for the dinner he's so graciously complaining about now.

"You know that isn't your strong suit, Whitney." He turns the water inside the shower on.

What is my strong suit is what I want to ask, but I doubt he would give any answer that isn't laced with condescension.

He's a prick, and if it weren't for my children, I'd say it to his face and rid myself of him once and for all. I honestly don't know what I saw in him before I lost my memory. Was I like him? Did I find his *I'm better than anyone else* attitude attractive?

Surely not. And if I did, maybe the accident was a godsend. Maybe I should stop praying for my memories.

I watch as he loosens his tie before disappearing into the closet. Quickly pulling the hand towel from where it hangs, I pat my face dry before he finishes undressing.

Walking out of the bathroom, I grab a pair of pajamas from the chest of drawers underneath where the television is hanging on the wall in our bedroom. After tossing them onto my bed, I pull my dress over my head, letting it drop from my hands to land in a pile on the carpet. I slip my arms through the silk camisole and finish by pulling up the matching set of teal shorts before climbing into bed.

It's a good fifteen minutes before he emerges from his shower. I quickly close the notebook I had been writing in, leaving the pen inside the page marking my spot, then place it in the drawer of my nightstand before he has a chance to inquire what I'm doing.

I know he didn't notice when I catch a glimpse of the tick in his jaw from across the room. He's eyeing the dress I purposely left on the floor.

"Is it so hard to put dirty clothes in the hamper?" He stalks over, shaking his head. Blake bends at the waist to grab the material. I chew on my bottom lip to stop myself from smirking.

He returns half a minute later, joining me in our bed.

The smell of his shampoo wafts up my nostrils, crinkling the bridge of my nose. The scent is too strong—*too wrong.* The thought of him on top of me makes my insides fist. I don't have to think about the idea too long because his hand snakes around my middle as he scoots closer to my side.

I can do this. I've been chanting the same mantra since I started prepping dinner. I knew it was coming. I even wanted it this time. *For my daughter's sake.* She doesn't ask for much. She's not like other kids I see her age asking their parents every five seconds for a new toy—or a new anything. Her friends are all spoiled little brats, but she's never taken any of her things for granted or been selfish. She's a great kid despite our constant battles.

His palm slips up my camisole at the same time his nose runs along my jaw, moving my long hair out of his way.

"You really should get this cut, honey. It's getting a bit too long, and you know I hate it dangling in my face when you're on top of me."

I mentally calculate when the last time that was. I don't remember. You'd think with the limited memories I have, it would be easy to recall an instance where we were making love with me straddling him, but I can't. Then again, it isn't like we have intercourse that often. Missionary is fine, don't get me wrong, but a girl—this girl—gets bored with the same ole same ole every time.

His hand latches onto my breast, squeezing. My throat tightens as bile threatens to spew. *I can't do this.* It's like this every time, and I can't figure out why. Other women like sex—love it even. So why don't I? What's wrong with me?

"Blake," I whine.

His lips touch my neck. My body squirms on its own accord.

"It's been a long damn day, Whitney. I need this."

"This weekend," I promise. "It's been a long day for me too, and—"

"Goddammit," he blows out as he pulls back. "You don't know what a long day is. Try dealing with the shit I have to deal with on a daily basis." He shakes his head, moving back to his side of the bed. Seconds later, the lamp is turned off, and we're cloaked in darkness.

Relief floods me even as his words burn a fire in my belly.

Lying is wrong.

Deceiving is wrong.

So why doesn't it bother me that that's what I'm doing? It goes against everything I've been told by Blake and my parents about the person I was before my car wreck. The good girl. The rule follower. Those two sentences alone make my skin itch. There's something inside me that craves disarray. Chaos, even.

Order is overrated.

Maybe that's just what I'm telling myself to justify my actions. And now that I've given it more thought, sex wouldn't have gotten Blake to agree to allow our daughter to take the guitar lessons she's been begging for, for months.

No. I had to do it this way.

Somewhere deep inside, I know he's going to eventually find out. Whether it's Everly slipping up and mentioning it or when he notices the credit card statement. He's a banker, after all. It's bound to happen, and I'll have to deal with it when it does.

But am I prepared for his blow-up? I guess I'll find out when it happens...

"Thank you. Thank you. Thank you, Momma," she chants as we pull into the parking lot of the Memphis, Tennessee studio I found online that offers lessons on weekday afternoons.

When I spoke to the teacher, he had an opening thirty minutes after Everly gets out of school. It's an hour-long session three days a week. It's perfect. I have just enough time to pick her up and get there on time. How could I not sign her up? The studio and the private school she attends are on the same route to and from our house.

This'll be good. No, great, I tell myself as a smile forms on my face at the sight of my daughter's happiness.

"You're welcome, sweet girl. Let me get Em out of her booster seat, and then we'll go in."

She bolts from the back seat, opposite her sister, as I exit the driver's seat of my red metallic Mercedes SUV.

Excitement blooms where guilt should be festering, but I don't allow my mind to think too hard. Instead, I grab Emersyn and then catch up to where Everly is standing at the glass entrance.

I just hope this doesn't catch up to me sooner rather than later.

CHAPTER 5

SHANE

I slide my hand over, reaching for hers. Glancing at me, she smiles at me when I intertwine our fingers.

A flash goes off from the backseat of my Jeep Wrangler, courtesy of Trent's girlfriend.

"Knock it off, Kylie. You're screwing with my vision by snapping pictures every two seconds."

Jesus Christ. I'm starting to see dots, and we're late. Dinner with my folks ran long tonight, so Whit and I didn't pick up Trent and Kylie until after nine. We were supposed to be at Chance's uncle's by eight-thirty.

"Lighten up for once, Shane. We're graduates now. And in less than two months, we'll all be away at college and out of sight of our parents. This calls for a celebration tonight. Right, Whit?" Kylie eggs on.

"You know it," my girlfriend agrees, earning her a scowl from me. It only takes her giggle for me to falter. Her laughs are my undoing.

"Some of us don't have perfect parents like you, Shaney."

"Hey! Don't call him that." Whitney quickly chimes in as she swings her head toward the backseat, giving her best friend a scowl of her own. Kylie thinks she's being cute when she calls me that, but it irritates the hell out of me, and I wish Trent would get her to stop.

"What. Ever."

"*Whit and Trent may have a leg to stand on,*" I say. "*But what issues do you have with your parents, Ky?*"

"*Oh my God! Have you met my overbearing mother?*"

"*Yep. Several times. She's pretty normal in comparison.*"

"*In comparison to what?*" Kylie demands. "*Your parents are awesomesauce on top of awesomesauce with sprinkles on top.*"

"*I know, right?*" I laugh. My parents are far from perfect, but they are great. I don't have one complaint. I might have a moody little brother that's a jerk at times, but I wouldn't trade my family for another.

"*I hate you.*" Looking in the rearview mirror, I see Kylie glaring at me with her arms crossed over her chest.

"*She may hate you, babe, but I don't.*" I glance to my right. If there is one thing that is perfect in this world, it's the girl sitting next to me right now.

"*Hand me your camera,*" Whitney tells Ky as the sound of her seatbelt releasing registers in my ear.

"*Love, what are you doing?*" I ask without looking at her. It's starting to drizzle, so I flick the handle to make the windshield wipers come on.

"*I'm capturing moments,*" she calls out, trying to appease me. From the rearview mirror, I see Whitney take the camera from Kylie's hand. "*You two cuddle up and smile,*" she tells Trent and Kylie.

"*Whitney,*" I call out. "*Put your seatbelt back on.*"

"*Hush.*" Click.

From my peripheral vision, I see her turn back around to face forward, but then the flash goes off again, momentarily blinding me.

"*Whitney,*" I force out, blinking several times.

Just as I'm reopening my eyes headlights round the corner...

A sharp inhale of air not only forces my eyes to pop open but also causes me to spring up. Air. I need air.

When I let the same nightmare that's on constant replay fade, I find myself alone in my bed... as always. The comforter is missing, but I know it ended up somewhere on the floor during the night. The dark blue sheets have been kicked to the end of the bed, almost falling off. There's sweat sliding down my forehead.

I draw in a deep breath, trying to shake the rest of the dream away.

But it's never far.

And it always returns.

A sigh escapes my mouth as I climb out of bed.

I know there's only one way to push it to the back of my mind... for now at least.

Going to my chest of drawers against the wall, I pull out a pair of sweat pants and put them on, pulling them over my boxer briefs, followed by my socks and sneakers. Grabbing my earbuds from where they lie on top of the chest of drawers, I head for the door.

Running away from my past is what I've done for what feels like a lifetime now. The only problem is I can never get far enough away. Doesn't stop me from trying.

TEN MILES LATER, I MAKE it back up the stairs to my third-floor apartment just as daylight breaks through the dark sky.

I have roughly two hours before I'm due at the children's hospital for a full day in the ER, but I have no plans for any more shuteye. A long, hot shower, though, is just what I need.

I pull the earbuds of my headphones from both of my ears just as *Torn to Pieces* by Pop Evil winds down.

As I get closer to my door, I see Roxanne's door swinging open before she walks out.

Her sharp intake of air isn't lost on me, but I act like I don't catch it.

"Hey. Where are you headed so early?" I ask, stopping by my door. Our apartments are directly across from each other. Rox is one of the interns I'm training in the Children's emergency department. As a third-year resident, I have to work in the ER for three months out of this fiscal year. This month through the end of December, that's where I'll be—some days, some nights. My schedule rotates every quarter. Nights are the worst. Working 7 p.m. through 7 a.m. will wear on a person's body—at least mine it does. I prefer day shift hours.

"Morning, Shane," she greets. "I promised my sister I'd take her kids to school this morning. She has to take her husband to the airport for an early flight for a business trip. What are you doing up already?"

I glance down at the sweat pouring down my chest.

"I'm usually up at this time every day unless I'm working. I like to run before the day officially starts."

I do like to run. I've always enjoyed it. Whitney and I used to run together every evening before dinner. Now, I don't know, maybe it makes me feel connected to her somehow. I often wonder if she still runs too. I shouldn't, but I do. Letting my mind wonder about those types of things makes it harder to breathe. Makes life harder.

"Well..." She pauses, allowing her eyes to run down my body. "Looks like it pays off." She gives me a coy smile once her eyes sweep back up.

It's not that she isn't an attractive woman, she is, very much so, but that doesn't mean I'm interested. For starters, I'm practically her teacher and somewhat her supervisor, in a way. All third-year residents are assigned first-year interns to help mold them into the doctors they need to become. It would be wrong—unethical—to pursue any form of a relationship. Casual or not.

"I'm going to hit the shower. See you at work." I nod in her direction.

Without another word, I go inside my apartment.

CHAPTER 6

WHITNEY

"Whitney." *His voice vibrates through the strands of my hair and into my ear like a caress, drawing out a moan from my lips. His free hand, the one not laced around my waist that's keeping me against his body, moves into my hair. His fingers comb the damp strands away from my ear, pushing my hair to my right shoulder. "God. I love you, Love."*

"Harder." *I fight the words out as he pounds into me. Sweat—his sweat from where his forehead presses against my temple—drops onto the apple of my cheek. Another moan, this time louder, escapes. I can't control it. I know I'm supposed to be quiet, but it's impossible.*

"Mmmm."

My voice jars me from the dream I was having.

"Mmmm."

Wait. That isn't my voice.

"Blake." Ughhh. Not this again. He usually doesn't try this hard, which suits me just fine.

"You were the one rubbing against my dick." He paws my breasts.

Always the boobs, and I don't get it. They're small. Not what I would consider my best feature either. I don't see what his interest in them is. His hands on them certainly aren't turning me on.

Then again, do they ever?

I'm still hot from my dream. *The dream.* The same recurring one I've had for a couple of years now. Little by little, I'll get more of it. I had hoped when they started occurring it meant my memories were coming back to me, but so far, no such luck.

"It's too early. You know I'm not a morning sex person."

I leave out that I'm not a sex person no matter the time of day, although he'd have to be dumb not to have figured that out by now with our lack thereof. And one thing I'm certain of is Blake Lane isn't dumb.

"Tonight. I promise." I push on his chest. "The girls are staying at my parents, remember? We'll have plenty of alone time then, okay?"

"And we're going to my friend's house after dinner at your parents, remember?" he stresses.

"Of course, honey," I confirm. "But after we take the girls trick-or-treating through my parents' neighborhood," I remind him.

He releases me, then rolls away. I sigh, thanking the heavens above.

Sitting up in bed, I pull the sheet to my chest.

"I don't see what the big deal is. They certainly don't need the candy." He walks around the foot of the bed with a disgusted look marring his pale face. He never agreed to my plan, but I'm taking them whether or not he joins.

"Because it's fun." I throw the sheet off, then slide out of bed. I need to jump in the shower quickly before Emersyn wakes, so without continuing this conversation that'll only lead to an argument, I jet into the bathroom.

I've learned with Blake that you pick your battles. And this is one I'll deal with if needed, but usually when I'm adamant about something and walk off—leaving him no room to worm his way out—I stand a better chance of getting what I want.

WHAT'S BUGGING YOU? I ask Blake as I eye him from the passenger seat of his black Lexus SUV. His head briefly swings toward me, his irritated brown eyes flashing at me.

He's pissed. That's easy to tell and not uncommon these days.

"You went behind my back, Whitney." Air rushes out through his clenched teeth. It's dark inside his car except for the glow of the LED lights coming from the navigation system in the center of the dashboard. I can't see his expression clearly, but I can hear the swoosh of air he makes when it exits his mouth. "You allowed her to take music lessons when you knew I specifically said no."

"Guitar lessons," I correct, which makes my husband inhale deeply. And before he can lash out at me, I continue. "She earned them, Blake. She made straight A's, and it's all she has asked for. She has wanted them for two years now. She deserves this."

"She deserves what I say she deserves." I gasp involuntarily at his response. My blood boils. "We're going to table this discussion until we're at home. I've had a long day at the office, and I still have to work tonight. This get-together, as you know, is at the Forsythes' home. If I can gain Dr. Forsythe's trust, I can gain him as a client. Tonight is very important, Whitney. I'm asking you not to give me any more grief."

The comeback is on the tip of my tongue itching to burst out. I want to tell him to *go fuck himself* more than I want to take my next breath. But I can't do that. I have my girls to think about, as my mother loves to remind me when I bitch about my husband and our crap-ass marriage.

So instead, I close my eyes for a moment as Blake pulls up behind a black Chevy Tahoe. When the car is in park, I open my lids, forcing a smile on my face.

When we reach the Forsythes' front door, Blake knocks. Seconds later, it opens to reveal a man that appears to be in his mid-to-late thirties with sandy blond hair and light green eyes encased in dark lashes. His eyes crinkle, welcoming us into his home.

"Mr. Lane, you decided to come. I'm so glad." The man's smile is genuine.

"Call me Blake, please, Dr. Forsythe."

"Okay then," he laughs lightly before turning his gaze to me. "You must be Blake's beautiful other half. I'm Gavin." He presents his hand in front of me, which I accept and shake.

"I'm Whitney. Thank you for inviting us." I release his warm hand, bringing my own up to my face, tucking a strand of my dark hair back behind my ear.

"It's a pleasure, Whitney." He takes a step backward. "Please, come in. There are wines and appetizers in the kitchen and several coolers of beer on the back patio. Help yourselves to anything you like."

"Thank you, Doctor," Blake chimes.

"Gavin," the man corrects as we enter his house.

Entering the foyer, I take in the warm decor. The walls are navy blue with a soft, eggshell trim in an off-white shade. Hung on the walls are scattered black and white portraits of people. It doesn't take a genius to see it's his family. From the look of it, he has two small kids—a girl and a boy. Twins, I think. And his wife is stunning. They all have similar fair features.

Moving along, following the guys, we walk through the living room where Blake and Gavin stop.

"The kitchen is through there." He points across the room to a wide opening. I take that as my cue to leave them.

The kitchen is large, with a formal dining room to one side and a kitchen nook off to the other side. The walls are the same navy color as the entrance, and the trim and cabinetry match the other room as well.

I swipe a small slice of cheese from the platter on the island, placing it in my mouth as I glance around. I see several bottles of wine across from me with clear, plastic drinking cups close by. I don't think I'm in the mood for wine, though. I enjoy a glass sometimes, but beer sounds more appealing. But I know if I decide on anything other than water or wine, Blake will have a conniption. *Ladies don't drink beer.* I can hear him now. *It's unladylike.*

He and my mother are like broken records.

Fuck it.

Blake is already angry with me. What's one more thing? The thought is almost welcoming.

Pivoting, I head for the back door that looks like it leads out to the patio. I remember Gavin telling us that's where the beer is.

Just as I open the door, a beautiful, soft melody rises. It makes me halt before stepping outside. Familiarity hits me, but I'm not sure why.

At the same time, I'm compelled to sing like I often do when it's just Emersyn and me at home alone.

Words I've never spoken fall from my lips as easily as if I've sung them recently. My eyes close involuntarily, eating up the peace and serenity I feel.

Believe me when I tell you
You are my forever
Because baby, no one can break through the way you do.
You're an ache I can't shake.

You're the one I can't shake.
You are the one.

I open my eyes when the music stops, and everyone is staring at me. Unease creeps up my arms. I don't like being the center of attention. In fact, I hate it.

"I'm so sorry." I laugh. Giggle, actually, as my embarrassment wanes. "I have no idea where that came from?"

Where the hell did that come from?

"Love?"

My head snaps toward that voice—*that voice.* I know that voice. It's...

Our eyes meet, causing me to stumble out the door. My breath pulls in on a quick inhale. He's beautiful, but that's not what made me have such a reaction. I'm not even sure why I did, but my heart starts beating faster. Too fast.

I can't stop looking at him. *It can't be. Can it?* My eyes squint, scrutinizing him.

"Oh my God!"

The shock in her voice pulls my eyes over. A few feet from the guy my eyes were locked on stands a young woman with golden-blonde hair looking at me as though she's just seen a ghost. One hand covers her mouth, and the other grasps another man's forearm. He's tall. He's big, and the arm she's digging her nails into is covered in ink. The art is beautiful—stunning even. I've always admired tattoos. Maybe even wanted one, but that's not a battle I'm willing to start.

When I look back at the guy that called me by my middle name, butterflies erupt in my belly. There is something about him, something that makes me... want him? It doesn't take long for me to realize I'm attracted to the man standing in front of me. I don't feel this way about Blake. I don't think I ever did. Something about this stranger draws me in, and it's scaring me but exciting me all the same.

"Um—" I'm about to ask him if he knew me before the accident that erased my memory when meat hooks grip my biceps yanking me backward.

"We're leaving." I don't have to look behind me to know it was Blake. His tone was harsher than I've ever heard it before. It was venomous hatred, but hatred toward who?

I don't want to leave. Not because of Blake and his apparent temper tantrum, but because it feels wrong. Moving from this spot feels wrong.

I make an attempt to shake his hand off me, but it's futile. His grip is borderline painful.

"Stop," I whisper, glancing over my shoulder.

"Release her."

Looking back in front of me, I see it's *him*. The one that had been playing the guitar when I walked out—the man I want to reach out and touch. And I almost do. I catch myself raising my free arm, but quickly drop it back to my side. He's standing a few feet from me now.

You know him.

Maybe, but how?

My dream from this morning flickers through my mind. Is it *him*? That voice. I know that voice.

Could it be...

Anger flares across his breathtakingly beautiful face, but he's still just as hot. Anger doesn't look right on him, though. It looks foreign, like he doesn't get mad very often.

"Whitney, I said we are leaving. Let's go!" Blake ignores the guy's demand to let my arm go.

I try to pull away again as my own anger bubbles up. *Why is Blake acting like a dick?* I want answers to my past. I've always wanted answers—wanted my memory to return—and something is pulling me to the stranger in front of me.

But something deep inside me tells me he isn't a stranger at all.

His eyes flick down to where Blake's hand is still firmly gripping me. The sight must make him more upset because his blue-green eyes darken, turning stormy. Then his hands ball into fists at his sides. *Does he want to hit my husband?*

"You should probably let her go if you know what's best for you." My eyes dart to the other guy, the one the blonde girl was holding onto before. They've both walked over too. She's back to standing next to the younger guy with the tattoos. She has the same stunned expression on her pretty face.

"Shawn." The guitar guy warns, breathing hard through a beautiful set of straight, white teeth.

"You're hurting her, so you really need to do what my boyfriend says." That was the blonde female speaking to Blake. Her expression has changed to anger too.

"Whitney." Blake's tone is seething.

"Blake, let go," I demand. "How do you know me?" I question the man in front of me. His eyes instantly soften at the sound of my voice. But then they turn sad. Stricken...

No, don't be sad. I don't like sadness on him. My chest constricts painfully. *What the hell?*

"I... Oh, Love." He shakes his head, pain reflecting at me through *those* eyes.

"We're leaving." Blake squeezes my arm, pulling a yelp from my mouth. "I won't tell you again." His grip tightens.

Hatred, madness, and even disgust wash over the guitar man's face right in front of my eyes. He doesn't scare me, but I may be afraid for Blake the way he's looking at my husband. I force my feet to step forward. I want to place my palm on his chest to calm him. As I do so, something flies past the back of my head. I'm ripped from Blake's grip and then pulled toward my left. My face plants into the hard chest of the tattooed guy.

"Shawn." His name comes out like a scold this time.

When I look up, I'm rewarded with a mischievous smile. Something flashes in my mind like I've seen this same look before. My insides warm, my lips tipping with a small smile.

Glancing behind me, my husband is face down on the deck. Unmoving. He's out cold, and I don't have one shred of sympathy for him. *Why is that? Shouldn't I?*

I turn my head again to see the guy I now know as Shawn looking sideways.

"What?" Shawn shrugs, letting go of my forearm and steadying me as he continues speaking, "You would have done the same thing had I not. Don't tell me otherwise, brother."

Are they brothers? Looking back and forth between them, they look nothing alike. Shawn has dirty blond hair with brown eyes. He's about the same height as the other guy, but Shawn is bulkier, whereas the guitar guy is lean. And Shawn has tats down the left side of his arm. Guitar guy has dark, maybe black hair with glowing eyes I have to look away from. Something about him stirs up feelings I don't understand.

I shake my head, trying to clear it.

Something is going on here, and I get the feeling everyone but me knows what it is.

Why was my husband in such a rush to leave? Why did I start singing a song I've never heard? And who are these people that for the life of me, do not feel like strangers?

So many questions are swarming around in my head, wanting answers. Needing answers.

My chest is heavy. I need air. There are too many questions pressing to get out of my head.

I look to my guitar guy and do something both crazy and stupid.

"I need to leave." Panic flashes before me. "Will you get me out of here?" He exhales heavily, then nods as his body visibly relaxes.

I turn, looking down at Blake before stepping over him. And as I walk past, I realize I don't care if he gets back up. What does that say about my marriage?

Hell, what does that say about me as a person?

CHAPTER 7

SHANE

She's here.

She's here, standing two feet from me, and I can't even speak. I've waited for this moment for a long time. A moment to simply be in her presence again—to be able to breathe again. But my breath was stolen the second I heard her unforgettable voice for the first time since the night of our high school graduation.

It was as though life had flowed back into my body—finally after so long without it—then lost again when the realization hit me square in the heart. It's her, my Whitney in all her beauty, even more beautiful now than when we were teenagers. But she's married to someone that isn't me. Someone I want to walk back into Gavin's house and finish off.

How is it possible she's married to *him*?

Whit couldn't stand that jackass any more than I could.

Her parents.

It's the only explanation.

They tried for so long to fix the two of them up, even when we were in junior high school.

"I don't mean to rush you, but I want to be gone by the time Blake wakes up." She looks at me from over her shoulder. "Blake, that's my husband. That guy, your brother... or Shawn—I don't know if he's your brother or not—hit."

"I know who he is." My words exit with a bite. I don't mean for them too. It was always a rarity for me to speak to her in any way that wasn't with love. Even when she irritated and pissed me off, I still had a sense of calm around her. She was that calm. Her chaos was my calm.

I look at her with what I hope is an apology. She's walking backward but staring at me with curiosity in her violet eyes.

Damn. *Those eyes.*

Any look she gives me has the ability to render me at her mercy. I've missed them. I've missed her more than words can say.

"You know a lot, don't you?" Her brows turn inward. "About me, I mean. You know more about me than I do."

She doesn't remember me or anything of her life before I wrecked my Jeep. I knew she didn't. Had she remembered, she would have come back to me a long time ago.

"What do you know about yourself?" I can't stop the question from leaving my mouth. "I'm in the Tahoe over there." I point behind her.

Turning, she makes a beeline for the passenger side door. Taking my keys out of the front pocket of my jeans, I press the button to unlock all the doors, then follow her to my truck.

When I slide into the driver's seat, she's clicking the seatbelt into place. I have to look away just to shake the memory from my head, the one on constant replay whether I'm sleeping or awake.

If I could just go back and change one thing...

As soon as I start the vehicle, I pull out onto the street, driving silently and praying she doesn't ask me to take her home. Her home, her real home, should be with me. But it isn't.

We're both quiet for the first few minutes I'm on the road, but when I exit Gavin's gated neighborhood, she speaks. "Can you explain why I wanted to leave with you—only you—and not my husband?" She doesn't wait for my response. She was always straight and to the point. "Why I wanted to smile at the sight of my husband lying on the ground unconscious? And why I have no care in the world if he ever gets up again?"

"Can you stop calling him your husband, please?" I beg.

"Why? He is, you know."

"Because it kills me a little more each time you say it. That's why."
Fuck, this is hard. I grip the steering wheel harder than necessary. My
hands itch to touch her. To pull her close to me. To kiss her.

I glance over when she doesn't say anything. There's confusion
marring her features.

"Get on the interstate and head north."

I don't question her. I just do as she requests. I-55 is close, so that's
the way I head.

"I have amnesia. I don't remember anything before ten years ago. I
was in a car wreck when I was eighteen."

"I know, Love. I was there." I pull a long stream of air in through my
mouth, hating the tone of my voice. I sound bitter, and I don't want to act
this way with her—ever.

"Wha... what do you mean you were there? How?"

I look away from the road, only for a second, to glance at her again.
The last thing I want to do is relive the worse night of my life. But for her,
I'll do it. I'll do anything she asks me to.

"I was the one driving the car."

"The one I hit head on?" she questions.

"No," I reply, shaking my head in disbelief. *What the hell?* "The one
you were in. My old Jeep—the one I drove back in high school. The
one you flew out of the windshield of because you weren't wearing your
seatbelt." My voice cracks. I haven't said those words out loud in years.
It's like reliving that scene over again. I just can't...

"That can't be right."

"Really?" I bark. "I think I'm the one with the memory here," I
breathe. I'm getting mad. I shouldn't be getting mad—at least not at her.
"Shit. I'm sorry, Whitney. I didn't mean to sound like an asshole."

"You don't sound like an asshole," she tells me, but I know she doesn't
believe that. It's an automatic response that makes me even madder than
I already am at the douchebag that yelled at her. The asshole that grabbed
her too harshly, probably leaving bruises on her arm.

I should have hit him myself. But I'm not confident I would have been
able to stop had I taken the first punch.

"I'm acting like a jerk. You know it, and I know it. I'm sorry. Okay?"

"Okay." She sounds surprised. "Why do you call me Love, and why do you say you were the one driving the car the night I lost my memory?"

She's picked up on my use of her nickname. I wasn't doing it on purpose. It's simply what I've always called her the most. It's a habit that hasn't gone away.

"I told you I was the one driving because that's the truth. It's a fact. A fact I wish every day I could change because then you wouldn't have gotten hurt, and you wouldn't have lost your memory."

I look over once again when she doesn't say anything. She's staring at me as if she's wondering if she can believe me or not. The thought of her not believing me feels like a noose around my neck, choking me.

Finally, she breaks her silence. "How can that be? My parents said I was driving alone."

"Of course they did," I rush out, regretting the words.

"Head east on I-240," is the only thing she says.

"Where are we going?" I ask.

"Germantown, Tennessee."

"Is that where you live?" Do I want to know?

Yes, I do.

"No, it's not, but it's close. I live just outside of Memphis."

"Is that where we're heading now?"

"No. And I'm not planning on going home. Not yet, anyway. My girls are at my parents'. I need to get them before my hus—before Blake does."

I notice she catches herself not saying 'husband' like I asked her not to. I like that she did that for me. I also don't miss her mention of girls, meaning she has more than one child she has with that asshole.

They should have been my kids...

I force those thoughts to the back of my mind. Whitney with another man only makes me want to hit something.

"If you'd have said so sooner, I could have driven a little faster."

My cell phone goes off inside my pocket with an incoming text message. I'm guessing it's my brother letting me know Blake is awake.

Carefully maneuvering, I reach into my pocket to retrieve it. I don't check it, though. Instead, I hand it to Whitney.

"It's a text. Probably from Shawn, and yes, he's my brother. Can you read it since I'm driving?"

"Sure." She takes it, her fingers brushing my wrist in the process, igniting a fire I haven't felt in far too long.

Fuck, I've missed that feeling.

Her breath hitches, making me aware she felt the same thing. It gives me a moment of joy knowing she's still affected by me the way I am her. How much? I'm not sure.

"You felt that too, didn't you?" she asks.

"Of course I did." I go for honesty. What else am I going to say?

"We were more than friends, weren't we?" She presses the round button on my phone, turning the light from the screen on. "That's why you call me 'Love,' isn't it? What's the code?"

"0314," I tell her, wondering if she's going to catch the date of her birthday.

"That's—" I cut her off.

"Yeah, Love. We were more than friends."

"Will you tell me as much as you can in the next ten minutes before we get to my parents'? Get on I-385, then get off on Kirby Parkway. The message says, 'Blake just stormed out of Gavin's house.'"

I accelerate, wanting to get her to where she's asked me to take her, even though all I really want to do is turn this vehicle around and take her home with me instead.

"If Judy and Martin said you were the one driving and you were alone, then they lied." It figures as much. They lied to me too. They lied to my parents about Whitney. "After our high school graduation, we had dinner with my parents. After that, we picked up Trent and Kylie, our best friends. We were all heading to meet two other close friends of ours, but we never made it there. Another teenager that had also graduated that same day, from a different school, was driving drunk. I swerved to miss him and lost control in the process, hitting a patch of slick dirt on the side of the road. My Jeep slammed into a tree, and you went through the windshield."

I breathe hard, trying my damnedest to push back the raw emotions surfacing.

"Was I cheating on Blake with you?"

What the...?

"No! Hell no." I shake my head, only making it throb more.

I exit onto Kirby Parkway as she instructed.

"In three miles, turn right. My parents' house isn't too much farther," she warns. At least I think it's a warning to hurry along. "Why would my parents lie to me about the accident?"

"From the looks of that dress you're wearing, the color of your hair, and the simplified way you're wearing your makeup, I'd say they saw the perfect opportunity to turn you into the daughter they always wanted you to be. I'd say they succeeded too."

"What's that supposed to mean? What's wrong with my clothes, my hair, or my makeup?"

"Nothing is wrong with them. They just aren't you, Love."

She relays the rest of the directions to her parents. Within minutes I pull up alongside a curb in front of an enormous house. Too big of a house for my liking, but then I grew up in a modest-sized one.

The click of her seatbelt releasing is the only sound inside my truck.

I look over, waiting for what's going to happen next. I don't want to leave her. Especially if that bastard is on his way here. I'm not confident I can drive away from her.

"I have two daughters in that house." She points out the window to her right side. "I want to know more. I want to know everything, but I need my girls with me. Can I—"

That's not a question I ever want her to have to ask me.

"Go get them. I'll wait here unless you want me to come in with you." She nods, then reaches for the door, but stops.

"Um..." She looks afraid to speak.

"What is it? You can say whatever you want to say. Never fear telling me anything."

"I don't want to offend you," she admits, making me laugh for the first time tonight.

"Since when are you afraid to offend someone? Especially me?" Her face falls, and my smile immediately vanishes. "I'm sorry. I shouldn't have said that."

"No, it's okay. It's just... I don't know your name."

"Shane. Shane Braden." A smile spreads across her face.

"Whitney. Whitney Lane, but I guess you already knew that."

I don't say I only found out forty-five minutes ago that her last name is Lane because she's married to Blake Lane. I think I'm more pissed off at myself for not putting it together years ago.

She exits the car, and watching her walk away from me causes my chest to hurt. It feels wrong. I don't ever want to witness her walking away.

My cell phone goes off with an incoming text, gaining my attention. Reaching into the cup holder where Whitney placed it, I pick it up, seeing it's a message from my brother.

SHAWN

> I filled Gavin in the best I could after that guy left.

Thanks.

> Where you at?

Her parents in Germantown.

> Anything you need?

I don't know, man.

> Holler if you do. We're gonna head home soon.

They were already going to head back to Oxford tonight. That's why we rode in separate vehicles.

When I hear what I think is Whitney's name being yelled, I look out the passenger side window. Whitney is walking swiftly across the lawn in my direction. Jumping out of the truck, I round the back. In her arms, pulled to her chest, is a small toddler. Whitney has one arm wrapped around the back of the little girl's body.

"Whitney, don't do this," a voice shouts, pulling my gaze toward the house.

Her mother stands in the doorway dressed in a long nightgown. I shouldn't hate that woman, but I do, and there isn't a damn thing I can do to rein in how I feel toward her. She took *my* Love away from me.

"Momma," a softer voice calls out, bringing my attention back to the two people getting closer to me. The voice belongs to a slightly older little girl. She wasn't as small as I was expecting.

Taking a step toward them, I freeze, rooted to my spot. My eyes zero in on the young girl about the same height as Whitney, with the same slender frame that mimics her mother's. She's wearing dark pajamas— solid-colored shorts and a loose top with tiny white skulls covering the material of the black shirt and flip-flops on her feet. Her long, dark hair almost matches the color of her bottoms. But it's the eyes I can't stop staring at. *My eyes.* Or the face that's a carbon copy of my mother's when she was ten. My grandmother has always loved pulling out old photo albums every time we visit. I'm often reminded of how much I look like my mom.

The realization was instant.

Air expels from my lungs in a rush as I crash down on the concrete below, my knees hitting hard, but the pain not registering because the searing pain inside my chest is so excruciating I think I might pass out.

Someone asks if I'm okay, but I can't speak to say anything.

"What's wrong with him?" The girl in front of me turns her head sideways, asking her mother.

"Um... Shane?" Whitney calls out slowly. I can't move. Words fail me. "What's..." She trails. "Oh my... I-I... oh my God..." I'm finally able to turn my face toward Whitney. She's looking from the girl to me, her face volleying back and forth between the two of us until suddenly Whitney's hand flies to her mouth.

She knows. She sees it too.

"Momma, what's going on?"

"Everly, please," Whitney calls out. *Everly.* My strength vanishes, and I fall forward, barely catching myself with my palms before my face plants on the ground. "Take your sister and get inside that vehicle over there."

"Why?" the girl asks. "Who is he?"

"Ev, just do as I say. Okay?" Whitney sounds like she's pleading with the girl. Everly. Our daughter.

A door on my Tahoe closes, telling me she did what her mother told her to do. A minute passes without words before Whitney finally breaks the silence that feels like it's going to crush my windpipe. "We were a whole lot more than just friends." It's not a question. It's a statement. One that's truer than she understands. She may realize I'm the father of her oldest daughter—it's obvious. How could she not? But she still doesn't remember *me*. She doesn't remember *us*.

"We were together almost five years," I tell her. God, I wish she could remember.

"I don't understand. How? Why?" She breathes. "What the hell is going on?"

"They lied to you," I bark, my voice cracking. "They didn't just steal you away from me." The words are bitter on my tongue. "They stole my... They stole everything."

"I can't even..." She sighs heavily, shaking her head. "Look, I don't mean to rush you. It's just that Blake will be here any minute. We gotta go. I don't want to deal with him yet."

"I can't drive," I confess. But I probably shouldn't stay here any longer either, or I'll end up leaving in a car with blue lights.

"I'll do it," she rushes out. "Just get in. I'll drive."

I look up, then push my palms off the ground, sitting back on my boots. I stare at her as I rub my hands on my pants to dust the dirt off them. Whitney looks more confused than broken, like I am.

Finally, I stand up and walk aimlessly to the passenger side and get inside.

As I pull the seatbelt across my body, buckling, I can't stop myself from looking over my shoulder to the backseat at the girl I now know as Everly. *Foreverly after.* I have a daughter. I've had a daughter for nearly a decade, and I had no idea. If I'd only...

"Where do I go?" Whitney breaks my thoughts.

Fuck if I know. Where do we go?

"Head back the way we came," I finally instruct. "Head to Oxford."

"Mississippi?" she questions, and I just nod. "Is that where you live?"

"No."

"Then why are we going there?"

"Because I'm going to need my brother to keep me from murdering someone tonight." A sharp intake of air comes from the back, and I instantly regret my choice of words.

I'm going to have to be careful what I say from here on. I don't want to scare her.

It's silent for nearly fifteen minutes until Everly opens her mouth. I can't help but twist my head around to look at her. She's sitting behind the driver's seat.

"Mom, where's Dad?" That question is like a rope cording around my heart. I have to look away, so I turn back around, facing forward. Whitney glances over, but I remain quiet.

"Ev, sweetheart, um..." Whitney pauses. I guess she doesn't know what to tell her. Even I realize she can't spring the truth on her right now. Hell, I'm still trying to understand it myself—absorb it.

I have a good idea why, but still... Who does something like that?

"We're going to hang out with my friend Shane here. Uh... he and I used to—" The sound of my cell phone ringing through the car speakers cuts her off.

Reaching for the phone, I have every intention of ignoring the call. I'm not in the right frame of mind to speak to anyone. The display shows Kylie's name along with her smiling picture. I hit decline, sitting it back in the cup holder between Whitney and me.

"It's not important," I mumble. It's about the only words I have the energy to say.

Ringing comes through the speakers again, and I do the same thing as before, declining the call.

Why do people call at the worst times?

Before I can set the phone back down, Kylie calls a third time.

Jesus fucking Christ. Not today.

"She's obviously not going to stop until you answer it," Whitney chimes in without taking her eyes off the road. I guess at some point she saw Kylie's name, or maybe her face on the screen.

My thumb hovers over the screen briefly before I sigh, accepting the call.

"It's not a good time."

"Don't you dare hang up," she demands, her voice streaming through the car speakers. "You haven't taken any of my calls in almost two freaking weeks." She sounds hurt. I suppose she is, but she can't expect me to be okay with her decision not to move. I'm pissed at her, and that's not something I'm used to when it comes to Kylie Morgan. My anger with her deepens just thinking about it.

"Have you changed your mind?"

"No," she fires back.

"Then I have nothing else to say to you until you do," I spit right back. I'm done. If she can't see logic, there's nothing left to say. I tried talking sense into her, but she doesn't see it—or doesn't want to.

A woman the same age as Kylie was murdered last month in the apartment directly across from hers. Kylie refuses to break her lease and move. "Kylie," I say through clenched teeth. "I don't need this right now." I breathe hard, inhaling and then forcing the air back out through my mouth.

"You!" she shouts, but then goes silent for a moment. I already know what's coming. I can already hear the whiny words fall out of her mouth before she even speaks. "Shaney," she whispers, in a voice begging me to stop being mad. She usually succeeds, but not this time.

"Don't call him that." Whitney immediately reacts, shocking me. There's an audible gasp on the other end of the line. Recognition was instant. "I-I don't know where that came from. I'm so sorry. Please, ignore me," she tells us, embarrassed.

"Wh-Whitney?"

Whit's head whips to the side, looking at me in confusion. "How does she know who I am?"

Before I can answer, Kylie's voice breaks in. "Oh my God! It really is you." Whitney looks back to the road but glances over again, waiting for an answer. "Shane, what's going on?"

"Ky, listen," I start. "I can't get into that right now. Yes. Whitney is with me, but there are also kids in the vehicle, and I just can't." My anger dissipates, and I'm hoping like hell she understands. She is my best friend. I love her more than words can say, but I can't deal with her shit plus my own right now.

"Okay." She sighs but quickly follows up with, "When?"

I lean my head back against the headrest, taking in a deep breath of air. I look up at the roof of my Tahoe, trying to come up with something to tell her, but I'm at a loss.

"I don't know," I confess. "I can't think right now. I'll call you later. That's all I can give you."

Silence ensues.

"Do I need to come home?" she asks. I shake my head. Why can't she take a hint?

"You can't, and you know it." I let out a breath. She's working in the surgical intensive care unit for the entire month of November. "There's just no way."

"But—" I cut her off.

"Kylie, please. I can't talk to you about this right now. I'll call you when I can. Let that be enough for now." Please, God, let that be all.

"Okay. But I need you to call me back tonight, Shane." I hear a whimper come out of her. "Promise me."

Hell...

"I promise," I tell her, conceding.

The line goes dead, and then there's silence.

Five minutes go by as we merge onto I-55, heading south.

"Pom-poms," Whitney whispers. It takes me a second to understand. "Is she Asian?"

"Half Korean." She's remembering. "And she was a cheerleader in high school."

"She's one of the ones you mentioned earlier. You said she was one of our best friends, right?" She does a quick glance my way. Then peeks through the rearview mirror, I'm guessing at Everly. I can't bring myself to look at her again. Not yet. I'm barely holding myself together, and I don't know what to do.

"That's correct. She was your best friend. The three of you, Eve included, were pretty tight."

"But I was your—"

"Can we wait until we get to Shawn's to talk about this?" I nod my head toward the kids. I'm not worried about the little one. She's too young to understand us, but Ever... I close my eyes, reaching for a reprieve that's nowhere in sight.

Movement from the backseat makes me turn my head, opening my eyes before I realize what I'm doing. Everly has her hands wrapped around herself, rubbing her arms up and down.

"Are you cold?" I ask her.

When she nods, I lean forward, turning the A/C off and the heat on. It was chilly when we picked them up.

"Crap," Whitney blurts. "I'm sorry Ev. I didn't think." She rolls her head toward me. "Thank you." I nod in response.

A truck passes us on the interstate, flying by at a higher rate of speed than Whitney is driving. It's my brother. His truck is unmistakable, with the Wicked Ink logo covering most of his back glass.

I grab my cell phone, shooting Taralynn a text.

> Tell Shawn to slow down. Whit's driving and I need her to follow him.

TARALYNN
> Done. You okay?

> No.

> What's going on?

> You'll know when we get there.

> Okay.

There is no doubt in my mind that Taralynn will instantly know Everly is my daughter, just as my brother will. My mom's been more of a mother to her than hers ever was.

I shake my head at the memory of Katherine. She was Trent's

biological mother, but Taralynn's stepmom. When Taralynn and Shawn were going through a rocky part of their relationship, she learned her father was having an affair with a woman that worked for him, a woman I faintly remember from when I was younger.

Lynn, Taralynn's biological mother, was my mom's best friend. Sadly, she committed suicide when Jacob, Taralynn's father, wouldn't leave Katherine to be with her. She carried Taralynn to term but then took her life the same day she gave birth. *Fucking tragic.*

I see brakes flash down the road as Shawn slows down.

"Follow the white F150 up there."

"O-okay," she stutters.

"It's my brother. I sent his girlfriend a text telling her you were gonna follow them."

"Gotcha."

I look at the dark-haired girl in the back. I recall something Whitney told me once. *They're the color of the sea with the moonlight shining down.* In the darkness of the truck, her eyes do seem to glow. I wonder if that's how Whitney saw mine once upon a time? *I wonder if she'll ever see them that way again?*

CHAPTER 8

WHITNEY

His brother parked his pickup truck a few minutes ago in the driveway. Both he and his girlfriend went inside the older two-story home afterward. More like after Taralynn drug Shawn from the front yard, where I'm guessing he was waiting for Shane to emerge from this vehicle.

We're still sitting here, in silence, with Shane's truck turned off.

Not knowing what else to do, I remove the keys from the ignition, then hold them out in the palm of my hand for Shane to take—which he does without looking at me.

I want him to look at me. I want to know what he's thinking. He looks like he's on the verge of a breakdown. There's a crease in the center of his forehead, and he's gripping his thighs like maybe that's what is holding him together.

I was so focused on driving that I didn't let any of the things I discovered tonight sink in.

I've been lied to.

I've been deceived.

I've been... Fuck, what the hell has everyone in my life done to me? I don't even know where to begin. *Everly.* I close my eyes to rein in my emotions. I'm not a crier, but suddenly that's all I want to do. I can't, though. I have to hold myself together for my girls. For Everly, mostly, because she'll know something is wrong. *If she doesn't already.*

Have my parents really lied to me? Would they do something that despicable?

Not now, I tell myself.

Glancing up, I look into the rearview mirror, seeing my oldest daughter staring at me expectantly. Yet, I have no answers to give her. None that she would understand. But one thing is for sure: she isn't Blake's daughter.

Oh, hell. I have a daughter with a man that isn't my husband. A man I don't know yet is capable of making my insides twist in ways Blake never has. Why is that?

I shut my eyes, pressing them together tightly. But the sound of a door opening has them popping back open. Looking over, I see Shane climbing out.

"Let's go," I tell Everly.

Hopping out, I round the back of the vehicle to the other side, grabbing Emersyn from her booster seat. Thank God I had enough sense to leave it with my parents in case they had to go out.

Everly waits for me at the front of Shane's truck, so when I reach her, we both walk toward the front of the house where Shane's walking up a set of steps.

"Mom," she whispers.

"Not now, honey. We'll talk later, okay?"

She doesn't answer.

I kick myself for not getting her to change into warmer clothes, but I was in such a rush to get out of there before Blake arrived. I know he went to my parents' house. I don't need someone to confirm it. He's probably livid right now, but I don't care. There is so much more I need to find out before I broach the subject of my husband.

Husband. That word disgusts me now. *If* any of this is true, then I feel so... violated.

No. I can't go down that road. Not yet. Strength. I need to muster up everything I have inside me and hold on to it for a little longer.

We enter the house without Shane knocking, but maybe he has that type of relationship with his family—with his brother. The one where you can go over to someone else's house, and even if they aren't expecting you, you just waltz right in. I don't have that kind of relationship with my parents or even Blake's folks. An invitation is always expected.

We enter a small foyer with a staircase directly in front of the door. Shane waits for all of us to come inside before he closes the door. When our eyes meet, he gives me the saddest smile I've ever seen. A knife stabs at my chest at the sight. I don't like it, but can I blame him? After what he's learned, I'm honestly surprised he's holding up as well as he is. When he crashed to the ground at my parents', it was all I could do not to drop down next to him. I don't know him, yet this pull inside me recognizes him. Then again, maybe it's just wishful thinking.

Fucking memories.

Shane nods his head toward an entryway to the right of me. He heads through it after a beat, and we follow.

Emersyn lets out a small cry; I shush her the best I can. When I look down, I see she's still asleep, so it must have been a baby dream. She does that often. She'll cry out once but never wakes.

The entryway we go through leads into a large living room.

"Mom," Everly whispers. I strain my head to look over my shoulder. "Why are we here?"

"I said we'd talk later, and we will. Just know everything is fine." Great. Now I'm lying to my daughter. How on earth will I ever explain any of this to her when I don't even understand it myself?

"Mom," she whines. I shake my head, giving her a warning with my eyes.

There's a TV playing a football game, but the sound is turned down too low to be audible.

Shawn enters through another opening at the back of the room. It's the same type of wide entrance, sans a door, we just walked through. He comes to stand in front of a recliner as Shane walks around the coffee table to stand in front of the couch but doesn't sit.

Shawn first looks at his brother, then his eyes cut to me. There is no emotion on his face. Now that I see him in a lit room, and from a distance, he seems larger than when I was pressed against him earlier tonight. A little scarier, even. But something makes the tension in my head lessen.

Something also tells me I'm going to like him. Like he could be a friend.

Hmmm. Interesting.

His dark eyes drop to Emersyn lying in my arms as he brings a Corona to his lips. Everly brushes against my side, coming from standing behind me. Sometimes she is shy in front of people she doesn't know.

There's an intake of breath beside him—Taralynn. I didn't see her enter the room, but when I look over, her eyes bug from their sockets. I don't have to guess why; she's looking at Everly.

Damn. Is it really that noticeable?

Shawn stops mid-sip, staring at her too. Finally, he lowers the beer bottle, slowly letting it drop to his side. "Oh, my hel—"

"Hold up, Shawn." Shane raises his palm, indicating he wants his brother to shut up.

Once he's sure Shawn isn't going to say anything else, he turns to face my daughter. *His daughter.* "Everly, I'm Shane." He takes the same hand he used to stop Shawn from finishing his sentence and holds it out in front of her. She looks up at me. I nod, giving her my approval, and then she extends her slender arm, placing her palm into his. My breath catches in my throat, but I force the air out despite the clog.

Shane's torn, but he's doing a decent job covering it. Those eyes that match Everly's glance down to where their hands are enclosed in each other's.

"You're cold again, aren't you?" he asks her. She nods in quick succession. Shane looks at me, releasing her hand as he does, "Does she have more clothes?" He inserts his hands into his blue-jean pockets.

"No." I shake my head. "I rushed and didn't grab her overnight bag."

He twists his head to the others in the room. Taralynn speaks up. "Whatever she needs, I'm sure I have something that'll work." She cringe-smiles. And I think she's unsure of what's going to happen. Hell, I'm unsure too.

I move closer to Shane, placing my hand on his forearm. It's warm and firm, and the spark I felt earlier ignites once again, all from a single touch. I like the fire between us, and by the look on Shane's face, I can see he feels the same way too. It's weird feeling this connected to someone I just met, especially since I can't remember ever feeling this way before. Is that crazy? Something deep inside me thinks it's not crazy.

"Are we... are we staying here tonight?" I don't want to make assumptions, but I have two girls that need sleep. And I don't have anything—no purse, no cell, no money. In the escape, I forgot to grab my things. I left my purse in Blake's car, but I had my phone. Now I feel stupid for laying it on the kitchen island in Gavin's house right before I walked outside. I'm at Shane's mercy. And I still need answers. I'm sure he does too, so...

"Yeah." He looks away, looking at his brother. Shawn tips his head up, silently giving him the okay, I'm guessing.

"My old room is vacant, with a bed. Oh, and Matt is out of town, and Mase is in Orlando, so those are both options as well."

This house is large, so it makes sense Shawn and his girlfriend would have roommates. They seem younger than Shane and me. Maybe they're still in college. We are in Oxford, so maybe they all attend Ole Miss.

"Thanks," Shane replies. Then he looks down at his watch. I look around for a clock. I know it's gotta be late. Spotting one on the wall, I see it's a few minutes after eleven. Jesus. My kids should have been asleep hours ago. And they were when I got them from my parents. Luckily the little one doesn't seem to be fazed. Then again, I think this child could sleep through an earthquake.

"Why don't I take the girls upstairs," Taralynn offers. "I can get Everly some clothes and then get them settled while you guys talk." She walks toward me. "Is that okay?"

"I—yeah, it's fine. Thank you."

"Mom." Everly pulls on the thin material of my dress.

"It's fine, Ev. I'll be up in a bit. I promise." I glance down at her, forcing a warm smile onto my face. "This is my friend, Taralynn," I tell her, hoping she buys it. I don't know these people. But saying that feels wrong. They seem to know me, after all.

Turning to Taralynn, I introduce her to my youngest daughter. "Her name is Emersyn, but we call her Em mostly, so that's fine too." I place my daughter in her hands, but her eyes bug even more than they did a few minutes ago. Alarm flickers through me. Looking at the two brothers, I see the same shocked expressions. Shawn's eyes flare as he grasps Shane's shoulder. "What did I say?"

"I'll get the girls upstairs. You talk to Shane, okay?" Taralynn walks away, carrying Emersyn toward the front, where I remember seeing the stairs leading to the second floor when we walked into the house.

"Go ahead, Ev. She'll get you some warmer clothes, or since you're going to sleep, it's fine if you just want to sleep in your pj's."

Everly looks behind me, eyeing Shane briefly before turning to follow Taralynn.

Does she see it? Surely not. She's too young to put all that together. At least I think she is.

When they're out of earshot, I turn around to face the guys. "Okay, spill it. What now?"

Shawn speaks. "Emerson is Shane's middle name. It seems you've named both of your kids after him."

"Both?" I cock my head in Shane's direction.

How can this be? How did I name Everly after him? I don't even remember him.

"Now's not the time, Shawn," he says, sighing. Shane looks worn out as if he's aged since I first laid eyes on him tonight.

"No, I think now is as good as any time. Tell me." I left my husband wanting answers. I'm getting those answers.

He pulls up his T-shirt, and as he does so, my eyes roam up his lean abdomen taking in tanned skin over ripples of flesh, finally stopping just over his pectorals. I don't have a chance to fully appreciate the sight in front of me when my eyes land on a tattoo. Over his heart is a script that says *foreverly after*. It takes me longer than it should, but then I see it, and chills break out over my arms. *Everly.*

My eyes skim down. On his side, in larger script, is my name. *Whitney.* The name is in black ink with small, blue flowers that look so alive on his skin. The flowers make the tattoo pop. It's beautiful and causes my heart to swell, but I can't focus on that right now, ignoring the warmth coursing through my veins to ask the question sitting on the tip of my tongue. "What does foreverly after mean?"

"It's what I used to say to you instead of happily ever after. It was just..." He trails off, not finishing his thought. I decide not to press him anymore.

"I think we should call Mom." Shawn's deep voice pulls me away from Shane. Glancing over, he's eyeing his brother.

"Of course you do. You always call mom at the slightest adult situation that arises." Shane sighs again, and then he falls onto the couch behind him. A breath whooshes out of his mouth.

Sitting down sounds like a good idea to me too. My legs are wobbly as it is. I'm not sure how much more information I can take. Yet I want to know everything.

Finally, there's someone willing to be more than vague with me about my past. Only now...

"I do not," Shawn argues.

"You do." Shane looks at me. There is longing in his eyes, and as much as I want to go to him, I stay put. My body, on the other hand, doesn't agree with my head. I have this insatiable urge to touch him. It's need. I recognize it.

"Can I have one of those?" I ask, interrupting their spat. I point to the beer Shawn seems to have forgotten is still in his hand.

"Sure." He pivots, leaving the room.

"I, uh... hell, I don't know." I walk over. "May I sit?" I ask.

"Of course." He scoots to the far end of the couch, and I take the empty space at the other end.

"Where do we go from here?"

"I wish I knew." He shakes his head. "I wish I knew, Love." He faces me. "You still don't remember me, do you?"

I shake my head. It's the truth, but at this moment, I wish I did. I wish I could make that sad look disappear. It doesn't belong on his beautiful face.

A beer is placed in my hand. I down it in seconds. Oddly enough, another is jutted out in front of me. I greedily take it too.

I want to remember.

I need to remember.

For him. For my daughter. *For me.*

CHAPTER 9

SHANE

"What you wanna bet this has to do with you?" Shawn flashes his ringing cell phone at me. Chance's name is displayed on the screen. His finger swipes across the screen. "Hello."

Chance's voice sounds further away as it comes through the phone's speaker, and it has me wondering if he's calling while driving his motorcycle. He does it often. I've told him countless times to stop doing that. He does it often, even after Trent's death. It only pisses me off more when he calls me while riding his motorcycle. He can argue all he wants that there's nothing wrong about it or unsafe, but he's wrong.

"You talked to your brother tonight?"

"Yeah," Shawn drawls.

"What the fuck's going on, then?" The wind against his machine makes it sound like he's in a tunnel. "It's true? Whitney's with him?"

Whit whips her head toward me with her eyebrows drawn tight as she listens to the call.

"I guess you could say that."

"You guess or you know, motherfucker?" I shake my head. "Because Kylie is blowing up Eve's phone. Eve is blowing up mine, talking about flying to Mississippi. That dickhead won't answer anybody's calls, and I had to cancel on one of my regulars to come home to calm Eve down. So, please, man, give me some straight fucking answers."

"She's here. He's here too. But Shane's dealing with some major fucking shit right now. They both are. Maybe y'all could give him some breathing room, yeah?"

"Maybe the motherfucker could answer a goddamn phone."

"You don't know what he's dealing with. Give him some room. He'll call you guys when he's ready."

"Fuck that. This isn't just somebody we went to high school with that didn't mean shit. This is Whitney, man. She was one of Eve's best friends. One of mine too," he barks. "Maybe you were too young to remember—" Shawn's quick to cut him off. His face turns heated.

"He's my goddamn brother. And yeah, I fucking remember too. I was there when my mom told him she was dead, fuckface." Whitney gasps, pulling in air through her mouth. And I've had all I can take. I reach, snatching the phone from Shawn's ear, earning a glare from him that clearly tells me he wanted to give Chance more of a piece of his mind.

I take the call off speaker, shoving the chair back as I stand.

"I'm here, and you're a fucking ass, you know that?" I lay into him. "And stop talking on your phone while you're riding your motorcycle."

"It's coming through my helmet, douchebag."

"I don't care. We're done until you stop riding." I hang up, ending the call before he can say another word. "I gotta call Kylie before she loses it. And Eve too, apparently. Can you fill her in on who that was?" My brother nods. I glance at Whitney before I leave the kitchen. "I'll be out on the back patio if you need me."

"Okay."

Once I'm out the door, I call Kylie's number. I don't feel like talking to anyone, but she deserves answers. The little I have anyway.

"Shawn?" she answers.

"Nah, it's me."

She's silent, and it helps me to get my thoughts straight. I take a seat on the small outdoor couch that's pushed up against the house, and I lean my head back, resting it against the brick.

"She's here," I start with. "But she still doesn't remember any of us."

I pause, remembering what Whitney said during the car ride. "Well, she may be remembering you. She said she pictured pom-poms after I got off the phone with you earlier."

She's still quiet.

"But, uh." My voice cracks. "Ky." I choke up and hear the air Kylie blows out of her mouth from the other end of the line. "There's something else."

How do I tell my best friend I have a daughter I never knew about? I'm not sure I've fully comprehended it myself.

"What is it?" she asks me, frustration evident in her voice. When I don't say anything, she speaks again. "Just tell me, Shane."

"She has a daughter."

"I know that. You told me that months ago. I'm so sorry, Shaney."

"No, Ky. She has another daughter. A nine-year-old—I'm guessing." There's silence once again as she takes in my words. There's no way for me to brace her, so I just say it. "A nine-year-old with my eyes." She gasps. "And the same color hair as mine." I blow out air. "The same everything. She's my daughter, Kylie."

"Oh, Shane. I-I don't even know what to say to that," she sniffs. "I'm coming home. I don't care about my job. This is so much—"

"No." I'm more forceful with my tone than I should be. "You can't. But I get it, so why don't you fly up on the two days you have off next week."

"I don't know if I can wait that long."

"I'm not letting her go anywhere. I'm not letting them go anywhere. She'll be here when you get here."

The phone beeps with an incoming call. Taking it away from my ear, I look to see who it is. Chance Manning.

"What do you need right now?" I can hear Kylie's sweet voice, even with the cell phone in front of my face. I put it back against my ear to hear her say, "I gotta do something."

"Will you call our bastard friends in Vegas and fill them in?" I ask her. She half laughs, but it quickly dies.

"Sure. I can do that. But I can't promise Eve won't call you. You know Eve."

"Yeah, I do. Chance already called Shawn's cell. That's why I'm on it, but I didn't tell him much. He was..." I leave that hanging, knowing she'll pick up on it. Trent's death is still too heavy for both of us. "And I wanted to tell you first."

"Thanks. I'll deal with them. And I'll see you in a few days."

"Thank you."

I drop the phone, letting it land on the cushion next to me, and I just stare up at the sky. *What did I do to deserve not only Whitney to be taken from me, but my daughter too?*

WHEN I FINISHED MY CONVERSATION with Kylie an hour ago, Whitney wasn't where I'd left her and my brother. Taralynn told me she had gone upstairs to check on the girls. I didn't want to talk anymore. I needed a minute of reprieve. So against Shawn and Taralynn's wishes, I headed up the stairs and went to Matt's room.

Apparently, he's in California until next week. I think I remember Taralynn mentioning his parents moved back there when he left for college. He and Taralynn became friends in junior high when his parents uprooted him and moved to Tupelo. I've noticed the two of them haven't been close in the last year, and I'm not sure why.

Movement brings me from my thoughts. My head rolls down from where it rests against the headboard.

Love. She's standing in the doorway I purposely left open, hoping she would see me in here.

"Everly is finally asleep." She crosses her arms, then leans against the doorframe. "That's where I went when you walked outside to talk to your friend."

"You know she's mine, right? Like, you don't just think there's a chance. You see it, don't you?" I sit up. My right leg falls off the edge of the bed, but I don't care. I leave it there. It helps anchor me.

"I'd say it's... clear." She pushes off the door, walking inside. She stops in front of the dresser and looks around, taking in the room until her violet eyes land on me. She braces her hands, cupping the edge of the dresser, then leans against it. "Can we..." She bites the side of her bottom lip. "Can we talk?"

"Yeah." I glance down at my hands lying between my legs. Glancing back up, I say, "I'd like that."

"Can we start with the past?" Her eyebrows furrow. "I'm really trying to wrap my head around you being my daughter's father and not... Blake."

I grunt, shaking my head.

"I'm trying to wrap my mind around you being married to that dirtbag. You couldn't stand him," I force out.

"Okay," she whispers. "Let's start there, all right? Please," she stresses, pushing off the dark wood of the dresser. She comes closer. "May I sit?" She points to the corner of the bed furthest from me.

"Of course." I take a deep breath, relaxing a little as she gets closer to me—closer to where she belongs. "And yeah, we can start with that, but, Whit," I pause, staring at her. "She's mine. I'm not losing another day with her."

She just nods. And even though she doesn't say she agrees with me, I can tell she feels the commitment behind my declaration.

"What do you want to know?" I ask.

"Everything." She sits on the bed, crossing her legs together, facing me. "Tell me about myself. The *me* I don't know."

I bang my head on the headboard as I lean back. I look directly at her, so there's no way for her to misconstrue what I say. "She was mine. She was mine from the moment I laid eyes on her, and she was mine until the night she was taken away in an ambulance."

She's silent for at least two minutes, but her eyes never leave mine. She doesn't cower. She doesn't scare. *My* Whitney is in there somewhere, and I'm determined to do whatever it takes to find her.

I decide to hammer my point home. "You were mine." I run my palms up and down my jeans. The itch intensifies.

She must notice because she asks, "What's the matter?" Her head dips, and her eyes follow my movement.

"It's taking everything in me right now not to grab you, not to kiss you, hug you. Not to..." I slam my eyes shut. If I don't, I may just grab her and toss her down on the bed anyway—to hell with the consequences. The need to be inside her is excruciating.

Opening my lids, I finally continue. "I know this isn't easy for you either. I do. But, Love... for me, you were and have always been the love of my life." I lay my truth on her. I lay it down thick. "And you're here. But you're not. You don't remember. I remember everything. And not touching you makes my skin itch. It's making my chest burn. You're so close but so far away, and then on top of it all, I have a daughter. God, if I thought you being stolen from me was hell." I breathe. "I could've had a family for how long now? She's nine, isn't she?"

Whitney bobs her head.

"She'll be ten on December second."

"December?" That can't be right. "I did the math. She should have been born in January."

"How do you know that?"

"We only forgot to use a condom once," I inform her.

"She was born five weeks early." My chest seizes. "She's okay, though. She's always been on the smaller side. Don't call her tiny, though. She hates that."

"Was there something wrong that made you go into labor early?"

"Me. Or so Blake loves to remind me." She sounds bitter. "I was stressed the whole time. More so in my last trimester."

"You lost your memory. Of course you were stressed."

"Yeah, I know, but that wasn't..."

"It wasn't what?"

"My parents planned my wedding, and I felt like they were forcing it on me." Her eyes cut away from me as if she's thinking. "I guess they were." Her brows pinch together, then she looks back at me. Anger burns in her beautiful eyes. "They did this. They did it all. Why? You said something about them finally getting the daughter they always wanted or something like that. What did you mean?"

"You weren't obedient. Well, not with them. Not with your mother. Judy wanted you to act a certain way. She wanted you proper." I let out a dry laugh. "You were far from proper. You did you. You did whatever you wanted to do. Other people's opinions didn't matter to you. You didn't follow anyone else's way or path. You went your way."

"What about your way? Did I follow your way?"

"No." I'm honest. "You followed you. I'm not saying you were bad because you weren't. You didn't get into much trouble, not anything substantial. But you weren't foreign to a fight or two if someone pissed you off or you didn't like something someone did." This time I chuckle, remembering something she did. "Our junior year of high school, a girl that thought she could come between Trent and Kylie. It was before our last class of the day. Everyone was in the halls, changing classes. The girl—Renee, I think—walked up to Trent when we were standing by some lockers talking. You and Kylie were probably coming to find us. This chick just walked right up to Trent, planting her lips on his, and I swear he went ghost white and became a statue. He didn't push her away, but not because he liked it. The poor bastard couldn't move; he was in so much shock. You, though, you walked up right behind her, grabbed her by the hair, and yanked her back. Then you slammed her face into a locker. You got in-school suspension for three days."

"Huh." She blows air out of her mouth.

"What?" Does she remember something?

"My parents said I was homeschooled." For the love of God. These people are something. Something despicable. Fucking evil is what they are.

"You weren't. We went to the same school since the beginning." She was mine longer than she's ever known. She was mine from the start. I just never told her that until a few minutes ago. The old Whitney thought I didn't notice her until junior high. That is the farthest thing from the truth.

"So I was so out of control my parents invented someone else? That's what you're telling me?"

"No." I spit, getting frustrated. "Not even close. You weren't out of control. Your parents have always had a skewed view of a person's worth. They only deem someone worthy of their time if that person can benefit them somehow."

"You seem like a nice enough person. Why didn't they want us together?"

"They didn't know me. They knew who my parents were, but uh..." I watch her, not sure I should tell her this. I'm not certain it's why they never cared to meet me or accept me in Whitney's life, but I have a feeling it's the very reason they didn't like me. At least why her mother dislikes me.

"What?"

"Your mom had a thing for my dad at one time. They even went on a couple of dates years ago. I never knew that until… until after the wreck. It was maybe in college, I think, but they didn't hit it off—at least not for my dad. Then he met my mom around the same time. I remember now; it was during grad school." I draw in a breath, needing a moment. Needing the knot in my chest to go away. "I guess your mom didn't take that too well. She wanted him, and my mother didn't come from money. Judy didn't understand why he could pick my mom over her."

"So, everything they did to me, to us, you're telling me is because my mother got dumped?"

She's finding it hard to believe, I'm sure.

"Maybe." I run my hand through my hair. "I don't know, Love. It's the only reason I can come up with."

"It doesn't change the fact that I have to go home." She holds her hand up. "There are things I need. Things my girls need. Hell, Ev has school on Monday. I need to figure out what I'm going to do."

"You're not." I feel like I'm preaching to a brick wall. "Anything you need, I'll get it. Anything they need, you tell me what it is, and I'll get it. Just don't go back. Please, Whitney. I can't take it." My fingers wrap around my knees, digging into my skin through my jeans. "Don't leave me again."

You damaged the sheetrock on my ceiling yet?

The ball falls back into my hands as my eyes flick to Matt's bedroom door. Since he's out of town, I crashed in his room since it's on the second floor and closer to where Whitney and the girls are sleeping. Only sleep hasn't reached me.

I pull air into my lungs, then push it out with a hard sigh.

"Gavin called your cell." Shawn walks into the room. "You left it in the kitchen, and I answered it. He said to take a personal day." He props up against the dresser, crossing his heavy boots one over the other.

Work is the last thing on my mind. And there is no point. I'd be useless.

"Okay." I go back to throwing the miniature basketball toward the ceiling, waiting until it falls back into my hands before doing it again, like I have for the last half-hour.

"She in my old room?"

"Whitney?" I ask for clarification. He nods. "Yeah. She went in there with them about two hours ago."

We're both quiet for a minute, but I see Shawn through my peripheral. His head is hanging, and his forehead is creased.

"I wish I'd taken more than one swing."

"You and me both." I catch the ball, but instead of continuing to toss it up, I place it on the bed, then scoot up into a sitting position against the headboard. "I'm surprised he didn't press charges, but maybe he didn't know who you were."

"I don't give a fuck. Let him," Shawn spits. "That motherfucker took what wasn't his. The question is, what're you gonna do?"

That's the question sitting in the pit of my stomach. What am I going to do?

I swing my legs off the bed, sitting on the edge before I answer him. "I don't know." I shake my head, then stand, running my hand through my hair. "I don't know what to think. Or do. So much is running through my head, and I'm getting nowhere. I just..."

"He needs to pay. Her parents need to pay for what they've done too." He's pissed. When Shawn's angry, it's unmistakable. "You have a fucking kid, man."

"Keep your voice down," I scold, gaining a huff of frustration from my brother.

"Why aren't you mad? I'd flip the fuck out." He pushes off the dresser only to turn, facing it. I see him close his eyes in the mirror. "Fuck, I'm mad for you. I want to rip him apart."

"You think I'm not mad?" Mad isn't the right word for what I am. I'm numb, and that's so much worse. I don't know what to do or what not to do. Logically, I know I'm still in shock.

"You're too calm. I don't get it." He starts pacing.

"What do you want me to do?" I ask. "Should I go find him? Beat his ass?"

"Yes," he bellows. I shake my head.

"I'm not saying I don't want to do that, Shawn. But it wouldn't help. It's not going to get the time back that I've lost with both of them." I head toward the door. My hands are itching, but I don't tell my brother that. I do want to hurt Blake Lane. I want to hurt him like he's hurt me. Like her parents have hurt us all. "I'm going to shower."

"That's it?"

"That's all I've got right now, Shawn. I'm exhausted, but sleep is futile at this point." I pull the door open but stop to look back at my brother. "I don't know what I'm going to do. Or what to do."

"Mom would know," he jabs.

"I'm surprised you haven't already called her."

"Not my shit to tell our parents." He steps closer, heading out of the bedroom the same as I am. There's a hall bath on the second floor I plan on using. Since it's next to Matt's bedroom, my feet don't have far to walk.

Walking is an effort.

Thinking is an effort.

"Do me a favor," I tell him. "In the back of my truck is a gym bag with a set of scrubs. Get 'em for me?"

"Sure."

"Hey, Shawn?" He stops before descending the stairs. "They're gonna find out eventually." We stare at each other until he nods, answering my plea, then his feet hit hard going down the stairs.

I close myself inside the small bathroom, planting my palms on the edge of the sink and staring at myself in the mirror. A fire kindles somewhere inside me.

I am mad. Angry. Hurt. But it's me I'm furious with the most. If I'd tried harder, kept trying to get to Whitney, would we...?

CHAPTER 10

WHITNEY

Sleep.

That's a joke.

Like I could actually shut my eyes and drift off into a peaceful slumber after learning everything I did last night. In reality, it was only a few hours ago.

I roll over onto my side, away from the girls. There's a small clock sitting on the nightstand that tells me it's a quarter to seven in the morning. Even though it's Saturday, I'd normally have been awake over an hour ago. I enjoy the alone time before the girls get going. On the weekend, it's nonstop with two.

Another ten minutes go by, and I can't lie here any longer. The constant thinking will not stop. My mind is on repeat, replaying the scene at that doctor's house, the revelation outside my parents, and my conversation with Shane a few hours ago.

None of it will stop.

I just need a few minutes...

Getting gently off the bed so I don't wake Everly or Em, I decide to go to the bathroom I remember seeing next to the room Shane's sleeping in.

I wonder if he got to sleep.

The look on his face has been haunting me since I left that room.

Don't leave me again.

It wasn't my choice to leave to begin with. Why can't I remember? Why is God keeping my memories from me? Was I so awful before that I deserved this? Shane says I wasn't, but then he was in love with that version of me—maybe he still is.

The way he looks at me. It's so nerve-racking, yet it calls to me. How does that make any sense?

I turn the knob on the bedroom door slowly. I'm not worried about Emersyn. That girl could sleep through anything. But Everly is a light sleeper. She always has been.

Slipping out, I pad down the hall. The lights are on in the bathroom, glowing through the crack at the bottom of the door, telling me someone's in there. My money is on Shane, seeing how I would imagine his brother and Taralynn have a master bath connected to their bedroom.

I lean against the wall across from the hall bath. As I wait, I look around me. The walls are a creamy, warm beige color with white trim. There are a few decorative wall art pieces hanging up. None of them match, but it's the cross that my eyes linger on. There's something about crosses I've always admired. I go to church every Sunday with my family, but I've never felt close to God there. Yet when I see a cross, I feel settled inside. It's really the only time I do. Being in a church with Blake makes my skin itch. I think he only goes for show.

"Whit?"

I was so lost in thought I didn't notice the door had opened. When I look over Shane is coming out. The light has already been shut off, and he's dressed in scrubs. That makes me wonder...

"Are you a doctor?" Gavin's a doctor, and Shane was at his party. Maybe they work together. Maybe I'm being presumptuous. Nurses wear scrubs too, along with others in the medical field.

"Yeah," he confirms. "I work at the children's hospital in Memphis. I'm in my last year of residency."

He works with kids. Why does that make my body hum?

I can see it, though. I know I don't remember him, but there is something gentle and caring that pours off him.

"You need in here?"

"Yeah." I nod.

"It's all yours. I'm going to head downstairs. I need to throw this in the laundry." He holds up his wet towel and the clothes he was wearing last night. "Taralynn will have a meltdown if I leave them on the floor in there."

"Okay."

I watch him pass me. I even watch him disappear down the stairs.

He's so... different from Blake. Polar opposite, actually. Blake looks at me as if he owns me—and not in a good way. As if I'm property. I hate it, if I'm honest with myself. But there's always been Everly, and then Emersyn came. She wasn't planned, but I love her so much. Both of my girls are my whole world.

Now there's Shane, and he looks at me as if I'm a treasure. It's weird. *It's exhilarating.* But I'm not treasure. I'm just me. But do I really know myself?

When I'm finished using the bathroom and washing my face, I smell something delicious as I exit. Bacon, to be exact. I descend the stairs.

As I walk the short distance from the foyer and down the hall that leads into the kitchen, voices ring out. They're familiar to me now. Shane's brother is talking. His voice booms, but I don't get the feeling it's raised. I think this is his normal tone. "How are you so fucking calm?"

I stop just before I enter. Shane's sitting at the round kitchen table with his elbows resting on top. Shawn's opposite him, leaning back in his chair.

"I'm not," he answers, and I wonder why Shawn can't see it. It's in the way Shane's jaw tics. How his skin is flushed along the column of his neck and how his leg is dancing up and down underneath the table. He doesn't exude calm—not to me. He's boiling beneath his skin. Why can't his brother see it?

A better question is why do I recognize it so easily?

"Then why aren't you doing something?" He leans forward. "Anything at all, man."

"I'm not you, Shawn. I don't get pissed and start throwing punches before I know what's going on." Shane's voice is soft. Maybe that's why his brother thinks the way he does.

Shawn's dark eyes cut to me, then Shane turns, seeing me too. Sadness overtakes the fire I feel coming from him. *Don't leave me again.* My chest constricts. I want to tell him I won't, but I can't make that promise. Everything is so messed up. I don't know which way is up or down. Right or wrong.

"Y'all don't have to stop talking because of me." I move my feet toward him. *Home.* The word pops into my head, catching me so off guard that I have to look away from him.

"Mornin'," Taralynn greets from the stove. "Hungry?"

My stomach is in knots. I don't think I could keep anything down at this moment—even if it smells divine.

"Do you maybe have any coffee?"

"Of course. Have a seat with the guys, and I'll bring you a cup." She places a spatula down next to the stove. "How do you like it?"

"Cream, no sugar." I turn my head. It was Shane that answered her. "Is that still how you like it?"

I nod. After a beat, I make my way over. Pulling the chair out, I sit down, joining them at the table.

"I was just saying," Shawn's forehead crinkles, "he should be pissed about..." He raises his hand, palm open, gesturing toward me without finishing his sentence. It doesn't take a genius to figure out where he was headed.

I peek at Shane, who's scowling at his brother. Turning my attention back to Shawn, I'm about to tell him Shane is mad—boiling mad, even—but the sound of the front door opening followed by a woman's voice stops me.

"Shawn Douglas," she calls out, and my insides instantly warm. Her voice calls to me. Not in the same way Shane's does, but the warm sound of her voice comforts me. Does that mean I know her too? Or rather, the *me* that doesn't remember knowing her?

"In here, Mom," Shawn calls out, shaking his head. I'm betting Douglas is his middle name. Everly hates when I bring out the 'Everly Michelle.' The thought makes me want to laugh, but I don't.

"Okay, what did you do now?" she sighs. My back is to her, but I know she has entered the kitchen. "Shane?" Her voice doing a one-eighty, becoming softer and surprised. "You didn't tell me your brother was here."

"Yeah, well..." Shawn brings his coffee to his lips as his eyes meet mine.

"Hey, bud," she greets Shane, and he gives her a small smile—a forced one.

"Boys. Taralynn, that smell alone is going to make this old man fat."
A man chuckles. Their dad. It must be.

"Mom. Dad." Curiosity gets the better of me, so I twist in my chair
to face them. "He called you for m——" Shane doesn't get to finish what
he was saying.

"Oh, my..." Her hand covers her mouth as I take her in first. It's not
just the short, dark hair cut into a bob that gets me. It's not her sparkling
eyes that pool with tears while she stares back at me. It's the look, the
facial features, the... *everything*. My daughter could easily pass for her own
daughter. They favor *that* much. "I can't belie——" Her hands slowly slip
away from her face. "I can't believe you're here."

"Mom," Shane calls out.

She doesn't answer him or even acknowledge he's in the room. She
just keeps looking at me.

"Oh, Angel." A tear falls down her cheek as she takes a step forward.
"I've missed you so much." She clasps her hands around my biceps, gently
pulling me up and out of the chair and into an embrace, wrapping her
arms around me. She squeezes tightly.

Angel. Why does that give me butterflies? She called *me* Angel. But
from what I took away from Shane last night in the car, it sounded as
though I was a tough teenager to handle—certainly not an angel.

"Here, Pam. I made it just the way you like it." Taralynn tips her lips
up, looking at me like she knows I need rescuing. Pam lets go, reluctantly,
then takes the steaming cup from Taralynn. "Strong and more strong."

"Thanks, honey," Pam says to her retreating back as Taralynn walks
to the stove. She takes a small sip, slurping the liquid into her mouth. But
she keeps looking at me. I have to take a step away, walking backward.

It's on the second step that a hand touches my hip, covering the long
T-shirt and yoga pants Taralynn let me borrow. I know it's Shane even
before I look over my shoulder. At first, it feels like heat coating me from
the outside, but the shaking of his palm makes the warmth retreat. He
quickly removes it.

I was about to back into him. That's the reason he reached out to me.

He swallows hard, then looks around me. I slide over so he can see his parents better.

"Mom," Shane calls her again. "Dad, you too." He presses his teeth to the corner of his bottom lip. "Can I talk to you both? Out back?"

"Of course, bud." His mom bobs her head.

"Momma." Everly's shy voice drowns out everything around me.

"Momma." Another voice—Emersyn—copies her sister, making me chuckle. She's been doing it for over a month now.

Twisting around, Everly is standing at the entrance of the kitchen. Her sister is wrapped around her leg, hiding behind her. Em isn't shy, but she clings to her sister every chance she gets, and luckily it doesn't seem to bother Everly. I think she likes it.

"Your sister wake you up?" I ask Ev.

She nods, but a gasp makes my insides drop. *Not again.*

Looking over, I see Shane's mom bringing her hand up to cover her mouth as her eyes grow large. As if to keep from speaking—or maybe screaming—she slides the side of one finger between her teeth and bites down.

She sees it. Of course she does. She sees the resemblance to her son—to herself.

"Mom." Shane tries to get her attention. When she doesn't acknowledge him, he stands, takes two steps in her direction, and places a hand on her shoulder. "Whit will introduce you to the girls later. Let's go talk, okay?" He turns her gently, then moves his hand from her shoulder down to her elbow, then guides her to the back door.

His dad follows. But as he does so, he glances between my daughter and me with the saddest look on his face. That sadness quickly turns to anger. *Can I blame him?* It's then I notice the resemblance to Shawn. Shawn looks like a younger version of his father. He favors his dad as much as Shane favors his mom in looks. Shane alluded to Shawn's quick temper earlier. I wonder if his dad is the same?

I see the damage that's been done to them as clear as a blue sky. *The damage done to you* I hear somewhere in the back of my mind. But I push it farther back.

Not now. Not yet.

Keep it together, Whitney.

CHAPTER 11

SHANE

I look behind me before exiting the back door that leads to my brother's backyard. Everly is standing there, eyes wide, looking at everyone while her little sister pays no mind to anyone but her. Confusion and uncertainty mar her precious face.

My daughter.

The suffocation in my lungs thickens every time I think about her— see her. It's heavy, and it's excruciating.

Going through the door, I turn left and take a seat on the patio couch that's underneath the wood awning. My parents sit in the two chairs facing me. My mom is in a daze with her eyes glazed over. She's staring off into space—thinking, I guess.

"Whitney called her Everly, didn't she? That's your daughter's name?" my dad asks.

"Yes."

"You have a daughter, Shane." He looks down at the ground for a long time. I don't say anything. There's no point confirming something that's plain as day.

When he looks back up, his dark brown eyes reflect something I've never seen in my father before. Hatred. I'm not so naive that I think my dad is a saint. No one is. But he is a good man. The best man I know.

He and my mother both have preached to me since I can remember that there's nothing in this world worth hating. There's nothing worth in life to allow that feeling to set up residence inside you, he's told me. But they were wrong. And he knows that now too.

"What the hel—" he stops before finishing. It's not that he doesn't cuss. He does, on occasion. But I didn't grow up in a house where my parents raised their voices when they got mad. My father and brother are a lot alike, but where Shawn is quick-tempered, my dad knows how to control his. He takes a deep breath, then forces out a rough exhale. "What in God's name is going on? Why do you have a daughter none of us knew anything about?"

"She was pregnant when we were in that wreck," I tell him. My mom is still lost somewhere inside her head. "I didn't know that until last night." It takes everything I have inside me not to lose myself and break down in front of them. I'm trying. I'm trying hard to keep it together. But I'm slowly losing the battle.

"That wasn't in her chart," he bites out. "I would have seen that, Shane. I would have told you."

I know that. I know he never would have kept something so huge from me had he known. He wouldn't have kept anything from me. It's because of my father that I even knew she survived the wreck. Her mom told mine she was dead. When I heard those words spill from my mother's lips, I died.

"I know, Dad." My eyes burn. "But she was, and they kept that from me. Hell." A dry laugh breaks from my lips. "They..." I can't tell them without choking up.

"They what?" he asks, wanting me to push on.

"You don't remember a guy named Blake Lane from when I was in high school, do you?"

My father shakes his head. "No. Should I?"

"No," I confirm. "He's just some guy her parents tried to get her to date for years." I pause, trying to gain the strength to force the words out. "She's married to him. Her parents—maybe her mom, I don't know— told her Blake was Everly's father." The words are bitter on my tongue.

"Please tell me this is all a goddamn dream?"

"I wish it were, Dad. I wish it were."

He leans back, looking up. The sky is gloomy, with dark clouds in the distance, like it's going to rain this morning. There's humidity in the air, making my lungs want to collapse. Or maybe that's just all the pressure sitting on top of my chest making me feel that way.

After a minute, his head falls, landing back on me.

"How'd you find out? How did you get here?" I scoot forward as he speaks. "Does she remember?"

"No." It's all I can say at the moment. I wish like hell she did. I told her last night that she may be here, but she's still far away from me. So far away from us when I need her here. I need her in my arms more than I need the air struggling to get to my lungs. "She doesn't remember. I was at Gavin's house last night. She showed up, and well... shit happened." The sound of her beautiful voice floats into me. The memory coats my insides, warming me. She gave me life last night, and she doesn't even know it.

"This is my fault. That bitch did this because of me."

My mom finally comes out from whatever place she was. "Like hell it is." Her voice is fierce. My mom isn't someone you mess with. She's fearless. Whitney was fearless once. I think that's what drew me to her, to begin with. I love that my mother is strong—a force to reckon with but tender at the same time.

"Pam." Dad shakes her words away. "It is."

"No, Dad. Mom is right. This isn't your fault. It's them. This is on them. All of them." I don't know who all of them are, but I'm going to find out. And I'm going to destroy every single one of them.

Judy Reed.

Blake Lane.

Her dad, Martin Reed. There's no way he wasn't a part of it. He might not have been the family man mine is, but he's not stupid either.

"So, what are you planning on doing?" It's my dad that poses the question. Yet I haven't a clue how to answer him, so I do what I always do. I go for honesty.

"I don't know." I let out a long sigh as I lean forward, placing my elbows on my knees and lacing my fingers. "I can't get those years back." My head shakes as I hammer that point across. I don't have a plan. Not yet, anyway.

"I just..." My mom doesn't finish her thought.

"What have you and Whitney discussed?" He gets right to the point.

"Just the past, her past, from before the accident," I inform them.

"She knows, right? She knows you're that child's father?"

"Yeah, Dad. She knows. She's still trying to wrap her mind around it all."

"I called my dad last night." We stop talking, and we both look toward her. Taralynn is braced against the door. I didn't hear her come out. "I hope that's okay, Shane, but I had to do something."

"Jacob." My mom whispers Taralynn's father's first name. Jacob Evans.

"He's out of town, but he'll be back home tomorrow evening. His flight lands in Memphis, actually. He said he could come by your apartment or here, wherever you need him to come." She pushes off the door. "He wants to help, Shane."

"It's not a bad idea, bud," my mother chimes in. "Jacob's... well Jacob, but he is a lawyer. A good one. And you're gonna need one, fast."

"He is, Shane. He's good at his job, and he'll know what you should do. What you and Whitney should do."

Taralynn's right. I know she is. I can't believe I didn't think of him myself. I nod, telling her I'm good with that.

"Thanks, precious," I tell her. She rewards me with a small smile.

I may not have any say in Whitney's younger daughter, but I'll be damned if I let mine go back to *him*. I love Whitney, I do, more than I've ever comprehended, but now that I know I have another life—my daughter's life—I'm responsible for, I won't allow anyone to stand in my way.

Not even the love of my life.

M¥ PHONE B|ASTS FOR THE NINTH TIME TODAY.

I know she's not going to stop calling—not until I answer and give her whatever it is she'll demand. Whitney. It's not what she'll want; it's who. But Whit can't handle her yet. She won't remember her, but Eve will try to force her to.

I love Eve. She's one of my best friends. But she's a lot to deal with on a normal day. Now that Whitney's within reach, she'll stop at nothing to get to her.

The only reason Kylie isn't here is because of her job. She's working in the SICU all month, and it's only the first of November today. It'll be next month before she can request time off. She'll probably take her few days off—days she needs to rest—to fly home. Even if it's for a day. I'm already expecting her to show up by Thursday of this coming week.

I exhale and answer. "You're not going to give it a rest, are you?"

"Fuck you, Shane Braden. Answer your fucking phone, and I wouldn't be psycho dialing you." Eve breathes heavily on the other end. "You and damn Kylie. It's like you don't want me to see or talk to my friend. My friend, Shane! She was my friend too." Her voice cracks.

"I know, Eve. I'm not disputing that. Not at all, but give her a minute."

"I need to talk to her. I need to see her. It's been fucking forever."

"Eve," I call out, trying to get her to stop.

"Don't. Just don't. I'm coming home whether you like it or not. And you won't stop me from seeing her." She sniffles, telling me this is affecting her just as much as it's affecting me. "Maybe I can help her remember. What are you doing to help her remember?"

"What did Ky tell you?"

"Fuck her too. She's just worried about you. She told me to give you breathing room," Eve spits out like she's disgusted.

"So she didn't tell you?"

"Tell me what? She said I wasn't allowed to call you until the middle of the week. Like that bitch can control what I do."

I'm taken aback for a minute, and then it dawns on me. Kylie didn't tell her for a reason. And Eve is going to flip out. But I know why she didn't. Eve would have been on a plane here already.

"Can you wait till Kylie comes? I think she's coming toward the end of the week. She's off Thursday and Friday."

"Shane," she whines. "Don't ask me to wait that long."

"Please. Just give me a few days alone with her."

She's silent, and a minute goes by without words.

"Fine, then I'll be there Thursday. I'll be there, so if I were you, I'd prepare her for me." Even she knows she's a handful.

"Thank you."

"Fuck you." The line cuts off. She didn't mean that in a bad way. It's just the way she's always told me goodbye.

CHAPTER 12

WHITNEY

He's going to hate me. I feel it in my gut. But I don't have a choice. Tomorrow is Monday, and Everly can't miss school. She's never missed a day of school since she started K-3, and I'm not about to let that change now.

"I need to go home." I perch against the door leading into the living room from the foyer. Emersyn is taking a nap upstairs, and Everly is in the room with her, watching television. I get the feeling these people watch a lot of television. I've seen a TV in every room, including the back patio when I peeked out the window earlier.

"Like hell you do." Shane's face snaps up from where he's sitting on the couch, as do Shawn and Taralynn's at the sound of his voice. She's sitting on her boyfriend's lap. Shawn has his arm wrapped snugly around her middle. They're both eyeing me, waiting for me to speak.

Roaming my gaze over to Shane, I declare, "Yes. Yes, I do." It never fails. Butterflies erupt in my belly whenever his eyes are on mine, when he's speaking to me, when his flesh grazes mine.

"Not happening." Fire ignites behind his eyes as his head shakes from side to side. *Are those eyes daring me?*

"I don't have clothes," I divulge, ignoring the fighting urge to fire back at him. I don't know where the feeling inside is coming from. "The girls don't have any clothes. I have no money, no cell phone, no nothing, Shane." I finally let out a sigh, trying to remember to put myself in his shoes. "I get it, though."

"No. I don't think you do. I'm not telling you 'no' to tell you what you are or aren't going to do, Whitney. They stole you from me. They stole *her* from me." His voice raises as he points behind me, toward the stairwell, and I know he's talking about our daughter.

I swear a crack opens somewhere deep inside my chest. I feel it forming.

"I'm just asking you to give me until I have a chance to speak to Jacob tomorrow evening." His eyes beg, pleading with me not to leave. It's pulling at the spot in my chest, deepening the split that's forcing my heart wide open.

I don't think he can just give me tomorrow. He wants more. *He wants me.* It's written all over his face for me to see. It's open, honest, and laying it all out.

The problem is... can I give him what he wants? I don't even know him; not really. Not the me I am now, anyway.

Goddamn memories. Where are they? My head falls back, looking at the ceiling above, cursing the higher power beyond it. *Why?* Why can't I remember anything? Why are you keeping them from me?

If I just had the right key to unlock them...

His cell phone rests in my hand.

I compromised—for now. For now, I won't leave. At least not until I talk to my parents. Everything they have done may be written on the wall, but I need them to tell me the truth. I need to hear it from their mouths.

But will they?

They have to. I have a daughter with a man I'm not married to. *A man that rips at the flesh in front of my heart.* Just being in the same room with him makes me forget everything I've ever been told. I don't feel like my life is so... borrowed when I'm near him. That's what the last ten years have felt like. My insides harden at the thought of my family betraying me. I'm a mom. I could never do something so wrong to my girls.

Bile threatens to come up.

I have to know. I have to hear her say it.

Without waiting any longer, I punch in the 4-digit code Shane told me in the car last night. Just twenty-four hours ago, everything I thought I knew crashed.

She answers on the third ring.

"Hello?"

"Mother." I bite out.

"Whitney? Where are you? Blake is worried sick." There's a scold in her tone.

"Oh, he should be," I can't help but say.

"Don't use that tone with me. What has that boy done to you? Has he ruined the daughter I got back?"

"That boy is a man, Mother. That boy is Everly's father."

"Blake's been her father since the day you found out you were pregnant with her. You should be grateful he stepped up like he did."

She doesn't deny it. Holy fuck. She doesn't dispute it at all. *Was a part of me hoping she would?* My heart plummets. My parents really did do this to me.

"Why did you do this?" The whisper falls from my lips. "Why did you take him away from me? Away from Everly?" My chest cracks, and I have to rub the pain with my free hand.

"Whitney." She says my name in that peevish voice. "It's time for you to stop acting like a petulant child and be the adult you were before that boy showed back up. It's time for you to come home to your husband and bring his children home."

"Tell me why, dammit." My anger builds.

"I'm not entertaining the way you're speaking to me, Whitney. When you come to your senses, you'll forget all this and remember the life Blake has provided for you and those girls. His girls."

"Everly isn't his, Mother."

"DNA doesn't change the facts."

"DNA is the facts. Why-how-I..." She doesn't care that she's caused damage to so many people. *My daughter.* My little girl doesn't know her father isn't really her father. And Shane. Fuck. This is... I don't even know what this is.

When I realize she hasn't spoken in over a minute, I pull the phone away from my face. The call has ended. She hung up on me.

That bitch.

Anger creeps in further inside me. My hand squeezes the cell phone so tight it burns my palm.

Someone is going to pay for this. And I'm not talking about money. I want someone to bleed.

A PHONE RINGS, THE VIBRATION making it dance from where it sits on the coffee table in Shawn's living room. Shane picks it up, then stands as he eyes the device like he doesn't recognize the number.

"Hel—" He doesn't finish his greeting. The shouts on the other end of the line can be heard from where I'm sitting at the other end of the couch. My head quickly whips toward Shane.

"Put my goddamn wife on the phone," he demands. Blake. My hus—

Hell, now even I don't like that word coming out of my mouth. The thought makes my stomach roll. The sick betrayal is so fresh.

My mom didn't even try to deny any of it. It's only been half an hour since I spoke to her. That tells me, without a doubt, that she's the one that gave Blake his phone number.

I don't want to speak to him... ever, let alone right now. I haven't grasped everything. How could they? How could he go along with it? I get Shane said he had a thing for me in high school and my parents thought we should be together, but to do this? And not just to me. What they've done to my daughter. To Shane. Hell, to his family. I just don't get it. I have no words for any of this.

No! You know what? I do have words. The only reason I stayed with that man was because of Everly. And then the surprise we got when I became pregnant with Emersyn. I didn't leave because of my girls. I thought they needed both parents. I wanted them to have both of us. Even through all the shit—all of Blake's shit—I was never attracted to him, but even then, I never wanted my kids to have part-time parents. *I never wanted to be away from them, ever.* I would have rather dealt with my asshole husband every day than miss any time with my children.

But now? Now I wish I had left and taken my girls away. I wish... I don't know what I wish. I wasn't given a choice. I wasn't told the truth. I was betrayed, lied to, tricked. Shane's voice breaks my thoughts.

"I don't think so, asshole. You'll never—"

"MY WIFE!" Blake screams. "She's mine." Shane's eyes flare as he tightens his grip on the phone.

Jumping off the soft, microfiber couch cushion, I rush to him. I don't know why I do it, but something tells me his strength is slipping. He's been strong since last night. He only had one moment of weakness when he saw Everly for the first time and realized she was his daughter. She looks so much like him. The same hair. The same eyes. Those eyes. *How did I not recognize them the moment I met him at Dr. Forsythe's house?* I don't know how Shane is keeping it together.

Hell, I don't know how I have kept it together. Then again, I've always disconnected from most emotions. I learned early in my marriage that's what I had to do in order not to lash out.

"No the hell she isn't," Shane bites out.

"Let me have the phone," I plead, calmer than what I'm feeling below the surface of my skin. I hold my hand out in front of him, waiting for him to hand it over. He pushes it away with his free one. "Shane."

"She was never yours!" There's so much anger behind his words. If Blake was here, I'm not sure what he'd do to him. I don't sense he's a fighter—not in the physical sense—but the way his eyes burn right now, I think he could kill him given the chance.

"Yes," I continue. "Shane, let me talk to him." He shakes his head, making me grit my teeth. I'm sick of everyone not doing what I ask. Blake. My parents. His parents. Now Shane? No!

Whatever Blake says, I don't catch. It was loud, but the phone is too muffled by Shane's hand covering it so tightly.

"He's my husband," I bark, instantly feeling like shit for saying that word. Shane's anger morphs into pain as his beautiful eyes fall on me. Shit. He's looking at me like I'm the one that's betrayed him. "Please. Just give me the phone," I plead, using a softer tone, ignoring the hurt I've caused him by that one word.

He stares. He stares for a long minute before relinquishing it. After he drops it into my hands, he turns away, walking out of the room.

His brother looks from me then to where Shane left. A door slams seconds later, telling me he went out onto the back patio. Shawn looks back my way, his dark eyes telling me he's not happy I upset his brother. Frankly, I don't care what Shawn thinks of me. However, I do care what Shane thinks, and I do care that I've hurt him. The pit of my stomach aches from the pain I'm causing him. Other than my girls, I've never cared so deeply for another person's pain.

A second later, Shawn turns, leaving in the same direction as his brother. When the back door closes louder than before, I drop my eyes to my palm.

Silence.

He must have heard me ask for the phone, and now Blake is waiting for me to speak. Well, why should I keep him waiting then? I've held back for ten years. I think it's time I start giving as well as I've gotten.

"You sick sack of shi—" He cuts me off.

"Don't you dare use that tone with me, Whitney." His words only fuel the furnace inside me more.

"I'll use whatever tone I want." I'm done holding back. "What did you do? Tell me, Blake. What did you and my parents do?"

"Shut up! Shut the fuck up," he roars. "You bring my daughter home right now."

"Your daughter?" Fucking bastard. "Don't you mean daughters? Or is Everly no longer yours now?" I don't wait for a response. "Maybe," my voice drips with sarcasm, "it's because she never was yours, and you've always known that, you piece of shit."

"Get your ass home. I won't tell you again."

"You don't have that right." A dry laugh slips from my lips. "You won't be telling me a goddamn thing anymore."

"You are my wife. You'll come home now, and you'll bring Emersyn with you. Do you hear me?" He's livid, and I don't have an ounce of care in me. I'm the one that has the right to be mad. To be angry. And I've only grasped a small part of what they've done.

If I could just remember.

"I only married you because I thought I was pregnant with your baby. She isn't yours, Blake." The only sound coming from the other end of the line is his heavy breathing. "Say something. Tell me why."

"I don't have to justify anything to you. You have an hour to show up with my daughter or so help me God..."

"So help you God, what? What do you think you're going to do, exactly?" What can he do? I don't know, and that worries me. I won't let anyone take my girls away from me. I won't.

"I will do whatever it takes, Whitney. Do you hear me? Whatever it takes." His voice is devious, leaving me no doubt that he would do anything. *But what is anything, exactly?*

Shane is right. I don't need to go home until I've spoken to a lawyer. And how can I take Everly away from him? Even for a little while. He's missed so much time.

What have I missed? What could've been if I hadn't lost my memory? Were Shane and I meant to be together? Would we be together now if I hadn't lost my memory?

"Until I know exactly what you've done, I won't be coming home. Neither will the kids."

"Don't you dare test me, woman. In the eyes of the law, I am Everly's father. You need to tell that fuck you've decided to shack up with that. I can—and will—take her too if you don't come home, Whitney." It's eerie how calm his voice has become. Instead of focusing on that, my chest builds with pressure as tension cords along my shoulders. "Don't push me."

He's threatening me. He's threatening to take both of them away. I don't think so. I won't let it happen, but I know there is no telling him that. It'd be like beating a dead horse. He only believes what he wants to believe.

Hmm... Is that why? Did Blake always believe I was his?

"Why, Blake? Answer me. Why did you marry me when I was carrying another man's baby?" He's silent again. "I'm not going to do what you say, so you might as well tell me the truth. You were never Everly's father, so why did you say you were?"

"You should be fucking grateful I made you my wife while you were carrying his child."

"That's not what I asked. Tell me what I want to know, dammit."

"I don't have to." His tone is laced with arrogance. "But you do have to bring *my* daughter home."

"Yeah, well, that's not gonna happen."

Pulling the phone away from my ear, I press the button on the screen to end the call. And even though it's not my phone, I flip the switch to silence it. I know he won't stop calling. And I don't want to hear it right now. I have too much to figure out. He's not denying anything, just like my mother didn't. Everything I've seen and everything I've heard is leading me to believe everything the man that makes my heart jump says. There is no instinct telling me to run from him; quite the opposite, actually.

"Mom?"

Ah, hell.

CHAPTER 13

SHANE

She didn't leave. Thank God for small miracles.

But it's Monday, and I had to report in this morning, working a 7 AM to 7 PM shift. It's going to be a long-ass day. It's already been a long three hours. How am I supposed to shove them to the back of my mind? Whitney. My daughter. Even Emersyn. It's impossible. They are at the forefront.

It's still surreal that she named Emersyn after me. Subconsciously, of course, but she still did it. That has to mean something.

I got Whitney to drop me off at work this morning so she wouldn't be without a vehicle. I was adamant. I didn't want her to go back to her house even for her car, and I can just Uber it home.

I'll do whatever it takes to ensure she doesn't go back to Blake's, even if it means maxing out my credit card or taking out a loan to get her another car since mine is paid for. My parents did a lot for me while I was in medical school, and even when I moved here, they helped me a lot. I'm not ungrateful. I know my parents struggled when they were in my shoes because they started their family before they finished medical school.

"Shane?"

Twisting around to Roxanne's voice, I see her standing in the entryway to our dictation room. Well, it's not really a room. It's more of a small, semi-secluded space with three computers tucked away along the hallway for doctors to finish patient charts. I've been in here for the last half hour doing dictations on three of the patients I treated this morning.

"Yeah?"

"You finishing up?" She smiles shyly at me. I'm not sure why. She's not shy with anyone else. Just me, yet she always finds a reason to talk to me. I'm not blind. I knew she had a crush even before my brother pointed it out a few weeks ago. I don't know why she continues to pursue me. I've given her no reason to think there could be anything between us.

"Yep," I inform her. "All done. What's up? Any new patients?" I stand after logging off the computer.

"Nothing new on the board. There are still four patients roomed." She braces her palms on the entrance walls, preventing me from slipping out. "That's not why I stopped by." She chuckles.

"Oh, okay. What's up then?" I ask once again.

"Some of us are going out after our shift tonight to grab a bite to eat and have a few beers. Wanna come?" Her lips tip up.

"Nah. I can't." I shake my head.

It has become a weekly ritual that Roxanne or one of the other residents invites me to hang out after our shift, and even though I've accepted their invite a few times, it's just not my thing. Okay, they aren't my thing. With the exception of Gavin, I really haven't connected with the others to consider them friends. Then again, I really haven't tried. Maybe it's because I don't want to get close to others. Maybe it's because I have enough friends already. *Maybe it's because you don't want to replace Trent.* Yeah... maybe.

"Oh, come on," she whines. "What do you have going on that you gotta rush home for, huh?"

"A lot," I breathe out. More than I ever imagined possible. The problem is, I'm not certain I'll get to keep them. The pain slicing through me at that thought is almost unbearable—which is why I keep trying to shove it to the farthest section of my mind.

"Huh?" she questions, dumbfounded. "You don't even have a dog, Shane."

"I have a daughter." It just slipped out. I wasn't planning on telling anyone besides my boss, but now that it's out of my mouth, it feels good to say it out loud for once. I have a daughter. *I have a daughter.*

"I'm sorry, what?" She leans closer, making me step backward.

"It's a long story." I shrug. "You know the woman that showed up at Gavin's Saturday night? The one I left with?"

"Yeah, what was up with that? That isn't like you."

It's not, but she hasn't known me long enough to make that call. It's not like I hit Blake, even though I should have been the one to do it.

"Maybe not, but it happened, and again, it's too long of a story. But I have a daughter. My girl..." I pause. I've always referred to Whitney as my girlfriend. But she's not. She married someone else. Pain shoots through my chest at that fact. "That woman was a girl I dated a long time ago. Her name is Whitney. Anyway, I have a daughter with her, and they're at my apartment, staying with me," I clarify.

Shock crosses her face. One look transforms into another: disappointment and even anger, I think. But maybe this is what she needed to hear to make her understand I'm not interested. It's always been Whitney. This weekend confirmed it. It'll always be her.

"I appreciate the invite. Maybe another night, okay?" I gesture for her to step back to allow me to exit.

Just as her stunned silence evaporates, my phone buzzes from my back pocket.

"I can't... I mean... but I don't..." She continues, not making a full sentence as I reach into my pocket, pulling out my cell phone.

Kylie's bright smile lights up the screen. It feels like it was just yesterday that I took that photo. But it wasn't, and too much has happened since she was that happy.

"I gotta take this." I flash the screen at her, but she stares dumbfounded at me. I guess I get it. It's still a shock and something I haven't fully let myself embrace because Everly doesn't know I'm her father.

Not yet anyway. But she will.

I turn away from Roxanne—who still hasn't acknowledged my phone call. I'm being rude, I know, but I'm also not up for explaining further. It's none of her business anyway.

"Hey, Ky."

"I got another resident to cover me through Sunday." She sighs. Her voice sounds almost as broken as I feel. She doesn't need more heartache this year, or ever. "My flight is Wednesday night after my shift."

"Okay," I resign. There's no talking her, or even Eve, out of coming. They want to see their friend too. I'm being selfish. But shouldn't I get to be selfish? I've missed too much. I've lost time I'll never get back.

No. I can't deal with all that yet. I close my eyes as I brace my forearm on the white wall at the back of the dictation room.

"Okay? Just like that? You're fine with me coming?"

My head falls, landing on my heated arm.

"Yeah, Kylie. It's fine. Come. I could use a friend." In all honesty, I could. I'm still upset that she won't ask to get out of her lease. I'm still mad at her for not agreeing to move. If Trent were still alive, he'd be livid that I let her stay in an apartment where another tenant—a girl the same age as Kylie and a girl that looks a lot like Kylie—was murdered. Maybe if they'd caught the person responsible, I'd be okay with her decision. But they haven't, and I'm not fine with her decision. She's one of my best friends. She is my best friend now that Trent's gone. And if anything happened to her too...

"Okay. Good." Her spirit perks up. "I love you, Shane. So much, and I'm coming for you too. Not just for Whit. I'm coming for you."

"Doctor Braden, you're needed in room two," the female voice from the intercom filters in from the hallway.

"I heard," she says. "See ya in a couple of days, Shaney."

God, I hate when she calls me that.

"CALL IN AN ORTHO CONSULT for me for the upper extremity," I relay to Roxanne on the other side of the patient's bed as I look over the x-rays from the computer I have rolled up next to the bedside.

"Got it." She squeezes the five-year-old boy's arm. "You're gonna be okay, little man."

He has a fracture to his femur from a trampoline accident. They've become more common in the last few years with the increased number of trampoline parks opening. Luckily, he isn't one of the cases that end up with damage to their spinal cord.

"She's right," I confirm, turning away from the monitor. "You'll be in a cast for several weeks, but you'll be okay soon enough." I cut my eyes over to the boy's mother, who is chewing on her bottom lip from the chair she's perched on. "I want one of the orthopedic surgeons to reset his bones. Did the nurse ask you what pharmacy you prefer?" I finish.

"Yes."

"Good. I'm going to call in a prescription for pain. If he needs it, give it to him, but if he's fine, you don't have to. So just as needed." I eye her to make sure she fully understands my instructions.

She nods her head, then stares at her son with pain in her eyes. It makes me think about Everly. Obviously, I like children. I chose pediatrics because the thought of any child sick, in pain, or even worse, made me sick to my stomach. I wanted to help them. I wanted to do anything in my power to make sure they grew into healthy adults. But now... Now I have a child, and I'm seeing things in a different light. Whereas before, I *wanted* to help, now I *need* to. The feeling is different. I hate to say it, but it's more real somehow. It's a deeper feeling.

My eyes skirt over to the door. Roxanne enters, walking to my side. Calvin Anderson, an orthopedic trauma surgeon, follows in behind her. He looks directly at my patient, smiling.

"I hear you took a dive off a trampoline." His voice is playful as he curls his fingers around the plastic at the end of the hospital bed the boy is lying in. The kid's face turns from in pain to looking scared in a matter of seconds. "It's okay, little buddy. I'm just messing with you. I'm Dr. Anderson."

The kid apparently didn't understand his attempt to lighten the mood.

He cocks his head toward Roxanne and me, his expression turning professional. "Dr. Braden, pull up the x-rays for me."

"Got 'em on the screen for you already." I step back, showing the computer screen to my right as I get out of his way so he can view them. Roxanne follows my steps, staying a little too close to my side for my liking. Another intern, or anyone really, and it wouldn't bother me. But I think she does it purposely.

He takes a few minutes to scan the images before turning his attention over to the boy's mother.

"Mom," he greets the boy's mother. She's still chomping down on her lip, but she's now standing by the bedside, clutching her son's hand. "Can you tell me what happened?"

"He was fine one minute, then an older kid jumped on the section he was on, and he bounced too high, I guess. He landed awkwardly." Her lip trembles like she's holding back tears, and I suppose she is.

"Yeah," Calvin comments. "That's certainly a recipe for disaster, but the break is clean. We'll get him to surgery to reset it, then it'll be cast, and it should heal fine. What questions do you have?"

"How long will he be in the cast?" she asks.

"Usually it's six to eight weeks, but sometimes longer. Most patients return to normal activities within twelve to eighteen weeks. I'd like to see him in my clinic in two weeks for a post-operative check-up." Dr. Anderson looks my way. "Will you put that in the discharge notes so he'll get scheduled timely?"

"Of course." I nod.

"Great. Let's get you to the OR, young man." He steps away from the boy's bed, addressing the mother as he walks. "Mom, if you'll follow me, we'll head up."

After the kid is wheeled out of the exam room, I linger to finish up the notes inside his chart on the computer.

"So a kid, huh?"

Roxanne brushes against me as I hit the acceptance button, saving my notes. With a few more clicks, I quickly sign off.

She's been quiet all day. Since I told her I couldn't go out tonight because I have a daughter at home, I've been expecting her to say something. I didn't expect silence. I was thankful for it. It's not something I want to discuss with people yet. I still don't know what the future holds.

I won't let either one of them go without a fight this time.

"Uh-huh," I affirm.

"How old?"

"Nine. She'll be ten next month."

"So what?" Her shoulders rise, then drop. "She never let you know? That's kinda shitty, Shane. I'm so sorry. If you need—"

"Look, Rox, it's a long story. One I don't feel like getting into, but she didn't keep me from our daughter on purpose. She didn't know." She gawks at me, telling me she thinks Whitney must have slept with more than one guy in high school. "It's not what you're thinking, but I'm not going to explain. It's too much, and I need to wrap up before our shift ends."

"Okay," she whispers as she turns to leave the room. I'm momentarily relieved until she halts, pivoting to face me ten feet away. "If you need anyone to talk to, my door is always open. I don't have kids or anything, but you know I help out with my sister's kids when she needs me."

I nod.

"Thanks. Kylie, my best friend, is coming up from Florida in a couple of days, so..." I trail off just as my phone vibrates through the back pocket of my scrubs. "Excuse me, will ya? There's something I need to check." I walk around her and out the exam room door.

Pushing through the emergency room door leading out of the ER and into the hospital, I find the stairwell entrance down the hall. I pull open the door, secluding myself inside for privacy before retrieving my cell and opening the message.

JACOB

> Just landed. Once I get my luggage, I'll be en route.

> Thanks. I still have another hour, but Whitney is at my apartment. Feel free to go on over.

> See you then, son.

I shoot a message to Whitney, letting her know Taralynn's dad is on his way.

> Jacob's flight just landed. He'll head there next. Will you let him in? I'll be home in about an hour and a half.

Love

> Sure. I can do that.

> Thanks!

Love.

When she texted me earlier letting me know her new number, that's what I logged her name as. I didn't do it intentionally. It was after I saved it that I realized I had.

She is my love. She'll always be my love. I just have to get her to remember. And if not... I squeeze my eyes shut, pushing the stinging sensation back. If she doesn't, then I'll make this Whitney fall in love with me.

Because I can't go another day without her in my life.

I won't.

PUSHING OPEN THE UNLOCKED DOOR of my apartment, I enter to the smell of something that makes my stomach growl. It also has me wondering if Taralynn is here. That girl can cook as well as my mother, and anytime I'm rewarded with one of her meals, it makes me wish for what my brother has.

If his stupid ass can keep her, that is. But I can't worry about their relationship now. I have my own worries with all that's fallen into my lap in the last few days.

"Love," I call out as I close the door behind me. Everly looks up from the couch where she and her sister are watching television. There's a cartoon playing. I remember me at Everly's age, and baby cartoons weren't on any list of fun activities I wanted to do. She's a good big sister. I can see it just in the couple of days I've been watching her.

"We're in here," Whitney calls out from the kitchen to the right of the living room.

"Everly." I greet my daughter, who hasn't taken her eyes off me since I walked through the door. She's been looking at me strangely since we left my brother's house Sunday night. I guess I'd be looking at me that way too if I were in her shoes. A man she's never met in her life is now not only a part of it, but she's living with him. Yeah, I think I'd be weirded out.

"Hi," she finally whispers as I walk past the couch toward the kitchen.

"Hiiiii!" I chuckle as Emersyn copies her sister because it makes me remember when Shawn did it. It annoyed me. I'm glad it doesn't seem to do the same with Everly.

"Hey, Em," I tell her, looking over my shoulder.

Entering the kitchen, I see Whitney and Jacob sitting at the small, round table in the corner. My kitchen is small, but for an apartment, it's not that small. I have enough room for the small table and a tiny island in the center of the space.

"Shane," Jacob greets. "How are you, son?" I eye him as I walk over to the granite counter next to my refrigerator, dropping my keys and wallet and hooking my cell phone up to the charger that's already in the outlet. "Scratch that, don't answer."

"Thanks for coming." I walk over to where they're sitting, taking a seat in one of the two remaining empty chairs. "I appreciate it."

"It's no problem. It's not like I have anything besides an empty condo to return to."

"How are things with you and Taralynn?"

I know she's trying to forgive her dad. He kept so much from her. Since Shawn told me, I've had a tough time deciding whether I should tell her I suspect Trent knew the truth. He was extreme when it came to watching out for her. He argued with his mother at least once a week over his sister. He didn't like the way Katherine treated them differently. In fact, he hated it. And something about it got to him. After I learned the truth, I remembered something he said once when he was pissed off at his mom. *She's never accepted Taralynn as hers.* Now I know what he meant. I didn't back then, but now it makes sense.

She may be the only one that understands what I'm dealing with, and here I am keeping something else from her. The only difference is Trent is dead. Whitney and our daughter aren't. What purpose would it serve to soil the way Taralynn remembers her brother?

"I need to check on dinner. It should be ready soon." Whitney rises from her seat.

"You cooked?" I ask, surprised.

"Yeah." She smiles. "Who else would have done it?" A laugh breaks through her lips as she passes behind Jacob's chair to walk to the stove.

He smirks as he looks at me, knowing I thought it was his daughter. I shrug. We all benefit from her skills.

"I hope you're both hungry. And haven't eaten yet." She looks over her shoulder. "I guess I should have told you I was cooking. Sorry. I didn't think to do that."

"It's fine, Love. Anything you need help with?"

"Uh-uh." Her head shakes.

"Ahem." Jacob clears his throat, getting my attention. "Whitney has filled me in on a few things my daughter didn't tell me. I am sorry, Shane. I know this has to be tough."

I look behind me, making sure Everly isn't in earshot. I want her to know I'm her father. I want that more than anything, but I don't want her to find out because she overheard someone say it. I want Whitney and me to tell her together—and soon.

After turning back to face him, I nod.

"What do we need to do first? She's my daughter. I want her last name changed. I don't want Blake to have any rights to her."

A dish clatters, making me look over at Whitney. Her back is to us, but her body is still. She knew I had to want all of this. I'm not sorry either. She doesn't fully understand what her parents did to us—to me. Or what Blake Lane's part was in keeping us apart. I lost the first ten years of our daughter's life. Everly isn't the only thing I lost either. If I hadn't wrecked that night, she would have never lost her memory. We'd be married, raising our daughter together. We'd be together and maybe even have another child by now instead of her having one with someone else.

I can't change the past. If I could, I'd go back to do things differently. But I can make damn sure the future is one we both want. I just hope I'm what she wants when this is all said and done.

I turn my focus back on Jacob. She needs to hear everything. She doesn't have to agree to all, and I won't push her, but I will be a part of Everly's life, even if Whitney chooses not to be a part of mine.

"If Whitney wants one," I curl my palm around the edge of the seat

I'm sitting on, "what's the quickest way to start a divorce? And can one be rushed?" I want everything out in the open, so I continue, letting not just Jacob but Whitney know what I'd like to happen. "Can both girls be kept from Blake?"

I don't want the man ever around Whitney or the girls again—Emersyn included. I don't trust what he'll do now that the truth is out. If he's capable of lying to a woman to get her to marry him, then what else is he capable of? I don't want to find out.

"Well," Jacob starts. "I can have a judge order a paternity test tomorrow. Then you can contest the birth certificate. I have a good friend that's a judge here in Memphis. That shouldn't be a problem. I'll call him tonight. Since Whitney has the girls in her custody now, he can't just come take them, nor can the law remove them without just cause. I can try to get an emergency hearing later this week or early next week to get a court-ordered custody arrangement if that's what Whitney wants. It sounds like we have a justified cause for it. Plus, that'll keep him from leaving the state legally *if* his daughter is ever in his custody."

He looks at Whitney, who's still standing on the other side of the room. She's facing us now.

"You and I talked. Am I correct that you pretty much want the same things Shane stated?"

Her eyes glide to me, but she just stares without saying anything. Her chest rises high, then falls just as quickly. Finally, she walks over without losing eye contact. My heart feels like it's lodged in my throat, waiting for her to speak.

"I want a divorce." She sits, still looking at me. "I don't want to stay married to him any longer than I absolutely have to. And I don't want him anywhere near either of my girls. I want full custody of both of them." I keep my emotions in check the best I can. For the most part, she's saying what I wanted her to. But whether she realizes it or not, Everly is half mine, and I'm going to have joint custody of her if she and I aren't together. I will not spend another second that I don't have to without my little girl. "Whatever we need to do," she turns to Jacob, "let's get it started as soon as possible."

"Okay. I'm going to clear my schedule tomorrow and remain in

Memphis tonight in case I need to file anything with the county. Did you get married in Tennessee?"

"Yes," she tells him.

"Okay, then. I need to make that call and find a hotel." He pushes the chair back before standing.

"Can't you stay for dinner? I made plenty, and I promise I'm not a horrible cook."

"Thanks, Whitney. I know by the smell alone it's incredible, but I won't stay. This is time-sensitive, and I'd like to get started."

"I'll walk you out, Jacob." I stand as well, following him to the door.

Everly looks up from the TV as he passes, looking bored.

"Night, girls. It was a pleasure meeting you both," he tells them, pulling the door open.

"Niiight!" Emersyn shouts.

Closing the door after I exit, I cross my arms and then lean against it.

"I really do appreciate all this. Thanks, Jacob." He turns to face me with his palm reached out in my direction—which I uncross my arms to shake.

"No thanks are needed."

"What do you think? Is all of this going to be easy or a long process?"

"Son, it isn't going to be easy. I doubt that man will go down without some kind of fight."

"Yeah," I sigh.

I doubt he will either. He hasn't stopped blowing up my phone since Sunday night. I finally had to block his number to get it to stop.

CHAPTER 14

WHITNEY

Shane keeps warning me that his friends will be arriving this week. I don't understand why he keeps mentioning it. Is he trying to prepare me for something? Taralynn assured me I'm going to love them, although she keeps referring to them as my friends. But I don't remember them. And not anything more than the thought of a cheerleader comes to mind when Shane talks about Kylie.

Shane has a picture of her and himself with another guy I learned was Shane's best friend up until New Year's Eve last year. Apparently, the guy, Trent, was killed. He was young too, only twenty-seven. Shane told me Kylie still isn't dealing with his death. He thinks she's avoiding it. But I can't say anything about that. It's not like I know what she's going through or even remember the guy Shane tells me was one of my best friends too.

He showed me a few photos from our past. I couldn't stomach many. Not because I don't want to. I do, I really want to know more, but just the thought of knowing I've been deceived the way I have is soul-crushing. Thinking about it makes my chest hurt too much. And I can see how badly Shane wants me to remember. Everything is heart-grabbing and heavy.

He's going to be so pissed when he finds out what I'm doing—and where I'm at. I can already tell Shane's a very passionate man. For the most part, he's calm, but with me, it feels like there's a beast underneath his skin waiting to jump out. He did say I'm the only one that can get a rise out of him. For some reason, when he told me that, it made me smile. And something inside wanted so badly to try to do just that.

That's not why I'm sitting out front of my husband's office, though, in the back seat of a cab.

Once a week, I take Emersyn to a local church that offers a *Mommy's Day Out* so I can have a few hours to myself. I usually write—something no one knows I do—but not today. Today I need to get things from my house, and I want to do it when my husband is nowhere near. The bank he runs is thirty minutes from our house, so I'm here to make sure he's working before I go home.

His Lexus is parked on the curb in front of the building, as it always is, in the vice president's designated spot. At twenty-eight, he's the VP of an investment banking company his father owns.

I'm about to tell the cab driver to take me to my house when I see him exit the glass doors. I quickly duck down in the back seat, not wanting him to see me.

"Lady, you okay back there?"

"Yeah. Just give me a sec, okay?" I ease back up when Blake doesn't look my way. His attention is focused on the black Mercedes double-parked in front of his building. Another car honks, making me look at the vehicle. More specifically, at the driver of the car, a woman. A woman that looks vaguely familiar, but I'm not sure why. I can't see all of her face, just her side profile.

Blake gets into the passenger side, and then they speed off in the opposite direction the cab is facing.

"Can you follow the black car that just went that way?" I ask, pointing my thumb behind us. He stares at me through the rearview mirror, looking annoyed, but he doesn't say anything. Instead, he pulls out, doing a U-turn in the middle of the road. A slew of honks are geared our way.

Within a few minutes, less than ten, the car we're following pulls up to the front of the Madison Hotel.

"I can't stop here, lady."

"Just a sec, okay?"

A man dressed in all black rounds the vehicle—the valet, I'm sure. Blake steps out, as does the woman. It's then I realize who she is. Courtney Harris. She's his father's executive assistant. Blake waits for her to walk to the other side of the car where he's standing. When she reaches him, he pulls her to his side, and then he plants a kiss on her lips.

I'm stunned silent.

Is he really doing what I think he's doing? What the...?

How long? I've only been gone for four days. In four days, he's found someone to bang?

Yeah. Right. All those times he shut me down about meeting for lunch. I bet this is what the bastard was doing all along.

Cheating.

"Lady, come on."

What a fucking pig.

I quickly snap a photo with the new cell phone Shane arranged for me to pick up from his carrier.

I have cash at home. I'm always stashing extra cash away for when I want to buy something I don't want my husband to know about, and I plan on paying Shane back if I'm able to get my hands on it.

Blake places his hand on the small of her back as they enter the building.

"You can go," I deadpan. I can't believe my eyes. He's been calling Shane's phone almost nonstop, demanding I come home. Threatening God knows what, because Shane won't tell me, and all this time he's off fucking some... holier-than-thou, uppity bitch I never liked to begin with.

Good riddance. I don't love my husband, sure, but I've always been faithful. Even when it's been hard. When he's been difficult to deal with, I never once thought about cheating on him.

"You still have the address I gave you?"

I gave him my home address right after he pulled up to Blake's work. I hadn't planned on staying. I just wanted to make sure his car was there before going to our house.

"Yeah. That's where I'm taking you, right?"

"Yes."

He finally pulls off, and I'm left to my thoughts, wondering if she's the only woman he's cheated on me with. The thought sickens me, and not for the reasons they should. My stomach rolls at the thought of what he might've caught from someone. *What he may have given me.*

I HAD TO LET THE CAB DRIVER LEAVE.

I ran up a forty-five-dollar fare by the time he pulled into the driveway of our home. When I dropped Shane off this morning, he left me with sixty dollars in cash. I'm praying I'll be able to get inside with the spare key I have hidden for emergency situations. Blake doesn't know about it, so I should be good.

I punch in our four-digit code on the garage keypad, and then the door rolls up with ease.

So far, so good, but I don't waste any time. I'm not stupid, and it wouldn't surprise me if Blake has notifications on his cell phone that tell him when the alarm has been unarmed. There have been too many times he's made little comments about the times I've gotten home late from picking up Everly from school. That tells me he knows when I come and go. Logically there are two ways: the alarm and my car.

Shit. I really hope he doesn't have something installed on my car. I plan to take it with me. In no way do I want to become any more of a burden on Shane than I already am. But I also don't have a choice. It's not like I can go to my parents. They're the cause of this whole mess.

They basically sold me to someone like they were selling a used car. Lying in bed last night, that's what I kept thinking over and over. How is what they did much different from human trafficking? I might not have been physically abused, but I was forced to marry a man. I didn't know I was being forced, but even back then, that's what it felt like. My mother said over and over *think about the baby you're carrying and how she'll be part of a broken home if you don't marry and raise her with Blake.*

Once the door is open enough that I can duck under, I do and quickly jog over to Everly's bicycle. I keep the spare key inside her empty water bottle attached to the frame.

In less than a minute, I have the key, and I'm inside my house. The code worked, making me sigh in relief.

I spot my purse sitting on the island. I snatch it up as I race down the hall and up the stairs. I hit the girls' rooms first, throwing as many clothes as possible into Everly's duffle bag and large tote she keeps her old stuffed animals in. I grab her tennis shoes too.

When I picked the girls up from my parents Saturday night, she only had flip-flops and her UGGS. She's been wearing her boots to school and complaining afterward because it's been hot. I guess my nine-year-old hasn't grasped our jacked-up weather in the South yet.

Next, I grab most of Emersyn's clothes, throwing them in with her sister's. I'll have to rewash everything to get the wrinkles out, but I don't care. It beats taking too much time and chance running into Blake.

I quickly take the bags and my purse out to the garage, throwing everything but my purse into the trunk of my car. I place my purse in the driver's seat for now, then head back inside.

The primary bedroom is on the bottom floor, so I go there, grabbing the biggest suitcase I own from underneath the bed. I toss as many of my clothes inside without bothering to take anything off the hangers. I'd rather bring less than take too much time. I have no idea if Blake knows I'm here or not, and I would rather not find out.

I'm fast. It takes maybe five minutes with how fast I'm rushing. I don't bother with my cosmetics. I can always buy more.

With what money, I have no idea. I'm not mooching off Shane, no matter how many times he tells me it's not mooching. It is to me.

Once I load my suitcase into the trunk, I get into the driver's seat. My keys should be in my purse, and after grabbing them from the side pocket, I start the engine to crank the car.

I feel like there is something I'm either forgetting or that I need to do, but as I rack my brain, I have no idea what, so I put the vehicle in reverse, pulling out of the garage. Before I get to the end of the driveway, it dawns on me. My cell phone. Of course. I stomp on the brakes, and then I check the inside of my purse. Sure enough, it's in there.

I huff. I don't want to take it. I have a new one, and this one is connected to Blake. No matter what happens, I need a fresh start. I don't know what road Shane and I will go down. I know he wants to be in our lives. He wants me. I'm not blind. And dammit, there is a part that feels something for him too. Sure, he's attractive. Okay, he's freaking hot. But besides that, it's the electricity, the spark, the goosebumps I get when we're in the same room. When he speaks or when he looks at me, it's overwhelming and exhilarating at the same time. I don't need him or anyone else telling me what we had was something more than just high school love. I feel it. I see it when I look into Shane's eyes.

The question is, can we have it again? And is it something I want?

Only time will tell, I guess. It isn't like I have any business rushing into another relationship before I end the one I'm stuck in now.

I don't feel guilty for being attracted to Shane. My cheating husband certainly isn't having any problems sticking his dick in someone else.

Granted, I haven't given him any in months, but that's beside the point.

I roll down the window and toss the phone in the grass, not giving a shit. I'm done with this life.

Now I just have to find my old one again.

CHAPTER 15

SHANE

I about lost my shit when Whitney picked me up in *her* car. Had the kids not been with her, I don't know what I would've said. She specifically went against what I asked her not to do. It shouldn't surprise me. It's not like she ever did or didn't do something simply because I requested it unless it was something she wanted to do.

That was a quality I used to like—loved, in fact. But right now, I could strangle her.

For all I know, that jackass could have LoJack installed on her car or some other tracking device for recovery purposes. When I mentioned it, she shrugged like it wasn't a big deal. It's a huge deal. And on top of it all, I'm frustrated because I haven't a clue where to check to see if it does. I don't have time until Friday to take it to the dealership. And even if I do that, he could have reported it stolen, and who knows what bullshit we'd have to deal with if he did.

Luckily, Jacob called me today. We have an emergency hearing scheduled for Friday morning at the courthouse. Thank God I'm already scheduled off. Asking my boss for more time off isn't something I want to do. I have a lot of responsibilities in my third year, not to mention being chief resident adds so much more to my plate. I have administrative duties to get done when I'm not scheduled in the ER.

I have to stop complaining. I should be grateful this happened. It might have all fallen into my lap at the worst possible time, but I'd rather it have happened now than go another day without knowing I have a daughter or having Whitney back in my life again.

She may be staying in my apartment, but until I can get her to remember—if that's even possible—I don't know if I have a real shot at getting *us* back.

Taking a sip of the beer I've been nursing since we got home, I watch Whitney and the girls from where I'm braced against the small island in my kitchen. Whitney is going through all the clothes she brought from her house, sorting everything.

We haven't spoken since I first got into her car. To say I was a tad livid is an understatement.

The doorbell rings, gaining my attention. I'm not expecting anyone. Kylie is on a plane at this very moment. She'll be here later tonight. She had an hour layover in Atlanta.

"Mom, you didn't bring my Kindle." Everly pouts as I walk to the door. Everly pauses, looking up at me. It's something she keeps doing, and I can't figure out why. I meant to say something to her yesterday, but I didn't want to scare her away from me. I like that she seems curious, but it's something else. I know it is with the way she tracks my movements.

I can't worry about that now. I have to answer the door. It's likely Roxanne. It's not unlike her to stop by to say hi. I hope like hell it isn't Blake Lane.

Someone pounds on the door harder, making my insides tighten with dread. But when I pull it open, I'm met with the colorful, loud presence that is Eve Matthews. She throws her arms around my neck before the door opens all the way.

"Where is she?"

"It's good to see you too, Eve." I pull away. That's when I see Chance behind her with his hands shoved into the pockets of his jeans.

"Hey, bro."

"Hey, man. I wasn't expecting y'all... yet." I shake my head.

"Move," Eve demands. And before I can stop her, she sidesteps me into my apartment. "Holy shit."

"Language, Eve," I bark.

That's when she looks away from Whitney and over to the girls.

"Shit's a bad word." Emersyn points her little finger at Eve. "Right, Momma?"

I see Everly crack a smile, but then she suddenly stops when she sees me watching her.

"Come on in, Chance," I tell my buddy. Once he's through, I shut the door. Whitney and the kids look at my guests.

"Y'all, this is Eve and Chance."

Everyone's silent until Whitney speaks up. "Hi. I'm Whitney."

"We know." Chance rocks on his heels with his hands in his pockets.

"I'm sorry. I've stayed quiet long enough. I can't keep standing still."

"Eve," I call out, fearing what she's about to do. Eve is an amazing friend. I love her to death, but until you get used to her, she's a lot to handle.

She stalks toward Whitney—who has a deer caught in headlights look on her face. Eve has to round the back of the couch to get to her. When she reaches her, she yanks her into her arms, wrapping her in a tight hug from the pained look I see on Whitney's face.

"Eve, chill, please." I try again, but either she doesn't hear me or doesn't care. I'm betting on the latter.

Eve pulls back, placing her hand on Whitney's shoulder then she kisses her. Yeah, full-on Eve Matthews affection right there.

"I've missed you so effin' much. You have no idea." I think I see tears in Eve's eyes.

"Did you... just kiss me? On my mouth?" Whitney eyes her. Eve just shrugs.

"Whit, meet Eve," I say. Chance laughs.

"She already knows me, jacka... ughhhh!" She grits her teeth in frustration at not being able to cuss.

"You got a beer, man?"

"Fridge. Help yourself," I tell Chance.

"Bring me one," Eve hollers at her best friend.

"Eve, you can let her go now." Eve glares at me out of the corner of her eye but finally does as I ask by letting go of Whitney to turn, facing the girls. They're sitting on the couch, facing backward, watching them.

Lord only knows what's going through their minds.

"Who are these little ones?" She looks at each girl, taking them both in one at a time. With Everly, she glances at me, her eyes somber, telling me she sees what's clear as the sky being blue. When she looks at Emersyn, her face scrunches. "What's she doing?" Eve asks, making me look to see what she's talking about.

Emersyn's eyes are huge. Then suddenly, she starts to clap like she's excited. "Mommy!" she yells, clapping some more. "It's Ariel." Chance bursts out laughing as he comes back through, carrying four open longneck bottles of beer.

"Here, brother." He hands one to me, then walks a couple of steps to Eve and Whitney, handing them one. "Ariel is my favorite too."

"You like The Little Mermaid?" Her small face is full of shock.

Chance lifts his white T-shirt, showing the mermaid tattoo on his left side. The top of the redheaded woman's head starts on his ribs with the tail ending right below his hip. Only a part of the full tattoo is on display for Emersyn to see.

"Sure do. What's your name, blondie? You look like a little Elsa yourself."

Lord, he's throwing it on thick for a three-year-old. There's no one Chance can't win over. Kids included.

"Emsin." She juts her hand out toward him, crashing against her sister's face as she leans forward. Chance grins, shaking her little hand.

"It's Emersyn," Everly corrects, grabbing her little sister by the waist and gently pushing her to sit on her butt on the couch.

Chance raises an eyebrow at me because of her name, but he doesn't say anything.

"And you?" He addresses Everly, who tells him her name too, earning me another knowing look from both Chance and Eve.

I rarely show my skin, so most people don't know I have tattoos. I don't do it on purpose. There's no reason to walk around shirtless unless I'm home. And until very recently, no one else was living here with me.

All my friends and family know about my tattoos and have seen most of them. They've seen the *foreverly* tattoo and know exactly what it means.

"Girls, it's late. Everly, take your sister and brush your teeth, please. I'll come tuck you into bed in a few minutes." Whitney moves from behind the couch, walking behind Chance and me until she reaches the loveseat. She sits, tucking her legs underneath her.

"Come on, Em," Everly says, grabbing the clothes from the couch and taking them with her.

After the kids vanish down the hall, Chance leaves his spot next to me and walks until he reaches Whitney. He doesn't say anything to her at first. He just stares down at her. Whitney looks uncomfortable. I guess if I didn't know him, I would too. Chance is covered in ink from the neck down. Whereas my tattoos are usually covered, his are on full display. I'm not sure if there's a surface left on his body he hasn't tattooed. He's tall like me, and lean too, but his presence can be intimidating like my brother's.

I watch his eyebrows go from smooth to scrunched several times before he finally breaks his silence. "You don't remember me, do you?"

So that's what he was looking for—recognition. He obviously didn't get it. *Neither did I, brother.* It's the same thing I keep hoping for. Every day this week, I've woken up begging for her to have remembered... something. Anything.

"No. Sorry." She shrugs, but her eyes are sad, telling me she wants to remember. At least that's something, I guess.

Chance keeps looking down at her.

"I'm fucking tired of losing friends," he says. He's not angry, just defeated. "Find your fuckin' memory, would ya?" He turns, steps to the recliner positioned between the couch and the loveseat, and drops into it.

Whitney looks at me briefly before excusing herself to put the girls to bed in my spare bedroom.

If I lose her again, it'll destroy me this time around.

I scrub my palm down my face, trying to rid those thoughts from my head. Luckily, I'm saved by a knock on the door.

I don't think it can be Kylie yet, though.

When I open the door, Roxanne says, "Hi," making me inwardly cringe. This isn't what I need right now.

"Whatcha need?" I ask, getting it over with.

"YOU WANT ME TO SIT THIS ON YOUR PATIO?"

I maneuver myself and the large pot I'm carrying for Roxanne inside her apartment door without denting the doorframe or chipping the clay.

"Ugh." She shakes her head as I enter. "I haven't decided whether I want it out there or inside here somewhere," she says, pointing to the sliding glass door that leads out to the small patio. "I guess you can just sit it in the corner, over there." She points to the wall her TV is on. Our apartments are mostly identical, except hers is a one bedroom whereas mine has two.

"Here, right?" I ask before sitting it down on the carpet.

"Yep."

Squatting, I gently place it down. It's not that heavy, but I don't want it to slip out of my hands.

I've been over here longer than I originally thought I would when she asked me to help her. Kylie should be here soon, so I need to hurry. I don't want to leave Whitney alone with Eve too long. There's no telling what she'll do in an attempt to *help* Whitney remember herself and the rest of us.

She texted me when she landed in Atlanta, Georgia not to worry about picking her up from the airport, saying she'd grab a cab. And knowing Kylie, there was no point in telling her differently, even though it wouldn't have been a bother to pick her up.

"If that's all, I'm going to head back across the hall." Three beers in me, and I'm already itching for something strong, even though I have no business wanting it. I have a full shift tomorrow, plus things I need to make sure get scheduled before my three days off. I've already let too much pile up. I'll be lucky to make it home tomorrow night before Everly goes to bed.

"Actually..." She grabs my arm, halting me before I'm all the way out the door. I pause, one foot inside her apartment and the other in the hallway. "Can't you stay for a few minutes? Have a beer, maybe?"

Ah, hell.

"I—"

"Shane, if you don't get in here right now, I will personally bite your junk off." I turn my head to see Eve leaning against my opened apartment door with her arms crossed. She smiles, giving me one of her, *don't fuck with me* smiles, yet her eyes are daring me.

A moment later, she cuts her eyes to Roxanne. "Hi." Eve's smile widens. "Yeah... he's not emotionally available right now—or ever." A chuckle breaks through her lips as Eve stalks toward me. "Bye-bye," she says to Roxanne as she grasps the scrub top I'm still wearing, pulling me across the hall and into my apartment.

"I'm sorry," I mouth in Roxanne's direction, letting Eve control my movements. But I'm grateful she came out here, saving me from being rude. I knew even before I stepped out she was just asking for my help to get near me. "Night," I say, closing the door.

"Did you just fucking pinch my ass?" Eve whips around, facing me.

"I'm going to pinch more than that if you don't reel yourself in." I grab her arm gently, pulling her into my chest with one hand and picking her up underneath her legs with my other.

"What the hell, Shane?" I walk toward Chance with Eve cradled in my arms. I catch Whitney's eyes on mine as I near. They're wide with shock at first, then she pulls in a deep breath as her eyes change, darkening. She doesn't like me carrying Eve.

Well, would you look at that. She's jealous, and I bet she doesn't even realize it.

"You know, if I'd known you were into kinky shit, I'd have gone after you back in the day instead of letting Whit have you." She wraps her arms around my neck, but she slips away when I dump her into Chance's lap. He's still sitting in the lone chair between my couch and loveseat.

"Handle her, would ya?"

"She isn't tamable," he mumbles as his palm glides up her bare legs until he reaches the top of her thighs, pulling her closer into his body. "Chill your ass out." Then he smacks her inked skin just below the bottom of her butt cheek. The way she's sitting, her shorts have ridden high up her legs, gaining his attention.

I'd laugh, but I don't find it as funny as I used to. Chance uses any opportunity to touch his best friend intimately but won't tell her how he really feels about her. And Eve? She's clueless. That, or she's as stupid as he is about admitting there's something more between them than a friendship.

He'd shit a brick if she even thought about letting someone else tattoo her. She's his personal canvas. The man signs his initials onto her skin next to every single one like a painter would. And she lets him tattoo whatever he wants on her. It's a bit weird, but that's them. Does she even realize who the mermaid tattoo represents? Better yet, does she realize who the merman inked on her right side really is? How could she not? It looks just like the fucker.

I hope they figure their shit out one of these days, but I can't worry about my friends when I don't have life mastered myself.

THE DOOR OPENS, CAUSING US to stop speaking as Kylie bursts through. I stand up, placing my beer down on the end table as she drops her purse on the floor next to the door before meeting me halfway.

Without words, she wraps her arms around my middle, squeezing so tight I wonder if she's purposely trying to cause me pain. She's not. I've been numb to physical pain for so long that I don't know if the feeling will ever return.

"Bitch, you can't knock?" Eve chimes. "You two don't live together anymore. It's rude to bust up into someone's apartment, you know."

"Kiss off," Kylie mumbles through the material of my shirt that her face is smashed into. "Stop being mad at me. I can't take it, Shane."

"Not this right now."

"Yes, this," she demands. "We deal with this first. I'm not moving, so you need to get that through your thick skull and get over it already. I miss my bestie." Wetness leaks through my shirt. I'm not sure if she's upset at me or overwhelmed that Whitney is *really* here. They were as thick as thieves, the same as Trent and I.

I look down at her, squeezing Kylie tighter. Even though I'm not happy with her, I have missed her. We lived together for a long time. And since Trent left us, we've become closer.

Her eyes are open, glistening with tears, but it's Whitney she's looking at. And Whitney is looking at me. When our eyes lock, my skin burns as if I've done something wrong. Instinct tells me she's not enjoying watching me hold Kylie in my arms, just like she didn't like me carrying Eve moments ago.

My heart flutters with emotions, but I press them back like I've been doing for days. I don't know if I have the strength to keep doing it much longer. The thread that's holding me back continues getting thinner and thinner every single time she looks at me that way.

When I go to step back, releasing Kylie, she takes a step with me, not letting go.

"I mean it, Shane. Tell me you aren't angry anymore and that you aren't going to ignore any of my calls ever again."

"Ky," I warn.

"Goddammit," she hisses. I see Whitney's eyes flare. "You will stop this shit." She releases me, then steps back.

"PMSing much?" Eve comments, earning her a glare from Kylie.

Kylie turns her heated brown eyes back on me, reminding me of her mother. Mrs. Morgan is a tremendous force in a tiny body. You do not want to get on her bad side.

"I said not now. We'll deal with our shit later." I walk around with the intention of grabbing my beer as I contemplate something strong.

"Trent wouldn't be happy with you right now."

I turn around so fast I almost knock her down. Grabbing onto her wrist and pulling her into me is the only reason she doesn't fall on her ass.

"Don't you dare bring him into this. Do you think he'd be okay with you living there when someone was killed next door? Huh?" I ask but don't wait for an answer. She had to know this would be my reaction before she opened her mouth. "What if the person who killed that girl comes back to do the same to you?"

"That's highly unlikely."

"And you know this how?" I roar.

"Enough," Chance calls out. "Both of you stop. Neither one of you are accomplishing anything. Let it go, Ky."

"Why are y'all even here?" she barks out instead of addressing what he's told us. "Y'all weren't supposed to come until tomorrow." She sounds like a whining brat.

"Yeah, well, we changed our plans," Eve tells her. "Get over it. He doesn't belong to you, you know." She points at me.

"What the hell does that mean?" Kylie gets defensive real quick at Eve's comment.

"You think Shane belongs to you now instead of dealing with your fiancé's—" I cut her off. The last thing that needs to be brought up at this moment is Kylie's lack of dealing with her emotions since Trent was killed.

"Knock it off, Eve. We aren't going there. Chance is right. We all need to stop and chill. And you," I force Kylie to look at me by pulling her chin up so she's facing me. "You need to say hello to Whit."

Kylie steps back, nodding as she does, and then slowly her eyes trail until they land on Whitney.

"You look... too clean. Even I look dirtier than you. And that's saying something."

"Look, pom-poms..." Both Kylie and Eve gasp, taking in a quick breath of air, making Whitney stop speaking. Kylie's mouth drops about the same time I glower in Whitney's direction. "What?"

Kylie's lips tip just before she rushes away from me, bouncing in Whitney's direction. Within seconds, she's kneeling and has Whitney wrapped in a tight hug.

"Bitch, I've missed you so much."

"Someone want to explain, please?"

It's me that sighs out a long breath before I tell her. "You called her pom-poms. It's what you always called her. Especially if you were irritated at something she said or did or if you just wanted to get under her skin. That was your go-to name for her." I rake my fingers through my hair. "You remembered something."

Just not something about me.

I shouldn't be upset. Logically I know this, but when will she remember anything about me—us? What if she never does? It's the question that keeps pounding inside my head.

"Shane," Kylie calls out. "Whit remembering anything is a good thing." She gives me her best fake smile, knowing exactly why it is I'm frowning.

Instead of replying, I turn, escaping into the kitchen.

I don't want to be hurt. It's stupid, and I know it. But I am. Logic goes right out the window when it comes to her.

I pull the bourbon down from the cabinet over the stove, needing something stronger than beer in my gut.

"Love," I call out as I take a small glass out, placing it next to the whiskey.

"How'd you know it was me?" I pour two fingers of liquid into my glass.

"Your skin ever heat when I walk in a room you're in?" I've always been able to feel her presence. The earliest I remember it happening was first grade. I hated it too. Back then, I didn't understand why it would happen. I knew she was the cause, but I didn't know how to make it stop. It was embarrassing. I'd stop anything I was doing to stare at her. My friends eventually caught me and teased me about it. So in turn, I teased her as often as I could.

"No." My stomach plummets. "I get lightheaded, though. And my belly feels like it's full of butterflies."

Her admission makes a smile ghost my lips.

"Hey," Kylie's voice soothes as she walks up behind us. "Let me talk to him, okay?"

"We're good. Thanks."

Whitney's curt with her, but Kylie places her hand between my shoulder and neck, squeezing anyway. I know she means well, but what she's doing is going to piss Whitney off. In her defense, she and I have had to lean on each other for comfort and support these past months. Not in a sexual way, but we have a deep friendship.

"It's fine. Really. I don't mind."

"I got this." Whitney's tone is firm, borderline rudeness, but it makes me feel a little better that she isn't backing down. She's inside herself... somewhere. I can't imagine Blake Lane would have allowed her to be bold, assertive, or strong like this.

"Okay, jeez." Kylie retracts her hand. "I'm just trying to help. I'm not the enemy, Whitney."

The sound of her shoes stomping on the floor tells me she stormed out.

"Bet she's regretting coming in here now." I turn, resting my hip against the counter. "You said she lives in Florida, right?"

"Orlando," I confirm. "But she's fine. Don't sweat it. That was no big deal."

I grip the glass, about to lift it when Whitney places her hand on my wrist, halting me.

"Do you really need that?" She tilts her head toward the amber liquid. "It's already late, and you have a long day tomorrow. You'll only feel like shit if you drink that."

I look down at the glass, realizing the heaviness of my chest isn't unbearable anymore. The pressure is still there, but it's nothing I haven't lived with for years.

I take my fingers off the glass.

"No, I don't need it." My head shakes as Whitney's hand slips off me. "Do you love him?" The question falls from my lips, and I instantly regret it. It's not something I want to know. *But yet, I need to know.*

"Who, Blake?"

I nod, but she doesn't respond.

"You can tell me, you know."

"No, it's just..." She trails off, not finishing.

"Just what?" I ask.

"I've never thought about it. Not... really." Her eyebrows crease together.

"You're married to a man, and you've never thought about whether or not you love him?"

Her eyes cut to mine, annoyance present in them. "When you put it that way, it sounds bad." She releases a puff of air. "Blake is an asshole. I stayed because I thought he was the father of my child. But loving him— it's never crossed my mind. I've never felt it, so I guess to answer your question, I don't."

"But you had another child." God, I'm a dick. I had to go there.

"Emersyn was an accident." Her eyes go wide. "Shit, that sounds worse. I meant she wasn't planned. Failed birth control."

I raise an eyebrow but don't say anything. Maybe she doesn't take them as regularly as she should. Then again, it's not unheard of for the pill to fail with some women.

"You're right. It is late." I look at the clock on the microwave, confirming it's almost midnight. "Let's go kick the others out and get some sleep. You look tired."

"I am, and maybe a little overwhelmed. They are..."

"A lot," I finish.

"Yeah, they're a lot. All three of them seem like great people, though."

"They are. Come on." She follows me out of the kitchen. When we enter the living room, Kylie is walking toward us from the hallway. "Where'd Chance and Eve go?"

"Left," Kylie tells us as she squeezes the water out of her hair with a towel. I didn't realize Whitney and I were talking long enough for my friends to leave or for Kylie to have time to shower. She has another towel wrapped around her body. "They're staying at the Marriott two blocks over."

"Good," I nod. "I'm beat and ready to crash out."

"So am I," she stresses, tossing the wet towel she was using on her hair onto my carpeted floor. I raise an eyebrow at her and then glance at the towel before glaring at her. "Oh my God! Really?"

"Since when did you become a slob?"

"Since I've been awake since three this morning, lost a patient today too, and then had my luggage misplaced by the airport. I'm ready for this day to be over." She bends down, grabbing the towel. "I'm sleeping with you, right?"

"What?" Whitney comes from behind me, looking between us both.

"Nah. Whitney's going to sleep with the girls while you're here, so you get my bed all to yourself. I'm fine on the couch."

"Shane, that's stupid. We've slept in the same bed dozens of times." I cringe at her choice of words, peeking at Whitney from the corner of my eye. Sure enough, her mouth drops and her eyes fall on me in an accusatory manner.

Obviously, I have nothing to feel guilty about. Kylie will always be my best friend's girl. And sure, Kylie's beautiful; I'm not blind. I've just never had any feelings for her other than friendship. I see her no differently than I see Chance, Eve, or how I saw Trent.

"I'm fine on the couch, Kylie." I hope she lets it go.

"Whatever, I'm not arguing with you. I am, however, raiding your closet."

"Have at it." I laugh.

"I have clothes." We both look at Whitney. "What?" She looks are me. "We're about the same size. I'm sure I have something that'll fit her. You said we were best friends, right?"

"Yeah, I did." I laugh at her obvious jealousy.

Even if Whitney hasn't remembered anything about me, she's gotten jealous a couple of times tonight. Knowing that makes my chest swell and the pressure I was feeling ease a little more. I'll take every bit she gives.

"Thanks, but I'll be more comfortable in Shane's clothes." Kylie turns, mumbling a dry, "night" over her shoulder as she leaves Whitney and me alone.

I roll my head to the side, looking down at her. She glances up.

"Do one thing for me tomorrow, okay?" She raises a brow. "Go to a car shop or the Mercedes dealership to have your car looked over. Make sure there's no tracking device on it. I'll leave you my credit card before I leave in the morning."

"Shane." She shakes her head.

I know I sound like a crazy person, but frankly, I don't care. "No arguments. Just do that one thing for me. Please."

"Fine." She grits her teeth. "Goodnight." She starts to walk away.

"Night, babe." The endearment slips out, making her halt, but she doesn't turn back round.

I know she heard me. Yet, she doesn't choose to address it. Instead, I hear the door to the spare bedroom close after she walks away from me.

I sigh as I shake my head.

I'm not sorry I said it. There will be more of them. She's just going to have to get used to it.

CHAPTER 16

Whitney

I wipe the lipstick I borrowed from Kylie off my lips using a tissue I snatched from the bathroom. It's just not my color. I'd rather go without. It's not like I enjoy wearing it to begin with. I'm more of a ChapStick girl.

I like makeup, and I experiment with my eyes often. The more dramatic, the more I love the look. I just don't like having to reapply lipstick constantly, so I typically go without.

Blake can't stand when I get a wild hair up my ass and leave the house in a shade of shimmer eye shadow that matches my eyes with thick black eyeliner. As much as I enjoy the way I feel when I wear bold makeup, it's the thrill of pissing my husband off that I love more.

Does that make me a bad wife?

Is that one of the reasons I'm in this predicament now? Maybe I've been trying to sabotage my marriage for a long time. What if my consequences for being a shitty wife are having my babies taken away?

"Are you nervous?" My eyes meet Kylie's through the mirror on top of the dresser I'm leaning over.

Tossing the tissue down, I take a seat on the end of the bed in the room the girls and I are using.

"Am I doing the right thing?"

"What do you mean?"

"What if he takes my children from me?" Oh my God! What if he does? My heart starts to race.

"Whit, calm down."

My hands are encased in Kylie's before I realize she has come to sit on the edge of the bed next to me. I look up, seeing love, acceptance, friendship, and much more staring straight at me through her dark eyes. She has a heart-shaped face I didn't notice before. I'm starting to understand why she was my best friend. She's easy to talk to. Something about her that makes me want to open up and spill everything I keep bottled up.

"I can't. What if Blake takes the girls from me?"

"Stop," she commands, forcing me to pull back. There's an air of authority in her voice. "Sorry." She takes a deep breath. "I sometimes have to get firm with my patients." She bites the side of her dark red lips, looking at me. "Look, we both know Everly is Shane's. The paternity test will prove that today in court. And hell, once the judge knows what all that sick bastard did, there's no way any sane person would award custody to him. You got this. Think positive, okay?"

"Easier said than done." She squeezes my hands.

I'm not used to all this affection. It's overwhelming. I don't know how to handle so many people invading my personal space. Shane is the only one that has kept a distance from me. And the only one I don't want to.

I couldn't sleep at all last night, and not because I was worried about today. I was, but something else was weighing me down more. I tossed and turned most of the time. Between my dream boy and the reality that is the man, I'm so confused.

I've dreamed of Shane every night since he walked back into my life. Only now he isn't a teenager. He's all six feet, two inches of lean masculinity that has my libido in overdrive. My desire for that man is thick.

Maybe that's why it was so easy to leave that party with him. I already knew him, even though I don't really remember knowing him. I haven't told him—or anyone—about my dreams. They've always been mine. I've never wanted to share them with anyone. And maybe there was always a small part of me that was embarrassed that I kept dreaming and wanting *that* teenager to make me feel in real life the way he always did in my dreams.

I know Shane wants me to remember. It's killing him that I can't recall something about us. But maybe it's because I've had the dreams for so long. And I know it's him. Their voices are so much alike. The *real* Shane has a deeper, more penetrating voice than the boy from my dreams, but they are one and the same. This one's just matured.

"Maybe you're right," I finally concede. There's no point in stressing over something that may or may not happen. She is right about Everly, though. We haven't seen the test result, but there is no doubt in my mind that she is Shane's daughter. My own mother didn't refute it, nor did my husband.

"Of course I'm right." She bounces off the mattress. "If you didn't like that shade of lipstick I gave you, I have more."

The airport finally located her luggage yesterday, so Shane stopped by to grab it after taking Everly to school this morning. She's not a believer in a weekend bag—that's for sure.

"I'm okay without any. Thanks, though."

"All right. I'll be in Shane's room finishing getting ready. Shane said we needed to leave in thirty minutes."

A pang of jealousy shoots through me because I know Shane is in his room getting dressed too. The thought of him seeing another woman naked makes my insides roll.

Logically I know these thoughts have no merit. I'm the one that's married. Neither of them is. He said she's leaned on him this past year since her fiancé was killed. *And I can't imagine what that's like.* Still...

What all has she taken, I wonder?

What all has he given her?

I CAN'T HELP BUT FIST MY HANDS together from where they're lying in my lap. I didn't want to bring Emersyn with us. Luckily, Eve volunteered to stay behind, offering to keep her. Shane talked me into letting her. I didn't have much choice, and so far, trusting Shane hasn't let me down.

I don't know what will be said or if there will be any shouting on mine or Blake's part. I don't want to be forced to give her over *if* the judge doesn't find anything that Blake has done wrong.

The judge's voice rips me from my thoughts, and I look toward the bench where he's seated.

"In all my thirty-two years behind this bench," he leans forward, interlacing his fingers together in front of him, "I don't think I've ever heard anything as atrocious as this. And I've witnessed quite a lot sitting up here." His eyes roam from mine, then to Blake's side of the courtroom, and back to mine multiple times before continuing. "Mrs. Lane," he addresses me, and I bite the inside of my cheek, trying to hold myself together. "Do you wholeheartedly believe your husband has done the things your friends have testified to?"

"Yes." My voice sounds stronger than the war raging inside of me. "Your Honor, I don't have to remember my life before to know I was tricked, deceived."

I catch Blake out of the corner of my eye, leaning in, whispering something into his lawyer's ear.

"Your Honor, I object." Blake's lawyer stands, buttoning his suit jacket. "There is no proof to back up Mrs. Lane's claims."

"Your Honor." Jacob stands. "I can personally testify on my client's behalf. She may not remember herself, but I do. And the paternity test did prove Everly Michelle Lane is the biological daughter of Shane Braden. Not Mr. Lane's."

"Not necessary, Mr. Evans. I've heard enough. I'm granting the birth certificate contest of Everly Lane and awarding Mrs. Lane as legal guardian of the child. Mrs. Lane and Mr. Braden, you'll need to get your lawyer to file a request through the state to change the name on the birth certificate. And Mr. Braden," he addresses Shane. "You need to understand the implications of doing this. You will be obligated financially for the child. You may even be required to pay child support to her mother."

I tilt my head to the side, watching Shane nod at the judge's statement.

Child support? Jeez, we haven't discussed anything yet. What if he wants partial custody? My thoughts are cut off as Judge Harrison continues.

"As for Emersyn Rose Lane." The man lets out a long sigh, shaking his salt-and-pepper-covered head. "I wish I could do more, Mrs. Lane, but within family court, I have found no evidence to support that you or Mr. Lane are unfit parents or have done anything to put the child at hand in danger." I take a quick peek over at Blake as my skin prickles. He's staring at me with a devious grin taking form. Blake thinks he's won. Breathing in, I face forward, waiting for the judge to seal my daughter's fate. "I'm awarding joint custody to you both. Emersyn will remain with her mother until you both meet to determine the living arrangement."

"Your honor," Blake's lawyer calls out, his voice giving away the surprise in his tone.

"Mr. Perry, please be seated. I'm not done speaking." Judge Harrison turns his attention back to the rest of us. "You both have two weeks from today to come to an arrangement, or the court will come to one for you." He looks directly at me, but my vision is blurred from the water pooling in them. "I'm not happy with this, Mrs. Lane. I'd personally rather your husband never see his daughter again, but I'm bound by the law. I am truly sorry that I can't give you what you want." He glares in Blake's direction, shaking his head again, then moves his eyes back to mine. The sound of the gavel hitting the small block on the judge's bench, punctuating his ruling, makes me jump. "This ruling is final. The court is now adjourned."

That's it? How can he...? My tears fall. I can't stop them. I hear Shane pull a sharp breath into his mouth right before he moves from his spot next to me, storming off. I can't move, though. I'm stuck to my seat—rooted to it.

"Whitney." My name is called. "Sweetheart," Jacob says, putting his arm around me and pulling me to his side. "This isn't over. We'll fight the custody ruling. And go as far as you're willing to take it against the people that have caused this mess of shit."

Yeah, this mess.

This mess that makes it feel as though my baby girl is being taken away from me. Away from her sister.

Who's going to bathe her? Read her stories when she's with Blake? He isn't going to do it. He does nothing. None of the important stuff anyhow. He's never helped with her necessities. And she's attached to her sister more than she is to me. She's not going to want to go if Everly doesn't.

And there is no way in hell Shane will agree to let her go. Not that

I'd even considered asking. I wouldn't do that to him or put our daughter through that.

I doubt Blake would even go for it either.

Everything makes so much more sense now that I know Everly isn't his. How did I not put it together before? I'm her mother. It's my job to know things, to see them clearly for their sake.

I should have pushed more. I should have made my folks tell me more about my past. Asked for pictures. I never saw many. Not any after I turned five, anyway.

I feel so dumb. I never considered myself naive. What word would you call what I've let myself be for the past ten years? *Ten years.* What life could I have had? How would things have been different? Would I be married to Shane instead? Would I have another child by him instead of the bastard I'll be linked to for the rest of my life?

"I'm going to need a number to reach you by, wife."

I look up. Blake is leaning over the table I'm still sitting at, peering down at me with gloating in his eyes.

"Go to hell." The words fall from my lips, and for once, I don't care.

"Whitney, you're going to have to provide him with a phone number to reach you at. I'm sorry." Jacob squeezes my arm, offering a little comfort.

Fuck my life.

Someone gains Jacob's attention, and he turns away from me. When I look back in front of me, Blake leans down, placing his palms on the table, inches from mine. I slide them off, away from him, and lean back in my chair.

"I could stop by that apartment you've been at since the night you left me face down on the ground last week."

What the...? He knows. He knows where Shane lives. How does he know?

Then it hits me. My car. My fucking car did have an anti-theft device on it when I took it in to be checked.

"What's the matter, wifey?" I glare up at him. "Didn't think I knew?" He bends lower, inching closer to me. "Don't ever forget how smart I am." His smile vanishes. "And don't ever forget you're mine."

"No." I stand. "I'm not." And with those last words, I walk out of the courtroom without looking back.

CHAPTER 17

SHANE

"FUCK!" I scream, pulling at the roots of my hair as I slide down the door. "Give me strength. Someone. Please," I beg.

The back of my head rests against the wood as my body shakes. Nothing I do seems to get it under control.

That's why I'm hiding in the men's bathroom, looking for anything to grant me a little reprieve. Just a moment...

My heart is racing a mile a minute, and my head pounds with the memory of Whitney's shattered face when the judge said that piece of shit could have equal rights to Emersyn. Those tears made me see red.

How? How does any sane person let that man within a mile of that little girl? If he's capable of what he did to Whitney, what would he do to their daughter?

"Shane?" My dad's voice breaks through from the other side of the locked door.

"Give me a minute," I tell him, mustering up all the bravado I have left in me.

"Son, I think..."

There's silence as I wait, listening for him to finish. But it doesn't come. What does come is the sound of the handle being jiggled instead.

I stand, breathing in deep as my lower lip quivers. I will not lose it.

Just as I blow the air out, there's a soft knock, followed by Whitney's voice. "Open, please."

I turn the lock without hesitation, opening the door to face her. Sadness still clouds her eyes, making my chest constrict even more.

Without words, she steps forward and into my space, wrapping her arms around my middle. The side of her face meets the center of my chest, and this feels like home. The tension my body is holding releases. I can't help but wrap one arm around her back as I bring my other hand up and behind her head, pulling her into me, fusing us together.

At this moment, she feels like mine again.

I want so badly for it to be real, but logically, I know she's just seeking some form of comfort. Whitney was never the type of person who would let many people see her vulnerable.

She pulls on my polo shirt, fisting it and pulling as if she can't get me close enough.

Running my hands down her sides, I stop just underneath her ass, then I hoist her up, making her wrap her legs around my waist. I'm not planning on kissing her. I'm not planning on doing anything further than holding her. But right now, I need all of her in my arms.

She doesn't say a word. Nor does she try to get me to let her go.

Whitney wraps her arms around me and stares, looking me in the eyes the same as I look into hers.

"This feels so..."

"Right," I finish for her, and she nods.

"I want to remember, Shane. I really do."

"I know." And I do know. I can see the want, the need for her memories every time she looks at me. I can hear it in her voice when she speaks. "Can I ask you something?"

"You can ask me anything," she says, nodding. "There's no need to ask permission. Just ask me."

"Will you take that wedding ring off, please?" Seeing it daily is only a reminder she isn't mine. I already have the fear inside my head that she never will be. I don't need the visual.

"Oh." Her eyebrows scrunch together.

"You don't have to if you don't want to." I need her to, but I won't tell her that. She has to want to.

"I didn't realize I still had them on." Her hands fall away from my neck, but I have a firm grip on her—she's not going anywhere. She brings her left hand between us. "What do I do with them?" She removes both rings.

"Throw them on the floor. Toss them in the trash. I really don't care as long as I never have to see them on your finger again."

She scowls, making me scowl right back at her.

"I'm not throwing them on the floor. Do you know how much they're worth?"

"I don't care, Whitney."

"Well, I do. I'm jobless, with no money and two kids." Her fingers fold around the two rings. "These could help until I figure out what I'm going to do."

"What does that mean?" My grip on her ass tightens at the thought of her leaving me. My lips fall open, and I can't control my labored breaths. She can't leave...

"I-I... I didn't mean I'm going anywhere, but..."

"But what?" My breath fans her face, making her hair fly up.

"I don't know." She shakes her head. "But you can't stop your life," she pleads, "just because I can't remember who I was. I don't know if I'll ever remember, Shane."

"I would, you know." The whisper of my admission is as honest as it's going to get.

"You would what?" she asks.

"Stop my life. Change it if need be."

Her eyes drop to my mouth. A second later, her tongue juts out, wetting her lips. My cock hardens, and I do something I shouldn't.

I lower her, making her feel me. Her eyes instantly flick up to mine. Watching them darken only makes me swell even more.

"Maybe I need help remembering." She wets her lips again. Her free hand runs up my arm, causing tingles to trail behind her touch. My eyes close, and my head falls to my shoulders. I can't do this. We can't do this.

But my dick disagrees. It wants her. I want her so fucking bad I can almost taste her solely from my memories.

She leans forward. Her breath tickles my throat, making me nearly lose my shit.

"Love," I warn.

"Help me remember, Shane." Her voice is intoxicating. She's not asking. She's demanding, causing every fiber inside of me to come alive.

I bring my head forward, looking her in the eyes. I can't chance looking at her mouth. I can't. I'll lose what little strength I have left.

Our faces are an inch apart. It would be nothing to meet her the rest of the way, but what would that accomplish? I don't see it gaining me what I need the most. I don't know if I can settle for anything less than what we once had. I need it back.

I shake my head. "No."

"Yes." She grips my bicep, tightening her hand around me and digs her nails into my skin.

Fuck.

She doesn't know it because she doesn't remember, but her aggressive side had always amped me up, just as it's doing now. My own fingers dig into her, making her eyes widen and a cocky smile take form on her lips.

I back her up against the wall.

"I said no." And before she can ask why, I tell her. "I'm not going to kiss you. I'm certainly not going to fuck you—not in a bathroom. And not until you remember."

She breathes out, making me blink from the force of the air rushing out.

I'm frustrating her. Good.

I drop her legs, but I crowd her space, looking down at her. "You're married. Remember?"

"My marriage is a sham. You know this. I know this. I don't need a memory to know that. I've always felt it. I've always felt it was wrong. And now I know why. So..." She pushes on my chest, so I step back, giving her a little room. "So why are you throwing that in my face? Huh?"

"I'm not." Maybe I am, hell. "I'm not going to add to your confusion, Love. I want you. There are no ifs or buts in that statement. But I want the *you* that's buried somewhere inside. I want what's mine."

"And what if I don't get my memory back?"

"Then I'll wait."

"For how long? What if it never comes back, Shane?"

Yeah. That's the question burning inside my skull. Because if she doesn't remember soon, I don't think I'll be able to keep my hands off her again.

I don't answer. Instead, I open the door, holding it open until she walks out.

CHAPTER 18

WHITNEY

I don't think I've ever been more pissed off and turned on at the same time in my life. Well, in the last decade, anyway. Hell, for all I know, Shane used to do this to me often. My skin is on fire, and the pulsing between my legs hasn't stopped.

I thought walking out of that bathroom without relief was torture. No, six hours later, and I'm about to go insane. I keep yanking on my long hair, trying to replace my need with pain. But I swear I'm only making it worse. On top of everything else, I can't get the memory of the way he held me against his erection out of my head.

I've never felt an ounce of this madness, this desire with Blake.

A part of me realizes exactly what was missing from my marriage. Shane fucking Braden. Bastard cock-sucking asshole worked me up and then refused me. If it wasn't for the same torture I see reflected in his ocean-like eyes as I do mine, I'd dick-punch him so that he could feel some semblance of what's burning inside me right now. If anything, he looks a little worse than I do.

Since leaving the courthouse and after our meeting with Jacob, we both needed something to help ease the pain of the judge's ruling on Emersyn's fate. As if that weren't enough, we added the intense desire to fuck each other senseless to the list of things we have to try and fight.

We picked up Everly after school, and since this is Chance and Eve's last night here, Shane's parents stayed with the girls for all of us to go out to dinner. I didn't want to go at first. I'm still hesitant to leave my kids with people I don't really know. I might have known them at one time, sure, but I don't know them now. I'm trying hard to trust Shane on this.

He hasn't looked at me since he asked me if I wanted him to order me a beer.

"Hey, what do you guys think of these?" Eve leans over, bumping into my shoulder with hers.

It takes an effort to stop looking at Shane. He's sitting at the other end of the long wrought iron table we're all at, talking with the guys. Shawn and Chance are down there with him, and I met Mason—Kylie's little brother and Shawn's best friend—an hour ago. I can already tell he's trouble wrapped in the same beautiful, flawless skin as his sister. He's funny too. I've watched him make a handful of jokes already.

I finally look at what Eve is holding out in front of me. It's her camera. She's a photographer who works for a tattoo magazine. These shots she's showing are proof that Eve is a damn good photographer. I'm not used to people invading my personal space—other than my girls.

Taralynn and Kylie come to stand behind us, looking at the image on the back of her camera. It's Shawn.

"Damn," Taralynn sighs, making Kylie and I laugh. Yeah, her boyfriend isn't hurting in the looks department. He's got a bad-boy, Brantley Gilbert thing going on. Only one of his arms is covered in ink, but he's got a massive tattoo covering his back. It looks like different colors of ink splattered across his back like paint splatter. It's a cool, unique piece of art.

Eve flips through the shots she took today. She and Chance went to Oxford early this morning before our court appearance to photograph Shawn in his tattoo shop.

"What are these for?" I inquire.

"Shawn is gonna be on the January issue of the magazine I work for."

"Seriously?" I'm surprised. Shawn doesn't seem like the model type. I almost laugh at the thought.

"Yep," Taralynn pipes in. "I can't believe he agreed."

"Girl, me either." Eve chuckles. "That boy puts the 'I' in difficult." She switches the camera to her left hand and then grabs her beer, taking a long pull from the amber bottle.

"You don't have to tell me that." Taralynn's voice fans my hair, making it tickle my face.

"Since they're down there shooting the shit," Kylie nods in the guys' direction as she sits back down into the chair to my left. "What's up with you two?" she asks. I follow her line of sight to see who she's looking at. It's Taralynn who takes on a shy expression like she doesn't want to answer her.

Eventually, she goes back to sit on Kylie's other side, and Eve leans away from me.

"We... working on us, I guess. It's the best answer I can give you."

"How about you just tell us like it is instead." Eve finishes off her beer, pushing the bottle away from her.

Out of the corner of my eye, I see Shane grab the waiter, motioning down to our end. His eyes catch mine for a split second before he goes back to talking. I can't hear their conversation, but the guys all have easy smiles on their faces, except Shane. His is forced.

In an effort to ignore the ache in my chest, I clue myself in on the conversation at my end of the table.

"I wish I could just forget what happened. If I could erase that memory, it'd be so much easier." Taralynn sighs, then her eyes widen, and her head snaps toward me. "Crap. I'm sorry, Whitney. I didn't think. I didn't mean it like it sounded."

"Yeah, you did," Eve calls her out, earning a scowl from Taralynn.

"It's fine," I tell her. "You don't have to guard your words or tiptoe around me. Actually, I prefer it if you didn't. Just be yourself."

She nods, but she still looks embarrassed, if her rosy cheeks are any indication.

I move my eyes back to the table, where Eve has gone back to looking at the images on her camera. The way her face changes, going from happy to not every few seconds, I'm not sure if she's scrutinizing Shawn or herself. I'm going with herself. The pictures I saw were beautiful; so lively.

"They're good," I tell her, making her eyes flick up to meet mine. "Thanks."

"Ladies." A man's voice rings out as four new beers are placed on our table.

My eyes roam, finding Shane staring at me over the bottom of the glass bottle he has tipped up. Flames stroke my skin the longer our eyes stay connected. I finally have to look away.

"How bad does it hurt?" I say after racking my brain for something that would get my mind off the man at the other end of the table.

"How bad does what hurt?" Taralynn asks.

"A tattoo."

"You want ink?" Eve sits her camera down on the table, then turns her focus on me. Her eyes are big, happy, I think.

I shrug. "Just curious is all." That was a lie. And as soon as it came out of my mouth, I regretted saying it. I've secretly wanted one for years.

"Tell me you don't have any." Eve is giddy. Now I wish I'd told her the truth.

"Nope. None."

"Chance is gonna blow his load." Does she mean...? "Not literally, Whit. Damn." She laughs. The other girls follow suit. She twists her head away from me. "Hey, Chance."

He stops speaking, turning toward her voice. "Yeah?" The way his eyes fall downward makes me think he's taking in more of her than a friend normally would. When he licks his lips, I'm sure of it. I'm positive he's staring at all the cleavage she has on display. She's not overly endowed like Taralynn is, but she's got enough to make me jealous.

"Guess who has a blank canvas?"

His eyes dart to me, taking on a hooded, half-mast look that I saw Shane give me when he was turned on in the bathroom at the courthouse earlier. A slow smile forms—a look that resembles a tiger pacing, waiting to catch his prey.

"You want a tat? Then I'm your man, darlin'." Shawn's voice pulls my eyes away from the way Chance is looking at me, making me squirm.

Chance turns toward his friend, taking on a fierceness that might make most people back away from him. "Whoa, motherfucker! You got

Shane. Your brother is yours, yeah?" Shawn just smirks as Shane shakes his head. "You don't honestly believe you get her too, do you?"

"Why not?" Shawn tells Chance, obviously not scared of him. Shawn's bulkier than Chance, but I doubt either is intimidated by the other.

"She was my friend long before you ever knew her." Chance turns, training his diamond blue eyes on me. "That skin," he gestures at me, "is mine."

"I think you should tattoo her tonight before we leave." Eve doesn't look up from where she's still looking at her camera. For the life of me, I don't know why she's still looking at them. She took them. Surely, she must know every photo taken by heart.

"Maybe another time," I tell them. I've had about all I can take for one day. Yes. I really do want a tattoo—one day. But all the attention looking my way right now is unwanted. It's too much.

I watch as Shane stands. "I think it's time to call it a night. I'm going to handle the check."

He walks off, our eyes meeting as he turns, telling me he ended the discussion for me.

It doesn't take a memory or even a genius to know he's a good man. I can see what I must have seen in him back then. He's good, thoughtful. He's kindhearted.

My own heart swells.

"So what kind of tattoo do you want?" I look at Eve, shaking my head. I think I see why she and I were friends. She's a lot to process, but I definitely like her. I like them all—a lot.

CHAPTER 19

SHANE

In the two weeks I've known my daughter, she hasn't stopped watching me. Sometimes it's out of the corner of her eye. Other times it's more obvious when her head turns, following my movements with her eyes.

She hasn't spoken much. A word here and there but nothing substantial. It's like she's curious, yet shy.

It boggles my mind. I don't want to scare her, but I want to get to know her. I just don't know how.

I stand my guitar on the floor, propped against the end table between Shawn's couch and the recliner. Twisting to my other side, I face Everly. She's sitting at the other end of the couch with her legs tucked underneath her.

"TV boring you?" She glances at the football game playing on the TV that's mounted to the right of the window in the living room. "You can change it if you want to watch something else."

The guys will probably flip if she does. Saturday afternoons are usually spent watching college football. Even Taralynn loves watching her beloved Ole Miss Rebels.

It's Blake's first weekend alone with Emersyn, so I thought it would be a good idea to get out of town in an attempt to get Whitney's mind off the situation. Obviously, shared custody isn't ideal. I don't want him near

Emersyn any more than I'd want him around Everly. So we're spending the weekend at my brother's. My parents are coming over tomorrow after church for lunch. It'll give my parents some time to get to know their granddaughter.

"No, it's fine," she shrugs, then looks back at me. "I'd rather watch you play that." She points to the Fender acoustic guitar. "If that's okay."

Joy spreads through my chest at her admission to want to listen to me play. I wasn't playing anything in particular. Just messing around with some chords.

I left it at Gavin's the night Whitney showed up. Thankfully, my brother—or it could have been Taralynn—had enough sense to grab it, bringing it with them. But in all the chaos, they forgot it in Shawn's truck that night, so I didn't take it home when we left.

"Of course that's okay."

"You're really good," she whispers. This is the most she's spoken to me. I'm not fond of the way she's so soft-spoken. It's such a contrast from the way her mother was at her age. I'm not complaining, though. Sure, I'd like her to be bolder, but she's still perfect the way she is. "When did you learn to play?"

I think back, smiling at the memory. "I started learning in middle school."

I first picked up a guitar in sixth grade after hearing Whitney sing in the school choir. I needed something I could use that would give us something in common. By then I'd stopped feeling embarrassed over my attraction to her. But I can't sing, so it left an array of instruments to choose from. Guitar just made sense. What other instrument is so... intimate between a small group? Between two people?

I took lessons for a whole year before I let anyone know.

It worked too. It got her to pay closer attention to me. And eventually—by the time we got to eighth grade, and after a lot of time hounding her—it got her to go on a date with me after I helped her put music to some lyrics she had written.

"Wow." She gleams.

"Do you like guitars or music?"

"Uh-huh. I've had lessons." She points to the guitar, then her body sags. "Well... I've had two lessons."

"When?" My voice is excited knowing she's taken guitar lessons. That must mean she's interested in the instrument and wants to learn.

"A few weeks ago," she tells me. "But my—" She stops as if catching herself saying something she wasn't supposed to. "He found out Mom was taking me and said I wasn't allowed to go back." Everly's voice sounds crushed, making my chest ache.

She doesn't clarify who the 'he' is, but I'm guessing it's Blake. The way she stopped from saying, 'dad,' though, is... odd. Whitney would have told me if she said something to Everly about Blake not being her dad. In fact, we discussed telling her after her birthday in three weeks.

I don't ask her if Blake was the one that told her she wasn't allowed to learn how to play. I don't need to, but I can remedy it.

"Do you want me to teach you?"

She beams up at me. "Really?"

"Sure. I'd love to, Ev." She grins, showing all her teeth. The ache starts to recede.

"Okay then. First lesson, forget whatever you've already learned."

She laughs, giving me that big, bright smile again. It's the first time she's looked happy instead of guarded. It thrills me to no end.

I mute the TV. Then I grab my guitar, pulling it onto my lap.

"Come closer." I motion for her to take a seat next to me. "We're going to start with the basics: how you hold the instrument." I twist, facing her, but that's not going to work. "Everly, come sit on the coffee table in front of me."

She hops up, doing what I've told her to do.

"You want to position it comfortably on your thigh. Right about here." I indicate the spot on my leg where it's sitting, and she eagerly nods. "Are you right handed?" I ask her before moving on.

"Uh-huh."

"Good. Me too. That will make it easier. Okay, next, rest your forearm over the body of the guitar, like this." My right arm touches the cool, smooth, black wood on the face of the guitar. "Then you want to place your palm, lightly, on the bridge at the base so you can pivot your hand easily. You following?"

"Yes." She wraps both hands around the edge of the coffee table, watching every step I tell her. I'm impressed. She's a good girl. From everything I've seen, I know Whitney has great kids.

"Now, with this hand," I hold up my left hand, palm facing her. "You want the pad of your thumb on the back of the neck. Make sure it's the pad of your thumb, not the tip." I hold mine up, rubbing my thumb and index fingers together. "Then, you want to wrap your hand around the neck, placing the tips of your fingers onto the fret when needed." Watching her watch my movements lifts a weight I hadn't realized I had. This feels good. It feels right—me teaching her. "Am I going too fast?"

"Nope," she says without looking at me.

I grab the pick that's lying on the end table. "Going back to this hand," I wave my right hand with the pick clasped between my thumb and index finger. "You can either hold the pick between your thumb and index finger like I'm doing now, or you can add your middle finger too. I only use these two," I show her, taking my middle finger off the pick. "Come here. I want you to try everything I just showed you, and then we'll do chords."

She stands as I scoot as far into the corner of the couch as I can, motioning for her to come sit between me and the guitar.

Once she's seated comfortably between my legs, I pull the guitar toward us, placing it on her lap.

"Like this?" she asks after she performs everything I showed her.

I lean over her, inspecting. She's done well.

"You need a gap between your palm and the neck for your fingers to arch correctly," is the only thing I correct. "Perfect," I tell her once she's adjusted. "Okay, so before I have you pick the strings, I'm going to tell you the names of each one. Let's start with how they are numbered. From the bottom to the top you have,"—I place my arm over her, putting my finger on the top string—"this is six, then going down, you have five, four, three, two, and one. There are letters associated with each string. Going back to the top, you have E, A, D, G, B, E."

She looks at me over her shoulder, asking, "How am I supposed to remember that?"

"You'll learn, trust me. And we can always come up with a phrase later if it'll help." She nods. "Take the pick, placing it at the top. Pick down for me."

That first sound is like a balm coating my heart in warmth. It soothes and settles something inside me.

"Great job, Everly. That was a down stroke. Now pick up." She does. "That's an upstroke. You can alternate picking up and down."

"This is so cool!" I laugh, enjoying her enthusiasm.

We continue, and she picks a few chords I show her.

"What's going on in here?"

We both look up to see Whitney, beer in hand, walking in with Taralynn and my brother following. Matt and Mason are home too, but they must still be out back drinking.

Weekends around here have always been party central. People usually just show up without an invite. But I guess tonight isn't one of those nights, or maybe my brother called off any plans they'd had when I asked him if we could come down.

Whitney takes a seat at the other end of the couch. Shawn falls into the recliner, pulling Taralynn with him.

"You were playing that song that night. I forgot." Whitney stares off into space, probably thinking back to the night she re-entered my life, the night she awoke my soul again. "I sang that song. In all the chaos that's..." She trails off, not wanting to say too much in front of our daughter, I imagine. "I'd never heard it before."

"Yeah, you had," I admit, making her eyes lock on mine. "You wrote that song."

"I did?"

"My mom wrote a song? No way." Everly beams, looking at her mom.

I move the guitar from her hands, sitting it on the floor. "Your mom is a very talented songwriter."

"I am?" Whitney's lips are snarled as if what I'm saying isn't believable. If my daughter wasn't sitting here, there's no way I'd be able to keep myself in check.

How does she not believe she's capable of so many things?

"Yes, you are." Mason's voice fills the room as he comes through. "I remember you used to sing things you'd written when you were at my house visiting my sister. You're a good singer too." He turns, addressing Shawn and Taralynn. "Matt and I are heading out. We're gonna go to Mac's for a little while. May hit up Level a little later."

"Have fun," Taralynn tells him.

Mac's is a small pub-like bar in town. He mainly has a blue-collar, older crowd, but when Taralynn used to waitress, my brother and his friends started hanging out there. She's no longer waitressing that I know of, but I guess they still frequent there. Level, however, is a club on the outskirts of town, but it won't open until around ten.

I look at the clock hanging on the wall, seeing it's just past eight thirty, so they have a little time to kill before they head to the nightclub.

"It is getting late. Ev, why don't you go upstairs and take a quick shower. Do you remember the room we slept in a few weeks ago?"

She sags against me but nods at her mom. Standing, she turns to face me. "Thank you for teaching me a few things."

"We can practice more tomorrow if you'd like."

Her eyes light up. "Yes! Please."

"Sure, kiddo. Night," I tell her as she starts to walk off.

I'll teach her how to play. Maybe it could become our thing, like Whitney and I used to have. But this'll be how I bond with my daughter.

Until tonight, I'd forgotten how far down I'd buried the need to play. It started out as a way to get Whitney's attention, but I quickly discovered I loved it. Since Trent's death, I've only strummed a song here and there. I was forcing something by doing it. I'm not meant to play alone. I need my Love. I need our family.

Family.

I look at Whitney. She's watching my brother and his girlfriend. Taralynn is cuddled in Shawn's lap, and he's whispering God only knows what. But whatever it is, even I can see it's turning her on.

The look in Whitney's eyes says a lot. There's need behind those dark, violet eyes of hers. But I can't do anything about it—not yet anyway. I won't chance messing up a future with her.

I don't plan on being some fling to satiate her needs at this moment. I want it all. And I want it for as long as I have air in my lungs and a pulse in my body.

It's not long before Taralynn hops off Shawn's lap, spouting how tired she is. Shawn mumbles a goodnight, and they head upstairs to their room.

Whitney and I stare at each other until I can't handle it anymore and get up to find a beer.

AFTER SHOWERING, I COME DOWN the stairs to find Whitney in the kitchen, bent over the island, staring at the cell phone in her hand. Her eyebrows are set in a frown, and her lips are pursed as if she's thinking hard.

"What're you looking at?"

She blows out a thick stream of air. "A text."

My body goes still. I hate that she gave him her new cell number. Logically, she had to, and I know that. Doesn't mean I have to like it, just as I don't like Emersyn being with him this weekend. Or that the judge awarded him joint custody. Makes no fucking sense. But like Jacob said, we'll fight it. At least I hope she will.

I make my way over to where Whitney is propped over the counter. I can't stand it. I need to know what he has said to her, so I peer over her shoulder, reading the text message I know is from *him*.

BLAKE

> Our daughter misses you.
> Misses her sister too.

> It doesn't have to be this way, babe. You can come home. We can be a family again.

> I still want that. Just come back home.

My insides turn. I can't stop my hand from wrapping around her front and pulling her against me. She's mine. She will always be mine.

But I'll also never stand in her way if she doesn't want me.

She hasn't replied to the text messages, but that doesn't mean she doesn't want him. It'd probably be easier for her if she thought about it long enough. She knows him. Knows that life. She doesn't know me that well. Not yet anyway.

"What do you want, Love?"

"What do you mean?" She leans up, pressing her back into my chest. Her head rises so she's looking up at me. I glance down at her.

"Do you want to go back to him? Do you still want your family... with him?"

"Do you want me to go?"

"That wasn't what I asked."

"Well, what do you want?"

"It doesn't matter what I want. I want to know what you want."

This passive shit is grating on my nerves. It's not her. The road to her memories may be in getting her to find the woman locked up inside herself. That's the girl I want.

I tighten my grip on her, lifting her onto her tiptoes and bending so my mouth lines up with her ear.

"Do you want him? Do you want to stay married to him and raise your kids with him?" She shakes her head, but that's not good enough. I want words. I push her front into the hard surface of the countertop. My dick swells, and right now, I don't want to do anything to stop it. I push my jeans-covered crotch into her ass, eliciting a moan from her lips. "Answer me, Love."

"I want you." My cock grows, hardening to the point it's painful against her body.

"I asked if you wanted him." My words are harsh, coming out as a bark and entering her ear, making her spine straighten.

"I don't love Blake. I don't want to go back to what I had. I want my girls, but... I don't want him."

I push myself away from her so fast that I end up backing into the refrigerator. I was seconds away from kissing her. And as much as I want to do that and so much more, I can't. She's married. She doesn't remember who she is. I can't.

I open the fridge, pulling out a Bud Light, and after removing the cap, I down the whole thing, trying to cool my body down. When I finish, I toss the empty bottle into the trash, then grab another, handing it to Whitney.

I know her body is as on fire the same as mine is. I don't need to touch her again. It's written all over her face and in the flames staring back at me through her eyes.

"I'm sorry."

"No, you're not." She calls me on the lie. "Why don't you tell me why you keep stopping it?" She twists the cap off the beer, then she takes a sip. "I was clear a week ago. My marriage is done. And I know you want me. Hell, I felt it clearly moments ago." She looks down at the hard-on I'm still sporting.

"I am sorry," I admit. "I'm confusing you, and that isn't what I want."

"Stop saying that. I'm not confused. I may not remember everything, but I've remembered more in the two weeks I've been with you than I have in the last ten years. Quit, stopping this." She gestures between us.

"I can't, Whitney." I turn away from her, bending and resting my forearms on the counter.

What am I really fighting against?

She comes to stand behind me. I feel her even before she touches me, placing her hands on my hips. "It's late. We don't have to figure this out tonight. I want my memory back too, Shane. I do." She sighs, her breath fanning my T-shirt. "Let's call it a night, yeah?"

"I do want you."

"I know you do. And I've said what I want and what I don't want. Bed, Shane." She makes me smile, but when she lets go of me, my smile fades. I want her so badly I can almost taste her on my tongue. She is the biggest craving I've ever had.

"You sleeping in the same room you did last time?"

"Nah. Matt's home. That's his room. And Mason has the other one down here. I'll crash on the couch. If you need me, just shoot me a text if you don't feel like coming down the stairs." I turn around.

"The couch?"

"Yeah."

"Um..." She pauses, thinking about what she's about to say. "Come sleep with us. The bed is big enough without Em here."

"I don't think that's a good idea, Love." After what just happened, it's definitely not a good idea.

"Sure it is." She sounds like she's trying to convince herself but not buying any of it. "Everly will be between us. It'll be fine."

"And what happens when she wakes up and doesn't understand why I'm in bed with you both?"

She's the last person I want to confuse. She knows her mother is married to Blake. Fuck, she still thinks he's her father.

"You underestimate our daughter." Hearing her say, 'our daughter,' does something to me. I swear it warms my soul. "She'll be fine. She won't think anything of it. You aren't sleeping on the couch, Shane."

"I'm not, huh?"

"No. Not when there is a comfortable bed we can all share. Come on. Let's go to sleep. I'm tired."

Without argument, I follow her.

I'd follow her anywhere.

CHAPTER 20

WHITNEY

I never responded to Blake's text message Saturday night, and he didn't bring it up when I picked Emersyn up yesterday. I'm surprised but also grateful he didn't. Maybe it was because Shane sat perched against his truck while I retrieved my daughter from the doorstep of my former home, I don't know. Don't really care if I think about it.

Just like I didn't care that I only got six grand for my rings that appraised for over ten. The way I see it, it's a small fraction of what I've paid being married to him. *The time lost...*

I walk out of the bank, Emersyn on my hip and my purse dangling from my other side, feeling lighter today. Maybe it's that I have a little money of my own now and I don't have to rely so heavily on Shane anymore. Not that he seems to think I'm a burden, but that doesn't stop me from feeling that way.

My cell phone chimes, indicating a text message, but I leave it in the back pocket of my jeans until I've crossed the parking lot to my car and get Emersyn strapped into her booster seat.

"Momma." The way she says my name sounds like a statement coming from her. It makes me chuckle. "I want ice cream."

"Not right now, sweetie."

"Yes, Momma. Shaney said I get ice cream today."

Ughhh, I want to kill Kylie. Before she left, she kept calling Shane, "Shaney" in that whiny voice she uses, trying to get what she wants out of him. And it ended up rubbing off on my daughter. Now she's calling him that. It's annoying, but she is a three-year-old. What am I gonna do? She says she likes it better than just plain ole Shane.

"Then maybe you'll get some after dinner. We're going to be late picking up your sister if we don't hurry."

We won't, but I'm not telling her that.

I walk around, getting into the driver's seat. Once the car is cranked and my seatbelt is on, Emersyn starts chanting, "moosic, moosic, moosic, Momma."

"One sec, sweet girl. Momma's gotta check her phone." I pull it out of my purse, only to regret doing so. Blake.

"I wanna phone."

I ignore the comment from the back seat as I glance down at the message.

BLAKE

I miss you, baby.

Stop this and come home.

I roll my eyes. My fingers itch to type even though I shouldn't respond... but fuck it.

"Evlee. I want my Evlee." I look at Emersyn through the rearview mirror. The girl is dancing in her seat. Not actual dancing, more like moving her shoulders side to side and bobbing her head.

"We're going in just a sec, Em. I've just got to talk to Daddy for a minute."

"Daddy," she singsongs.

Courtney Harris isn't doing it for you anymore?

?

> Don't play me. I saw you
> go into a hotel with her.

I send the photo I snapped of the two of them before he tries to give me some bullshit excuse.

I watch the dots come on the screen, telling me he's responding, but then they go away and come back on a few more times before his text comes through.

"Daddy says we comin' home."

I turn my head quickly, looking at her. "What was that, Em?"

"Daddy said we come home soon."

Did he now? The fucker. Figures he'd lie to his daughter. Surely, he doesn't actually believe that. Hell, maybe he does.

> Honey, what you saw isn't what
> you're thinking. I promise.

I don't bother with a response, even if I could throw that kiss I saw in his face. It was exactly what I saw. I'm not stupid.

I place my cell in the cup holder without looking at the next message that comes through. I won't be late, but I also won't be the first car in line to pick up Everly when school lets out at three like I usually am.

I flick the radio on as I pull out. Emersyn loves music. Loves to sing too.

I don't remember singing when I was pregnant with Everly, but with Emersyn, I sang every day. I sang just for her. That was when I realized I was actually good at it.

I think I also know why Blake hated it every time he caught me singing. He'd tell me I was tone deaf and couldn't recognize my singing as bad. I knew he was wrong. I recorded myself several times when I started to let doubt creep in.

He just didn't want to take a chance on me remembering.

No matter what the future holds, one thing's for sure: Blake Lane and I are done.

Shane wants me to pursue criminal action, but I just want that part of my life left in the past. Because the more I think about what they did—what he did—the sicker I get.

FUCKEDY, FUCK, FUCK.

I pop the pill into my mouth and down it with a gulp of water.

With the exception of the two days I was without my birth control when I left Blake, I've never once forgotten to take my pill in the morning. I have my routine for a reason. I always take it while I'm preparing Emersyn's breakfast. I don't know how I forgot this morning. I did everything the same. Except...

The images from this morning reappear vividly in my mind.

Shane. Shane damp from a shower, coming out of the bathroom, wrapped only in a white towel.

He was rushing. He is normally showered and dressed by the time I get up, but this morning I walked straight into his chest as he came out and I swear my brain lost every cell it had.

I'd seen his stomach briefly, and half of his chest when he showed me the foreverly tattoo over his heart. But I'd had a messed-up head that night. I don't remember him looking so... delicious.

And I don't even think he realized he had stunned me silent. He smiled. Oh, he smiled that smile that made me want to sink to the floor in a puddle. He told me good morning, then he bypassed me, going into his room. I'm pretty sure I caught sight of a tattoo covering his back, but I couldn't see or think straight at that moment to know if he actually does or if I saw a blur.

He's a distraction—a very sexy distraction. And I'm a very stupid woman if I once had that and then lost my damn memory, which ended up causing me to lose him.

He's the reason I forgot to take my pill. Yeah, it's his fault.

I know the girl across the hall likes him. She's come over at least once a week asking for help. Like this morning, apparently, she stopped him after his morning run because her heater wasn't working. That's why he was running late. She asked him to look at it like he's fucking maintenance.

Yeah, I know what kind of help she's looking for, and it isn't the handyman type. Not unless she's into role-playing anyway.

She wants him. And I want him.

I've never experienced jealousy before. Not until Shane. Every woman he comes into physical contact with makes my heart race and my skin burn. I was so happy when Kylie left to go back home to Florida that I helped her pack her things.

It's dumb feeling this way, but I don't know how to stop doing so. He isn't mine. *But he wants to be.* Unless I'm reading him wrong. But he wants the other Whitney back. The one I can't remember. Sorrow etches around my heart. What if I never get it back? What if he can't love this me?

"What's burning in here?" Taralynn's voice penetrates my ears, breaking me from the thoughts running wild.

"Oh, shit!" I shout, pivoting toward the stove.

"I told you I would've helped."

She did, but I didn't need it. At least I didn't think I did at the time. With what I saw this morning and the feel of his hands on me Saturday night, my brain is fried. I can't do anything right.

When I found out Taralynn was coming to Memphis to bring Shawn to the airport, I invited her to dinner.

"I wasn't paying attention," I admit, getting to the stove. Ah, hell. The asparagus is done. Trash. They're burnt to a crisp.

"Toss it," she says. "It's no big deal. I saw a text flash on your cell right before I came in here. Shane's stuck in traffic. He'll be a few minutes late."

It goes in the trash, and then I turn off the oven, but I leave the smothered pork chops inside for now. The peas I turn down on low to keep them warm.

"Well, so much for that."

"Are you kidding? The chops cooking in the oven smell divine. I can't wait to scarf them down. And from what I'm told, you could give me a run for my money in the cooking department."

"Uh-uh, no way."

"Apparently so. Shane doesn't exaggerate when it comes to food."

"I'll take your word for it," I tell her, coming to sit down at the kitchen table next to her. "So why did Shawn go to South America?" Shane told me, but for the life of me, I can't remember.

"A tattoo convention." She plays with the condensation on her beer bottle, drawing on it with her finger. "The whole studio closed down and went with him. Chance and Eve are there too. They go to several each year, but this is Shawn's first."

"And you didn't want to go to Brazil with him?" She looks up, stopping what she's doing.

"No. He's going to be so busy. I'd never see him. Eve wanted me to come, but I know she's working too. I'd just be in the way. Besides, I can get more writing done with him gone this week."

"That's right. Shane mentioned you're a writer. That's cool." I beam.

"Coming from someone who's written a ton of songs?" she says, surprising me.

"I have?"

"Shane hasn't shown you any?"

"No, he hasn't."

"Well, I know he has all your notebooks. When Shawn helped move him from Oxford down to Jackson years ago, he told me he had a box full of stuff labeled 'Whitney's, and I doubt he got rid of any of it."

I wonder if he still has them? And if so, why hasn't he mentioned it?

The door closes. A little harder than usual, making both of us jump. Before I can get up to make sure it is Shane coming in, he walks through the kitchen entrance looking tired. His hair is a mess as if he has run his fingers through it multiple times. His scrubs aren't the same ones he was wearing when he left this morning. And they're wrinkled.

He tosses his keys and phone on the counter. "Do I have time for a shower before we eat?" he asks me.

"Sure," I tell him. "It's done, but we can wait a few more minutes. Go ahead."

"Thanks." He sighs as he pulls a beer from the refrigerator. Before opening it, he walks over. "Hey, precious." He kisses the top of Taralynn's head. She gives him a soft smile, but even she notices something is wrong.

When she wraps her arms around his middle, giving him a hug, I'm struck by the realization that I'm not the least bit jealous of their interaction. I guess I don't see her as a threat. That should make me feel good, but whatever is up with Shane tonight isn't giving me joy.

"Everything... okay?" I ask when he releases her to twist the cap off his beer.

"Yeah." He shrugs. "It could have been better. Just a rough day in the ER. I think I'll be glad when this rotation is over. Today confirmed emergency medicine isn't my calling." He bypasses me, speaking over his shoulder, "I'll be quick. I just need to wash this day off me."

"That doesn't sound good," Taralynn comments after he's out of earshot as she picks up her beer, polishing off the contents.

"No. No, it doesn't." I hope nothing bad happened, but I'm guessing it must have.

I get up, going into the living room to check on the girls.

Everly is seated on the floor in front of the coffee table, working on her homework. Her sister is bouncing on the couch. Cartoons are playing on the television, but I don't think she cares about them. She is too into entertaining her sister that it makes me chuckle.

Picking up my cell phone from the small home office setup Shane has nestled off to the side of the kitchen toward the back of the living room, I check for any other notifications.

I have eight unread messages—all from Blake. I breathe out my frustration. I just want him to go away and never come back. But I might as well read them and get it over with.

It wouldn't surprise me if he could somehow use my lack of communication with him as some form of leverage.

CHAPTER 21

SHANE

Finishing my shower, I turn the hot water off, pull the shower curtain open and then step out, grabbing a towel to dry off.

This isn't the first time I've worked in the emergency department. I've rotated several times through the ER throughout my residency. But it is the first time I've questioned my career choice.

Good days are great. When you've helped a child that's injured or sick, there's this feeling I don't even know how to describe. It's more than joy. It's even part pride. It's an amazing feeling.

But bad days wipe you out. They crush your soul and bring you to the edge of breaking down.

I lost a patient.

It's not the first time, and it won't be the last time, but God, I wish it were.

It was a senseless accident that should never have happened. A guy was running from the cops in a truck. He t-boned a school bus. There were eighteen students on board. Fifteen, including the driver, had serious injuries. Two of those were life-threatening. The second kid was still in surgery when I left the hospital.

After dressing and hanging the wet towel on the rack behind the door, I scoop my dirty clothes up, taking them to my room.

When I come back through the living room, Whitney is staring at her cell phone with the same look on her face she had two nights ago. Must mean another text from that dickhead. When I step back, looking at Whitney's situation objectively—at least I think it's objectively—how is he much better than a rapist? He took from her what she would never have given willingly if she didn't have amnesia.

Her parents. How do I call them that? They didn't do what was best for their daughter like they were supposed to do. They did what they wanted, and for whatever reason they did it, it wasn't what was best for Whitney. It wasn't right. It wasn't her choice.

Someone needs to pay for what's been done to her. It's not about me. She was touched physically by a person she would not have allowed to touch her. It's taken everything inside me not to do something about it. I want him to pay. I want them all to pay.

I'm not used to these violent feelings. I don't know what to do with them.

Jacob told her to say the word, and he'd file a motion in civil court. So far, she hasn't mentioned doing anything. And financial means won't make up for the damages he has helped cause. But if it's a choice in losing a good chunk of what he has in the bank, it might put Whitney in a position to bargain for sole custody of their child.

It's her choice where this is taken. I get that she just wants it over, but until she does something, he'll always be in her life. And in Emersyn's life. He doesn't deserve to be that little girl's father.

At this point, I don't want to know if she's reading a message from him. So instead of walking over to Whitney, I ruffle Emersyn's blonde hair as I round the couch. Crouching down next to my daughter, I cock my head to see what she's doing. Homework, from the looks of it.

"I think we're about to eat dinner." She stops writing to look up at me. "But after you finish your homework and shower, if there's enough time before bed, we'll do a lesson on the guitar. You want to?"

"Yes!" She beams. "I'm almost done now."

"Good deal." I stand, scooping Emersyn into my arms. "Let's go wash your dirty paws before we eat."

"I not got paws, Shaney." Her nose scrunches up as she shakes her head. "I not no cat."

"I don't know," I tell her, walking down the hall. "Those green eyes look catlike to me. You sure you aren't part kitty?"

Placing her down onto the vanity next to the sink, I grab the hand soap.

"You think I'm part kitty?" I laugh, soaking it all up and letting some of the ache in my chest ebb away. I needed this.

"Hold your hands out." I squirt foam into her palm. She rubs them together without being told to do so.

Leave it to a three-year-old to lift a weight from my shoulders.

"Thanks, Em."

"For what?"

"For being you." I place a light kiss on her forehead.

"For being a kitty?"

"No, sweet girl. Just for being you."

Once she's done, I pick her up off the counter. "Let's go eat."

When I walk through, Whitney catches my attention. She's picking up Everly's homework from the table in front of the couch and placing it into a pink binder. It's not what she's doing that has me pausing.

She's humming.

She's humming the song I'm teaching our daughter on the guitar. She's humming a song she wrote.

Another weight is lifted, and I pray this is progress toward her unlocking her memories.

WHEN YOU HAVE SOMETHING YOU look forward to coming home to, it's amazing how fast a person can complete tasks that usually take all day.

That's why I'm coming in the door to my apartment just after lunch the following day. Working the long hours I do, I haven't gotten nearly as much time as I'd like with Whitney and the girls. I know Emersyn will never be my daughter biologically, but I've become attached to her in the three weeks they've been here the same way I've grown attached to Everly.

"Whit," I call out. When I don't get a response, I listen. Emersyn is probably down for her afternoon nap, and maybe Whitney is too.

I peek into the spare room but only see Em sprawled out across the bed, with her head at the foot, sleeping.

I ease the door closed, not wanting to wake her.

I didn't check the kitchen; maybe Whitney is in there. Before I get back down the hall, soft music makes me pause by my bedroom door.

Maybe she decided to rest on my bed to give herself a break. She has Emersyn twenty-four seven, except last weekend when she was at Blake's. Before that, she's always had her. I didn't think about it until now, but I should offer to keep them on one of my days off so she could get some alone time. As much as I want all my free time with her and the kids, she deserves some time to herself.

I don't knock. Not because I want to sneak in, but because if she's sleeping, I don't want to disturb her. But what I get, I don't think I'm prepared for.

"Holy hell," I whisper, unable to take my eyes off the bed. My bed. My bed with Whitney in it—naked. Naked with her hands between her legs and her eyes closed.

I need to close the door. I need to, but I can't. I'm rooted to the ground with one hand cemented around the doorknob and my other wrapped around the frame. I can't move. And I certainly can't stop watching the scene laid out in front of me.

My dick hardens. I don't have to look down to know my hard-on is trying everything possible to break through the fabric of my scrubs.

"Goddamn." The words fall from my lips as she pumps her middle finger in and out of her pussy.

She must have heard my voice because her eyes fly open. A moan, which sounds more like a curse, falls out of her mouth.

I swallow.

"Don't stop, Love," I tell her when her fingers slow and the other hand she was using to rub her clit falls to the mattress. Seconds go by without any movement at all. "Please," I beg her to start moving her fingers between her legs again. To allow me to watch. Finally, her fingers slowly start pumping, picking up speed.

Her eyes stay locked on me as mine stay trained on her beautiful pussy. *My pussy.*

"Rub your clit," I instruct, and she complies, running her other hand over her hip bone and down until she comes in contact with that sweet, sensitive spot. Her teeth clamp down on her lip, suppressing a moan.

Taking a step inside my bedroom, I close the door behind me without looking away. "Release your lip. I want to hear you." I can't stop myself. I take another step forward. And then another until I reach the foot.

"Mm." Her moan is low and soft, but it strikes my ears, piercing them, making me feel her all the way down to my toes.

"That's beautiful, Love. Pull your heels up to your thighs and open your legs wider."

Another moan—this time louder—slips through those red, full lips. Both of her hands are between her legs, causing her beautiful tits to push together and sit high on her chest.

"Fuck yourself harder."

"I-I can't," she stutters as she tries to pick up speed but can't keep the momentum circling her clit.

"Move your hand from your clit up to your breast, Love." My knee meets the mattress as she moves her hand, running it up her torso until she palms her gorgeous tit, squeezing.

I bite the inside of my cheek to keep myself under control. I'm quickly losing the battle, but I have to push on.

My hand comes down, meeting the soft material of the comforter. I fist my hand around the fabric, bending down as I do. When the intoxicating aroma of Whitney's juices hits my nostrils, my tongue juts out, wetting my lips.

She still smells the same. Just the way I remember her. I could drown in her scent every day, and it wouldn't be enough to sate me.

Some people's vice is drugs or alcohol; mine was always Whitney. The sweetest, most powerful of anything in existence—and I want nothing more than to overdose on it right now.

But I won't. Not yet anyway.

"I won't touch," I assure her, watching as goose bumps trail down her inner thigh from my breath fanning her leg. "I promise," I swear to her, even though it's taking all the strength inside me not to.

Lowering my head, I blow on her clit. "Oh, my fu—" A smile tugs the corner of my lips.

"T-touch me. Please, Shane."

I lift my eyes to hers. "No. You're almost there. You got this, Love." Then my gaze drops to the most beautiful sight in the whole damn world. "Pull your fingers out. Run your juices up to your clit and make slow circles, baby."

She follows my command. Her glistening finger runs up the path of her slit, connecting with the bundle of nerves that will set her free.

I blow a soft breeze over her fingers and clit, eliciting a long, drawn-out moan from her lips. Her abdominal muscles contract as her ass lifts. I have to pull back so I don't come in contact with her hand.

Voyeurism isn't new to me. I used to love watching Whitney make herself come undone, and she got off on watching me watch her. Just like she's doing now.

Only this time, I won't be slamming myself home.

"Faster," is all I say, and then I blow another stream of steady air. Seconds later, she screams out her release, and it's music to my ears.

She pants, sucking in and releasing air in rapid succession. I push off the bed, backing up to give her room. Her cheeks pink when her eyes open, meeting mine. And I smile.

Whitney moves off the bed and walks toward me—my smile falters. What is she doing? She just watches me, her face blank, not giving me any idea what she was thinking.

Was I wrong? Should I have not...

Her hand rises in a gesture I remember all too well. Her fingers, including the one still slick with her juices, run down my lips. My eyes close, savoring her touch. But when her hand starts to lower, I catch her wrist in my hand, pulling it back up. My lips tip of their own accord as my eyes flutter open.

"May I?" Without words, she bobs her head, granting me permission.

Pulling her wrist to my mouth, I close my lips around her middle finger. Her eyes dilate as sweetness coats my tongue, spreading a static-like sensation around my scalp as tingles flow over my shoulders and down my spine.

I don't want to release her, but I do, pulling her finger from my lips.

"So beautiful." Her cheeks turn pink again. "You are the most beautiful thing I've ever seen in my entire life. I thought that when I was a kid. I thought that when I made love to you the first time. I think that now."

Tears pool in her eyes. She breathes in deep, schooling her emotions that threaten to spill down her cheeks.

Stepping back, she lowers her eyes, and then a sexy smirk forms on her lips as her eyes flick up to mine. "Your... scrubs are a little wet."

Fucking thin pants and pre-cum. Nice.

I look down, surprised I didn't blow my full load from what I just watched, if truth be told. "Thank you, Love, for letting—"

"Momma," Em's voice came through the door, cutting me off. "I peed the bed. I'm sorry."

Whitney's palm meets her forehead as laughter pours out of me. Luckily my hard-on dies down, and the interruption helps break up what just happened between us without any awkwardness or tension.

I shake my head.

"Go clean up, babe. I got her." And then I slip out of the bedroom door.

CHAPTER 22

WHITNEY

Holy bejesus.

I take a deep breath, running the events from moments ago back through my mind. *Seeing him watching me.* Jesus Christ. Just picturing those hungry eyes is making me hot all over again.

I tip my head back against the door, dragging air into my dry lungs.

I've never come that hard in my life. My body is still scorching, and my jumbled mind is a mess, but one thing is certainly clear... That was the best damn orgasm of my life. If he's that skilled without laying a finger on me, what the hell is he capable of?

Shane's voice filters in through the door. "Well, hello, naked." His voice beams and I laugh, covering my mouth so they don't hear me. Shane must be in the hall. Emersyn must be as well.

"I not stay in no pee clothes. That's just gross, Shaney." I can just picture her scrunched-up little nose. "And pee was everywhere!" I snort, not able to hold it in any longer.

Shit, I hope she is exaggerating.

"Come on, let's get you in the tub, monkey."

His use of a pet name washes over me, caressing my insides. It's the first time I've heard him use one, with the exception of his brother's girlfriend. It's sweet. And fitting.

Pushing off, I walk to the side of Shane's bed where my clothes are and quickly dress.

Lord, I hope the mess isn't too bad. I hope she didn't ruin his mattress.

When I walk out of Shane's bedroom, the door to the bathroom is halfway closed, obstructing my view, but I hear splashing, telling me Shane is giving her a bath. My hand pauses on the door to the room the girls and I have been staying in. The strangest sensation hits me. This feels right. Being here, Shane cleaning my child, him watching me minutes ago when my body shattered with his assistance. I feel calm. My chest doesn't ache. I'm not walking on eggshells around someone. Is this what peace feels like?

Emersyn's giggles pull me out of my thoughts—my revelations.

"Thanks, monk." Shane breathes out a short laugh. "I needed that."

"You wet."

Oh, dear Jesus, what has she done?

Instead of going to find out, I leave Shane to handle it and enter the second bedroom, turning on the light.

Ah, hell. Did I give her a gallon of juice before she went down? Fuck. That's a lot of piss in the center of the bed, spreading out and covering over two feet.

I shake my head, knowing there is no mattress cover under those soiled sheets. How am I going to get urine out of a bed?

"Momma. Momma." Emersyn barrels into the room where I am. Looking down, I have a naked toddler hanging on my leg with long, wet hair.

"Sorry," Shane says from behind me. "She escaped the towel."

"Go put some clothes on, little lady," I tell her. Turning toward Shane, I say, "Thank you for cleaning her, but I think she ruined the bed. She has a protector on her toddler bed at..." I almost say home, but stop, knowing that isn't a word I can stomach coming out of my mouth. And from the look on Shane's face, he knows that's what I was about to say too. "At Blake's."

Shane just nods, lowering his head.

"I'll get the bedding into the washer, then I'll Google how to clean this up. I'm sorry."

His eyes snap to mine. I watch them darken as if I somehow pissed him off. Eventually, he shakes his head and tells me, "You don't have anything to be sorry for, Love." Tingles wash over me every time he calls me by my middle name. "Kids piss beds. It happens. It's life. It's not a big deal. So what if the bed is ruined? Another can be bought. Don't tell me you're sorry again for anything you don't have control over."

"Yeah, well—" He cuts me off.

"No, Whitney." He says my name in a tone that ignites a furnace in my gut. Not in a bad way, though. In a challenging way, making me cock my head to look at him. "It's just a bed. Beds are replaceable. People aren't." He steps backward and out of the room, then turns, leaving me alone with Emersyn.

I can't help but think he has a double meaning by what he's just said. *People aren't.* People meaning *me*, I'm guessing.

Blake would have never reacted the way Shane did. He would have blown up. *He would have blamed me.* They're both so different. And only one is breaking through to that muscle in my chest.

"Okay, you." I turn, looking down at Emersyn as she pulls leggings up her legs. She chose a Mermaid T-shirt she owns to go with her pants. Ever since Eve and Chance left a few weeks ago, she's worn that shirt at least three times a week. I can't wash it fast enough before she's asking for it. She says it reminds her of the pretty girl with all the colorful drawings on her arms. "You're gonna help me take all these covers off the bed, and then we will clean up this mess."

"Ewww, Momma. Gross. Do I have to?"

"Yes, ma'am, you do."

"Is it time to go get Evlee yet?" she asks, ignoring what I've just told her.

"Nope." I squat down to her level. "We have plenty of time to clean this up before we go get your sister from school."

When she stomps off toward the bed, I smile even more. She's going to be trouble when she gets older.

"Hey, Whit." I stand, looking at Shane in the doorway, holding a box. "Taralynn said she mentioned your old journals to you." He raises the box a few inches in his arms as he steps closer to me. "This is them if you want the notebooks." He sighs, as if not wanting to give the box to me.

"I would," I say, honestly. I've been wondering if I should ask him since she mentioned it. I'm too curious not to want to look at them.

I take a step toward him, taking the box from his hands. He doesn't say anything else. He just blows out a tired breath of air, then steps back out of the room.

Sitting on the floor, crisscrossing my legs, I bring the cardboard box onto my lap. It's not taped up, but the flaps are all tucked around each other so nothing spills out. Flipping them open, I stare inside the box, seeing numerous journals. There has to be more than ten, maybe closer to fifteen, inside the box. All are different in color and size. Some have words on them; some don't.

"Momma!" I glance up. Emersyn has her hands on her hips, looking at me. "I not do all this by myself." I just raise my eyebrow, having had enough of her sass for one day. When I don't lower it, she eventually raises her little hands in surrender. "Okay. Okay. I do it. But I not happy 'bout it."

She goes back to the bed, her small hands pulling the sheets off and huffing out her exaggerated frustrations with each jerk and pull.

I giggle. Maybe I shouldn't. Maybe it's wrong. But it's funny.

Looking back inside the box, I reach in, pulling a teal journal out. Fanning the pages, I can see all the pages are written on, so I stop on a page and read.

I push you away
But you just won't leave
No matter how hard I shove
I don't deserve you

You're a saint
I'm a sinner
It'll never work

I don't read the rest. That shit is sad and makes my chest ache. And supposedly I wrote that?

Yeah, there is no *supposedly*. This is my handwriting. I wrote it. Deep down, I feel these words, and I don't like them. This girl, this *me*, she sounds broken and sad, like she doesn't believe she's worthy of love. *Shane*. I wonder if that's who she—no, I—am referring to. Probably. He did say we dated off and on for years.

Why would I ever push him away? That's crazy. Just in the few weeks I've been here, I know he's perfect. As I sit here, looking at these words, I wonder how my parents could have ever disliked him.

I haven't spoken to my mom since that first call. I know I need to man up everything I have in me and talk to her. But I'm so mad. And I don't understand why. Shane is amazing. He's a doctor, for Christ's sake, as are his parents, and I know my parents are all about appearances and money. Two things I've never cared about.

He's not flashy, and from the little I've seen of his family, I don't think they are either. So I guess... I suppose I see it. My parents, Blake's parents, are all about what someone else can do for them. They hold money in the highest regard.

I jump when something touches my leg. Looking down, it's a photo. It must have fallen out of the journal. I pick it up and my breath hitches. It's a picture of Shane and... me. He's behind me with his arms around me. I'm looking at the camera. He's looking down at me. If there were any questions before, there aren't anymore. He loves me. Or he loves this me, anyway.

"Momma! Momma!" I look up to see Emersyn barreling toward me. "Get it off, Momma!"

"What?" I question, shoving the box and the photo to the side so I can jump to my feet.

"Pee-pee! I got pee-pee on me!"

Oh, Lord. Is she for real?

"Come on."

CHAPTER 23

SHANE

"You got this?" I look up from the computer I'm standing in front of to see my boss leaning against the wall opposite me. He's changed out of his scrubs and white coat into jeans and a polo. "I'm about to cut out."

"Yes," I confirm as I finish typing out the sentence I was writing before he interrupted me.

Interruptions are all I've gotten today. Between the nurses and an intern that's steadily grating on my nerves, I'll be good to make it home before Whitney gets in bed.

"You book our flight, hotel rooms, and rental car for the conference next month in Orlando?"

Before three weeks ago, I had been looking to get away—to spend time with Kylie, just the two of us. I'm presenting at the hospital she works at, but other than a few hours plus a dinner the night before, I had two full days to hang out and catch up with her. And two days to convince her to move if I'm not able to do it before going down there. And since I haven't yet, I tabled the discussion because of everything that's happened, but I haven't forgotten. She'll be moving from that apartment one way or another. I'm damn sure of it.

"It was done two months ago." As soon as he asked me to accompany him and told me the details, I scheduled everything the next day, except for a hotel room for me. I'd planned on staying with Kylie.

He bobs his head, acknowledging what I've confirmed.

"I swear, I should have booked this trip to coincide with the conference next month but Marie..." He shakes his head. "She wanted to take the kids to Disney World for Thanksgiving. Start a family tradition, she said."

Even though he rolls his eyes at the thought, I know there is nothing he enjoys more than time with his wife and two kids. I'm beginning to understand why. I've always known time with family is the most important thing in life. It was taught to me early on. But until Whitney and the girls, I had never felt it. Now, there is not one thing I wouldn't give up or not do to make sure they remain with me, safe and happy.

"Yeah, okay." I exaggerate my belief in his statement. "Get out of here, would ya? I got this today and tomorrow. Roderick is on-call until I return Saturday."

"Roger that." He pushes off the wall. "Wife's out front waiting. Flight's in," he flicks his wrist up to peer down at his watch, "less than two hours."

"Later."

He turns, walking toward the doors that lead out into the waiting room of the ER. My cell phone chimes with an incoming text, so I save everything I'm documenting and then sign off the computer.

I don't like taking calls or answering messages anywhere close to patient rooms. It sets a bad example for the interns as well as nurses and other staff. I only do it in emergencies, and even then, if I can do it away from everyone else, I do.

Pulling my cell from the back pocket of my scrubs, I take a seat on the stool in front of another computer in the dictation room. It's a message from my brother. I see it before I unlock my phone to reply.

SHAWN

Are we really not going to Georgia?

I type a reply to him, then sign onto this computer so I can finish up what I started before Gavin left.

> I'm not. You can do what you want.

Another message comes through, but I'm almost finished, so I take a minute to wrap up my documentation inside the patient's chart. When I'm done, I sign back off and pick up my phone from where it's lying next to the keyboard.

> Asshole

I shake my head. I get it. I do. Shawn has always loved going to Georgia, to our parent's vacation home, for Thanksgiving. It's been a tradition since I was in high school, and I've only not gone once, the first year I interned at the Medical Center in Jackson, Mississippi.

My parents used to take us on trips a couple of times a year to ride ATVs at an off-road park. I loved it from that first trip we took when I was a teenager. There is nothing glamorous about it. It's dirt, dust, and mud inside your nose and mouth. Exertion and sore muscles for days. But it's fun. Shawn loves it more than I do. Our friends even started coming years ago too. Thursdays used to be reserved for just family, but my parents quickly welcomed all our friends, making most of them part of our small family.

I type another response that quickly turns into a full conversation, back and forth between us.

> Emersyn has to go to her dad's Friday.

> Why?

> Shared custody

> That's BS

> I agree, but it is what it is.

That fuck shouldn't be allowed around them.

Don't I know it.

What's Jacob doing to make it where he doesn't see them anymore?

We'll talk Thursday if you're at Mom and Dad's.

I'll be there.

I'm not surprised. Shawn is a momma's boy through and through. He's not going to miss a holiday with our family. He comes off hard and dickish, and he is, but he values family the same way I do.

Until this moment, I never thought about it, but I see now he'll make a great dad one day. He's a lot like our dad.

"Hey, Shane?"

Standing, I place my cell phone back into my pocket as Roxanne steps into the narrow space with me.

"Yeah?"

"I was wondering if I could catch a ride home with you." She smiles, hopeful. It makes my gut tighten.

"I guess." I cock my head to the side, looking at her. "Something going on with your car?" She has a relatively new Honda Accord. Or so I think it's fairly new, maybe a few years old.

"I dropped it off at the dealership for a service, but apparently, they couldn't get to it today, so it'll be tomorrow before I can pick it up."

"Sure," I tell her. "It's no problem at all. Will you be ready to leave in about an hour and a half?"

I need to round on all the patients and ensure everything has been done that needs to be done since the next shift is about to come on.

"Yes." She's a little too eager, making me raise an eyebrow. "I just have one patient right now. Once I bring Dr. Monroe up to speed on her,

I'll be done."

"Okay." She bounces around, leaving me.

I don't know why I have such a reservation. It's not like we aren't going to the same place.

"You Okay, Shane?"

Her soft, almost whisper of a voice penetrates my thoughts, making me cut my eyes off the road for a split second to glance over.

I haven't said more than two words to Roxanne since we got into my SUV and left the hospital. My night went to shit, and before Whitney came back, it wouldn't have fazed me. But here I sit, pissed off because it's fifteen minutes till eleven at night, and I haven't seen Love or the girls in over twenty-four hours.

I'm torn. I'm torn in two.

I love my job. It wears on my heart, but I enjoy helping children. Making them well. It's all I can imagine doing. But it's going to keep me away from them longer than I want. Longer than I may be able to handle.

"I'm all right," I finally tell her, pulling into the apartment complex. "You know how it is. You have plans, and like what happened tonight, they get squashed because you can't leave."

"Yeah, of course, but that's what we signed up for."

She's got me there. I know one hundred percent she's right. I chose this. I wanted it. But I also wanted Whitney and a family. I wanted that more than I wanted my next breath.

I thought I'd go to college, then medical school, and then Whitney and I would get married. And by the time I was settled into my career, we'd start a family. That was the plan. One that never saw the light of day. We never had a chance.

And now...

I let out a breath as I cut my wheel to turn into a parking spot in front of our building. I look up, seeing the window of my apartment—lights off.

I raise my arm, cutting off the ignition, but before I can pull the keys out, Roxanne places her warm palm on my forearm, running her heat down toward my wrist. I snatch my keys out and my arm out of her grasp. "What are you doing?"

"You're obviously upset, Shane. I'm your friend. Tell me and let me help." She closes her fingers into a fist, pulling away from me.

I give her a look that clearly says none of my other friends touch me the way she just did.

I get out of the vehicle without addressing it further. I'm done with today. I did the nice thing and gave her a lift. I didn't ask for the other shit.

I've dealt with enough for one day. Two teenage overdose admits, a child abuse case, and now I got my intern trying to cross a line I want no part of like this is Grey's Anatomy or some shit.

"Shane, wait," she calls out, making me reluctantly stop. "Look, I didn't mean..." She trails off, just looking at me with something resembling anger in her eyes. When I'm about to tell her to forget it, she grabs my arm and slams her lips into mine. I'm too shocked to pull away at first, but when I feel her tongue sweep across mine, I jump back, pushing her away.

"What the fuck?" My anger erupts, and there's nothing I can do to stop it. "This stops!" I yell. "This stops now."

"No!" she argues. "You have someone right in front of you that wants a chance, Shane. I know you. She doesn't." She points to my apartment without looking, indicating Whitney, and it only pisses me off more. "She doesn't remember you. She has a family with another man. She's married, Shane, or have you conveniently forgotten that?"

"That." I point in the same direction she did. "Is none of your business. Whatever future she and I have or don't have doesn't concern you. But let's get one thing clear. This," I point between the two of us, "is not happening."

"Because of her," she floors.

"No." I shake my head, my voice coming down. "Not because of her. Because I don't feel that way about you. Not to mention it's morally wrong. I'm your superior at work. It would never have happened, even if Whitney never showed back up." I tip my head back, trying to pull air into my lungs.

"What the hell does us working together have shit to do with anything? If anything, we have a lot more in common than you do with her," she says, disgust evident in her voice.

My calm is weaning.

"Just go." My head falls forward, and my eyes land on her so she can see how serious I am. "For fuck's sake, leave this and be done."

I don't wait for her. I don't know if she follows, and frankly, I hope she doesn't.

Guilt from the memory of her kissing me seeps into me, and I need to get her taste off my tongue. The longer it's there, the shittier I feel.

By the time I make it up to the third floor, anger is rolling off me. It's a good thing Whit and the girls will be asleep. I need a shower and to crash on the couch since they have my bed because Emersyn refuses to sleep in the "pee" bed now. Whitney did everything she could to clean it, and it's probably clean enough, but even I can't go in there and sleep, so I've been crashing on the couch for the last couple of nights.

CHAPTER 24

WHITNEY

He's late. Later than he's been before. I don't know why I'm lying here, waiting and hoping he'll message me. Shane sent a text right before I started dinner telling me he would be late and not to wait for him to get home before I put the girls to bed.

But he didn't say if he wanted me to stay up. I'm being crazy. I'm being stupid. I'm being a girl and not acting like a twenty-eight-year-old woman.

But what happened last Friday... What he watched me do only three days ago? I can't get it out of my head. I can't get him out of my head. I've never had this want so deep inside, burning, needing something—someone—to put it out. I can't look at him now without my desire shooting through the roof.

If I could just freaking remember!

Ughhh. I have too much pent-up aggression. I tried calling my mother this morning, but she conveniently didn't answer her phone. When I called my father, his receptionist said he would be unavailable through the holidays. *Yeah, okay.* My dad has never spent one holiday with his family. It's always work, work, work for him.

If I think about it, the man probably has a mistress on the side. There's never been love between my parents. Not that I've seen anyway.

Still, I will have a conversation with them. They will know what they've done is wrong. I'm starting to think face-to-face is going to be the way to do it. I want them to see what they've done. Though, I doubt it'll faze either one of them.

Just when I'm about to send Shane another text—since he didn't answer the first one I sent—I hear keys in the door, and my heart starts to race. Not in a scared kind of way, either, but an excited one.

I overslept this morning, so Shane was gone by the time I woke up. Everly is out of school all week for the Thanksgiving holiday, so there was no need to set the alarm. I regretted that as soon as I woke and realized how late it was.

It's pitch black in the apartment when Shane enters. The light from the hallway outside the door illuminates him for a split second, showing me there's something... off. He's encased in darkness once the door is shut and locked, but his body movements are stiff, and I hear his hard breaths.

Is he mad? Upset?

What's happened? He wears his heart on his sleeve. He feels pain for others like no one I've ever met.

Instincts kick in, telling me to get up and go to him, but before I can, he storms past the couch without noticing I'm lying here. Seconds later, I hear the water from the bathroom running, followed by light pouring out of the hallway when I hear a door squeak open.

He doesn't come back to the living room, though.

Shane has started keeping some of his clothes in the spare bedroom since the girls and I have taken over his room. I shouldn't have let Emersyn sass her way out of sleeping in the bed she had peed in. I cleaned it. There isn't even a stain. Baking soda and hydrogen peroxide. Thank you, Google. So it's fine to sleep in. I even checked today—it's dry. But I'm not going to lie. I wanted to sleep in Shane's bed more than my daughter didn't want to sleep in the pee bed. It smells like him.

My phone lights up, making me groan. Another message from *him*, I'm certain. Fuck my life. Fuck my parents.

I open the messages I've been putting off all night to read.

Blake

You're keeping my kids from me, Whitney. I can't take this anymore.

And you think I didn't love Everly? I raised her, for Christ's sake. She's mine too. I don't give a damn what some sheet of paper says.

BLAKE
Come home.

Please. We're still married.
You're my wife. You can stop all of this.

You know, it'd be nice if you
would fucking respond.

Goddammit.

Respond.

Look, babe. You're killing me. I just
want my family back. I want you back.

I'm tired of this. I'm so sick of him sending all these "poor me" text messages. How about poor fucking me for what *he* did? How about that? When do I get retribution for all that's been done? Or for all that's been done to Everly and Shane.

I throw the phone to the other end of the couch, away from me. I'm not speaking to him unless it has something to do with Emersyn. Not happening. He can piss the fuck off if he thinks otherwise.

I think it's time I have a talk with Jacob. Something needs to be done— even if I get nothing out of it. At least Blake will know I'm serious. This has to be some form of harassment, right? But hell, look at everything my husband was a part of, and he still got equal rights to our daughter. The only reason I see her as much as I do is that he works and I don't, so I'm able to keep her during the weeks, and he's been okay with seeing her every other weekend. I'm surprised he hasn't pushed for more. Then again, he'd actually have to take care of a child. I've always been the one that has does everything for the girls.

A knock on the door rips me from my thoughts. Another rapid knock, louder this time, bangs on the door.

Jeez. It's nearly midnight. What the hell is so important that a person needs to bang on someone's door? I swear if they wake up Emersyn, I'll strangle them.

I'm about to toss the blanket off and get up when a shadow crosses over me in the dark. I blink my eyes above me to see Shane headed to the door. I didn't even hear the water shut off, much less him come out. He's shirtless but wearing scrub pants. But... I look harder. There is something on his back that I can't quite make out. I squint, trying to see better, but it's no use. It's too dark.

He opens the door, instantly shushing the person on the other side with a harsh tone. "Not so loud, would ya? Whitney and the girls are asleep."

He slips out the door, pulling it closed, but the latch doesn't catch because a crack of light eases into the room from the hallway.

"Really?" It's Roxanne. The neighbor and his coworker or intern that's training under him from what he's told me. "Why is everything about her? You can't even go out with us anymore—because of her. You can't hang out with me because of her. Jesus, Shane, what's next?"

"I don't know what the fuck your problem is, but I've had it. I told you earlier, this," he pauses a mere second. "This isn't happening. Whatever you thought could be between us would never have happened, even if Whitney wasn't here. Kiss me again, touch me again, or make any advancement again, and I'll go to HR."

Kiss. She kissed him?

My hands ball into fists so tight that my nails dig into the meat of my palms. A flame ignites, brewing a fire in my gut, heating me, making my blood come to a boil. She fucking kissed him?

"Shane. I'm sorry, okay? I thought—"

"I don't care what you thought anymore. I've told you. You know, and yet you keep pushing. No more! We have a work relationship only. No more asking me to do anything for you outside of work. Got it?"

I don't hear her respond, or if she even if she gives one.

Shane walks back inside, shutting her out by closing the door. He shuts it with more ease than I would've expected. I can practically feel his anger vibrating through my own body. He's pissed.

He told her to back off. What the fuck has she been trying to do? Maybe I should have been paying more attention...

He's walking out of the living room as I'm still battling these thoughts, these questions. He didn't notice me yet again. Looking upside down from where I'm lying, I watch as he goes into the kitchen.

That's my cue to get up. I need to feel him.

A light clicks on, but they aren't as bright as they usually are, telling me he must have flipped on the light above the sink.

My bare feet carry me toward him. There's a pull I've come to recognize anytime he's near. It's worse, heavier, whenever we're alone. I ache for him to touch me. He doesn't, though. And not for lack of wanting to. If anything, his agony seems worse than my own. It's written all over his face. He wants me as much as I want him.

He wants it more than you, my mind echoes. *He remembers.*

When I enter, my eyes trail until I find him standing in front of the sink. His arms are stretched out, away from his body, and braced against the edge of the countertop. His breathing is heavy. I can see his shoulders rise and fall with every breath. I stop next to the small island when his back catches my attention once again.

A tattoo covers the majority of his back. There's a woman—an angel—in the center. The top of her head starts between his shoulder blades, with her bare feet ending at the small of his back. Her wings are black, but that's not what draws me in. It's her face—my face—that has my palm covering my mouth as my lip quivers.

I blink, making myself take in the rest. Writing—no, lyrics—surround her in a script. I know these words. I know the song they go to. The song he's been teaching Everly on his guitar.

Blinding pain erupts inside my head, making me grip the edge of the island. The front of my forehead burns with fire so hot I think I might black out. But it only lasts seconds before an overwhelming tingle replaces the pain. A flood of heat releases, flowing down through my whole body.

I can see it all.

Memories.

I can see everything.

The day a boy asked if he could kiss me. I'd never been kissed before. I paled at his question. Everyone was looking at me, waiting for my response. I had to make the stares stop, so I... I punched him in the arm. What he did next knocked me on my butt. He smiled, and his eyes lit up like a Christmas tree. I was done for in that moment. And no matter how hard I fought, he owned me. That was the moment I became destined to be Shane's and only Shane's.

God, I was a bitch even that young. I bite my lip, remembering he liked, no, loved me that way. I remember it all. The beauty and the ugly—the chaos. Every time I refused him. Every time I begged him back. Every time he was inside me. Shit.

Before I realize it, I'm touching him, running my hands up his back, making his muscles tighten at first touch, but I guess he realizes it's me because he relaxes into my hands. He's welcoming it—needing it, I recognize. It's what I need too.

"Love," he chokes out.

I place my forehead to the center of his warm back.

"You broke my pencil in first grade because you accidentally stepped on it. You weren't paying attention to where you were walking. Then, the next day, there were ten brand new colorful pencils on my desk when I sat down."

"You—"

I cut him off. I'm not finished. I have too much to get out.

"In second grade, Tommy Wilson pushed me to the ground. You made him apologize. You were at least six inches taller than him, taller than every other kid in our grade. He was so scared of you that he peed his pants." I laugh for what feels like the first time in my life. It feels good too.

Fingers wrap around the loose T-shirt I'm wearing. *His* T-shirt. I swiped it after my shower because I wanted his scent to envelop me. I never bothered with shorts since the shirt was long enough to cover my thighs.

He pulls me around to his front, sandwiching me between the counter and him.

"You remember." I bite down on my lower lip to keep myself from attacking him. I nod. "What else?"

He hoists me up onto the counter, then Shane settles between my thighs.

"In third grade, I kicked you in the balls." His eyes flash. "You went down harder than Betsy Lincoln did when I cunt-punched her in ninth grade for—"

I don't get to finish. His lips smash into mine, making me almost fall into the sink bowl behind me. If it weren't for Shane's grip on my ass and tugging me back to him, I would have.

My panties are ripped off, leaving my ass bare on the cold surface.

Between memories returning and Shane's lips and hands going everywhere, I'm getting dizzy. But it feels so good I can't stop. It's the chaos I've dreamed of. And it's real.

"Fuck, baby," he says between kisses. "I need you, Love."

I need him too. I need him more than ever before. There's a burning fire inside that has always been there since the day I woke up in that hospital bed. I know he's the only one that can put it out. He's the reason there was a fire in the first place.

His lips work down my neck. My eyes close, and my head falls back to allow him all the access he wants to take. I need him to take it. Take it all. It's his. It's always been his.

"Please," I beg, pleading as if my life is on the line. "Fuck me, Shane. I need you inside me."

His hand jerks off me, and he shuffles. Before I comprehend what's happening, he rams inside me, pushing a scream I've been holding for such a long time out of me.

"Oh God."

"Love," he pants, pulling my head forward. Our eyes lock, and then he rams inside me again. "This is what living feels like."

His hand digs into my hip, making tingles skirt across my body. His lips find mine once again, and his tongue feels like bliss dancing with my own. Our eyes never leave one another, but his pace increases, and the pressure starts to build from deep inside my core.

He lets me see every emotion forming in his stormy eyes. It's beautiful and sad and happy and much more. Above all, there is love, and it wraps around me, coating me, penetrating me.

He slams into me one last time, his girth stretching me like I haven't been stretched in ages. And I haven't. This is everything. This is home. My orgasm rips me apart, shattering all the pent-up hatred I've been gathering inside for so long. Shane breaks me apart like no other man ever could.

His hands tighten, holding me in place, and before he comes inside me, I say, "I love you," as I'm coming down from the deepest high I've ever had.

His eyes open after he comes, and they tell me he isn't done with me yet.

"I'm going to show you just how deep my love for you is, Love."

And with that, he slips out of me to pull up his pants, but before I can hop off the counter, he pulls me to his chest, wrapping my legs around his waist, and then walks out of the kitchen.

Whatever he has in store for me, I want it. No, I'm craving it.

My lips find his bare neck and shoulder, where I pepper kisses all over him. When I bite down on his flesh, he sucks in a sharp breath of air, but he doesn't stop me. I remember he used to like this, and I plan on marking every inch I can get to before the sun rises.

I can't stop the smile that spreads across my lips at the thought: I have him, and I'll be damned if I ever let go. That bitch across the hall has something else coming if she thinks she has a fighting chance.

He's mine. He has always been mine. And he will always be mine.

CHAPTER 25

SHANE

A sense of peace washed over me when she said those three words I've longed to hear. *I love you.* I doubt she has any idea how much I needed them at that moment. I don't remember ever blowing that hard before. It's as though I was holding onto everything until she returned.

My Whitney.

My Love.

I tighten my hold on her as I walk down the hall to the spare bedroom. There's cum leaking from her, dripping onto me, and I love knowing a part of me is inside her.

When she bites me, she creates a storm deep within my gut. I squeeze tighter, planning to release it all inside her—again.

Whitney pulls back, stretching her torso away from me but keeping her fingers wrapped around my neck. She looks into my eyes as I walk us into the room and lock the door.

"I've missed you," she tells me when I lay her down on the bed. A tear forms in her eye, but she doesn't blink it away. It's as though if she closes her eyes, this won't be real. It's how I feel too.

"I've missed you more than you'll ever fucking know, Love."

"You cuss more now than you used to."

"Maybe. But then life didn't go like it was supposed to either."

"I'm sorry, Shane." Her voice falls somber.

"Don't you dare tell me you're sorry ever again. You didn't do anything, Love. And frankly, I don't want to discuss that shit right now. I'm starved for you. I just want us, right now, at this moment. We'll deal with everything else later."

"I want that too."

"Good." I rise, hopping off the bed to shed my pants and boxer briefs. I'm back on top of her in a matter of seconds. She giggles, and it's music to my ears. She has more than my heart wrapped around that tiny body of hers. She owns my soul. My being. She owns all that I am. She always has—always will.

Pulling her thigh up, I wrap her leg around me as I look into her eyes. Then I enter her slowly, inch by inch. Her eyes widen as I stretch her, and Whitney's breath hitches. This time I'm taking my time with her, and I plan on reacquainting myself with every centimeter of her succulent body.

"Mmm." Her moan reaches somewhere inside of me, tugging on my heartstrings. I pull my cock out, stroking her pussy lips, never wanting her to forget the feeling.

More moans escape her throat as her eyes flutter shut.

"Open them." I don't need to clarify. Her eyes snap open, finding mine immediately. "You'll look at me, Love. You'll look, and you'll never stop looking. Got it?"

"Yes." Her back arches and I take hold of her hips, raising her ass off the bed and pulling her toward me, thrusting into her harder.

"Mmm. I can't take this."

"You'll take it, baby. And you'll love it."

"Sh—Shane." I pull out, only the tip of my dick remaining at her opening. "You're torturing me."

"And I'm loving every damn second of it." I slide in slower. I need her to remember what I want. And as the thought filters through me, she rakes her nails down my shoulders, stopping at the bottom of my biceps. My fingers dig into her skin, painfully, I'm sure.

Getting that gleam in her eyes, her back rises off the bed. Her lips brush my skin seconds before her mouth opens and she bites my chin, clamping down before sucking. She sucks hard, and when she pulls away, I meet her and capture her lips with mine, raising her ass off the bed. A nip to my bottom lip ensues as my release cords inside my gut all the way down to my dick. My speed increases, and I continue until I'm fucking her hard.

"Harder," she demands.

I push back through her, my body rapidly chasing my release.

I push her ass down to the bed and off my cock, and then I rush back inside her one last time, using everything in me to muster the strength to give her what she needs, and then I'm gone, my seed exploding deep inside her. Inside her where it's meant to be.

I fall, giving all my weight to her. She greedily takes it, wrapping her arms around me to pull me closer.

After I come down, I roll off, bringing her with me. Whitney in my arms was always my favorite thing. And we lay here in silence for several minutes until I break the silence.

"I came inside you. Twice."

She doesn't flinch or even react to this fact. Instead, I get kisses and licks and playful bites peppered all over my chest. "Yes! And you should do it again."

"Love." My warning falls on deaf ears. She laughs without any concern. "The last time I came in you, we created a person."

"Yeah, well, this time I'm on birth control, so I think we're okay." She pushes up and plants a chaste kiss on my lips.

Then she lays back down on me again. All feels right until my conscience creeps back in as I'm stroking the back of her hand. "I think it's time to move."

"Because of... the woman across the hall?" I still, not knowing what to say. I didn't know she knew about Roxanne. "I heard most of your conversation with her when you went into the hall. I was on the couch."

Her admission both soothes me and ignites guilt. One, because she knows the truth. I don't have to hold back anymore. But two, because I do feel guilty and not just because of Roxanne putting her mouth on me, but because of the other women I remember being with. It always felt like a betrayal. Still feels like a betrayal.

"Hey, what is it?"

Whitney sits up and straddles me as she looks down, searching for what's changed.

"I've slept with other women." I can't keep that fact from her. I won't. I've always been honest with her.

I see it. The hurt that slices through her tears at my chest, trying to rip me open. It's the same pain knowing she's been with someone else too.

"I can't... undo it."

"No." She shakes her head as a tear drops onto her cheek. "It's..."

She looks at the ceiling for a second or two before her eyes fall back to mine. Her tear drops to my stomach. "I'm the one that's married." She says that last word with so much anger pouring out that it twists me up inside, knowing I should have done more to find her. *I could have made her remember.* I close my eyes, trying to rid myself of that thought. It's no use. I open them, seeing her beauty looking down at me.

"But I was the one with a memory. I knew you were out there... somewhere." *And I should have searched more—harder, longer.*

"Stop." She bends forward, propping her hand on the mattress beside my head, cupping my face with the other. "I'm not mad at you. I'm not asking you to undo it or even be sorry. We were dealt a shitty hand. But now we've found each other again and going forward, it's you and me."

"And the girls?"

"Yeah," she breathes out, then flicks her eyes up and away from me as if in thought.

"We tell her," I let out. I need my daughter to know I'm her father. I want her to know. She doesn't have to call me Dad or anything other than my name if she isn't ready or if she doesn't ever want to. But I need her to know. I need to start being her dad. Regardless of everything, I want to be a father to my little girl.

"I know. We will. Let's get through Thanksgiving, and we'll tell her then. Her birthday is next weekend and..." Whitney trails off, and I had completely forgotten her birthday is December 2nd.

"We need to plan something," I say before she finishes. "What do you usually do for her birthday?"

Whitney lowers her body onto mine, then slides off to my side. Her face fell when I mentioned a birthday celebration for our daughter.

"Whit?" I question.

"Nothing. Just a cake with candles and some presents. My parents and Blake's parents aren't really celebratory people. Hell, neither is Blake."

"So," I twist to face her. "Everly has never had a real birthday party?"

"No." She rolls to her back. "Neither of the girls have. I don't..."

"You don't what?" I inquire.

"I don't have any friends, Shane. I don't know any of the parents at her school. I don't mesh with them, so I've never gotten to know them or their kids. And Blake never wanted to have anything extravagant or even take them anywhere."

Hearing her say she doesn't have any friends cuts me deep. She had great friends, real friends, before the accident. And she still has them, but I'm not sure if she realizes that.

"You have friends, Whit. You have people that love you and that you can lean on. You have me. You know that, right?"

She's silent for a minute, drawing circles on my bare chest. Finally, her eyes glance up. "I do have you, don't I?"

"Yes, baby." I roll forward, capturing her lips in a long kiss. "I'll never go anywhere. And you have Kylie, and even Chance and Eve, though they aren't around here. My brother and Taralynn like you too."

"I remember my life before, but I'm still living the one I've had for the last ten years."

I breathe out, frustrated because she feels like she doesn't have her former life in her grips.

"Whitney." My use of her name sounds like a plea, and maybe it is. "You don't have to have that life. You don't even have to go back to the one before. I'm not expecting you to. But what I do expect—no, want—is for us, and the girls, to move on to a new life somewhere that isn't here. I'm done with this place. This city even. We both need something new. A fresh start."

"I just need you," she confesses. "You and the girls without Blake or my parents. I'm done with them. I can't even think of my mom or dad in a positive light anymore."

"You have me. There's no question about that. The question is, do I have you?"

"I've always been yours. Even when I wasn't, I was yours, Shane. I'll always be yours." She makes me smile, and it relaxes my mind.

"Will you move somewhere else with me? I am serious about moving from here. It's not even big enough. The girls need their own room and—" She cuts me off.

"Boy, I'll move anywhere you do. You're never getting rid of me again."

"Baby, I'm not a boy anymore." I jump up and out of the bed after planting another kiss on her plump, juicy lips.

"Where are you going?" She pulls the sheet up, covering her tits.

"To get your panties off the kitchen floor while you continue lying in that pee-ridden bed." Her nose scrunches up in disgust, making me chuckle. Hell, she did clean it, and it's now dry, but as I leave the bedroom, I catch her covering her eyes, causing a louder laugh to burst from my lips.

God, it feels good—so good.

CHAPTER 26

WHITNEY

I have to gain control over all these emotions running wild in my head. The pain. The betrayal. The elation that my soul finally feels whole again. The clarity and understanding of my memories brought me to how I've felt about Shane these last couple of weeks.

So many things are taking up space in my brain that I'm tripping over all of them. I can't focus on just one, and it's driving me mad. I want to pull my hair out. Too much is consuming me.

I've washed everything in Shane's apartment today just to keep my hands busy and my mind on other things.

It hasn't worked, though. I can't stop the questions from taking root, or the horrible, awful thoughts I wish would come to light, or even the *what could have been* if I'd never been in that accident and lost my memory.

"Momma, can I bring the Kindle he let me borrow?"

I stop, placing the laundry basket on top of the dryer. "Sure, Ev. Just make sure you don't leave it."

Shane lent her his eReader after she pouted because I forgot to pack it when I went to our former house to gather as much of mine and the girls' clothes as I could.

Now I wish I'd grabbed all of them.

"Hey, Ev," I call out. "Will you make sure your sister has packed enough clothes for two days? The correct clothes," I yell after her as she runs off—hopefully to find her sister and do what I've told her.

I have to say, she has given me a much easier time than I had first expected her to when I left Blake. We've had daily arguments for as long as I can remember. But I can't think of one since living at Shane's.

Once I pull the dry clothes out of the dryer, I close the door and lean against it after taking my cell phone out of the back pocket of my jeans.

Doing a quick Google search, I find the number I'm looking for and press the call button.

An auto-attendant comes on. "For store hours, press one. For the pharmacy, press..." I don't wait for the recording to finish before I press two.

While I'm holding, I hold the phone to my ear with my shoulder so I can grab the basket of clothes off the dryer. I take them to the couch in the living room and dump the clothes on it.

Ughhh. Is anyone going to answer my call or is it going to keep ringing?

It's been less than a minute since I dialed the phone number, so there's really no reason for being upset. I'm mad, frustrated, and pissed off, but not at this phone call. I'm furious at Blake for not sending Emersyn back with any of the clothes I'd packed the weekend before last when she went to stay with him. But even that isn't what's really bothering me. As frustrating as it is, I can buy Em more clothes. I'm certainly not asking her father to send more home with her.

I'm nervous. That's the truth behind my irritation. On top of everything going on in my head, add nerves to the list.

"Pharmacy, how may I help you?" A sweet, older voice comes through the line, ripping me away from my thoughts momentarily.

"I need to have a prescription refilled," I tell her.

"Sure. Can I get your name and date of birth?"

"Whitney Lane," I say, hating that Lane is still my last name, then I rattle off my birthday. I wonder if I can change it before my divorce is final? Probably not, but I could at least ask Jacob. I see how much it bothers Shane, just like my rings did before I removed them.

"Thank you, Mrs. Lane. Which prescription are you refilling?"

"My birth control." I'll take my last pill tomorrow before the placebo week starts. I want to make sure I get the new pack called in and picked up before I need to start them next Thursday.

"Wonderful. I'll get it entered, and we'll notify you via text message if your number is on file when it's ready. If not, we'll give you a call."

"Thank you." I hang up, feeling better now that I've accomplished one thing today.

Now to get two kids packed and then Shane and myself. He asked me to toss him a couple of changes of clothes into a weekend bag before he left for work this morning. We're leaving tonight after he gets home from work to go to his parents' until Friday.

I toss the phone onto the couch as I look up at the clock hanging on the wall. He'll be home in an hour. He told me not to cook, that we'd eat at his parents'. As much as I'm stressing about seeing his parents again, I'm also excited. I haven't eaten one of Pam's home-cooked meals in ages. It's the one thing I'm looking forward to, and I plan on enjoying it.

"Momma." I turn my head to face Emersyn as she saunters down the hall. My head shakes at the sight of her getup. "I not got no pants. I'm wearing this."

"'I don't have any pants,' is what you need to say. And no ma'am, you are not wearing a costume. Come over here." I motion her to where I'm standing in front of the couch. "I know I saw at least one pair in this pile. Help me sort."

"Why I got to help?" She puts her hands on her hips.

"'Why do I have to help?'" Lord, help me with this one. "And because I said you do, so get to it, little lady."

"But, Momma."

"Emersyn Rose, get your butt over here."

"Fine. But princesses aren't supposed to work."

"Says who?"

"Says my daddy."

Fuck my life.

"Well, your daddy doesn't know everything." I hate that man, but I push the smile forward so my daughter doesn't see that. "Look at the costume you're wearing. Maybe you need to re-watch Cinderella. She worked. She worked hard."

"She had a bad mommy too."

I give her a look that quickly shuts her up, and I don't feel one ounce of bad for doing it.

If Blake thinks he's going to use her to get to me, he has another think coming. I haven't answered one of his messages that weren't concerning Emersyn, and I don't plan to. It's likely he's only going to get worse, and I'll need to figure out what I'm going to do about him. I'm not going to put up with his shit. I think ten years was plenty. He's not getting another second of me.

"WHAT'S WRONG, LOVE?"

The butterflies haven't stopped since we left Memphis.

"Why do you think something's wrong?"

His head swivels toward me before going back to looking out the windshield as we drive down a road I fondly remember. *His road.* Well, his parents' road, leading to their house. "Because I know you." That's all he gives me, and I realize I don't need a more valid answer. We may have been torn apart for years, but he gets me better than I get myself.

I turn my head, looking at the houses we pass. I spent a lot of time here and at Kylie's when we were teenagers. That thought makes me think of something else.

"Do Kylie's parents still live in the same house?"

"Same house across the street from mine." He nods.

"Is she coming home?" I ask.

"You still haven't called her, have you?" A sigh leaves his lips. "No. She can't take off work, but she's planning on being here for a few days during Christmas."

At his mention of Christmas, I see a house lit up with Christmas lights, making me laugh. Thanksgiving isn't even over yet. And then I laugh harder because I know exactly what house it is. Or whose house it is. It's Shane's parents' house. Pam loves Christmas, and I remember she used to go all out. She had even won several awards when I was in high school for her outdoor decorations.

"Momma, look."

"Looooook, Momma." Emersyn tries to copy her sister. No doubt they've both seen the same thing I have.

"That's where we're going, girls. That's Shane's parents' house." I turn my head as he eases into the driveway. He isn't looking at me because he's parking the SUV, but he's got a smile on his face knowing I knew this was his childhood home.

The cell phone I'm clutching in my hand chimes with an incoming text message. Flipping my wrist, I groan at Blake's name above the preview of the message. I don't even attempt to read any of it. I'm sick of him.

"Love?" Shane questions, calling me by the name I can't get enough of hearing. I love that only he calls me that. I love the way it penetrates my soul every time he does. I've always been able to feel the meaning behind how he says it.

When I don't answer, he swipes the phone from my palm. He eyes the screen, reading what's there I know.

"Let it go," I tell him, unbuckling my seat belt. "Let's get out." I urge, but he just studies me. Then without breaking eye contact, he unlocks my phone. Oh, crap. Dread enters me, coating my insides. "Forget it," I say with a little power behind my words. "Let's get out and go inside your parents' house."

Nothing. He just keeps looking at me like he's trying to read if I've been keeping something from him. Sure, I haven't mentioned the text messages Blake's been sending, but I can handle them on my own. Shane doesn't need any more shit to deal with. He has enough to last a lifetime. We both do. I'm not adding more.

Breaking eye contact, he unbuckles his seatbelt, but he's still looking at the phone. I know he's not going to let it go. I know he's about to read every single message between Blake and me.

Turning in my seat, I look at Everly. "Unbuckle your sister for me, but both of you stay in here for just a second. I need to speak to Shane before we go in."

She nods, and I get out of the vehicle.

"Why haven't you told me about this?" He doesn't lift his head. He's intent on continuing to read more.

"Would you just let this go?"

"No. And I want an answer, Whitney."

"Don't say my name like that." I cross my arms, refusing to answer him and realizing at the same time how much of a child I'm acting like.

"Like what?" His head pops up, and then he steps toward me. I don't retreat, even though my instincts fight to make me do so. When Shane is passionate about something, he can be almost as intimidating as his brother. He never realized that when we were younger, and I doubt he realizes it now. I'm not scared. I've never been scared of him. If there is one person I'm certain of, it's this man in front of me now. He'd never do one malicious thing to me. That I'm sure of. Not even when he's angry with me for keeping something this small from him. "Like I'm mad at you? Yeah, you never did like it when you were on the receiving end of pissing me off."

He takes another step forward until he's towering over me.

"The girls are watching."

His face jerks to the windshield, and he instantly cools his facial expression. Shane breathes out, then looks back down at me. "You don't keep this shit from me," he says, holding up the phone. Placing it in my hand, he continues, "This is gonna stop. I'm calling Jacob first thing next week if it's too late to do anything tomorrow because of the holiday," he adds. "Something will be done to stop this. That has to be considered harassment." He gestures with a nod to the phone I'm clutching.

"Fine." I bark out, wanting this conversation over with. "But then," I say, forcing myself to speak softer. "I want you to forget about it and enjoy this. Enjoy us, Shane. We have each other again. That's what we need to focus on, okay?"

He licks his lips, and my core contracts, remembering what those lips did to me this morning. And from the look in his eyes, he knows what I'm thinking about.

Lowering his head, he whispers into my ear, "I have a bed I plan on reacquainting you with later, Love." I squirm as his voice penetrates, touching every nerve inside my ear and sending tingles down my spine. I remember everything we ever did in his childhood bed, and those thoughts, on top of what he's promising, set me on fire.

Leaning back up, he smiles that cocky grin that makes me want to skim my teeth down his cock just to watch him squirm the same way he makes me.

"Promises, promises, promises," he tsks at me, being the mind reader he is as he steps backward. "I got our stuff. You get the kids."

As I'm opening the back door to let Emersyn out, I can't help but bask in his words. It's like we're already a family. He's getting all the bags from the back, and I'm wrangling the girls out.

Is that what we've become? Can that even be possible this soon, and when I'm still married? Is it right? *It feels right. It feels good.* And since when have I cared what's right in other people's eyes? *Since you've been married to douche-prick for the past ten years,* I remind myself. Between him, my parents, and his parents, they tried to change me. They tried to mold me into what they wanted. And maybe they mostly succeeded. I kept so much inside me, never voicing my thoughts or wants because I knew none of them would approve.

In a lot of ways, I'm ashamed of that. I allowed them to push me to be someone I always knew deep down I wasn't. I can use the excuse of my child, but that only gets you so far.

I know I was trapped, figuratively and in reality. I didn't have any friends, any support. I had no means to leave Blake and make it on my own. In a lot of ways, I was a prisoner in his world and in my mind. Those memories were always just out of my reach. They were hidden behind a thick cloud of fog, and no matter how much I reached or how hard I tried to see through it, I couldn't.

Until Shane.

And now I just have to make sure I keep him. Because with those memories came more demons for me to battle. The same fears I had years ago still run rampant in my mind. Even back then, I didn't understand why he put up with me, why he loved me—still loves me, or always took me back.

I'm twenty-eight years old, and I still don't know what I want to do. Something is still missing, although I don't feel that emptiness inside me anymore. I haven't felt that since the night Shane walked back into my life—or maybe I walked back into his. Yet, there is something I know I'm meant to do. I love being a mother. I'm not sure if anything could ever surpass that, but I need more.

Fuck, maybe I just need to find a hobby to help control my never-calm mind.

CHAPTER 27

SHANE

Dinner was spectacular, as it is every year. My mother outdid herself, though. Between the Christmas decor that's always up by the last week in November and the food that could've fed at least twenty more people, I'm still stuffed from eating earlier, and now I feel settled. Being in my parents' house has had a tarnished feel until I walked through the doors two nights ago. I've never been able to get the images from the night I was told Whitney was gone forever out of my head. So it's a relief to be able to be at my parents' and enjoy being here with them.

And now, having my own family here, it's another feeling entirely. Whitney may not be my wife yet, and one day she will be, but she is my family—the girls too. I couldn't imagine what it would feel like if I were to lose them after just gaining them.

When she started spouting off her memories, I was both stunned and scared. Scared because I didn't want to believe it and then it not be real. Like now, as happy as I am to have the three of them in my life, I can't stop the terrifying feeling it won't last.

I think back on my conversation with Jacob.

"Blake's harassing her and I want it to stop. I want him out of her life, Jacob. There has to be something—anything—that can be done to get him out of her life and

out of *Emersyn's. He's using their daughter to get to her.*"

"*You have proof of that?*"

"*Just text messages he's sent her.*"

"*What kind of messages? What did he say exactly?*"

"*Sir, I don't know verbatim. He keeps telling her to come home. To stop the divorce. To put their family back together. Shit like that. Then he goes off when she doesn't respond to his messages.*" The man is a psycho if you ask me.

"*But he hasn't made any threats?*"

"*Not that I read,*" I admit through clenched teeth. "*Jacob, come on. This isn't right. No one, man or woman, should have to deal with what he's trying to do to her.*"

"*I agree, Shane. But I need to know everything, even the smallest of details, so I can proceed the right way.*" He's silent for a moment. "*Shane, he shouldn't have been awarded joint custody. No judge I've ever come across would have ruled the way he did.*"

"*What are you saying?*"

"*That it's possible he or someone else bribed the judge to make that happen.*"

I jump from where I'm sitting on the stool at the bar in my parents' kitchen when a firm hand shakes my shoulder. "Shane," my dad says, exasperated.

Turning my head, I realize he must have been calling me. "Sorry, Dad. I was lost in my own world," I tell him, shaking my head.

His brown eyes meet mine with concern. Flicking his chin to the side, he heads toward the table off to the side of the kitchen where we ate dinner a few hours ago. I swivel, sliding off the stool to follow. I drop into the chair seconds after he does.

"What's up, Dad?"

"She has her memory back." I kick my head to the side to look at Whitney. She's talking to my mom. They're laughing, and that warms my heart. I really never expected to be here—with her—again.

"Yeah," is the only word I have for him. They were elated to find out she remembered when we arrived two nights ago. I look back to see him watching me. "What is it, Dad? You obviously have something on your mind. Let's hear it."

"I know you've already been accepted into the fellowship program, but have you considered, with everything that's happened, maybe it's too much to take on right now?" He holds up his hand before I get a chance to say anything. "Just hear me out." We stare at each other for a few seconds before I nod for him to continue. "What about coming home for a year or two? Peds is where your heart is. I get that, just as it is for your mom. Go into general practice instead of the surgical fellowship. Just for now, what about joining your mom's practice when you complete your residency in June?"

"Dad, I don't—"

He doesn't allow me to say no.

"Just think about it. You don't have to decide today or tomorrow, but you do need something solid for *your* family."

The family indication doesn't go unnoticed. And it's not like I haven't thought about this. I have. I just haven't allowed myself to stress over it. With all that's happened, I haven't had a real chance to let my mind consider much about the future. But letting myself do that now makes me realize how much I hate when he's right.

Going into pediatric cardiology has been my plan from the beginning when I decided I wanted to be a doctor. Then when I decided I wanted to be a pediatric doctor, it was going to be the best of both worlds. I worked at my dad's clinic too in high school. It was fascinating, cool even.

"I..." I look up when Whitney's hand roams over my shoulder. She smiles, and I bring her down onto my lap. I wrap my arm around her. "Look," I finally say, glancing back to my dad from where he sits across from me. "I'll consider it."

"That's all I'm asking, son."

"Consider what?" she inquires.

"Just work stuff," I say, being vague because I really don't want to get deep into this conversation. In fact, what I really want is to spend time with my daughter. Between my mom and Shawn, I haven't seen either of the girls. Now is a perfect time to let Everly practice on the guitar. "Hop up." I pat Whitney on the hip, indicating I want her to get off my lap. "I'm going to go find Everly and see if she wants to practice the guitar."

"It's getting late, Shane." She stands, and I look at the clock on the microwave, noting it's half past nine. "Can you do it quickly and make sure she brushes her teeth and is in bed by ten?"

"It's a holiday," I comment.

"Yes. Which is why she's already gotten to stay up an hour later than she normally does."

"Get off her ass, Whit. Let the kid live a little."

"She's nine," she deadpans, making me laugh as I stand.

"Almost ten. And speaking of, Mom wants to throw her a birthday party next weekend."

"Really?" Her eyes get big, excited. She turns, facing my mom. She's walking away from the sink where she just finished cleaning all the dishes we dirtied. "You want—"

"Angel," Mom says as she settles on my dad's lap. "Of course we do. Besides, any excuse I can find to spend more time with my granddaughters, you better bet I'm going to use it."

The word granddaughters doesn't go unnoticed by either Whitney or myself.

"Thank you. That would be... Thank you, Pam. And Bill, thank you too."

"No need, Whitney." My dad pulls my mom tighter. "We're beyond happy to have you back, and we gained two beautiful girls in the process." He pats my mom's hip the same way I did Whitney minutes ago. "Honey, I'm beat. Please tell me you're ready to go to bed?"

"I am." They both stand as well. "Night, kids."

My dad scrubs a hand over his face, showing me just how worn out he is. Maybe Whitney is right. It may not be that late, but it has been a long day.

"Night," we both say simultaneously to my parents as they walk past.

Pulling on Whitney's arm, I stop her before she leaves. "If you want her to go to bed, then—" She stops me by putting her lips on mine and wrapping her arms around my neck. I smile through the kiss.

"Go teach our daughter how to play guitar. She gets to sleep when she gets to sleep."

"I love you." I've never been shy or uncomfortable telling her those words, and since her memory has returned, I can't stop them from flowing out of my mouth.

"I know you do." She shoots to her toes to kiss me once more. "Now, go. I need to go find the other kid and dump her in a tub or maybe just the bed and bathe her tomorrow."

Releasing her, I head out of the kitchen and walk into the living room, first seeing Everly with her legs crossed, watching TV. Swiveling my head to the side, I see Shawn lying down on the couch with one arm covering his eyes and the other wrapped around Emersyn. He's lightly snoring, telling me he's asleep. Emersyn is sprawled across his chest with strands of blonde hair covering her pretty little face. She's asleep too.

This sight does something to me. It makes me proud and tells me how blessed I am. I know Shawn is a great guy and a good brother. He's hard to handle, and Taralynn is probably the only woman in the world who can handle him. But people have always had to earn his love or friendship. Even Taralynn had to prove to him that he was worthy of her love. I say that, but now I wonder if he's actually accepted it. They seem fine. They look fine. But looks can be deceiving. All I can do is pray because this sight right here gives me a glimpse as to what kind of dad I hope he'll be one day. These kids—my kid—didn't have to earn anything. He loved them from the moment I brought them into his house.

Yeah, he'll make a good father, and hell, how could he not? Our dad is there for us during the easiest of times and the hardest.

I see her watching me out of the corner of my eye, so I turn my focus from my brother to her. She quickly moves her head back toward the television.

"Hey. Come on." I tell Everly as I scoop the guitar up. "Let's go in the backyard. We can practice out there and not wake my brother or your little sister." She unfolds her legs.

Once I'm back through the kitchen with her following behind me, I open the sliding glass door that leads out onto a deck that overlooks my parents' backyard. There's a wooden play gym for kids that's seen better days, a tire swing hanging from the big Bradford Pear and a pool that's covered for the impending winter.

Descending the steps, I head toward the outdoor lawn furniture that's alongside the length of the pool.

I sit, pulling another chair closer toward mine, and motion for her to sit down.

"Are you cold?" I didn't think to have her throw on a hoodie since it's breezy out here tonight.

"I'm... good." She tells me, sounding unsure and making it hard to tell if she's telling me the truth. I decide not to push.

"Here." I hold the guitar out in front of her. I've already decided I'm getting her one of her own for her birthday. I picked it out a couple of days ago on my lunch break. I rarely take one, but it was slow for once in the ER, so I walked down the street to a local music store.

When she takes the instrument, I grin proudly as she positions it on her lap and her hands on the guitar just as I've taught her.

"We don't have long. Your mom wants you in bed by ten." She nods as I hand her the pick I pulled from my pocket. Her eyes glance up, meeting mine, and I get the same feeling I've been getting for a while now. Like there's something her eyes are trying to tell me or ask me. "You sure you're okay?" I can't help but ask again.

Her head bobs in response, so I let it go.

"Same as before?" Her words are almost a whisper.

"Sure. Let's do that." I've been teaching her the same repetitive chords since she got the basics down. "If you think you're ready, we'll add more chords tomorrow. Does that sound good?"

She nods once, then dips her head down to the guitar and starts to strum the chords to the chorus. The same words and music notes I have inked on my back.

Of all the things that could've triggered Whitney's memory, I'd have shown her my back weeks ago had I thought that'd happen.

When I look up after the music stops, she isn't playing anymore, and she's staring. Again.

"What is it, Everly?"

I really do love her name, and although I technically have "everly" inked on my chest, I want her name on me somewhere.

"My... my fingers hurt."

"That's normal," I assure her, letting out a short laugh and remember mine when I first started learning. They hurt like a bitch until I built up calluses on my fingers. They still do now because I've only been playing again since Trent died. I'd stopped when I lost Whitney. She'd always been my reason for playing to begin with. Then my best friend got killed.

All the emotions I thought I'd closed off when Whitney was ripped out of my life came rushing back, along with the need to play. And now, I don't play that often. Halloween at Gavin's was the first time I've played since this past summer.

"They're going to hurt. At least at first and until you get your fingers used to the guitar. Feel mine." I open my palm, moving it forward in her direction.

"Your... fingers?" I nod.

Looking down, she reaches out, running her thumb over mine. "It's rough." Her nose scrunches up.

"Not as rough as they used to be when I played all the time." I pull my hand back. "They're called calluses. And your fingers will develop them too, if you keep playing. The more you play, the quicker they'll develop, and eventually, they won't hurt anymore when you play."

"Thanks..." Her eyes don't leave mine, as if she's searching for something.

I can't take it any longer. "Why do you keep looking at me like that?" I finally have to ask Everly. I've racked my brain. I haven't a clue what she's thinking about. It's as if there's something she wants to ask me but is too afraid of voicing it.

Shit, I hope not. The last thing I want is to scare her.

She's silent, biting her lip but finally speaks, "I don't know what... to call you."

I look at her. That's it? That's the big thing that's been lingering all these weeks?

"What do you mean? You know my name. Don't you remember I told you the night we met? And surely you've heard your mom and everyone else call me Shane at some point." She nods her small head.

"I know that, but..." Her words trail and she tucks her dark hair behind her ear. When she's nervous, she has to touch her hair in some way. I've noticed this about her in only a few short weeks.

"But what?" If there is one thing I'm determined to do as her father, it's to break this shyness. She needs to learn to be bold and strong like her mother.

Although, speaking of her mom, even she has got to come back into herself. *They've* tried to tame her, and it shows. I hate it.

"If you're my real dad, shouldn't I call you that and not your name?" Her words stop every thought in my head, and I stare. I stare at her, knowing I heard exactly what I did but not believing them. She knows I'm her father. She finally knows after almost a month of wanting to tell her. She knows. But how does she know? "I don't have to," she says way too fast.

"Wait, what?"

"I don't have to," she repeats. "I'll call you whatever you want me to. I just thought—"

"Wait, Ev. Stop." I take a deep breath. "How do you... know?"

"I-I..." Her eyes grow wide, and she stutters nervously as if she's done something wrong.

"Ev, it's okay." I let her know, reaching over and squeezing her shoulder. "Calm down. You don't have to be scared. You're not in trouble. And yeah, I am your dad, and you can call me that. You can call me whatever you're comfortable calling me. But Everly, how did you find out?"

My voice is a lot calmer than the emotions running through me. When she acted like she was about to get in trouble for doing something, I went into doctor mode. Kids are all too often scared and nervous when they come to the ER injured. Half the time, they're fearful they'll get in trouble for their own injuries. As sad as the thought is, I was a kid too once, and it's a normal feeling. Especially when you hurt yourself doing something you weren't supposed to be doing.

"Ev?" I try encouraging her. "It's okay to tell me anything." I should get Whitney for this.

How the hell did she find out? And why isn't she freaking out? If I'd just found out my dad wasn't my dad and someone else was, I'd lose it. Nine, ten, twenty, doesn't matter. I'd lose my shit.

"Well, Mom—" I cut her off, not meaning to.

"Your mother?"

There's no way Whitney would have told her without me. No. I mentally shake my head. She wouldn't.

"Uh-huh." But that thought is contradicted by my daughter's words.

"Wait a minute," I pause, looking down at her. "Whitney. Your mother knows that you know I'm your father?"

"Yes, but," she shakes her head vigorously, "I wasn't supposed to say anything. I'm sorry. I just never know what to call you and..." Her words get rushed as my blood pressure starts to rise. "I don't know. I just-I just..."

"Everly." I grab her gently by the shoulders, doing everything possible to rein in my anger so that she doesn't see it. "Slow down. It's fine." It's not, but she doesn't need to know that. "You are not in trouble whatsoever. Okay?" She just looks at me. "Okay?" I say again.

"Okay," she says, but it's soft, and we're back to that shy voice of hers. Her eyes start to fall from mine, so with the tips of my fingers, I gently raise her chin.

"Sweetheart, you can call me Dad, or you can call me Shane. Whatever you want to call me is perfectly fine with me. But you are not in trouble. It's fine that you know. I wanted you to know."

Her head bobs.

Surely, she has questions.

"Is there anything you want to ask me?" She just shakes her head. "You know this means Emersyn's dad isn't yours. He was never your father. You know this?"

"Momma explained it a couple of weeks ago."

"A couple of weeks ago?" I burst out, unable to contain the rise in my voice and scaring her at the same time. Her body jumps. "Crap. I'm sorry. I didn't mean to frighten you."

"Are you mad at Momma? Please don't yell at her. I don't like it when he yells. He's always yelling and being mean to her. I don't want to go back there. Please don't make us go back to my old home."

Without thought, I reach out and pull her onto my lap, into an embrace. It's the first time I've hugged my daughter or touched her this much. It feels good. It feels right. She's mine, and I've wanted this moment for too long now. It's been less than a month since I've known her, but right now, right here, it feels like I've had her in my life longer.

"Everly, you aren't going to understand this, but I'm going to say it anyway. I love your mother more than I'll ever be able to put in words. I've loved her for a long time. And even if I am mad or upset at her, which you should never worry about, it does not mean I stopped loving her. It doesn't mean I want her or you or Emersyn to leave. Because trust me, if there is one thing I can assure you of, it's that your mother, nor you, nor your sister are going anywhere. Ev, I don't know how to make you understand, but you guys, all three of you, are my family now, tomorrow, and forever. No one is going anywhere. But I do need you to go into the house and upstairs, brush your teeth, and get ready for bed. Don't worry about showering. You can take a bath in the morning. It's late, and I'm probably throwing a lot at you. I'm going to stop now," I breathe, holding her tight for a second longer. Finally, I let up on my hold, and then I help her off my lap. "We can talk tomorrow if you don't understand something or you need anything. Okay?"

She nods, smiling and tucking a stray hair behind her ear at the same time. "So I..." She bites her lip and looks away, toward the house.

"What?" I prompt, getting her to turn back toward me.

"I can call you Daddy?"

Fuck me if my heart doesn't stop.

"Of course you can." I grab her wrist, pulling her into another hug. "There's nothing in the world that would make me happier."

She steps back, yawning and covering her mouth with her elbow. "Night, Daddy."

Before my mind has time to process a response, she turns and takes off running toward the door.

Once Everly is through the door, I sit here for at least five minutes. One, I need time for my brain to catch up to everything running a mile a minute. Two, because I need a chance to calm down, because there is a certain woman inside the house I want to strangle.

How the fuck could she keep this from me? And why? I let out a long breath. It's going to take everything in me not to beat that woman's ass. Not literally, but she is about to hear a lashing from me that'll feel like one.

I push off the chair and stand. Then, I march my way inside to find out why the hell she hasn't told me before now.

I can't fathom any excuse or reason she'd keep that to herself and ask our daughter to do the same. Guess there's only one way to find out.

CHAPTER 28

WHITNEY

With all the excitement these past few days, I haven't had a quiet moment to myself until now.

Shane's family is amazing. I've always thought his parents were the best. I even envied him at times when I didn't understand why mine couldn't be more like his. Pam and Bill both have demanding careers, yet they've always found the time—wanted the time—to spend with their kids. They still do. I've seen that since we've been here. But it can also be overwhelming, especially since I'm not used to it.

Holidays spent with Blake's family or mine consisted of an hour, two at the most, in their company. Never days. But even if all this is a lot to handle at once, I'd still take it over one more day spent in the company of people that set out to sabotage my whole world.

And the thing is, I don't know why. It doesn't make sense, but then again, maybe shitty people are just that—shitty people. And for no reason at all.

If I could just wrap my mind around the why of it all.

Blake knew back in high school I didn't like him like that. I made it blatantly obvious.

No one is in the kitchen as I come down the stairs after tucking Emersyn in the bed. I left, coming down here once Everly started brushing her teeth. If I don't make sure that girl puts a toothbrush, with toothpaste, into her mouth, chances are high that she won't clean her teeth.

I plugged my cell phone into a charger yesterday morning and haven't checked it since. I have to say, it's been nice not dealing with Blake's crap. We were supposed to appear in court early next week about the petition to dissolve my marriage, but Shane heard from Jacob yesterday. The hearing has been delayed by an extra week. I don't know why, but probably bullshit.

I just want this fake-ass marriage over. The sooner, the better.

Grabbing my cell phone, I pull the charging cord out from the bottom and let it fall to the granite countertop. Then I twist around, resting my back on the corner of the kitchen countertop.

Of course I have multiple text messages from my child's father. That's what I need to refer to him as from now on. He's just Emersyn's dad. God, I wish he weren't, but there is nothing I can do about that.

I have a couple of missed calls and one voice message. One of the missed calls is from my mother, but she didn't leave a message. I'm surprised she even called.

I hit the play button on the voice message, then bring the phone to my ear to listen.

"Hi, Mrs. Lane. This is Betty at Dyer Drugs. I called because we don't have a prescription on file for you. If you could have your doctor's office call us or have someone submit one to us electronically, we'll get it filled right away."

What the hell?

That's impossible. I've always gotten my prescriptions filled there for as long as I can remember. And I know they have to have it. The last time I saw my gynecologist, she gave me a paper prescription because they were still behind in electronic submission technology. Blake dropped it off for me. And then he would pick them up for me each month. *Right?*

I pull the phone away from my ear as I rack my brain, thinking back. I can't be wrong. There's no way he got them from another drug store. I remember the prescription bag. The store logo was stamped on the bottom.

It has to be some mistake. Maybe she pulled up the wrong person. I'll have to call tomorrow and get it sorted out.

"Hey, have you seen Shane?"

I pause, looking up. Shawn is standing on the other side of the island with his hands in his pockets, rocking back and forth on the heels and balls of his feet.

"I think he's still out back." I tip my head toward the sliding glass door that leads to the back patio. "Ev came in a few minutes ago to go to bed."

He nods. "We're about to cut out." He looks down for a moment before his dark eyes rise, meeting mine again. "I'm glad you got your memory back."

"Thanks." Other than Pam, no one's made a big deal of it. And for that, I'm grateful. "Where's Taralynn? I want to tell her bye before y'all leave."

"Across the street getting Mason."

That's right. Kylie and Mason's parents still live directly across from Pam and Bill. I didn't go over there. Kylie didn't come home, and I was never close to her mom like I was to Shane's.

I put my cell on the counter, not bothering with the text messages I don't even want to read—like ever—to hop onto the countertop.

"Y'all are going to Georgia tonight? This late?" I've never been to their parents' vacation home. My parents never let me go, but I remember it, and I remember both Shane and his brother loved riding ATVs when they were kids. Apparently, that hasn't changed.

"Yeah," is all he tells me, or maybe that's all he gets a chance to say.

I jump at the sound of the door shutting with force.

"Everly knows?"

I look away from Shawn as Shane's words register. His voice doesn't match the fire blazing in his eyes.

A tickle starts to creep up my back. He's pissed. "She fucking knew." His words are slow and measured the same way he's stalking toward me now. And he's not asking. He already knows our daughter knows the truth. "And you didn't bother to tell me?" He's not just mad. He's hurt. His eyes are rimmed in red, and his face is flushed.

Taking a few steps, he inches closer to me.

"Everly knows what?" his brother asks, but I don't dare say a word.

Instinct urges me to move back, but I have nowhere to move to. There's a cabinet door directly behind my head.

I've fucked up.

Big time.

Everly has known Shane is her real dad since the day after I left Blake. She overheard the end of my conversation with him. What was I supposed to tell her? The truth was always going to come out eventually.

Shane is right, though. I never bothered to tell him she knew. In fact, I've led him to believe she still thought Blake was her father.

At the time, I didn't know how to deal with everything being thrown at me, so I asked her to keep it between the two of us. It was a mistake. I should never have done it, and I've had plenty of time to come clean since then, but I've chosen not to.

"Dude." Shawn is exasperated. "You gonna tell me what the fuck's going on?"

We both are too locked on each other to pay Shawn the least bit of attention. No way I'm breaking eye contact first.

When he steps in front of me, he doesn't stop. He pushes through my legs, getting an inch away from my face.

"How could you keep that from me?" I feel his hands wrap around the bottom material of my shirt, fisting it and using the fabric to pull me forward. "Say something," he barks.

Shane has never been one to get angry quickly. Even with everything that was stolen from us, he hasn't shown any of the resentment I know he's harboring. So this, what I've done to him, I know I've hurt him like no one else has the power to do. And I feel like dog shit—as I should.

The problem is, I'm at a loss for words. There isn't one thing I can say to make what I've done justified.

"Whitney, so help me fucking God. Do not sit there—"

He is yanked backward, away from me, making me lose eye contact with him. Shawn has one hand wrapped around his bicep and another around his throat, holding Shane to his front.

"Calm down," Shawn commands. His voice sounds like a threat.

"What on earth?" Taralynn's voice is panicked, but I can't take my eyes off Shane.

"Get off me," he demands but doesn't stop looking at me—maybe through me. Fuck, those eyes. "Shawn, let me go."

"Not until you cool down, bro."

"Take your hands off my throat, or I'll—"

"You'll what?" Shawn interrupts, making me wish he'd shut his damn mouth.

I hop off the counter, rushing forward. "Let him go," I order. Shawn throws his head back, looking at me like I'm crazy, shaking his head. After a beat, he finally lets him go.

Shane pivots, bumping into me as he turns around to face his brother, but I don't fall. His arm shoots out behind me, grabbing my hip in a gesture that is almost too gentle for what's transpiring. Shane's angrier at me right now than he has ever been before, but even so, he wouldn't let any harm come to me. He's still protective. And that right there shows me how different he is from Blake, from any other person I know. Someone else wouldn't care if I fell, hurting myself. Shane would.

"If you ever grab me like that again, I will lay your ass out. Are we clear?"

Shawn laughs.

Ah, fuck. Does he not have any sense?

"Babe?" Taralynn calls.

"I mean it, little brother. Don't ever grab me like that again."

"Then don't get in your woman's face like that ever again, and I won't." Shawn stands straighter, stepping into Shane's face as if to prove something.

I step up behind Shane, placing my hands on his hips. This is all my fault, but I still want him to know I'm on his side. I have his back before anyone else, even if I didn't show that before.

If he forgives me for keeping this from him, I want him to know and believe I'll always have his back.

"You're one to talk." Shane is taking his anger out on Shawn. That I'm sure of. "It took thinking she was dead for you to open your eyes." Shane juts his arm out, pointing toward Taralynn. I don't know what he means by that, but my curiosity has been piqued. "And she could have.

It could have been her on the back of that motorcycle. And all because you're an asshole."

Taralynn's face turns to horror, and the only sound is the sudden rush of air she pulls into her mouth.

Then silence.

"I'm out of here." Shawn's face is emotionless, but it's obvious what Shane said has gotten to him.

He leaves, exiting the kitchen. Seconds later, the front door closes with a loud bang. Shit, I hope we haven't woken his parents.

"You had to bring that shit up?" Taralynn looks at Shane like she's disappointed in him. Her arms cross over her chest, then she shakes her head. "He hasn't forgiven himself. He doesn't trust himself not to screw up again." She sighs heavily. "He didn't need that, Shane."

Shane takes my hands, pulling them around his middle, but he doesn't respond to Taralynn. Not unless he's communicating silently. I can't see his face with mine plastered against his back. Taralynn hasn't stopped staring at him, though.

We all stand in the kitchen. The silence is deafening.

Finally, after a minute, Taralynn turns, leaving the same way her boyfriend did.

His chest expands, then he lets an almost violent breath shudder out of him. I tighten my arms around his middle, feeling like the shittiest person on the planet for what I did to him.

"She was right," he says as he pulls away from me. A cold gush of air winds around my body, and I don't like it one bit. "I shouldn't have thrown that in his face."

"Which was what?" I prompt.

His shoulders square, and without looking at me, he says, "Not what you should be worried about right now." Then he walks out of the house, exiting through the sliding glass door to the backyard.

Fuck.

My shoulders sag, then my head falls back onto my shoulders.

Never once did Shane threaten our relationship back when we dated in high school. That was what I did. But this isn't high school, and we aren't kids anymore. Hell, we aren't actually in a relationship. I'm still married for who knows how much longer, and Shane and I haven't discussed a future—or us.

So exactly what is there for him to threaten?

Still, it feels like I've lost him, and that's what kicks me in the ass.

I'll be damned if I act like I did back then. I'm an adult. An adult with her memory back. It's my second chance. I can't lose him. Not again.

I follow, not sure what I'm about to walk into.

I FIND HIM SITTING INSIDE THE children's wooden play gym out back. He climbed to the top level, where there's a square section behind the big slide.

Putting my foot onto the ladder, I pull up, seeing him sitting with his back against the wood panels, his knees bent with his arms resting on top of them.

I stand here, feet on the ladder and hands gripping both sides of the handles on each side of the opening with my eyes on him. Shane knows I'm here, but he hasn't raised his head to meet my eyes.

Deciding I'm not going to wait for an invitation, I step up another rung, then another and another until I plant my shin onto the platform, crawling inside with him. Sitting on my calves, I face him and wait. I'm not leaving until he talks to me—until we've fixed this divide between us.

It's several minutes—several long, agonizing minutes before he does anything other than breathe. There's a slight chill in the air. It's not cold, but I can see a faint fog as his breath exits his mouth.

I'm about to ask him to talk to me when he lifts his head, his eyes meeting mine instantly. My words get lodged in my throat. A part of me wants to die—and maybe a small piece does—because what I see makes my heart plummet. My eyes sting, wanting to cry.

One lone tear drops from his lower eyelid. And that one liquid drop makes me spring forward. His knees part to allow me inside. I don't waste a second, fearing he'll push me away or close me off. I quickly straddle his lap and place my palms on his shoulders.

I need to feel him touching me as much as I need to touch him.

As if he knows that—and he probably does—his hands glide up and inside my fitted T-shirt. Despite the chill in the air, his palms are warm. He tips me forward so we're torso to torso. His eyes flick up to mine, making my insides contract and fist. They show just how badly I've messed up— I've *betrayed him*. And that makes me feel the lowest I've ever felt in my life.

My nose burns as all the feelings I've been holding in come forth. "I'm sorry." I press my forehead against his, pushing forward and trying to hold everything in. "I'm so sorry. Please don't. I'm sorry." I can't stomach his tears. I can't. I won't be able to hold mine in much longer.

"How could you keep that from me, Love?"

"I... I don't know. I'm sorry." I'll grovel. I'll beg. I'll do whatever will stop him from hurting.

"You do," he says through clenched teeth. His hands tighten ever so slightly around my waist. "Tell me why, Love," he says through gritted teeth. "Tell me something."

I flick my eyes away from his, looking up at the sky. There used to be a small roof covering this area, but it's gone now, and the stars shine brightly in the dark sky.

I let out a shudder of breath.

There isn't anything I can say that isn't an excuse. I don't want to give him an excuse. It is what it is. I kept something important from him, and for no good reason.

"It was just all too much, all at once."

"That's your excuse?" He sounds bitter. Hell, what did I expect? I could have avoided this had I just opened my mouth and told him.

I can't blame him either. I'm bitter, resentful. I'm enraged at what was kept from me. And here I am doing the same thing.

"No," I stress on a sigh. "I don't have any excuses for what I did."

"So then why did you?"

"Does it matter? I shouldn't have."

"Actually, yes, it does."

"Between everything you were telling me and everything I saw and believed about my life since I woke up in that hospital room." I sniffle, sucking up everything that wants to drain out of me. "Then I got my memory back. I just..." I look back down. "It was all too much. I didn't want to deal with one more thing."

"That was a real shitty thing to do to me, Love."

A sob breaks through my throat. "I know." Tears leak from my eyes, and there isn't one damn thing I can do to stop them. "I'm sorry. I wish I could go back and change what I did. I do." His hands slide around me, going up my back. His comfort just makes it all that much worse. I don't deserve his mercy, his love. I don't deserve him.

My heartbeat starts to increase rapidly, and my breaths speed up and shorten at the same time. My chest tightens, and my head feels too light.

"Love?" His voice edged with panic.

"I'm no... better than they are?"

"What?"

Anxiety creeps up my spine as too many emotions rush forward.

"They kept me from you, you from Everly. I did the same. I'm no better than my parents and Blake."

What have I done?

The harder I try to get air into my lungs, the more I feel like I can't breathe.

"Whitney, stop. You're going to hyperventilate." I hear him, and I know I'm looking at him, but my vision blurs. I can't breathe. Panic sets in. "Love, I said stop." Something tightens around my scalp, and my body shakes as if someone is forcing my movements.

Will he resent me like I resent them? No. He can't.

I try to shake my head furiously, but I can't move it more than an inch or so. It's like I'm not in control of my own body.

Suddenly it all stops. As quickly as it started, it's all washed away. I can breathe again. I can focus. Cool air rains down my nostrils, filling my body with the oxygen I was denied moments ago. Shane's lips are pressed against mine in an all-consuming, revitalizing kiss.

It was him. Realization dawns as the tightness encasing my scalp relaxes. His hand lets my hair go and roams down my back. His mouth releases my lips, moving alongside my jaw and down my neck, peppering kisses all over my skin.

Shane's cock hardens, growing and pressing against me, pushing through the material of our clothes. There is too much fabric between us.

When his hand reaches the small of my back, he takes the material of my shirt into both hands, then he pulls up, taking my shirt and forcing my arms above my head. In seconds, my shirt is off, and his lips are back on me again, kissing the other side along my collarbone, then up my neck until he reaches my ear. "I'm furious with you, but don't ever think I've stopped wanting you. Today, tomorrow, fifty goddamn years from now, I'll love you, Love. Even when I'm angry with you." His teeth latch onto my earlobe, biting and dragging downward until only his lips are left, soothing the area he just inflicted minor pain on.

His fingers slide up my arms and over my shoulders, pausing briefly, then the straps of my bra are yanked down my arms, taking it down my body where he leaves it around my waist. The chill in the air hits my nipples, hardening them and erupting goose bumps across my skin.

He grabs my ass next, squeezing my jean-clad cheeks and lifting me upward. "I love you too, Shane." When his mouth latches onto my breast, I almost lose all my thoughts. He has a way of getting inside me, consuming me. "So much," I finally force out when I regain my bearings.

His teeth pinch as he drags them off my nipple. "I've never once doubted that, Love." Shane's eyes flick up to mine, making me pull in a stream of air. He's silent only for a second, but in that second, those eyes penetrate me. One of his hands roams up my back and into my hair, grabbing the strands closest to my roots, fisting them. "Now I need you to stop doubting me." Then he bends me, bringing my lips to his. Yanking me off him, he looks deep into my eyes and says, "Us." Then my lips crash into his once more, and he's devouring me.

Wanting more, needing more, I drop my hands, finding his belt buckle. Once it's undone, I move to the button on his pants, unbuttoning and sliding the zipper down as fast as humanly possible. Thank God he helps me by lifting his butt so I can slide his jeans down his legs.

I leave his boxer briefs fully on, pulling his dick through the opening. No need for both of us to get splinters from the wood below us.

He does the same to me, getting my pants off as fast as he can before threading his fingers back through my hair. Then he pulls my mouth back to his hungry lips.

I can't help myself; I fist his cock in my hand, needing to feel his silky, smooth hardness. Pulling my hand down his length, I twist my wrist, sliding around until my hand reaches the head. With my thumb, I run the pad of my finger back and forth over his opening. His lips disconnect from me as he sucks in a sharp breath of air through his clenched teeth.

His pre-cum wets me, evoking a smile from me as I guide him to my opening.

Shane slips inside me effortlessly, thanks to how wet he's made me. "Fuuuuuuck," he draws out.

Once he's fully seated to the hilt, inside my pussy, I wrap my arms around his neck and look into his eyes. "I don't doubt us, baby. I doubt myself sometimes, but never us. I want us now and forever." Rising slowly, I drag his cock back out until just the tip is inside me. "I'm mad we lost so much time." I drop down, taking him back inside so quickly that I gasp for air.

"I'm mad too." This time, with his hands on my hips, he pulls me up. "So fucking mad." Then he plunges me back onto him, making me bite down on my lip to stifle a scream. It's late, and I don't want to wake his parents or the girls. "But what's done is done," he tells me through a locked jaw.

Shane holds me in place longer than I want, so I try to lift myself up. It's no use. He's keeping me where he wants me. "Slow down, Love. I'm about to blow my shit."

I shouldn't, but I do it anyway. Leaning forward, I brush my lips against his ear. "So come inside me."

"Fuck."

I'm lifted and yanked back down. He does this over and over again until his cock swells, and I'm starting to get dizzy. Shane leans into me, and a second later, his teeth latch onto my shoulder, biting down as his cum coats my insides.

When he's done coming, he licks the marks I'm sure he left on my skin. Then he kisses me, working his way over to my neck, up my chin, and then he takes my lips in a slow, torturous, but sweet invasion.

I'm lifted off him. Using his finger, he gathers his cum and runs it slowly from my opening to my clit. My legs clench automatically. "Oh," I moan. "Yes."

His fingers slip up and down, rubbing me just the right way. I can't make it last. It's impossible. He's too good at what he's doing. I come hard, legs shaking uncontrollably.

It takes more than a minute to regain my bearings, but when I do, I look around us. "Well," I draw out. "This is one place we've never christened before."

He chuckles. "Yeah, I guess not."

CHAPTER 29

SHANE

I may not be completely over being left in the dark. That was another month added to the time I wasn't allowed to be a father to my little girl. Another month lost that I can't get back. And a month Everly must have been confused. Hell, the kid is probably still confused.

But no more. Starting tomorrow, I plan on making up as much time as humanly possible.

We're lying in my bed in my old bedroom. There's a comfortable silence between us. My head is propped against two thick pillows, and Whitney is snuggled in my arms with her head on my bare chest and her thigh draped over and tucked between my legs.

I know she doesn't realize just how right her being here makes my world. Her presence settles me. It always did. Most people didn't get that I knew she was the one when I was fifteen years old. Everyone thought I was crazy and dumb. I don't think it happens often, but I'm proof that it is possible to find the other half of your soul when you're still a kid.

I could stay mad at her for what she did. I get it. I do. I don't like it, but I get it. And what would be the point in dwelling on something neither of us can change? We have the here and now and our future. And I'll be damned if the three of them are taken from me ever again. There is no Hell I wouldn't go through just to know they are mine until the day I die.

"Whit?"

I place my hand on top of where hers is resting flat against my chest, over my heart.

She lifts her head, tipping it back to look up at me. "Yeah?"

Before I can open my mouth, my cell phone chimes, alerting me of an incoming text message. I lean over, moving Whitney with me to reach over her to grab my cell phone from the nightstand.

It's a message from Kylie. When I open it, I see she's sent a video. She was supposed to FaceTime me tonight, but I guess she changed her mind.

Leaning back down, I get comfortable and hit play.

"Hey." There's a pause, then she looks away from her phone briefly. Toward the sky, I'm guessing by the angle of her head. After a second, her face comes back into focus on the video. "So I know I said we'd FaceTime after I got off, but as you can see, I chickened out. Plus, you got all your crap going on, and well, this is probably better. Happy Thanksgiving." She laughs, but there isn't an ounce of humor in her voice. "I said it. I've said it a lot to patients today and haven't meant it once. That's awful, isn't it?"

A tear drops, rolling quickly down her cheek, making my chest tighten. I hate that she's alone in a city too far away for me to drive over just to give my friend the hug I know she needs.

"I know I'm being ungrateful for everything I have, but there isn't anything I'm thankful for. And happy?" She snorts. "Fuck happiness." She stares at the screen, her eyes on the camera. "See why I didn't want to call live?" She blinks, and more tears cascade down.

Ah, hell. The weight piles back on my chest, taking root and cementing itself at center mass.

Wiping her face using the back of her hand, she blinks a few times to sniffle.

"And you can stop whatever it is you're feeling about this video too. I know you. And I know you're feeling guilty. You don't even realize you're feeling guilty, but I do, and I'm not even seeing your eyes. I just know you." There's a second or two pause before she continues. "Deep down, I am happy for you, and I'm happy you have her back, but at this moment, I can't fathom one shred of happiness for myself, so..." she trails, not finishing, and I get what she's saying about me feeling guilty because I do feel for her when she's hurting so badly. But I've waited too long to get Whitney back. Kylie and I have wallowed in sorrow together for a long time. It's time for me to be happy—I have a second chance. I'm not letting anyone, not even my best friend, make me feel guilty for having her in my arms.

Of course, it helps to know that wasn't Kylie's intent. She just can't see any amount of sunshine right now. She may never see it again. I hope that's not the case, but I've been where she is. At least on some level, I do. I know what it's like to lose the person you love most and think you'll never get them back.

"Anyway, I still want to talk to you. Tell you I miss you. Tell you I wish you were here instead of *there*. You know what I mean. Tell Whit I said hi and I'm thinking about all of you. I love you, Shaney. Tell her I love her too. I'm not sure I've shown her that yet. I will, though. I promise. Night. Oh, and let's never bring this crap up. Kay?"

The video ends, and I click the phone off without replying. I'll text her back in the morning. Reaching over Whit, I place the phone back on my nightstand, sitting it next to hers.

As I lie back down, I see Love grinding her teeth. A smile breaks out that I can't hold back.

"Are you jealous?" I laugh, unable to help myself, knowing I'm right.

"I don't know? Am I the crap in your life? According to her, I am." She moves off me, settling her head on the pillow next to mine and crossing her arms.

I'm stunned for all of a minute, watching her sulk. This is uncharacteristic of the girl I once knew. Then again, she isn't a girl anymore. She's a woman. A beautiful, sexy as sin woman that will hold my heart in the palm of her hand until the day I take my last breath. Probably even after that.

"Love," I draw out, waiting for her to look at me. When she does, I continue. "I see what it looks like. But you know Ky. And if you think about it for two seconds, then you know why she's coming across that way."

"No, Shane, I don't know. I haven't known her in years. A decade," she bites out. "And people can change in that amount of time."

I breathe hard, not wanting to talk about Trent but knowing I need to make her understand.

"Less than a year ago, her world, her future, was ripped away from her in a blink of an eye. One minute she was happy, in love, and planning a future. The next, she was alone. Kylie has never been alone in her entire life. She has never been without affection. You gotta remember how touchy-feely she was and how much she craved physical touch?" I pause, letting my words sink in. Eventually, she nods. "She craves attention, not in a bad way. She doesn't want me like that. But she does want something familiar she can cling to for a little while longer. She hasn't actually dealt with Trent's death. She'll only talk to me about him, and even then, she's closed off and distant with her feelings."

Whitney is quiet for longer than I expect. The jealousy has been wiped from her face, but something still remains. Something... sad. Something I want to crush and make disappear.

"I know all too well the things Kylie is feeling. And I owe her a lot." That makes Love's face turn, her eyes flicking up to mine, wanting me to continue. "The first semester of college, I'd show up for my classes, mostly, but I didn't participate. I couldn't tell you now what any class was about. I don't remember them. The only reason I passed those classes was that Kylie did all my assignments. I probably flunked my exams. My parents tried to get me to take off a year, but I refused. I couldn't come home. I couldn't be there and be alone."

"Why did this happen to us?" Before I can respond, she spouts out another question. "What were you going to say before she texted?"

Is she ready to hear this? I hope so, because I'm going all in.

"I need to know this is forever. No bullshit. Your parents nor anyone else can make you doubt us—this." I grab her hand, interlocking our fingers and squeezing tight, just before the point of causing her pain. I need her to know I want us solid, whole, unbreakable.

"You forgive me for keeping *that* from you?" she asks.

"Yes. And you knew that before those words ever left your mouth. I can be mad. I can be hurt and still want you. Still love you."

"I believe in us. I want us, too." She squeezes my hand back. "Forever."

Leaning down, I cover her mouth with my own, kissing her and making damn sure she feels everything coursing through my body. My dick twitches, coming to life and needing to be inside her. If I could live inside her forever, I would.

She drives me mad in both good ways and bad. But there's no one that's ever made me feel a shred of the things she does.

"YOU KNOW I HAVE PLENTY of leftovers from yesterday. I wish you would take some with you."

I look up from where I'm posted against the railing on my parents' front porch to see my mom pursing her lips at me as she steps out of the house.

"And it's better served by taking it to the homeless shelter in town, Mom." She was already going to do that anyway. I don't know why she's so insistent on making sure I'm fed.

"Fine." She closes the door behind her. "Have you thought any more on what your dad suggested last night?"

"No." I deadpan. "I haven't had time, but I will." She looks at me like only a mom can do, silently telling me I better. "I promise, Mother."

"You know if there is anything you need, anything at all, you just have to ask, Shane."

"I'm good. We're good." I nod my head to the yard, making her look to where Whit and the girls are waiting for me.

"I'm sure you are, but I know you have to get ready for your boards in July. I remember how stressful that can be, and if there is anything your dad and I can do to make your life—their life—less stressful, then we're here and willing to help wherever we can."

"You had a husband and two kids by the time you and dad were finishing residency. I got this, Mom. Stop worrying."

"I'll never stop worrying, Shane. It's impossible. You'll understand soon enough. Being a parent is the hardest and scariest thing you'll ever experience in life." She smiles. "You'll find out soon enough what I mean. It's also the most amazing and wonderful thing you'll experience."

A scream from the yard makes me twist around, ready to charge whatever has Emersyn in a fit.

"No," she hollers. "I don't wanna go." Her arms tighten around Everly's leg like she's holding on for dear life. "I'm not going without Evlee."

Blake.

It's his weekend with her. That's where we are headed as soon as we leave my parents. Even though the fucker has joint custody because he works and Whitney doesn't, she's able to keep Emersyn during the week and only has to part with her every other weekend.

Even that's too much.

Whitney grabs Emersyn, attempting to pull her off her sister, but by the looks of it, she's not succeeding.

My mother's laugh catches my attention, making me turn to face her once again.

"What's so funny?"

"Just remembering you and Shawn when y'all were kids. The only difference between them and you and your brother is that Everly doesn't mind Emersyn hanging all over her. Yet," she adds. "When Trent came along, you no longer wanted to play with Shawn."

"Thanks, Mom. Way to make me feel like crap." Not that I don't already for what I said last night.

"Bud, that's what siblings do. Some are inseparable. Others aren't. Some even can't stand each other. No pair is alike, just like all people aren't the same. Every human being is unique in some way, and that's what makes us all special. I wish we humans understood that more."

"I agree with you. Now give your favorite son a hug before I leave." That gets a chuckle out of her as she shakes her head. I embrace my mother, knowing I'm not her favorite because she doesn't truly have a favorite. But I know and she knows she's closer relationship-wise to my little brother just like I'm closer to my dad than Shawn is.

"I love you, bud."

"I love you too, Mom."

Pulling away, she looks out into the front yard where Whitney is still trying to pull Emersyn off her sister.

The kid has determination. I'll give her that.

"Take care of them." She turns, looking back at me with a more serious look.

"You doubt me?" I have a hard time believing that.

"Of course not. It's just..." She trails off, her head rolling to look back at them again.

"It's just what?"

Her eyes rise to meet mine, showing me she's worried. Maybe even borderline fear. "I have a bad feeling is what."

"Stop worrying, Mom. Jacob will get everything straightened out eventually." At least I hope so. Wednesday is the court hearing for their divorce, and I won't be able to attend. I can't take off with others already scheduled off.

She places her palm on my shoulder as she turns to head back inside but pauses, looking over her shoulder at me. "I had this same feeling before my best friend took her life, Shane. It's not a good feeling, and I thought, back then, if I had done something, maybe Lynn would still be here." She breathes, visibly trying to hold back tears that want to fall. "I don't want anything to happen to those three, or you, bud. Just be careful, okay?"

"Okay, Mom." I don't know why she's that worried. I would never take my own life, and I know Whitney wouldn't either. We've just gotten each other back. We have a future now, and I'm not letting anything jeopardize that.

When the door to my parents' house closes, I pull out my phone from my pocket and shoot a text to my brother.

> Call me when you get up.

Almost immediately, I see the delivered notification under my message turn to read, but after waiting, he doesn't respond, prompting me to type out another one.

> When you decide to stop sulking like a 5-year-old, call me.

SHAWN
> Fuck you.

I get out of the text app and call my brother. It rings once but then goes to voicemail, telling me he declined the call.

Shaking my head, I hammer out another text.

> I don't want to apologize in a text. Call me.

> AGAIN, FUCK YOU.

God, he makes me want to kick his ass.

I'm about to call him again when something tackles my leg.

Looking down, Emersyn starts trying to climb my leg. I quickly pocket my phone.

"Emersyn Rose," Whitney scolds.

Bending, I grab her under her armpit and the back of her leg, pulling her up and anchoring her to my side. She's profusely shaking her head from side to side. "Don't make me go, Shaney. I don't wanna." She wraps her arms around my neck and buries her little face in my neck, making my heart crack because I don't want her to go to her father's any more than she obviously doesn't want to go.

Something has to be done. It's not right that he has joint custody—hell, any rights at all.

I squeeze her. "Em," I began as Whitney steps up to the front patio. I shake my head, silently telling her to let me handle this. "Look at me, monkey."

"No," she refuses. "Momma's making me go, and it's not fair. Evlee doesn't have to."

"It's only for two nights. And I'll personally come pick you up on Sunday." Whitney's eyes widen, clearly not liking that idea. I don't care, though, not about that. It's high time I give that motherfucker a piece of my mind.

I raise an eyebrow, letting her know I don't want to hear any arguments. She huffs in response. Tough shit.

Emersyn pulls back, looking me in the eyes as crocodile tears fall from each eye. "Promise?"

"Yes, monkey. I promise."

"Fine," she pouts and then sniffles as she lays her head down on my shoulder.

"Let's go," I say to Whitney. Then I wait for her to descend the stairs, following behind her to my Tahoe.

Jacob is going to have to figure out a way to get Blake Lane out of our lives one way or another.

CHAPTER 30

WHITNEY

"See ya, Ev," I tell her as she gets out of the car on Monday morning to head into school.

"Bye, Evlee," Emersyn chimes in after me. Looking in the rearview mirror, she's smiling brightly at her big sister.

Everly waves as she shuts the door. Emersyn's smile drops, replaced with a scowl as she looks at me in the mirror. *Oh, she's going to be a handful today.* She crosses her arms as if confirming my thoughts.

"I'm not going back to Daddy's."

"Em," I say in a pacifying voice.

"I'm. Not." Her head cocks, challenging me, and if we weren't in a car, in the school carpool lane, I'd...

My train of thoughts is interrupted by the ringing of my phone. Grabbing it from the console, I answer. "Hello?"

"Where you at?" I'm taken aback for all of two seconds before that rough voice registers. "You there?"

"Yeah, Chance. Hey." Why on earth is he calling me at 7:30 in the morning?

"Hey, back at ya. Now tell me where the fuck you are."

"I just dropped Everly off at school. I'm about to go back to the apartment." Is he trying to piss me off?

"Scratch those plans. Come to Wicked," he demands.

"Wicked?" What's that and where?

"Yeah, Wicked Ink. Shawn's tattoo studio. Ring any bells?" He sounds annoyed that I don't know.

"Yes." I bite out through closed teeth. The nerve of his attitude. Jeez. "I just didn't know that was the name."

"One week with your memories back, and you still don't know jack shit." It's not a question. And he's lucky Emersyn isn't in hearing range right now, or I'd give him an earful.

"It hasn't been officially one week until about midnight tonight, A-hole."

"A-hole? Really, Whit?"

"My three-year-old is in the back seat listening to every word coming out of my mouth. I'm thanking myself for not putting you on the car speaker."

"Whatever. Just get down here."

"I don't know where 'here' is." Or why he's in Mississippi.

"I'll text you the address. Better see you in forty-five minutes, bitch." He hangs up without another word, and within a few seconds a text message comes through my phone.

Oh, he's going to see me all right. He'll be lucky if I don't kick him in the junk too.

An hour and a half later, after a pee stop, then a poop stop ten minutes after the pee stop, we arrive at Wicked Ink. It's a tattoo shop in a building that could easily pass for a medical or dental clinic. If it weren't for the large sign over the awning, I'd never think this was a tattoo parlor. There are no neon or flashing sign that reads "TATTOO" anywhere in sight.

"Unbuckle, kiddo, and get out."

"Where we at, Momma?" Her attitude is nowhere in sight now, making me sigh in relief.

"Where are we, Momma," I correct. Jesus, sometimes I think I'm raising a redneck. And I have no idea how. I don't talk like that. Her sister doesn't, and Blake certainly doesn't.

Ugh, Blake. I haven't missed the snide little comments he used to make when she started speaking either. Emersyn's voice even has a twang to it that no one in mine or Blake's family has.

"You remember Shane's brother Shawn, right?"

"Yep. He's pretty." I burst out in laughter. Shit, that's funny. Sure, Shawn is good-looking in a brooding slash meanie kind of way. But I would never put the word 'pretty' in context when describing Shane's brother.

"What's funny, Momma?"

"Nothing, baby. Let's go."

She beats me to the front door. It's wooden, with frosted glass in the top half with "WICKED INK" etched in all caps and the business hours in smaller, lowercase writing underneath.

"It won't open," she huffs.

"I got it," I say, coming up behind her and pushing the heavy door open. She jets inside, obviously excited.

I spot both of them over to the left after walking past what I'm guessing is a receptionist's area up front. The room is open and large, containing workstations on each side of the room. There's no one else but Shawn and Chance in sight. Chance is perched against a large mirror and Shawn's sitting on a stool, leaning back against a tattooing table. They're talking, but I'm not close enough to hear their conversation.

"Hey, guys, what's up?" I say, walking up.

"What are you doing here?" Shawn twists his head, surprise lacing his voice.

"Shawny." Emersyn singsongs before launching herself at him. He catches her midair.

"Hey, Em." He chuckles as he wraps his large arms around her in a hug, a smile tugging at his lips.

"We come to see you."

"Y'all did not come to see him?" Chance scowls at my three-year-old. "Y'all came to see me."

Emersyn twists around in Shawn's arms, but he doesn't let her go. Her face lights up as if just noticing Chance for the first time. "You're friends with Ariel."

"If by Ariel you mean Evie, then yes, sugar, I'm friends with her."

"She looks like Ariel," she states, as if disputing Eve's name.

Ignoring her statement, Chance asks, "Do you not remember my name, Emersyn Rose?" She shakes her head. "Guess memory loss runs in the family." For that, I kick his boot. He only shrugs, then pushes off the wall. After ruffling Emersyn's curls, he turns, grabbing me by the arm without a word and pulling me toward the opposite wall.

"Why am I here?" I ask when he lets go.

"Hop up there." He nods toward the tattoo table, ignoring my question.

I do as he asks but question again once I'm settled. "Why am I here, Chance?" He holds up a sheet of paper. "What's that?"

"This is your new tattoo. Look."

"Flowers?" I question.

I'm more girly now than I was in high school, but I still don't care for flowers, albeit really pretty flowers. They're a vibrant blue and the artwork is incredibly detailed.

"They're forget-me-nots."

"They're pretty." And they're familiar looking.

"They mean undying love—which you and Shane obviously have." He stares at me, giving me the impression he has more to say. "And they match your boy's flowers on his side. But most importantly, they're forget-me-nots, meaning, don't fucking forget me, not ever fucking again, bitch."

"Language!" I bark.

"I expect that out of Shane. Not you, mouthy."

"Wait till you have kids."

"Kids aren't on my agenda. Ever." I raise an eyebrow. "Kids are cute. Yours seem kind of cool, but I don't care for them full-time."

"What about you?" I turn my head to the side, eyeing Shawn as he and my child walk over.

"I'm just trying to keep my girlfriend as my girlfriend. Whatever comes later comes, just as long as it involves her."

"You know, I hear if you don't fuck up in the first place, then you don't have to worry about that shit." Chance relays.

Shawn grits his teeth but doesn't comment on Chance's jab. Shane finally got to apologize to his brother Friday night when Shawn called him, and I'm glad they patched things up.

I turn my attention back to Chance, wanting to get the subject off Shawn. His relationship with Taralynn is obviously a sore spot for him. It's easy to see how much he regrets what he did to her earlier this year.

"Who says I want that tattoo?"

"Oh, you're getting this inked on." He holds up the transfer paper, waving it in the air. "Today. I'll strap you down and get Shawn to hold your foot still for me." I scowl at him even though I really sorta want the tattoo now that I know the meaning—because that's what Shane and I have. "I know you, Whit. You're impatient. You'll decide you want a tat on the spur of the moment, and I won't be here. You'll get him to do it." He points to Shawn. "And he won't say no." Shawn smiles, confirming everything Chance has just said.

"You know." I pause, looking him dead in the eyes. "I don't remember you being the whiny, bitchy one of the group. Is my memory still jacked up?"

"Momma, that's a bad word." Emersyn's eyebrows are drawn together, and her face conveys the same stern look I give when she's done something wrong.

"Yes." Chance confirms. "Yes, Momma. That's a bad, very bad word. Good job, Shirley Temple."

"Who's Shirley Temple?"

"Someone I'm sure your mom is super happy to introduce you to."

Eww. I hate old movies. And by the smirk taking over Chance's face, he knows this too.

Bastard.

At least he's a bastard that obviously cares about me. The tattoo is proof of that. When he was here a few weeks ago, I saw my not remembering him hurt deeply.

I'm grateful my memory has finally returned, and I have a lot of years to make up with the few people I care about. He's one of them, so if this tattoo is something he needs, then I'm willing to get it placed on my body forever. It's a bonus that Shane has the same flowers on him too.

"Fine. Let's do this!" I swear his eyes dilate, but he blinks, and they're back to normal. "I have one alteration, though." And it's a must. Shane has my name inked on his body, so I want his on mine. I think weaving it into the flowers will look badass and pretty at the same time.

Holy shit! I'm getting a tattoo.

BY THE TIME WEDNESDAY ROLLS around, I'm a nervous wreck. On top of court this afternoon, I can't get in to see my doctor until next week, and she won't call in a prescription until she makes me take a pregnancy test. For the love of fucking God, it's just drawing blood. It shouldn't require an office visit with the actual doctor. A nurse can do it and have it tested. Surely they can.

My foot taps on the marble floor as I wait for Jacob to arrive. The hearing is scheduled for ten minutes from now, and I'd thought he would have been here by now. Luckily, I'm saved from more thoughts plaguing my mind by the ringing of my cell phone. After digging it out of my purse, I answer just after catching Eve's name across the screen before bringing it to my ear. "Hello?"

"If you fuck a dildo made in China, does that mean you fucked a Chinese cock?" I'm stunned silent. This cannot be a legit question. But then I remember the crazy crap she used to spout all the time when we were good friends. Not that we aren't good friends now, but... are we? The question stops me. "Well?" She prompts.

"Umm... I think no matter how you look at it, it's still a fake dick."

"Fake dick or not, it's still a Chinese fake dick, right? I've never fucked someone Chinese. Work with me here, Whitney. I want to be able to say I've fucked Chinese cock now."

"Okay, you've fucked a Chinese cock."

Exactly how many different nationalities has she slept with? The thought pricks my mind. We're the same age. Scratch that, she's five months older than me. She's already twenty-nine. But still...

"Good. Now," her voice turns sweeter, "how do you like your first tat? And when are we getting another one?"

"*I* like it just fine, and I," again stress the 'me' in this conversation, "am just fine with the one."

"For now," she draws out. "Whatcha doing?"

"Waiting for Taralynn's dad to show."

"Ah," her voice turns flat. "Court, right?"

"Yep." Shane must have told her because this is the first time I've spoken to her since she was here. I feel guilty for not calling her or Kylie when my memory returned. Over time I thought about doing it, but I felt awkward. Yet I don't feel that way now. Maybe it was all in my head.

"Don't sweat it, Whit. You remember now. Everything is going to work out. I know it will."

"You have more confidence than I do." I slump back against the wooden bench I'm sitting on.

"You don't take shit from anyone. You don't settle for less than what you want. You remember that person, right?"

"Yeah, but—" She cuts me off.

"Stop that train of thought right now. You don't take what they are giving lying down. Don't like it? Fight it. Fight it until that little girl of yours is grown if you have to. But you fight."

We're both silent, giving me time to think about what she has said. She's right. One hundred percent, she is right. The person I was before. The teenager I was would have fought tooth and nail and then fought more.

"That motherfucker better hope I never catch him in a dark alley."

"Thanks, Eve." I smile for the first time today.

"For what?"

"For being you. For calling me. I miss you." Tears suddenly prick my eyes, catching me off guard.

"I've missed you too. For a long time, but I don't have to anymore. You're back."

"Yes, I am." I breathe, seeing Shawn walking down the hall toward me. "Eve, I gotta run. Talk later?"

"Yeah. Go rip those fuckers a new one. Bye, babe."

"Bye." I hang up as Shawn reaches me. "What are you doing here?"

"Was in the neighborhood."

I raise my eyebrow. "Shane asked you to come?"

"No." He shakes his head. "Jacob mentioned it when I spoke to him an hour ago, and I know my brother's schedule, so I knew he wouldn't be able to be here. Figured you could use support."

"So we're friends?" I ask, not doubting that truth for a second.

"No. We're family." The look he's giving me tells me he means every word. And it eases some of my nerves.

Footsteps catch my attention, making me look past him, seeing Jacob heading in our direction. His expression doesn't give me any indication if I should be worried or not. I'm worried no matter what. At best, it'll still be a month before a divorce would be finalized. And after that... he'll still be a part of my life until Emersyn is an adult, and even then, he'll be a part of her life until he dies. Life isn't fair.

"Let's do this," is all Jacob says as he walks past us and into the courtroom to my left.

I huff, letting out a frustrated breath.

"You got this, Whitney," Shawn reassures me, holding out his hand for me to take.

"I hope so." But I don't feel one once of those words.

I HONESTLY DON'T KNOW WHAT to do with myself. Or how to contain every emotion that's been coursing through my body for the last three days. Joy. Relief. Excitement for the future. None of that even skims the surface of the happiness I feel inside.

Shawn held my hand every minute I sat inside that courtroom listening to the judge, to Blake and his lawyer, to Jacob. There was yelling. There was a lot of pounding from the judge's gavel.

Yet, there was mostly silence from me. I think I was in shock. I think I'm still in shock.

The judge, Kenneth McDonald—not the former judge we had last month—wanted to grant me an annulment. He said that wasn't an option, and my stomach pummeled at that moment. A tiny part of me had hoped, had prayed. But he did refuse Blake's motion for marriage counseling and then his objection to the divorce altogether.

And in surprising events, he overturned the joint custody ruling the previous judge awarded Blake, saying he was appalled the previous judge even thought such a thing was acceptable. He even mentioned bringing the man's ethics up to the Tennessee State Bar Association or something like that. Yeah, those were the words he used.

So, as it stands now, I'll be officially divorced in ninety days. Three months and I'll be free to move forward with my future. With Shane. And I have full custody of Emersyn. Blake can see her with supervised visits.

I swear I wanted to laugh in his face. I wanted to do more, but everything else would have been illegal.

So today, on the following Saturday, we are celebrating Everly's tenth birthday. A party would have been out of the question with Blake.

God, I disgust myself thinking back on the last ten years. I let him rule my life—every decision. I was weak, and for the life of me, it doesn't make sense. I've never been a weak person. At least before I lost my memory I wasn't. I allowed him and my parents to dictate everything, and I didn't balk at much of anything.

"Momma," Everly squeaks, bringing me out of my thoughts. She grabs onto my forearm and squeezes. "Can I open my presents now?" The excitement in her voice both thrills me and makes me aware of everything she's missed out on.

Neither my girls nor I am expected to act a certain way. It's obvious to me that Shane and his family love us just for being us.

"Yes. Where's your dad?"

Dad. My soul feels that word, and it loves it. Hearing her say it makes that feeling soar.

She lets go of me, turning and yelling for Shane. "Daddy." She runs off, calling him again.

It's a wonder how easily that word rolls off her tongue. It's as though she was meant to say it. And I guess she was. But only to Shane.

I don't think I've ever seen Everly this happy and relaxed. She and I haven't had one argument since we left Blake's home. I call it that because that's exactly what it was. It was never ours. We were never meant to be there.

Then at that thought, guilt slips in. Had things not happened the way they did, I wouldn't have Emersyn. I'd probably have another kid or maybe more, but not her. And I can't imagine my life without her in it.

I still wish I hadn't lost years with Shane, but dwelling on the "what ifs" is pointless and only takes away more time that I could be spending with my family now. My new family. My real family. Shane, our girls, his parents, Shawn and Taralynn, Chance and Eve, Kylie, Jacob even, and anyone else that comes along. Because I see a big family in our future.

"Hey, babe." I look up. Shane is leaning inside the door.

We're at his parents' celebrating Everly's birthday, and there are so many people here that I don't know half of them. I think most work with either Shane's parents or with him at the Children's Hospital in Memphis. Gavin, I remember from the Halloween party. That was the night that changed my kids and my life forever—for the better.

"Yeah?"

"Come on. She's ready to unwrap her gifts."

"Y'all are going to spoil her with the amount of presents in your parents' living room."

He laughs. "Well, you can thank my brother for at least half of them. Hell, a quarter of them, I think, are for Emersyn. I'm hoping Ev doesn't get her feelings hurt over that."

"She won't," I assure him. Knowing Everly, she'd let her sister open all of them.

I'm lucky in the children department. I don't have siblings, and from what I remember of Shane and Shawn when they were this age, the younger sibling isn't treated as nicely as the way Everly treats Emersyn.

I'm not sure yet if that's a good thing or a bad one. Only time will tell, I guess.

"I'm coming." I stand, making my way toward him. He bends down, pulling me into his chest and planting a chaste kiss on my lips.

"I love you, Love," he tells me, pulling away as he stands to his full height.

"Back at you." I jump, smacking his lips with mine once again before bypassing him toward the rest of the party.

Stooping down to the ground, I grab a beer from an ice chest, pulling an extra one out for Shane. Standing, I hand it to him, then turn toward the room where everyone is watching Everly and Emersyn on the floor near the fireplace where all the gifts are piled on top of the hearth.

"Okay, Everly, your parents finally decided to join us," the room erupts into laughter at Shane's dad, a jab at us being the last to make it to the living room, "you can open your presents."

"Presents." Emersyn jumps up and down. After the fourth jump, she loses her balance and falls into her sister. Everly pulls her into a seated position on her lap. And as I predicted, she lets her sister rip open the gifts.

After ten minutes of "oohs" and "ahhs," she gets to her last present. Noticing the look on Shane's face—a smile so big I want to bottle it up so I can open it every single day for the rest of my life—I smile too, facing him as he watches her.

Her gasp breaks my stare. I look over to see what he's gotten her, and my mouth drops. And not in a good way.

A phone?

My head whips over to Shane. He's not paying me the least bit of attention. All eyes, especially his, are on Everly. He's thrilled she likes it, and it shows. Of course she likes it. What kid wouldn't like a brand new smartphone? Hell, any phone.

Heat breaks out across my face, cascading down my neck. I have to get out of this room.

And I do. I fly out of the room so fast I almost trip over my feet.

What the mother fuck was he thinking? A phone?

I had to leave. If I hadn't, I would have made a scene. Everly doesn't need that. His parents don't either. I'm not ungrateful for what they've done today, and I'm not about to lose my shit in front of them and all their friends.

But my God! A phone?

The more I think about it, the madder I get. She's ten. She's in third grade, for Pete's sake. She's a child. She doesn't need a phone.

This is crazy. This is absurd.

"Whitney?" His cautious voice causes me to whip around. "What's wrong?"

As if he has to ask. It should be obvious. Why the fuck isn't it obvious?

"You got her a phone?" I blurt out, producing a surprised look on his face.

"Yeah. I did." He quickly defends himself.

"Are you... insane? She's ten."

His eyes cast down for a mere second before he stalks closer toward me.

When he reaches me, Shane's fingers clasp around my upper arm. "Let's talk upstairs." Then he's gently pulling me toward our bedroom.

I love this man, but this is ridiculous. Seriously, he has to see the logic.

I look over my shoulder right before he reaches the hall. Everly is scowling at me as if she knows exactly why I'm upset. Everyone else seems oblivious.

Entering Shane's old bedroom, he lets my arm go, then shuts the door and leans back against it.

I cross my arms. "Don't you think that was something we should have discussed before you got my daughter a phone?"

Fuck. As soon as the words come out of my mouth, I regret them.

"Your daughter?" His anger erupts as I cringe inside. Shit. Shit. Shit. I didn't mean it the way it sounded. "She's our daughter, Whitney. When are you going to see that?"

"I see it." I blow out a long stream of air. "I'm sorry. I didn't mean to make it sound like she isn't yours too. I just... Fuck, Shane. Come on. She's ten years old." I run my fingers through my hair in frustration.

"Look, you're right. We should have talked about it, but..." He pauses as he steps toward me. "I need the peace of mind knowing I can reach her whenever I want. And when she isn't with me, when she's at school or at my parents', or wherever, I can look on an app on my phone to see where she is. It was either that or get an actual GPS device placed on her body. I figured maybe that was extreme."

"Extreme? They're both extreme. Where do you think she's going?"

He grits his teeth. He's mad. Great. Just fucking great. I'm the one that has the right to be pissed, and it's all his doing.

"I can't fucking believe you right now."

"Well, fucking believe it, baby," he throws right back at me, pissing me off even more.

"Is this how it's going to be? You make all the decisions and piss on what I want or think?" I know he wouldn't. Even I think it's stupid after the words have left my mouth, but I can't help them. I won't go back to the way my life was with Blake. I won't allow someone else to dictate everything. I won't fall in line ever again.

My chest rises, not backing down from my question. It's shitty. I know it's shitty, but he didn't consult me. A phone is a huge decision. And not one that should have been made without us talking about it.

"You're making a big deal out of something that isn't a big deal."

"And you didn't answer my question."

"It was a stupid question, and you know it. If you think I'm going to stop calling you on your shit, you're wrong. If you think I'm going to make major decisions without you, you're wrong." He holds up his hand just as my mouth opens to speak. "Yes, I should have talked to you about it. But I didn't. It's done, Whitney. Let's move on from it. From here on out, we'll talk about things we want the girls to have and do." He shuts up, clearly waiting for my response. A response I don't give, so he prompts me. "Okay?"

My silence continues. Mainly because I know deep down he's right, but I'm too stubborn to admit I might have overreacted.

"Whitney," he warns.

"Kiss off." And with that, I push past him, open the door, and walk out like the petulant child I'm acting.

A goddamn phone. Jesus fucking Christ. What's next?

CHAPTER 31

SHANE

"Oh. My. Gosh." Her little palms go to her cheeks. Emersyn's mouth forms an "o" as she takes in all the sparkling jewelry. "Shaney, everything is so pretty." Her head tips back, looking up at me. "Ain't everything so pretty?"

"Isn't everything so pretty," I correct. Whitney is damn set on correcting her grammar. She's three. I don't see what the point is, but if her mother is going to do it, then I need to stand behind her and help. Even if the woman hasn't uttered one word to me since Saturday afternoon. Two days and she's still putting up a hard front. "I guess."

"There is no guessing about jewry." She cocks her hip to the side, giving me a serious look. "All jewry is pretty."

"Jewelry," I correct.

She turns, giving me her backside as she walks up to one of the clear cases in front of us. "Why are we here?"

"I have to pick something up. And remember, you promise not to say anything about where we've been to your mom or Everly. Right?"

I scoop her off the floor, placing her on the glass countertop above the jewelry cases. I think her eyes get even bigger as she looks down at everything.

"Surprise. I remember." Her head pops up for all of two seconds.

"My lips sealed."

"And why are your lips sealed?"

"Because we don't want to spoil anybody's surprises." Her head shakes from side to side, making her curls swing. "I like surprises. You like surprises?"

"Yep."

I don't, but there is no way I need her thinking about spilling the beans. I should have taken her to that Mommy's Day Out thing Whitney drops her off at once a week, but I thought the two of us could use time alone together. She may not be my daughter biologically, but I still want to bond with her as if she were.

She was the first one I saw last year when I found Whitney on Facebook. I think I loved Emersyn even then. I didn't know her. I knew she was another man's daughter. But I also knew she was a part of Whitney. And there isn't any part of that woman I don't love. She can act all kinds of mad if she wants to. She can go a week without speaking to me if she wants, but I still love her. I know she loves me. In the end, that's all that matters.

"Hi, can I help you?" a man greets us as he walks from the back room behind the jewelry counter. He's shorter than I am and probably twice as old. He's wearing a navy suit. His hair is solid white. He's not the man I dealt with last week when I picked out the ring, so my guess is that he's the father of Bradford and Son Family Jewelry.

"We want everything." Emersyn looks up, serious as a heart attack. I smile while the older man laughs.

"You're in trouble with this one," he tells me. I'm inclined to agree. "I'm Bradford Collins. The owner." He sticks his hand out for me to shake.

"Shane Braden." I grip his hand briefly.

"Ah." My name must ring bells. "You have a ring order to pick up, correct?"

"Yes."

"Give me one moment. It's in the back. I need to make sure it has been cleaned. I'll be right back."

"Sure. Take your time. We're in no rush."

Mr. Collins heads back to where he must have been when we walked in. There's no one else in the jewelry shop as I take in the rest of the small room. It's an old establishment, or so Gavin, my boss, babbled on about when I told him my plans to ask Whitney to marry me. She's not divorced yet, but that doesn't mean she can't wear my ring until it's official. And once it is...

"Shaney," Emersyn draws out my name, bringing my attention to her. Glancing down, I see she isn't looking at me. Her head is still down, and she's drawing circles on the glass with her fingers.

"Yeah, monk?" I ask, alarm setting in. The way she said my name wasn't her usual bubbly, happy self. She sounds sad.

"Why you want to be Evlee's dad and not mine?"

Her question halts my breathing. I don't know how to respond to that. *Does she want to be my daughter?* I already thought she was, even though officially I'll be her stepdad when Whitney marries me. Does she want to call me dad like Everly just started doing?

I pick her up off the counter, bringing her to my front. She wraps her legs around me, but her face is still downcast, and her hair hides her eyes from me.

"Look at me." She obeys immediately, her head snapping up. "What do you mean, Em?"

"You Evlee's dad now. She calls you that, but you not mine. Do you not like me like you like her?"

"Baby girl." I squeeze her. "I love you, Emersyn Rose."

"But why you not my daddy? My other daddy not as nice as you."

Air rushes out of my lungs, making me feel like I've been punched in the gut. What the hell?

"Emersyn." My voice comes out too harsh, making her jump in my arms. I've never spoken to a child like that. I've always had a soft, patient voice with kids, but then my patients aren't exactly my own. "Sorry, sweetie. I didn't mean to startle you."

"What I do wrong?"

"Absolutely nothing."

"Here you go." I look up as the jeweler walks back up.

Taking the box, I slide Emersyn to my side. "Thanks." I nod in his direction.

I'd say more, but I'm more worried about the little angel in my arms than being polite to a man I just spent a good chunk of my savings with. Worth every penny, though.

Exiting the shop, I walk down the sidewalk to the end of the block. There's a street vendor with a couple of tables and chairs. After buying her a cone of chocolate ice cream, I plop her onto the top of the wrought iron table, and then I sit in the chair opposite her.

I pop the top on the ring box. "What do you think?" I ask, flipping it around to show her.

She swallows her ice cream, some already dripping down her chin, but I didn't grab any napkins, so there isn't much I can do to clean it off.

"That for Momma?" She gives me a wide, chocolate-covered grin.

"Yes, and you cannot tell her. Okay?"

"I not. It's real pretty."

"Em," I prompt, waiting for her to look at me. When she doesn't stop staring at the ring like it's candy, I close the box and pocket it. She looks up then. "I do want to be your daddy. And with that ring, I'm going to ask your mom to marry me. Is that okay with you?"

"Then I can call you Dad like Evlee?"

"Monkey, you can call me anything you want, whenever you want. You can call me Dad, Daddy, or keep calling me Shaney. That's up to you. But I'd be honored if you decide you want me to be your dad."

"Then I want you to be my dad, and I don't want to go back to my daddy's house ever again." She shakes her head profusely.

"Earlier, when we were in the shop with all the pretty jewelry, you said your daddy wasn't very nice. Why isn't he nice, monkey?" The doctor in me can't help but probe, questioning everything this child is saying and trying to decipher it.

"He yells. A lot. And I don't like it when he says bad things about Momma or Evlee or you." I'm about to try to explain things when her eyebrows turn in, and she gets a mean look on her face. "And I don't like when he hurts my arms. He's a meanie, and I don't want to go back."

Alarm bells sound in my head as goosebumps ripple up my spine.

"Hurts your arms how?"

She sits her cone on the table. It falls over, the ice cream dripping out and onto the table. She doesn't seem to notice or even care. Leaning forward, she grabs onto my biceps and tries her hardest to shake me.

More alarms go off and anger spikes.

"He does that when I tell him to stop saying bad things."

As much as I'd love to find something—anything—to get Blake's rights stripped from him, to get him out of Whitney and the girls' lives forever, I don't want it to be because of this. I don't want this little angel to have been abused physically or mentally in any way.

The distinct text tone I set for work sounds off, stopping my thoughts and telling me the chief resident on call in the emergency department has sent me a text message. That typically only means one thing: I have to go into work on my day off.

ED PHONE

Can you run up here for a sec?

Sure. Be there in twenty.

Odd. Usually, Roderick gives me some form of a heads up or tells me why I'm needed.

"Kiddo, you want to come to work with me for a bit?"

Her eyes light up, and her mouth falls open, but no sound comes out. Then she claps her hands and bobs her head.

Her excitement makes me chuckle, but I'm looking forward to this time next month when I'll be rotating back in the children's clinic instead of the ER. That place will wear on a person's soul. And at least in the clinic, I'll have better hours—all daytime hours—and weekends off, meaning I'll get more time with my family. Maybe my parents are right. Maybe I need to try general pediatrics for a couple of years. I've already missed too much time. At least that way I'd be home for dinner every night, and my weekend would be spent making memories with the three most important people in my life.

I grab her off the table, bringing her to my hip, then I tap my pocket, making sure the little black ring box is secured. That ring is going to set our family on course to a solid future.

CHAPTER 32

WHITNEY

"*The results were positive.*" *She smiles.* "*Congr—*"
"*Say what?*" That's impossible.
"*You're pregnant, Mrs. Lane.*"

Those words are still playing on repeat as I pull up to the school to get Everly. It's still early in the afternoon. After I left the clinic, there wasn't a need to go to the pharmacy, and I wasn't feeling up to running the errands I told Shane I would do before I picked up our daughter at the normal time they get out.

So here I sit, still in a daze. Confused. How on earth am I pregnant? I've been on birth control regularly since after Emersyn was born.

Should I really be surprised, though? Emersyn was the result of failed birth control. Hell, maybe *that* should have told me to always use two forms of pregnancy prevention. I figured it was a fluke with her. I thought there was no way it could happen again. Fuck, what are the chances?

If I'm honest with myself, I'm not entirely sure I'm unhappy about this. Shock? Yes. Definitely. But upset or mad? No.

It's Shane's baby. That I'm sure of. Blake and I haven't had sex in months. Shane and I, on the other hand, have been fucking like rabbits for the past two weeks. It's still early. I don't feel pregnant. Then again, I never did with Everly either. I was eight weeks along when I even found out about her.

Oh, wow, things should have been different.

I brace my hands on the steering wheel, wrapping my fingers around the leather, letting a big breath of air flow out of my mouth. I don't want to think about the past. I want the future.

I've been a bitch too. And for no reason. I'm over the phone. Sure, it's ridiculous for a ten-year-old, but I get why he did it—why he needs it. He's lost so much time. Time he'll never get back, and if knowing where she is helps ease weight off his chest, then who am I to say no.

A good girlfriend would have understood his need from the start. A good person wouldn't have made such a big deal of it. A woman wouldn't have acted like a fucking child.

Thinking back on my reaction, I'm embarrassed. I shouldn't be. It's Shane. My Shane. My good, understanding, amazing man that loves all my crazy—has always loved my crazy and will always love my crazy.

I shut the ignition off and get out of the car.

I came straight here to get Everly, so I could get home to tell Shane the news.

I don't know how he's going to react. We aren't married. I'm not even divorced and won't be for three months. But something tells me he's going to be happy about this. He would have been happy about Everly, even though we were still teenagers. And this is his chance to be a father from the beginning.

The more I think about it, the happier I get.

I pull the glass door open, walking inside and stopping just to the left of the building's entrance at the secretary's office.

"Hi," I say to a young girl. She's not the normal lady that's always here. She may even be a high school kid. "I'm here to check out my daughter."

She looks up from her phone. Yeah, she has to be a high schooler.

"What's her teacher's name?"

"Mrs. Parks."

"And her name?"

"Everly Lane."

Her body jerks back a few inches, and her eyes do this crazy, confused thing. "I'm pretty sure her dad picked her up. About half an hour ago, I think." She stands, grabs the clipboard in front of me, and scrutinizes the page.

Shane didn't say he would pick her up. In fact, we discussed me getting her even though he's off. He wanted to spend a few hours alone with Emersyn. He thinks he needs to bond with her. Which is great and all, but I already know she loves him as much as he loves her.

"Yep." she says. "It's right here. He signed her out at 1:10."

She hands me the clipboard. The last spot, sure enough, has Everly's name scribbled down, but I don't have to look at his signature to know who it belongs to. I know that handwriting. I know *his* handwriting.

I gasp.

"Ma'am, are you okay?"

Why did Blake check her out? Why does Blake have *my* daughter? She isn't his daughter. Oh my God! Where's my daughter?

"Ma'am?" she calls again, but I don't have time to yell or scream for her or whoever let someone that wasn't her father take her. I removed his name from the list of people allowed to pick her up. The school was very understanding after I explained and showed them the court documentation giving me full custody of her.

I stumble backward, turning and running out of the school.

What purpose could he have had for taking her without my permission? Nothing is adding up. There is no logical answer coming to mind.

I left my purse in the car, which is where my phone is.

Running, I make it to the parking lot and into my car less than a minute after finding out my daughter wasn't where I thought she was.

I practically fall into the vehicle, tripping over my feet trying to get in. Once I find my cell, I unlock it, calling him without checking the text message that's showing up as a pop-up message on the home screen.

No answer. I call again.

Still no answer. What the fuck?

Chills run down my spine as my finger hovers above the text message app. I open it, seeing it's from him.

BLAKE

> I'm done playing games. Get your ass and my daughter to this address. NOW. 348 N. Brooks Road Collierville TN 38017.

That's just east of us, outside the city of Memphis.

Why is he there? Why does he have Everly there? Or does he?

What the fuck is going on?

I toss my phone, hearing it land on the floorboard of the passenger seat. I don't care. I need to find my daughter and get her away from him. My blood is boiling. He's taken this shit too far. This isn't a game to me. This is my daughter's life he's dangling in front of me, trying to scare me.

He's not going to fucking scare me. All he's done is fuck with momma bear's cub. I see crimson, and I'm going to rip that motherfucker's heart out with my bare hands. I'm going to make him wish he never laid eyes on me.

And then... then I'm going to do everything in my power to see that he never comes within sight of either of my children again. I don't care how long it takes. I don't care how many different judges we have to go in front of. I'm not above begging. I'll beg. I'll plead. Hell, maybe I'll even find a way to blackmail one. I'm not above it. Not when it comes to my kids. I'd do anything for my girls. Anything.

CHAPTER 33

SHANE

"This is fun."

"What's fun?" I ask Emersyn, walking through the automatic entrance doors to the ER.

"Getting to come to work with my new daddy." My legs pause. Those words cause my throat to clog up and my chest to warm. A smile finally breaks through my lips.

"What?"

I shake my head, continuing through the waiting room. "Nothing, kiddo. Just hearing you say that makes me happy is all."

"I'm happy too."

"Dr. Braden," a voice greets, surprise laced in her words. About the time I glance away from Emersyn, I realize who's spoken to me. "I thought you were scheduled off today. Am I wrong?" Catherine, another third-year resident, asks.

"No," I confirm. "But I got a text from Roderick. Have you seen him?"

"I'm pretty sure he ran to the cafeteria to grab lunch. Want me to page him?"

"Nah, I'll call his cell. Thanks, though."

What the hell? I told him I'd be here in twenty. Why call me down here when he wasn't going to wait on me? Making me wait on him is only going to piss me off. I enjoy my days off just like everyone else around here, and I don't appreciate—

"Shane." Roxanne stops my thoughts, making my eyes glance in her direction. She's standing, rocking on her heels, just inside the entrance to where the registration desk is. "It was me. I asked you to come down."

"What the...?" Jesus Christ. I don't need this. Not today.

For the last two weeks, since the night she blew up on me in the hallway between our two apartments, I've been professional. I've been cordial. I haven't been personable or friendly. She lost those two things when she thought she was going to shove her tongue down my throat.

"Just hear me out. Please." She motions for me to come through the door leading away from the waiting room area.

Against my better judgment, I go, hoping I won't regret it later. She sees I have Emersyn with me, and this is our place of employment, so surely, she wouldn't try anything inappropriate. *She better not.*

"Make it quick," I say, following her to the dictation room.

Before entering, I place Emersyn down into the plastic chair just outside the small room, handing her my cell phone to keep her entertained while I talk. There's a coloring app she likes on there. It'll keep her busy for at least ten minutes. I don't plan on being here any longer than that.

I hope Roxanne heard the seriousness in my voice when I said she better spit out whatever it is she wants.

"It's about Whitney's husband." My jaw locks. One, I still hate hearing that term used. I fucking hate it. And two, what do Whitney or Blake, or anyone concerning me, have to do with her?

"What about him?"

"He approached me a couple of weeks ago before she got her memory back. Before you and I had that fight in the hallway. He asked me to help him split the two of you up." Her cheeks flush, and she bites her lower lip, looking away from me for a split second before returning her green eyes to mine. "I wanted to. At first, I thought it was a brilliant idea. She would leave and go back to him. I would get you." She shakes her head. "Stupid, I know."

I don't say anything. I can't. Frankly, I don't know what to say to that. I shouldn't be surprised he'd try to get help to break us apart. We're stronger together. I see that now. I've always had this image of Whitney as strong, independent, and fierce. Not that she wasn't. But until she returned, and knowing what other people were able to convince her of, I didn't realize we gave each other strength. We gave each other courage. We're each other's rock.

"He's not right in the head, Shane. He's obsessed with her." This I already know. "He'll stop at nothing to get her back. Nothing, Shane. He wants to do something. Hurt your daughter, I think." My breathing stops. "I didn't want to become a doctor to hurt kids. I love kids. I would never deliberately cause any child harm. Not ever. I refused to help him with any plan. But Shane, someone's got to do something about him. He's crazy. I'm worried he really is going to try to hurt your kid. Hell, he may even try to hurt his child if it gets him Whitney back."

"Why..." Is he that fucked up in the head? "Why do you think he'd hurt one of the girls?"

"I asked him how I could help. I said I'd do anything if it got me you. But I thought he'd ask me to help it look like we"—she points between the two of us—"you know. That we slept together or something like that. Don't." She holds up her hand as if she thinks I'm going to say something. I wasn't, but I don't correct her. "I know how messed up that was. My sister made me see the light."

"You still haven't said why you think he wants to harm one of my kids." Her eyes grow, catching the fact that I consider them both mine. I do. There's no point in pretending I don't.

"He said something that made the alarm bells in my head go off. He said he just needed to get rid of Everly and things could go back to the way they were supposed to be."

Fury boils beneath my skin, the heat intensifying as it courses through my veins at the mere thought of someone thinking of doing harm to her.

"I freaked out and told him I wanted no part. I didn't wait for him to explain or change my mind. I hightailed it out of there. And shit." Her head falls back onto her shoulders. "I should have told you this before now. I just didn't want to overreact, and you think I was crazy. Well, crazier than you already do anyway."

I back out of the room, turning and dropping to my knees, next to where Emersyn is. "Monkey, I need my phone for a sec."

She hands it over without so much as a fight or a whine.

I locate the tracking app as quickly as I can. Within seconds the app pinpoints Everly's phone location. Chills crawl up my arms. She's not at school, which isn't that alarming. Whitney could have gotten done with her doctor's appointment and errands before school let out. She might have picked her up early. But she isn't at home. She isn't in the city. She, or at least her cell phone, is in another town.

I don't know what to do. What the fuck do I do? Panic sets in. There's no stopping it.

"Em, we gotta go."

"Shane, what is it?"

"She isn't where she's supposed to be. I gotta go. I have to call Whit, and I just gotta go."

"Why don't you leave her with me?" She nods to where Emersyn is still seated. "Maybe it's nothing, but she'll just slow you down. Leave her here. I swear I'll take care of her."

"Go find Gavin. Tell him what's up and ask him to take her home or see if Maria will come get her. Okay?"

"Sure. Just go."

"Monk, this is Roxanne. She lives across the hall. You know that, right?"

"Uh-huh."

"I have to run an errand, and I'll be right back. You're going to stay with Miss Roxanne, and she's going to take you to my friend Gavin until I can get back. Okay?"

"Does she have coloring on her phone?"

"I do," Roxanne says before I can speak. "Go." She juts her head to the side.

Fuck.

I kiss Emersyn on the forehead real fast, and I jet out of the hospital hoping and praying nothing is wrong. I just got her. I can't lose her. Not now.

Please...

CHAPTER 34

WHITNEY

I stand outside the building of the address he sent me in the text message. *The Landmark Group* is etched in the glass door in front of me. That's the name of the investment banking company my soon-to-be ex-husband works for. His father's company. But this can't be right. They don't have a branch here. They only have two locations. One is in downtown Memphis, and the headquarters is in Nashville.

Blake mentioned his father wanted to open a third location, but the talk was always Dallas, Texas, not one town over. I'd remember something like that. Maybe Dallas fell through? Where did this come from? And when? I've only been gone from his life for six weeks. Well, gone as much as I can be anyway. We'll unfortunately always be connected because of Emersyn.

Raising my cell phone to my ear, I call his phone once again. And again there's no answer.

What the hell is he playing at?

What stupid point is he trying to make?

I pull on the heavy steel door handle. It opens, but all is dark inside. I can still see, but there aren't any lights on. It's not open for business, that's clear.

"Blake," I call out, hearing my voice echo in the emptiness. I pause a moment to take in the construction. There's plastic everywhere, covering the concrete flooring and what I presume will be a large welcome desk in the center of the lobby. The smell of fresh paint wafts up my nose, making the bridge crinkle at the pungent aroma. "Everly," I say louder.

Where is my daughter?

I'm hit again with silence.

"Blake!" I bark. "Dammit, where is she? This isn't funny."

I turn in a circle, my eyes scanning every nook and cranny before the sense of being watched creeps up my spine. But from where? There's a glass elevator to my left. Looking right, I see a wide set of steel stairs. My eyes glide up, taking in the offices above me that are encased in more glass. The walkways and railing are all hard steel, and I can see everything. The flooring above me has an industrial feel. Nothing about this place says banking. At least not to me.

When I get to the third floor, I see *him.*

He's dressed in his usual: black suit, white dress shirt, and silk tie. His jacket is unbuttoned and opened with his hands positioned on his hips as he stares down at me. I see that wicked gleam in his eyes, but anger engulfs me so quickly I don't have time to think about it.

How dare he? How dare he think he can get away with this? Whatever the fuck this is. He's gone too far. He has to realize this isn't okay.

I dart right, taking the stairs two at a time. Adrenaline propels me upward. My legs are quickly tiring. I haven't run in years, and the burn in my calves lets me know how out of shape I am, but determination won't allow me to slow down. I'll get to my child, and he'll be lucky I don't push him over the railing before I leave with her.

He watches every step I make, not moving from his position behind the glass wall. I still haven't seen—I stop just before the last step. Everly. That's when I see her sitting off to his right. She looks so small sitting in one of the chairs at a vast, empty table. Conference room? Maybe. Probably. Her backpack is in front of her on top of the table, which is also glass. She's hugging the material, scared, I imagine.

There are two entrances leading into the room. I take the one closest to me—closest to my daughter.

Up here, there is no plastic covering anything. No dust. Everything

I'm seeing is already finished and cleaned as though the construction is being completed from top to bottom.

"What do you think you're doing?" I ask, not looking at him as I step toward my daughter. "Are you okay?" I wrap my hand around her head, gently pulling her into my chest as I meet his eyes from where he's standing.

"Step away from her." His body twists around, facing us. I glare, getting angrier by the second.

"You don't get to tell me what to do. Or her." I squeeze Everly tighter. "I'm here to get my daughter. We're leaving. When I get home, you better bet—"

"I thought I told you to bring my daughter with you. Where is Emersyn?" he demands, seething as his nostril flare.

"Not here. And I'm pretty sure I just told you I don't take orders from you." I drop my hands and take a step backward, giving Everly room to get up. "Let's go, Ev."

"I don't think so, wife."

I ignore the "wife" term used to refer to me, not wanting to drag Everly into more drama than he already has. There's no telling what's going through her head. It hasn't been that long since she learned he wasn't her father. I still haven't explained why that is. She's ten. What am I supposed to tell her? Eventually, I will. When she's older. When she doesn't still have her innocence of the evil that plagues our world still intact, I'll tell her everything. *That innocence is probably waning at this very moment.*

"I do think so. Pull this shit again, and I'll—"

My body steps sideways at the same moment Everly gasps for breath as I try to block her from his view.

"You'll what?" The small gun he pulled from the pocket of his slacks rises in the air, pointing in our direction. "Give me your phone." My cell phone is still clutched in my hand. "Place it on the table and slide it this way." When I don't do it or say anything, he yells, "Do it now!"

I quickly comply. "Blake? What do you—"

"Shut up. When I want something out of your mouth, I'll tell you when you can speak."

He steps toward the table, the gun trained on me—or us. He picks my phone up without taking his hateful eyes off me as he turns it off.

Why didn't I tell Shane? Or fuck, call the police. Why the hell didn't I? He did kidnap my daughter, after all. That's a crime.

God, this is bad.

He's lost his mind.

What do I do? I have to do something. I have to protect my child.

"Get over here." He flicks the gun, motioning for me to come toward him. I don't. I'm not stepping away from shielding Everly. I can't. "Don't make me tell you again."

"What do you want, Blake?"

"I. Just. Told. You. Now get your ass over here."

"I'm not leaving my daughter." Everly wraps her arms around my middle, squeezing. "Blake, put the gun down. You're scaring her."

"*Her?*" he snarls. "She ruined everything." His words startle her. I feel her body jump slightly against my back.

How do I get us out of this? Think, Whitney. Do something. You have to do something. But what? He has a gun. What if it's loaded? Blake hates guns. Always has. So maybe it's possible that it's not loaded.

"No," his words draw out in a whisper, as if they're meant for his ears only. "This is more your fault than hers, isn't it? They promised me you. And you violated what was supposed to be mine when you screwed him, producing her."

What the fuck is he talking about? I was promised to him? What in God's name does that even mean?

"Let her leave, Blake. She's scared. This is about me, right? Not about her, so let her go," I plead. God, please let her leave. But where is she going to go? No one knows we're here.

His eyes squint before he huffs frustration, then steps forward. Before I can make any move, my cell phone slips from his fingers, then he grabs my forearms, yanking me into his chest and away from Everly.

"No!" I yell, attempting to push him off so I can get back to her.

"Momma," she calls out, but I can't look at her in fear that taking my eyes off Blake could... *No no no. I can't think that.* I can get him to stop this madness. He wants me. I'm his end game, right?

"I said come here. Dammit, you come here."

I shove as hard as I can. "Get off." My body shakes with fear for my daughter's life, but I'm momentarily blinded when pain slices through the side of my head. Fuck, that hurts. My hand releases him to reach up to my skull. To the pain stinging the side of my head.

"No! Leave her alone," Everly yells.

The gun. He hit me with the side of the gun. At least he didn't pull the trigger. At least his attention is on me.

I blink rapidly, seeing him waving his arm wildly in her direction. "She's not leaving here. Neither are you."

Cupping my head, I look over at my daughter. The sullen demeanor that's been gone for weeks is suddenly marring her beautiful face again. If looks could kill, the one she is giving him certainly would.

It breaks my heart knowing I'm the one who allowed Blake's disdain for her to go on for so long. Even though I didn't know he wasn't her father, I shouldn't have put up with it. I should have left. I knew when I was pregnant with her that I didn't love him.

"Now, where were we?" He's still holding the gun, his arm outstretched toward my baby girl. "Sit your ass on the table behind you. We're going to have a little family discussion."

I take one step back, my butt hitting the hard edge of the glass, but instead of sitting on top of it, I perch myself against it. He says nothing, so neither do I. My mind is racing with a million things at once. I have to get him to point the gun at me. Not her. He's so angry he could accidentally pull the trigger. I can't let that happen. I'm responsible for her protection.

"Blake, please just stop pointing the gun at her. Point it at me. You're mad at me, not her."

"You're right, wifey. I am." The gun slowly moves. Relief floods me, even though now I'm in danger of him shooting me, either on purpose or by accident.

"No." Everly scream-cries. "Don't hurt my mom."

"Shut up, you little brat." His eyes cut to her just for a second, and I see the devil. I see the evil coursing through him. How have I never seen it before? He did, after all, play a huge part in convincing me I was someone I wasn't. Only someone with evil intentions would do that. My parents.

His parents. The doctors. Who else had a part in keeping me from the life I should have had?

"Blake. Honey." I call, trying to get his attention solely on me. Maybe she can run out of here.

"Don't fucking *honey* me. Remember, I know your memory is back, Whitney. Heard it loud and clear when you told the judge what a sick fuck I was to do what I did. You. Were. Promised. To. Me. You're mine. And I'm a sick fuck?"

"I shouldn't have said that." Is that what set him off? Were my words to the judge what caused this? "I'm sorry, Blake. Please let—"

"Stop. Talking." He breathes in deep.

"How did you get a different judge anyway? Your golden boy, the good doctor, is too good to blackmail a judge. I'm not, though. So." His head cocks to the side. "How did you get a different judge to preside over the hearing? You don't have any money. I made sure you had to depend on me all these years. So how?"

"You blackmailed the other judge?" Shane mentioned Jacob thought something fishy had to have happened for him to be awarded joint custody.

"You know, wife, it's a wonder what some people—influential people—keep in safety deposit boxes. They think they're burying their dirty little secrets and no one would be able to touch them. I can, though. And it just so happens our judge has a box at my bank in town. And he didn't want messy things leaked to the public. He was very happy to help me." His smile is sickening, making my stomach roll. "Many people have secrets they think they can keep hidden. Not from me. Not when they pay me to house their dirty laundry. Doctors. Lawyers. Judges. And not just people in Memphis. People from all over the United States. And you, of all people, should be grateful. It's how we got Emersyn, after all."

My spine straightens.

"What are you talking about?"

"You and your damn birth control. So thorough. I had to feed you fake pills for nearly a year before you became pregnant with her." I gasp, shocked. I have no words. My birth control didn't fail like I thought. He planned it. He made it happen. And I let him. I've let him pick up my prescriptions all these years. "This time, though, when we have our next child, there's no need for secrets. No need for you to continue taking those fake pills you've been on."

My eyes widen. He was trying again. Holy hell, that's why I got—

Fuck. Fuck. Fuck. I'd completely forgotten about my doctor's visit a few hours ago. The positive result.

I have to do something. He's crazy. Crazy people do stupid things. He's talking about when we have another child like I'm going to go back to him.

He's going to do something bad. I feel it. I feel it in my soul. And I can't allow him to hurt my daughter that's already here, breathing, alive, and scared, only a few feet away from me.

She has to be my number one priority. I can't think about anything else—or anyone else. Not until she's safe.

I react, doing the only thing I can think of that might get her out of this unharmed and away from him. I have to do something. Surely anything is better than doing nothing at all. Something has snapped inside of him, and there is no talking my way out of this situation. I'm just praying she'll be okay after this.

"Run, Everly!"

I don't look at her. Instead, I leap forward, pushing and knocking Blake backward as hard as I can while trying to reach for the weapon. His back hits the glass wall behind him. The gun goes off. Loaded. It was loaded. I stumble, falling onto him, my ear ringing.

No. Nooooo. *Everly.*

I push up, trying to see where she is. But I don't see her. She isn't in the spot she was before. I look out the entrance, still seeing nothing.

"You bitch."

A sting to my face both stuns me and makes me fall off him, to the side, landing on the carpeted floor.

He slapped me.

Please get to safety, Ev. Please, God, get her to safety.

That's all that matters. If this is it, if he shoots me and I die, all that matters is that she gets to safety.

CHAPTER 35

SHANE

My tires screech as my Tahoe comes to an abrupt stop behind Whitney's car. She hasn't answered her phone once in the dozen times I've hit redial.

My mother's feeling from the week before last comes crashing into me. *I have a bad feeling is what. I had this same feeling before my best friend took her life, Shane. It's not a good feeling, and I thought back then if I had done something, then maybe Lynn would still be here.*

I have a bad feeling too. I'm just praying I'm wrong. I'm praying there is a logical explanation for them being here. For Whitney not answering her phone. But then Roxanne's words come to mind. *He's not right in the head, Shane. He's obsessed with her. He'll stop at nothing to get her back. Nothing, Shane.*

That was after she told me Blake approached her to help him split us up. When she admitted she liked the idea at first, I could tell it embarrassed her to have to tell me, but she did it anyway.

But when she told me he planned to hurt Everly, I nearly lost it. And when I brought up the GPS tracking app I have on Everly's phone and saw she wasn't at school, I almost choked. My heart feared every worst thing a parent can feel when they don't know where their child is.

Thank fuck she kept Emersyn. I rushed out of the hospital so quickly

I couldn't explain to her why. I trust Roxanne when she said she would never hurt a kid. She'll take her to Gavin, and he'll take her home with him until I can figure out what's going on—and if my other girls are safe. *God, please let them be safe.*

The street is empty of people. It's late afternoon, but this block is mostly vacant except for a few cars. The buildings look new.

When I come to the glass door next to where Whitney's car is parked next to the curb, I read the name of the business. Chills crawl up my neck. That's the company Blake works for.

I don't have time to think. I dial 911 on my phone as quickly as my fingers will type the digits in.

"911, what's your emergency?"

"I need a police officer to come to my location. My girlfriend and daughter are missing and—"

My body flinches, hearing a loud pop from somewhere above me. A gunshot, I think. My head snaps up at the building in front of me. It came from in there. The pressure inside my chest mounts, building up. It's heavy. It's agony. *They have to be okay.* I won't be able to breathe without them. I can't do loss again.

I drop my cell, yanking on the door handle and rushing inside. I scan all around. There's nothing in here but dust, darkness, and sheets of clear plastic.

Movement to my right catches my attention, putting me on alert. My head snaps to a set of stairs. Relief floods through me when I see Everly running down them. My feet propel toward her, meeting her just as she's about to step off the last stair.

"Daddy." I grab her, pulling her into my arms, lifting her off the floor.

"Are you okay?" I set her down, pulling back to scan her from top to bottom. She nods, but there are tears coming down her cheeks, one right after another.

"Everly." I hear the panic in Whitney's voice. My eyes shoot up.

"Get outside now. My truck is unlocked. Get in and lock the doors."

"But Momma," she squeaks.

I look back down. "Go, Ev." I pull her back to where I came inside, pushing her out the door and into the daylight. "Get in the truck." I step backward. "Lock the doors."

Turning, I look up again, this time seeing bodies on the third floor as I run toward the stairs, taking them as fast as I can with only two thoughts going through my head: that motherfucker has a gun, and my woman is up there.

When I get to the third level, I jet inside the office space I saw them in. Blake is just getting to his feet, and Whit is lying on her side on the floor. And he has a gun, pointing it down at her.

"You stupid, stupid bitch!" he screams. His eyes never leave hers, and I realize he hasn't seen me yet.

I tackle him from the side, forcing him away from her. The gun goes off again. My ears can only process the ringing the blast caused. I don't know what direction the bullet went or if it hit something or someone. If it hit Whitney... *Fuck, no.* I didn't think. Not really. I was only trying to get him and that weapon away from her.

I crash into Blake, sending him into a glass wall, shattering it with the impact of our bodies.

"Shane." Whitney sounds panicked, but just the sound of her voice lightens me, telling me she's okay. I don't dare look at her, though. Taking my eyes off a madman would be stupid and dangerous to us both.

He starts moving under me, shoving, twisting.

"You have to die," he grunts.

"Shane, get away from him. Please," she begs. "He's crazy. He's lost his mind."

"Get out of here," I yell, pushing him back down. He kicks, bending my leg and making me lose my balance. I fall, landing on my hip. "Fuck."

"No, fuck you." He gets to his knees, blood dripping down his cheek.

"Whit. Leave. Go find Ev."

I push off the ground at the same time he does. He's not looking at me. My guess is he's looking at Whitney. I see the obsession in his eyes. I've loved Whitney for so long, at times it felt like an obsession. An all-consuming feeling where only she mattered. But this obsession he has isn't like that. Not at all. He only cares about what he wants. I've always cared. I've always loved her more than I love myself. The same way I now love my girls more than my own life. I'd do anything for them.

He'd do anything for himself.

How does he not see me?

"No. You aren't leaving, wife," he spits out. A small stream of blood trails from his lip and down his chin. "You're staying right here. With me." His arm slowly rises. "You won't be his. I won't allow it. You are mine fore—"

I move fast. My hands reach out, one grabbing his wrist and pushing down while the other turns his face to me. Surprise sparks his eyes, but only for a moment. I slam the back of his head into the doorjamb behind him. Anger quickly returns, and he headbutts me, thrusting my head backward and blinding me.

Fuck. The pain that radiates through me is squashed and replaced with something else when Whitney screams. I can't let him hurt her. I won't.

Shaking it off, I see through a haze his arm lifting. Without thought, I shove him out the door, getting him away from Whitney. I push again as my forehead throbs.

Blinking, my vision has finally fully returned, and I'm able to look him in the eye. I'm expecting to see hatred, but in its place is fear. What the...?

When I realize what's about to happen, I jump forward, leaping to the railing to grab him, to grab onto something to keep him from falling. But I'm not quick enough. He goes over the railing, his suit jacket sliding through my fingers. I'm not able to stop it from happening.

My stomach pushes against the hard steel of the railing. My head turns to the side, wincing when his body hits the concrete with a thud. All the air leaves my lungs in a gush.

Deep down, I know there is no way he survived that fall. But the physician in me urges me to make sure—to see if I can save him. He doesn't deserve it, but that's never been my call to make. My job is to save lives, not be the decider on who deserves life or not. I'm supposed to do anything within my power to give people another chance.

"Oh my..." Whitney steps up next to me, looking over. "Fuck. Is he...?"

"Go," I whisper. "Go check on Everly. She's supposed to be in the truck."

She doesn't say yes. She doesn't tell me she heard me. But she takes off running down the stairs. Seconds later, I'm doing the same, but for a different reason.

A part of me doesn't want him to be okay. Doesn't want him to be alive. And I curse myself on the inside for those thoughts. What does that say about the doctor I'm supposed to be?

CHAPTER 36

WHITNEY

When I raced outside, I saw blue lights all around, but I couldn't comprehend they were police officers. Seeing Blake go over that railing and then trying to find Everly, consumed my every thought. My thoughts were like a ping-pong ball bouncing back and forth.

Everly. Blake.

Where is she? Is he dead?

Everly. Blake.

How is all this going to scar her? How did he become that person?

My baby girl. A man that should have never been my husband.

"Ma'am," someone, a man, had called out.

"Ev. Everly." I looked all around, finally spotting Shane's Tahoe.

"Ma'am." I ignored him again, running toward the vehicle.

"Mom." Her voice made me stop a few feet from being able to snatch the door open. She wasn't inside. The sound of her voice was somewhere else, so I looked in the direction I thought I heard it. I looked left, across the street, spotting her sitting on a curb in front of a police cruiser.

"Ma'am, please stop. I need—"

I took off, running toward her.

"Sweetheart, are you okay?" I pulled her to her feet and clutched her to my chest. I was finally able to breathe again. She was okay. At least physically, she was okay, and that was enough for now.

That was two hours ago. Two hours that I've been able to take air into my lungs. Two hours that I've felt relief like nothing I've ever experienced before in my life. Not even the moment my memories returned did I feel this settled.

Blake's gone. He's dead. The father of one of my children died today, and I feel settled. What the fuck kind of fuckedupness is that? I don't voice any of this though. No, I keep all that inside.

"Buckle up, Ev," I tell her when we all slide inside Shane's Tahoe with me in the driver's seat, Shane in the passenger, and Everly safely in the back. Both are quiet. Shane is the quietest of us all. He's thinking. I can tell he keeps getting caught up inside his head.

We were questioned at the scene of the accident. *Accident, my ass.* Sure, Shane never meant to push Blake over that railing. That part was an accident, but the whole thing wasn't an accident. Blake planned it. I don't know what he thought the outcome was going to be, but he planned it. It was no accident. He's dead now because of his own selfish reasons. He did this.

I called Jacob, not knowing who else to call. He called Shawn, who was closer. Shawn met us at the bank, and Jacob arrived just as we got to the police station to give our statements about what happened.

Jacob says there will be an investigation into everything that happened. Protocol, he said. He also said not to worry. It's mostly over, and he'd deal with anything else that comes along. I'll probably be questioned again. He told me this, but I also figured as much. We'll all have to relive today's events at some point. But for now, it's over.

I'm taking us home. Shawn is going to follow. He wanted Shane to ride with him. Said we could all fit in his truck and he'd come back for our vehicles later, but I wanted to drive us. Driving helps me think. It'll help clear my head by the time we get back to the apartment. At least I hope so.

I shove the keys in the ignition and crank the engine. When I go to sit the bottle of water Shawn bought me into the cup holder, it won't go in, making me look down to see what's blocking the hole.

It's darker now. Dusk is upon us, so the inside of the truck is too dark. I reach in, pulling out a small box. It's velvet. I know this from the feel of it before I pull it up. It's unmistakable. It's a ring box. I open it before I realize I'm doing so. My eyes grow wide with shock. My mind sparks, and my chest swells.

It's a ring.

It's an engagement ring.

I don't have to be told that to know that's exactly what this is. I promptly sit it back down, not closing the lid like I should. I pull my hand back, still looking down at the diamond that sits nestled in the jewelry box. It's an oval cut with small diamonds around the band. I can't see beyond what's visible, so I don't know if the diamonds go completely around the brand.

Shit, that's pretty. That's freakin' gorgeous.

Oh my God! Another realization dawns. He was going to ask...

Fuck.

Focus, dammit.

I glance down at the open ring box again. *Stop it!*

I look over. Shane's head is resting on the headrest, and he's looking up. Eyes open. He's freaking out inside his head. I know he is. I see it. He saved us, yet a person is dead. This is going to eat him alive.

I look in the rearview mirror. Everly is biting her nails. She must be wigging out too.

Hell, I'm freaking out now too, but not because someone died. I'm freaking out because the man next to me wants to marry me.

Emersyn.

The thought pops up. Where's Em? Panic bubbles up my throat. Where the hell is Emersyn?

"Shane? Babe, where's Em?" I touch his forearm where it's resting on the console.

"Rox has her."

Rox? Who the fu—

"Roxanne, your neighbor? Roxanne that wants you? That Roxanne has my daughter!?"

Ah, fuck. I'm screaming at him, and I can't stop myself. *Roxfuckinganne?*

I just dealt with a crazy psycho. I can't deal with another.

"She's fine," he assures me. "I'll explain later. I can't... think." He sits up, abruptly taking his head off the headrest, and starts looking around, searching for something. "My phone! Where's my phone?"

"Here." Reaching behind the center console, I grab my purse.

One of the police officers found his phone on the ground earlier. They asked if it was mine when we were at the police station. It wasn't, but I took it, knowing it was Shane's. I pull it out it, handing it to him.

"I told her to take Em to Gavin's. I'll call him."

Relief doesn't come until he's spoken to his boss and confirmed he does in fact have Emersyn.

Thank God.

"He's going to bring her home. He'll meet us there," he tells me when he puts his phone down. His eyes stay cast down. When I look where he's looking, I see his eyes are on the opened ring box. "You saw it."

It's not a question. He knows I did.

I grab his hand, entwining our fingers, and I lean over. He looks at me, then my lips meet his. It's not a passionate kiss. It's not sexy or erotic. It's just a kiss. But it's a kiss that tells him everything he needs to know at this moment.

It says we're here together, forever.

I just have to figure out a way to get him past what happened today. To get our family past today's stupid, tragic events. But first I have to confront the people that put all this in motion to begin with.

Mommy and Daddy, I hope you're ready for me, because I'm bringing a shitstorm to your door very, very soon.

GAVIN WAS WAITING IN THE parking lot when we arrived home last night. Seeing her unharmed and as the same bubbly three-year-old she always is, killed the panic I felt when Shane told me he left her with that bitch. Maybe I shouldn't be so harsh, but she didn't care that his heart belonged to someone else when she kissed him.

Shane told me about his conversation with Roxanne. The one that prompted him to locate Everly's cell phone via GPS when he couldn't reach me.

If he hadn't bought that phone for her, I don't know if she or I would be standing here today.

I hadn't said one word to him until yesterday because of that phone. What a bitch I was. I was a fucking child who treated him like shit. That could've easily been the last thing I'd done. I could have really died this time, and he probably would have questioned my love. That thought sickens me. I don't want him to ever doubt the way I feel about him.

And he was going to ask me to marry him despite it all. God, I don't deserve this man I love with all my heart.

The same thoughts continue repeating in my head. Shane saved us. Yet he can't get past the fact that a man is dead. A man I've told him over and over in the last twenty-four hours deserved everything that happened to him. I wish it hadn't happened at our expense, but it did.

I pick my glass up, knocking the finger of whiskey back in one swallow.

Shane isn't the only one eaten up with guilt. So many emotions are rolling through me, and I'm trying to be strong, but fuck, it's hard.

All I want is to take the damage from yesterday and flush it down the toilet. What Everly saw yesterday can never be unseen. Shane may never get past someone's life ending because of a push from his hand. It doesn't matter that all this is Blake's fault. I can't flush any of this away. And I don't know how to make this situation better for my family. I don't know how to take Shane's guilt away. Guilt that should have never pierced his soul.

What if the permanent damage Blake has caused the people I love is too great? What if Shane can't get past it? He's in his last year of residency. He has six months left. He has to prepare for his board exams. He doesn't need this in his life.

My stupid head keeps telling me he doesn't need me in his life. My heart fights like it should. Like I need it to. I'm not weak. I tried to force myself to be weak when I didn't know who I was, but that person kept trying to get back up. That person was fighting to come back, I just didn't allow myself to embrace it. I allowed my parents and Blake to fill me with lie after lie.

I pick up the bottle on the counter, pouring more liquid into my glass.

I fill the glass, pouring a lot more into it than I should, and then I take it to the table.

I want to cry. I want to scream. I want to hurt someone for causing the people I love most so much pain. For causing me all this agony.

I want to give up too. The pressure in my chest is so great. The agony that consumes my head is too much to bear.

You'd think with Blake dead, life would feel easier. There's no one I have to share Emersyn with. No more taking her to her father every other weekend. No more excessive texts. I don't even have to wait for my divorce now. He's gone. Actually, I'm a widow.

But everything he left in his wake... What the hell am I going to do with it? I keep coming back to *how do I fix this mess?* And my problem is I don't know how. It's making me question too many things. It's making me feel undeserving when I know in my heart Shane and I are meant to be together forever. He's my foreverly after too.

I'm about to drink from my glass when I cringe, remembering the doctor's words from yesterday. *It's positive.* Shit. Fuck. Damn. Motherfucking son of a bitch, no, I didn't...

I sigh in frustration, mad at myself. Not only did I forget about being pregnant, but I also drank alcohol. Not much, just an ounce, but I still... I shake my head. *Seriously, Whitney.* Who the hell forgets they're pregnant?

I haven't even told Shane about the baby. Nor have I told him what Blake divulged yesterday about Emersyn and my birth control pills that weren't real.

I don't want to put too much on him. I just want to ease his pain, his guilt. I want to take it in my hands and squeeze the life out of it.

I sit the glass on the table, pushing it away from me, disgusted.

"What the hell, Whitney?" I look over to see Shawn stomping toward me with his arms crossed.

I think the feeling of wanting to cry outweighs everything. I push what I've just done to the back of my mind and focus my thoughts on Shane.

A tear drops, making me feel weak when I just want to be strong. I don't know how to fix Shane, and that is crushing my heart. Or maybe it's ripping it open. I don't know.

He grabs me, wrapping his hands around my biceps and hauling me up onto my feet, bringing me inches from his chest.

"Get your shit together!" Shawn yells in my face, making me rear my head back as far as possible after being hit with spittle. "He killed a man. Whatever you're feeling right now... Guilt? Loss? I don't know. Get over it. He. Killed. Someone. What's going through his mind is a hundred times worse than what's going through yours."

Does he think I don't know this? Really? What the fuck?

"I was a bitch. A stupid, stupid bitch to him. And Shane? Shane was going to propose anyway?"

"Of course he was. He loves you, woman. He's always loved you, and only you. And from what I remember and from what I've heard, you were a bitch in high school, but he still wanted you—still loved you despite all that. Some guys like that, the same way some girls like major dicks. Case in point." He points to the center of his chest.

"I don't think you're a dick." I sniffle, then wipe my nose with the back of my hand. Okay, maybe he is being somewhat of an insensitive dick, but I know he's just worried about his brother. I get it.

"Give it a few months. You haven't seen all my colors yet. And I've been on the best behavior of my life lately."

"Thanks, Shawn."

Some of the weight eases off my chest. He's right. He's so fucking right. Shane does love me for me. I know this. Shane's told me this countless times.

"For what?"

"Reeling me in. Getting me out of my head."

"Look, you gotta accept he loves you for you and nothing more and nothing less. Then, wherever that strong bitch-girl is, bring her out and go fix my brother. He needs you right now. And I need you to take care of him and make whatever demons crawling around in his head disappear."

I want to. I want to do that so badly. But can I?

Images of my parents flicker through my mind, hardening my chest. I need to face them before I attempt to fix my man. I have to fix the *me* they damaged first.

"I will." I finally say. "I will do everything in my power to help get him past this. But first, I have to do something for myself. You're staying here, right?"

"I can."

"Stay. I need to go see the bastard assholes that fucked with my life. Okay?"

He's silent. He's thinking. And then he nods his understanding of what it is I need to do. I don't know how he could understand, but I'm grateful he does. He has wonderful parents.

I bypass him, then stop, turning around. "Hey."

He picks up my glass, bringing it to his lips. "Yeah?" he asks over the rim.

"Maybe take your own advice," I offer.

He tosses the whiskey down his throat. "Meaning what?" He places the glass back on the table.

"She loves you for you too, you know. Truly loves you for the man you are."

I believe that too. I think he and Taralynn are meant for each other the same way I know Shane and I are.

He doesn't say anything. He doesn't nod or address it at all. Instead, he takes the glass to the counter, and I watch him bring a second glass down from the cabinet. He's going to make Shane one. I know it. And I'm okay with it. Shane needs something until I can get back.

"My parents said the girls can stay with them for as long as you need," he says with his back facing me.

I'm grateful for them. I really am, but as soon as I make Shane believe what happened, happened for a reason, then we're going to get our kids and we're starting our family. *The five of us.*

DO I KNOCK?

Or do I walk right through?

I don't feel like knocking. I don't want to treat them with respect. They didn't respect me. They didn't treat me like a human. They made me their puppet. But why? It's the one piece I do not understand. I don't believe it was because they didn't like Shane. They didn't know him.

I reach for the knob but stop. Looking at the brass door handle, my hand pauses midair. After a beat, it falls, and I let out a sigh.

I am going to be strong. I am going to be what my family needs. And they need me to be an adult. They don't need me barging in, even if it is what I want to do.

I knock, and then I wait.

Within seconds the door pulls open. Surprise crosses my mother's face. "I wasn't expecting you, Whitney."

"Is Dad home too?"

"Yes. He's getting ready to leave, though. For a business trip," she clarifies, waving her hand as she turns, leaving me on the doorstep. "It's awfully late, dear."

If I'd come this morning, she'd be telling me it was *awfully early*.

I step over the threshold, following her through the foyer and then into her sitting room, a.k.a. the living room for normal people.

"Have a seat, I'll fetch Martin."

She turns, leaving to find my dad the same at time my cell phone sounds off with an incoming text message. I take it out of my back pocket, then perch my butt on the edge of the couch arm.

SHAWN

> New plan. Taking him to my house. Go there after you tell off the fucks you call parents.

> Don't get him too drunk.

I have things I need to tell him.

The palm of my free hand goes to my belly. *I'm pregnant.* The shock is still there, but with everything that's happened today, it has been at the furthest section of my mind.

> If that's what he needs, then that's what he's getting.

"Whitney." I look up to see my father strolling in. He has a bag on wheels he parks next to the wide entryway. "What brings you here unexpectedly?" He walks up to me, stopping in front to kiss my forehead. I allow him, knowing there's a huge chance I'll leave here never speaking to my parents again.

"Blake's dead." There's no sense in sugarcoating it. Might as well rip the Band-Aid clean off.

"What?" My mother gasps for breath.

My dad takes a step backward, away from me, but says nothing.

"Blake's gone?" My mother's hand covers her mouth, and tears prickle her lower eyelids while my jaw drops. "The poor Lanes. Their only son. Dear, Jesus. This is..." She leans against the entryway across from us where my dad left his small suitcase. *Business trip, huh?* I want to laugh, but that's not why I'm here.

"He kidnapped Everly from school yesterday. I'm surprised you didn't hear the story on the news."

"Kidnapped?" My father's eyebrows turn in, scrutinizing what I've just told them.

"She's his daughter, Whitney." My mother stands straight, placing her hands on her hips. "If he picked her up from school, it wasn't kidnapping. The poor man hasn't seen her in weeks. You're the one that has kidnapped his children from him."

Wow. Just wow. I 've have nothing for that.

"She is Shane's daughter. She was never Blake's. How could the two of you do what you did? If it wasn't for Shane, she and I could both be dead right now instead of Blake. He had a gun. He was determined to hurt Everly because she wasn't his."

"That boy killed him, didn't he?" Her tone is accusing. How dare she.

"Fuck you. If the two of you hadn't played God with my life, Shane would never have been placed in the situation he was put in last night. He saved us. Which is a hell of a lot more than I can say the two of you have done. This is y'all's doing. Blake is dead because you both fed me lies. You both stole my life and gifted it to a man I didn't love."

"Don't you see why we never wanted you with that boy?"

"You didn't even know *that boy*."

"Christ," my dad blows out. "It was a business transaction, Whitney. Grow up. We gave you a good life with a man from a good family. And in exchange, Blake's father pulled my company out of a financial hole. Without their help, we would have gone bankrupt. You should be grateful instead of sitting there cursing your mother and me like you're doing." He flicks his wrist, looking down at the expensive watch adorning his arm. "I'm going to miss my flight if I don't hurry. Judy, deal with her."

My mother waves her hands like it's nothing at all. Like I'm nothing more than a snag in her pantyhose. I guess if I think about it, that's really all I am to her. That's all I've ever been to her. To both of my parents.

A fucking *business transaction* he called it?

"I need to call the Lanes. Give my condolences. Oh." My mother places her hand on her head. "I just can't believe he's gone. So sad. What am I supposed to say to them, Whitney?"

"How about, go fuck yourselves?"

My dad rushes out, apparently not wanting to face what he's done. And my mom? She's not addressing it either. She's too worried about Blake's parents and what they're going to think.

Like I give a rat's ass. They're probably responsible for making him the psycho he was.

Screw this.

Fuck them.

They'll never be sorry. They'll never regret the pain and years lost they've caused.

My boyfriend. The father of my children. *Children.* Plural. I place my hand against my stomach, remembering my doctor's appointment. I'm pregnant.

Shane is not only just Everly's dad. He's the father of my unborn child too. And he's just as much Emersyn's dad as he is the other two. Blood doesn't make a parent. Blood doesn't make a family. Love makes both of those.

These people aren't my family. And love is nowhere in sight in this house. It never was. It never will be.

"How can you be so crude?"

"How can you be so cold-hearted?"

She just shakes her head, and that's when I stand up. There's no point to this. They don't love each other. My parents never have. Their marriage was one of convenience, so why should I be surprised by any of this?

"Where are you going?"

"Leaving."

"You can't leave. You can't leave me to deal with your mess."

I snort. I mean, what else can I gonna do?

"Forget I'm your daughter. I've already forgotten you're my mother."

And with that, I walk out, knowing this was never my family. Before I reach my car, I take out my cell and type out a message.

> I need you to do something for me. Meet me at Wicked Ink. DON'T TELL SHANE!

> You're gonna have to give me an hour.

> That's fine. It'll take me an hour to get there. Leaving my parents now.

CHAPTER 37

SHANE

Problems don't get solved at the bottom of a bottle. It sometimes takes the edge off, but that's because it muddies your thought process. That's what my brother wanted, though. Shawn thinks I need to stop thinking about it, so he keeps shoving glass after glass in front of me. That's why I came up to his old bedroom at his house in Oxford.

That was two hours ago.

For two hours, I've been lying with my back propped up against the wooden headboard in this room. This small, closed-in room. It's both a reprieve from the sympathetic eyes downstairs, and like a noose, choking me.

Sleep won't come because my brain won't shut off. I used to love the twelve-hour shifts at the hospital. Sometimes even working longer than that. Before I moved to Memphis, I used to moonlight at another hospital so that I wouldn't be alone in my thoughts.

I hate being alone. I hate the silence.

Silence is never that—silent.

Unless I tire my body out completely, my brain never stops.

I need Whitney. *Where is she?*

I thought once she got her memory back, I'd finally be rewarded with peace. I wasn't. Sure, I could breathe again, and the heaviness in my chest was mostly lifted, but peace never came. My mind never slowed down. Instead, it took a sharp turn and continued racing, just with different thoughts.

I had her. There's been no doubt in my mind about that. She is mine—always and forever—heart, body, and soul. All three of them were. Are. Even when she was pissed and wasn't speaking to me, she was still all mine.

But a nagging worry would never ease up. Fear of losing them. Fear of someone stealing them from me. Fear of something just like what happened yesterday gripped me and wouldn't let go. Peace was never granted.

"Hey."

My eyes pop open. I didn't even realize I had closed them.

Looking over at the opened door, I see Whitney standing in the entryway with one hand holding the doorknob and the other raised, but behind the doorframe, out of my view.

"Can I come in?"

"You have to ask that?"

She shakes her head, walking through and closing the door behind her. "No."

"Then why did you?"

Her feet bring her toward me. Her hands are behind her back. "Something to say, I guess."

She stops at the side of the bed. My fingers tingle at her closeness, needing to feel her.

Reaching out, I grip her jean-clad thigh, pulling her onto the bed and then on top of me, straddling my center. She smiles down at me. With my other hand, my palm glides up her knee until I reach the column of her neck. Wrapping my hand around the back, I pull her down until her lips meet mine. I need them. I need to feel them, and I need her taste to filter through me.

She bites down on my lower lip. She always bites my lip when we kiss. And I love it. I'll never get enough of her. It's impossible.

She rears back a couple of inches away from me to look me in the eyes, but I keep my hand firmly wrapped around the back of her neck, keeping her close.

"What happened isn't your fault. You know that, don't you? You know you saved us, right?"

"I don't like that a man died because I pushed him the wrong way. I could have done a number of things, and he'd probably be alive right now."

"Shane, don't—"

I stop her words by pulling her back down and pressing my lips to hers again.

"Let me finish." She rises. My hand releases her but keeps her eyes locked on mine. "Who's to say if he hadn't died, you wouldn't have gotten hurt, or me, Ev, or even all three of us." I sigh and run my hand through my hair. I need to tell her. I need to say it out loud. I need to come to terms with the truth. "I felt relieved too. And I'm conflicted by it. I hate he's dead, but I also feel relief because he's out of our lives. Emersyn never has to go to his house alone again. The worry I felt that somehow I'd lose you all over again—lose all of you—is gone. And that feels good, if I'm honest."

When I ran down those stairs, raced to his body, with the instinct to save him—or try to save him—I dropped to my knees, checking for a pulse, only he didn't have one. All that worry vanished in an instant. That peace I was seeking settled into my bones. Sure, I felt guilty for my part in his life ending, but the peace that settled inside me knowing he no longer had an ounce of power in our lives outweighed that guilt.

And a part of me feels like those feelings are wrong to have.

I shouldn't feel relieved a man is dead. I'm supposed to save lives. Not take them.

"I feel horrible for feeling glad *he's* dead."

"Babe," she sighs, then bites down on her bottom lip.

"That's fucked up, isn't it, Love? That I get enjoyment out of a life ending?"

"It's not enjoyment, Shane." She shakes her head. Then she leans back down where her lips are centimeters from my own. Her forehead presses into mine, and her eyes bore into me. "I thought he was a thorn in our sides. Would always be there, not allowing us the pure happiness we deserve." She just looks at me. "But he wasn't a thorn. He was a knife waiting to gut us. He was a bullet in a chamber waiting to go off and end us." She waits, and I know she wants her words to sink in. They do. "Now he can't hurt us. He can't hurt us ever again. Baby, you didn't kill him. He killed himself. He took our daughter. He was going to hurt her. And I can't even utter the words rolling around in my head that I know deep down he was really going to do." *Kill Everly* is what she can't say. I know this because I can't say them out loud either.

Her lips take mine. Kissing me. She's trying to make me feel her words. Trying to make me take them in as the truth.

I know she is right. I do feel it.

"Love," I start to say, but she shoves her hand between us, over my lips, and then she rises back into a seated position on my lap.

"I have something I need to tell you."

Her smile, a smile that shows excitement and happiness, makes me smile back.

"Yeah?"

"Blake told me things." She lets out a breath. "He told me things before you got there. And..."

Her brows knit together like she's searching for the right words. Her smile confuses me. Why would something he told her make her happy?

"Why are you getting upset?"

I hadn't realized I was. I guess subconsciously, the thought that something he said could cause her joy angered me. "Sorry." It's the only thing I have to offer her.

"Shane?"

"You're happy, and I don't know why. I don't know how you can be happy over anything that man said."

A huff of air exits her mouth. "I'm not happy over what he said. Just give me a sec to explain. I'm happy for another reason, and I know you will be too." She leans down quickly, giving me a reassuring kiss.

"All right, Love. What is it?"

"Emersyn was never planned. I knew I didn't love Blake. I certainly didn't want another kid by him." I cringe at those words. "Hey, I didn't know Everly was yours. But I did know I didn't want another baby. Well, that's not exactly true. The thought of another baby was awesome until I factored Blake in. Anyway, you get my point, right?"

"Yeah, I do."

"Well, Blake wanted a baby. I understand why now. But I wouldn't get off my birth control. Not even when he kept pressuring me to. Apparently he was determined, because he switched my real pills with fake ones somehow. Oh, and he did blackmail that judge to get joint custody of Em, by the way. But that's a topic for later. So, I got pregnant with Emersyn because he made it happen."

What a twisted human being. Who the hell does that? And how?

"I have no words for that, Love. I'm sorry. I'm sorry I didn't try harder. I should have looked for you. I—"

"Stop that," she scolds. "We were dealt a shitty hand. We can't change it. There is no point in regretting what we had no knowledge of. So just stop that thought and let me finish."

"Go on."

"He wanted to do it again. That's what he told me. He was going to get me pregnant again." Bile bubbles up my throat. "But he didn't succeed this time. We found our way back to each other. And you made me remember. You gave me back my past, and because of that, I have the future I was meant to have with you." Her smile is larger than life, making my chest swell.

"I'm pregnant." My breathing stops. "We're pregnant." Whitney grabs my hand, placing it on her stomach. "I'm only a couple of weeks. I found out yesterday when I went to that doctor's appointment."

"You're..." I lose my breath.

"No. We're. We are having a baby. This is our baby. And Shane"—she lets out a big breath—"the pure joy I didn't get to experience when I was pregnant with Everly or Emersyn because of the situation that was forced upon me..." She shakes her head. "I have that. I'm so happy because I'm having your baby. It's a feeling I can't even begin to put words to."

I stare at the place my hand is resting.

She pulls up her shirt, the material sliding through my palms until my skin meets her skin. Her stomach is warm. The way it expands as she breathes...

My eyes shut. Feelings and emotions I can't even process zip through me. Bliss. I think that's what this is.

When I open my eyes, the words fall from my lips, "Marry me, Love." Her eyes sparkle. "You've already seen the ring." I shrug. This was not at all how I'd planned on proposing. "Will you be my wife?"

"Braden," she bends down. "I want foreverly after with you. Yes! I'll marry you."

Screw peace. Peace is overrated. I'm about to marry a woman and have three kids. I doubt peace will ever be in my life. And that's okay. As long as Love is here, that's all I'll ever need.

In a quick move, I rise and flip her onto her back. Her giggle washes over me, awakening my dick in the process.

"I need inside you, Love."

"Then I guess you need to get us out of all these clothes." She looks up at me, showing me the love and lust heating her up on the inside and promising me forever with those eyes.

When I finally slide into her warmth, I feel the shudder that ripples through us both.

We can never get back what was stolen from us, but we can walk into our future, making up for lost time and creating memories that'll last forever.

EPILOGUE

PART 1

SHANE

Maybe all the tragedies in life are meant to get us to the point where everything comes together at the right time. I don't know if destiny is predetermined or if the choices we make daily are what form it. I do know the woman walking toward me was always meant to be mine. My soulmate. My other half. Whatever you want to call it. She is mine.

Seven months ago, a man died. Maybe at my hands, maybe not. Whitney keeps telling me I didn't kill Blake Lane. She calls it a fortunate accident. It's not that she's happy the man she was married to for ten years is dead. He was, after all, the biological father of our middle daughter. Our soon-to-be middle daughter anyway.

"That for me?" I ask.

"Sure isn't for me."

Whitney hands me one of the glass bottles of beer in her hand and leans over me, handing the other one to Shawn before settling herself on my lap.

"Thanks." Shawn tips his head.

"Y'all both did an awesome job moving all the furniture where I wanted it, so I figured it was well deserved."

We bought a house in my parents' neighborhood a few blocks from them and just finished moving in. It took three days. Both my dad and brother helped, but my parents were tired and headed home half an hour ago.

When I finished my residency, I was apprehensive about moving back to my hometown and joining my mother's practice, but now that we're here? This feels right.

"You mean all fifty times I moved this couch? I think I deserve a twelve-pack." Shawn takes a long pull from the bottle.

"You're such a drama queen," Whitney throws at him.

"This is not the face of a drama queen." Shawn points at himself. "This is the face of a scary mofo. Watch yourself."

"Scary?" Everly questions my brother from the other end of the couch, where she's sitting down from him with her Kindle nestled in her lap. Her nose wrinkles as she cocks her head to the side and looks over at him. "Like... funny scary, or are we talking clown scary?"

She's doing great despite everything that happened. We did a few months of counseling for all of us. And I'm hoping I'm not missing anything because it's as though she wasn't affected all that much. She says she understands. We tried explaining—the best we could—why Blake did what he did. But really, what exactly are you supposed to tell a ten-year-old in this circumstance?

"Like mother-lovin' zombie world apocalypse scary. Clown scary? Jesus, girl." Shawn scowls at her. Turning his head, he looks down at Emersyn, shaking his head. She's sitting in her favorite spot—my brother's lap. "Can you believe your sister, Em?"

My brother and Emersyn are inseparable any time they're together. Oddly, it isn't weird.

"Uncle Shawny, you not scary." Her small palms shake his head from side to side. "You pretty!" Emersyn beams. "Like a kitty." She pets his beard, smoothing her hand down only to repeat the motion as if to hammer her point home.

I lose it. Laughter rips from my throat. Whitney and Taralynn follow behind me. Even Everly chuckles. But my brother looks horrified.

"Dude." My brother trains his brown eyes on me. "Your kids are annoying me."

"You're annoying," Everly counters.

"Bad Uncle Shawny." Emersyn shakes her finger in front of him as her head moves with the same motion. "You not make a good daddy talkin' like dat."

She's four now. Her birthday was a few weeks ago, and the baby talk was quickly going away a few months ago until we told the girls that Whitney is pregnant. If anything, it's gotten worse, and she's gotten clingier toward Whitney instead of how she clung to her sister all the time. Jealousy? Maybe. Probably.

"I'm not the one that's gonna be a daddy, sugar. Your dad and mom are the ones having a baby." Shawn's been more forceful about making sure he refers to me as Emersyn's father, more so than anyone else. It doesn't bother me, but I'm not so sure it should be forced upon her. She did, after all, have a father. A psycho twisted fuck, but he was still her father. *But now, I'm her father.* And I always will be, even if she decides not to call me Dad, Daddy, or any word to suggest she sees me as such.

"I know that, funny Uncle Shawny," she giggles. "But Aunt Tarry got a baby in her belly too." Shawn's eyes freeze.

"How did she know that?" Taralynn asks as shock washes over her face.

"We gonna have lots of babies." Emersyn claps her hands.

Maybe I was wrong. Maybe she is excited about getting a little sister.

"You're... pregnant?" Shawn questions his girlfriend. I can't tell if he's shocked, happy, or scared. Maybe a little of all three.

"Yeah," Taralynn sighs. "I was gonna surprise you with it." She sounds disappointed. Her face falls, confirming my thoughts.

"But we're not married."

"Yeah," Love laughs. "Neither are we," she points between the two of us, "but we're having another baby." *Another baby.* I missed my firstborn's birth. And Emersyn isn't really mine, even though I've been given the chance to call her mine. I've missed so much of my daughters' lives. The small things. I won't miss Ella's birth. I won't miss her anything.

I tighten my grip around Whitney's belly, and with my other hand, I sit my beer down on the end table. Then I reach for her wrist, bringing it to my lips to kiss.

They're my world—my whole world. And that's everything I've ever needed.

EPILOGUE

PART 2
WHITNEY

Shawn's lips slowly tip up as he eyes his girlfriend's belly. He's shocked, yes, but his eyes have taken on a brightness I've never seen before. It makes him appear softer—less intimidating. The news that Taralynn is pregnant makes him happy.

He slides Emersyn off his lap, beckoning Taralynn to come to him. I chuckle when Emersyn crosses her arms, pouting.

Warmth cascading through me pulls my attention away from everyone else as Shane peppers five kisses along the five roses tattooed over an infinity symbol on my wrist. I got it the night I asked Shawn to meet me at his tattoo shop. I never got to show Shane until the next morning. He scolded me pretty good too, before he told me he loved it.

How was I supposed to know you really aren't supposed to get tattooed while pregnant?

Chance was pissed when they came three weeks ago for Emersyn's birthday party. He's currently sulking like a two-year-old and not speaking to me. Eve said he thought I was going to let him—and only him—continue tattooing me. But right now, I think two tattoos are enough. I don't plan on getting more. I don't have the ink bug everyone else seems to have.

"How's Ella?" Shane asks.

We only decided on a name this week, along with a wedding date.

We wanted our whole family present, including the little girl that's currently sitting on my bladder. Our wedding is planned for next summer. We aren't in any rush. We're already a family. Making it official is just the final step. We're already whole. We have the rest of our lives upon us. And it seemed unfair not to allow Ella to be a part of our huge day—a day that's been a long time coming.

"Active," I tell him. "I'm trying to ignore her. I just went to the bathroom before coming in here, but she makes me feel like I need to go again."

He laughs. Shane's laughter is one of my favorite things. It does so many things to me all at once. He can make me smile with that sound alone. And he can turn me on fire with it too.

I let my eyes roam back over to Shane's brother. Taralynn asked Shawn to marry her earlier this year. And as happy as they've both been, I'm almost surprised Shawn hasn't flown her to Vegas to make her officially his. Then again, she already is, the same as I'm Shane's. No piece of paper can prove or show the amount of love we have for each other or the emotions swirling around in our hearts.

But we know. And we show it every day with each other and our girls.

This right here, this life with these people, was what my soul was missing. This was what I'd been yearning for. At this moment, I'm content. There's still a want inside me. And I'm still not a hundred percent sure what it is, and that's okay because I'm happy.

Shane starts working at Pam's pediatric practice in a couple of weeks. Everly starts a new school, and Emersyn starts preschool. And me? I'm going to college. At twenty-eight, I'm going to go to community college. For the first semester, I'll take classes online since I'll be giving birth soon.

I at least want to get an associate's degree, maybe something in music. I don't know yet, but that's something down the road I'll decide. For now, I'm the happiest I've ever been. I'm happy, enjoying the life I have.

Kylie and I aren't the best friends we once were back in high school because with her living in another state, it's harder to get to know her again. We talk. I'm glad she's back in my life again, but when it comes to best friends? Well, Shane is that person. He owns that spot. I think he always was, just a different kind of best friend than the one Kylie was.

"You need anything, Love?"

I twist to face him. "I have everything I've ever needed and wanted. I have my foreverly after. We have our foreverly after, Shane."

"I love you."

"I love you, too. Always. You've always been the one I loved." His nostrils flare, and his eyes darken.

He brings my face down to his. His voice comes out low, telling me he doesn't want the others to hear him. "Night cannot get here fast enough. I need my brother and Taralynn gone and the girls asleep." A promising smile graces his face. "We have a new house to break in, Love."

Shivers run up my spine, and my face grows hot.

Yeah, I can't wait for that either.

"Could you two stop making out?" Shawn chastises. My cheeks flame. I'm not as bad as I used to be about showing affection in public. I think my kids helped me with that, but occasionally I get embarrassed when I forget others are around. "I'm hungry. Someone needs to feed me for all the hard work I did today."

Taralynn is nestled in Shawn's lap, and he doesn't look like he wants to let her go. He keeps appraising her stomach and kissing her, so he has no room to talk. She's only six weeks along, so she's not showing yet.

Emersyn's at the other end of the couch now, by her sister. She's lying on her back with her feet practically in Everly's face, but Ev doesn't seem to care.

I lean up, getting ready to get off Shane, when I look at Taralynn and say, "Let's go start dinner." I'm getting hungry myself. Ella demands to be fed already, and she isn't even here yet.

Before I'm off his lap, Shane reaches up, wrapping his hand around my neck. "Later," he promises, making my heart speed up.

I give him a quick kiss, biting his lower lip in the process, unable to stop myself. He loves it as much as I love doing it.

I dash for the bathroom, feeling light with joy coursing through me.

Maybe memories aren't forgotten. Maybe they're just locked up until the right person comes along with the key to set them free, unlocking glimpses of our past. Or maybe every situation is different. Maybe happiness outweighs what has been forgotten.

I smile as I close the bathroom door behind me. I have the love of my life and our kids. The elation I feel is unexplainable. And we have the rest of our lives to make memories. Memories that I intend to remember and cherish until my last breath.

Thank you for reading Shane and Whitney's story.

ALSO BY N. E. HENDERSON

SILENT SERIES:
SILENT NO MORE
SILENT GUILT

MORE THAN SERIES:
MORE THAN LIES
MORE THAN MEMORIES

THE NEW AMERICAN MAFIA:
BAD PRINCESS
DARK PRINCE
DEVIANT KNIGHT

STANDALONE BOOKS:
HAVE MERCY
THE CONSEQUENCES OF LOVE AND VENGEANCE

ABOUT THE AUTHOR

N. E. Henderson is an Amazon top 30 best-selling author who can't stand a long drawn-out grovel by the hero in the book. If the heroine can't accept an apology and forgive the man she loves, does she even really love him?

When Nancy isn't reading books where the villain gets the girl or the latest supernatural epic romance, then she's likely creating the next badass heroine in her head. There are always scenes playing out, and she can't stand a weak heroine. Nancy can thank Jackie Collins for gifting Lucky Santangelo to the fiction world for that, and her mom who let a fourteen-year-old read Chances back in the late 90s.

Or she could be off playing in the dirt in her CanAm Maverick with her family. Characters create themselves when she's on vacation too. They never leave her alone.

Nancy lives in Central Mississippi with her husband, teenage son, and their bull terrier, Xena.

FOR MORE INFORMATION VISIT:
www.nehenderson.com

Made in the USA
Las Vegas, NV
06 March 2024

86824807R00164